MELISSA SCOTT
THE EMPRESS OF EARTH

THE EMPRESS OF EARTH

This is a work of fiction. All of the characters and events portrayed in this book are fictional, and any resemblance to real people or incidents is purely coincidental.

Copyright © 1987 by Melissa Scott

All rights reserved, including the right to reproduce this book, or portions thereof, in any form.

A Baen Books Original

Baen Publishing Enterprises
260 Fifth Avenue
New York, N.Y. 10001

First printing, November 1987

ISBN: 0-671-65318-4

Cover art by Alan Gutierrez

Printed in the United States of America

THE EMPRESS OF EARTH

This is a work of fiction. All the characters and events portrayed in this book are fictional, and any resemblance to real people or incidents is purely coincidental.

A Baen Books Original

Baen Publishing Enterprises
260 Fifth Avenue
New York, N.Y. 10001

First printing, November 1987

ISBN: 0-671-65364-4

Cover art by Alan Gutierrez

Printed in the United States of America

Distributed by
SIMON & SCHUSTER
1230 Avenue of the Americas
New York, N.Y. 10020

NO MIRACLES, ONLY POWER...

The woman leveled the gun. They were facing the charred ruins of one of the outbuildings. Beyond was the unmistakable mound of a newly dug grave. There were three more beside the first, one much smaller than the others, and Silence bit back a whimper of sheer terror. They could not have come so far just to die here. . . .

The woman's harsh voice cut through her concentration.

"All my life," she said, "they've been telling me the off-worlders are going to come for us, going to come work miracles and save us all. All right. Work me my miracle. Give me back my Javerry, and Ardis, and the babies. I've lost too damn much waiting for you not to get something back."

The sudden fury in her voice snapped something deep in Silence. The levelled weapons seemed to vanish from her perceptions; instead, she saw, with stark clarity, the way the harmonies of Earth's core rose around her, vibrating in the air to all sides. She lowered her hands, reaching out with her new-trained powers to grasp that dark music.

"I don't have any miracles, woman, and I can't raise the dead, but I have power!"

ALSO IN THIS SERIES

Five-Twelfths of Heaven
Silence in Solitude

OTHER NOVELS BY MELISSA SCOTT AVAILABLE FROM BAEN BOOKS

The Game Beyond
A Choice of Destinies
The Kindly Ones

CHAPTER 1

The grassland sloped gently down toward the low cliff and the scrub-covered mountainside below it, the red-tipped leaves of the clinging pines barely rising above the edge of the cliff. Beyond the dark line stretched the Silvermarsh, its vast expanse veined with blue-gleaming channels, the grey-white reeds rising and falling in a breeze that did not reach the clifftop. On the horizon, where the solid ground of the Shiled Islet lifted at last out of the marshes, the towers of Anshar' Asteriona were faintly visible.

Silence Leigh, lying halfway up the grassy slope, shook her head slowly, moved in spite of herself by the subtle beauty. She was a star-traveller, a pilot, inured to the scenery of a hundred different worlds, familiar with the significant beauties of purgatory, the voidmarks spread across a gaudy sky; a simple marshland shouldn't seem so exquisite. But then, this was Asterion, central world of the Hegemony, the greatest power in human-settled space, and this view, this hillside above a cliff, was part of the Hegemon's personal estates, all of which had been chosen to take advantage of naturally occurring beauty. Of course the Silvermarsh would be magnificent.

Sighing, she leaned back into the curve of one husband's arm. Julian Chase Mago shifted drowsily, adjusting himself to her weight. The other husband, Denis Balthasar, was soundly asleep, his head resting against her hip, one arm thrown across her thighs. Overhead, the sky was very bright, the

1

hot, hazed blue of Asterion's late summer. They said, in the
magi's hostel, that Asterion had been chosen as the capital
because it bore a close resemblance to lost Earth; sleepily,
Silence wondered if it were true. All human-settled worlds
resembled Earth to a degree: systemic and planetary harmonies related to the original notes of Earth and Earth's star
system in varying degrees, allowing the starships to travel
easily between them, but a close resemblance seemed unlikely. There would be ways to calculate the probability, of
course—her teacher Isambard would know them. . . .

She shook herself lightly, stretching a shoulder that had
stiffened. Chase Mago, disturbed by the movement, murmured an incoherent question, and promptly fell asleep again.
Silence smiled. This had been the first day in months she had
not spent studying, or, with her husbands, supervising the
refitting of the starship, *Recusante*, for the long voyage to
Earth. In fact, Chase Mago should have been installing new
dolor-crystal pipes in the harmonium that morning, a delicate, boring operation that would have kept all three of them
fully occupied for seven or eight hours, if the dockyard hadn't
failed to make its delivery. Isambard had left for the magi's
hostel in Savaid, Anshar' Asteriona's western suburb, a little
after sunrise, to be out of their way. If he hadn't left so early,
Silence thought, still smiling, she would have had to spend at
least a part of the day with him. Isambard had acknowledged
eight standard months ago that she was a magus—a theoreti-
cal impossibility that still made her laugh, so thoroughly had
she upset the magi's understanding of the worlds—but they
both knew she was still relatively inexperienced. Her skills
would have to be honed and polished before they made the
attempt on the Earth-road. Even so, she thought, I need
some time apart.

She sighed, her smile fading. The thought of Earth, of the
complicated web of obligation and unwritten contract that
kept her searching for a way to reach the lost planet, drove
away her lingering pleasure in the view. She had never
intended to spend her life looking for Earth, as so many other
star-travellers had done. That had been her uncle's obsession,
not her own; all she had ever wanted was to be a pilot, gain
the freedom of the star lanes. To a certain degree, she'd

gotten what she wanted, though the Hegemony's conquest of the Rusadir, and the imposition of the Hegemony's rigid laws on the losing planets, had severely restricted her opportunities. Still, her grandfather had been desperate enough to attempt to recoup his trading losses by sailing with a woman as his pilot—it had saved him enough money, Silence thought with a wry smile, hiring his own granddaughter—and she had had steady work. But then, with her grandfather's death, everything had changed.

He had left her the starship *Recusante*, called *Black Dolphin* then, but her uncle had acted to steal that meager inheritance, hoping to use it and her to further his own search for Earth. Silence had avoided that only by giving up her claim to the ship and taking the first job offered her. The Delos-born captain Denis Balthasar had needed a pilot aboard his half-and-half, *Sun-Treader*. More than that, he had offered her a three-way marriage, and that was the only way, under Hegemonic law, that Silence could free herself from her uncle's guardianship. It had seemed like such a simple arrangement. . . .

She smiled rather wryly. Balthasar, who never revealed more information than was necessary, had not mentioned he worked for the pirate combine Wrath-of-God until she was already committed to his plans, and Wrath-of-God had been preparing for its final battle with the Hegemony. *Sun-Treader* had reached the Wrath just in time to take part in the pirates' disastrous attack on Arganthonios, and she, with the rest of the survivors, had been captured and geas-bound to service in the Hegemonic Navy. Somehow—she still did not know how—the geas had triggered something within her, forcing her to begin to tap powers she had never suspected she had. She had broken the geas, freeing herself and her husbands, but their attempt to steal the mailship on which they had been serving had been foiled by the mailship's only passenger, the magus Isambard. Frantic, Silence had offered him a desperate bargain. In the starbooks she had brought with her from *Black Dolphin* was the key to the lost road to Earth; if the magus would protect them from the Hegemony, they would take him there. Earth was not just wealth, it represented metaphysical power beyond most of the magi's dreams, and Isambard was not the man to resist that temptation.

That wasn't the only reason, though, Silence thought, and sighed again. It was hard to like Isambard, even though she had to admit that he'd treated her fairly. The magus had recognized her anomalous power for what it was—the potential to become a magus, a power no woman should possess—and, more than that, he'd been willing to teach her to use it. After their first attempt to reach Earth had failed—though in the process Silence had been able to steal back the ship bequeathed to her so many months before—he had brought her to the magi's created world, Solitudo Hermae Trismagisti, and persuaded the rectors there to allow her, a mere woman, to enter the regular course of study. She had just reached the first rank beyond apprenticeship when disaster struck again.

The Hegemonic authorities were still looking for the three pirates who'd escaped the geas. The agents of the Rose Worlds, the six-world trading ring whose engines blocked the road to Earth, knew that she and her companions had learned the Rose Worlds' greatest secret, and were desperate to protect it. It had been the Hegemon's men who reached Solitudo Hermae first, circulating an inquiry about a woman pilot who might or might not show anomalous powers. Despite the fact that Silence had not completed her training, she and the others had decided to try to break through the siege engines' field, knowing that if they could achieve that, the Hegemon would be willing to forgive their escape in exchange for the secret of the Earth-road.

Their first attempt had failed, and in the process they had learned that sheer brute strength would not be enough to break the siege engines' distorting harmonies. However, during her studies on Solitudo Hermae, Silence had stumbled across a description of an archaic piloting technique, one that did not involve the active manipulation of the voidmarks, and so would not be affected by the engines' fields. If they could find a portolan, the roadmap-like compendium of voidmarks that was the key to the old system, Silence was certain she could learn the ancient technique, and bring them safely to Earth.

Isambard had been equally sure he knew where to obtain

the necessary book: he had worked for the satrap of Inarime, the most noted collector of curiosities outside of the magi themselves, a number of times before. If the satrap owned a portolan, and Isambard guessed he did, the magus felt certain he could persuade his former employer to let them take the book—especially since the satrap was currently at odds with the Hegemon. In fact, his plans had gone further than the magus could have known: a rising against the Hegemon was already in the planning stages. As Isambard suspected, Adeben Kibbe of Inarime did indeed own a portolan, but the price he'd asked for it was unexpected. His daughter, his only legitimate child, was being held hostage in the Women's Palace on Asterion itself, in hopes of stopping the rebellion. Only a woman could enter the Palace, and only a magus had any hope of rescuing the shazadi. If Silence would rescue the girl before the invasion force reached Asterion, the satrap had said, he would give them the portolan. If she did not try, he would leave them to their fate.

There had been no choice. Silence, disguised as the noble daughter of an admiral, had entered the Women's Palace, and, after weeks of effort, had succeeded in breaking through the elaborate security systems and effecting their escape. However, she had taken longer to do so than they had planned: *Recusante* had lifted from Asterion only to run into a pitched battle on the fringes of the system—a battle that Adeben Kibbe had been losing. Desperate, Silence had resorted to a dangerous, unproven trick, adjusting the music of the ship's harmonium to a note that would disrupt the Hegemon's fleet, and channeling that music directly through the sounding keel—in effect, using the ship itself as a destructive engine. It had worked, though Silence's hands were still slightly scarred from the uncanny heat of the harmonium's pipes. Adeben Kibbe, now the Hegemon by right of conquest, had kept his word, and the portolan now rested in *Recusante*'s strongbox, protected by Isambard's specially constructed locks. As soon as the refit was completed—*Recusante* had suffered quite a bit of damage during the battle—they would lift for Earth.

Silence shifted against Chase Mago's encircling arm, suddenly faintly impatient with the day's enforced leisure. It was not that she regretted the time apart, the laziness, but that she was ready to complete the adventure she'd begun nearly two years before. The engineer opened his eyes and yawned hugely, teeth very white behind his dark beard. Before he could speak, however, a flat voice said respectfully, "Sieuri."

Silence sat up, finally disturbing Balthasar, who muttered querulously and rolled over, rubbing at his eyes. She ignored him, and turned to glare up at the figure that stood patiently at the top of the slope.

"I left orders we weren't to be disturbed," she said.

The homunculus looked back at her. It was an expensive toy, finely detailed, its face an immobile, inhumanly beautiful mask sculpted by one of the Hegemony's greatest artists. "A priority call," it said. The voice issued without inflection from a pinhole in the slightly pouting lips.

Silence eyed the homunculus warily. She had never liked the created beings, though they did most of the heavy work in space. Even now, after she'd had to learn how to grow them from seed and matrix, and knew how to shatter the fragile pseudo-flesh with a single tone, she could not feel entirely comfortable in their presence. "Who is it?"

"The vizier n'Halian." The homunculus's voice did not change, but it lifted one grey-fleshed hand to its gilded forehead in imprinted response to the title.

"N'Halian?" Balthasar sat up, frowning. "I wonder what he wants."

Silence shrugged, and pushed herself to her feet. Halian n'Halian was the Hegemon's chief minister and his most trusted servant—not a man to be kept waiting.

Chase Mago stood, stretching, then turned to pull Balthasar to his feet. "Who knows?" the big engineer said, calmly enough, but his eyes were wary.

"I bet it isn't good news," Balthasar muttered.

"Don't be such a goddamn pessimist," Silence said, more sharply than she'd intended. Balthasar grinned, and she knew he'd recognized her own fear. She gestured quickly to the homunculus, cutting off the Delian's response. "Please inform the vizier we're on our way. We can call him back, if he doesn't want to wait."

"I beg your pardon, sieura," the homunculus answered. "The vizier is waiting in the garden room."

The three humans exchanged glances, and then Silence said again, "Tell the vizier we're on our way."

"Yes, sieura." The homunculus bowed over folded, grey-fingered hands and turned away, striding over the uneven ground with inhuman precision.

As soon as it was out of earshot, Chase Mago said, "That's very odd."

Silence reached for the thin, gold-flecked shawl she carried instead of the veil required by Hegemonic law, and wound it expertly around her head, covering her boy-short black hair, and tossed the trailing end over her left shoulder, just concealing nose and mouth. It would—just—preserve the amenities, but there was no time to change into full court regalia. "Very," she agreed.

"Come on." Balthasar was already hurrying up the hill after the homunculus; Chase Mago shrugged and followed. Silence clambered after them, frowning. There was no reason that she knew of for the vizier to come to the villa in person; all the obvious things could just as easily have been dealt with over the view-globe network. But there shouldn't be anything wrong, either, she thought, and ducked under a trailing branch from one of the allreds that formed a windbreak at the top of the slope. At the Hegemon's request, she had stayed out of sight for the past months, letting the Thousand, the members of the great families that governed the Hegemony, forget that Adeben Kibbe owed his throne at least in part to a woman magus. She hadn't been outside the villa, except to visit the magi's hostel or the star-travellers' Pale surrounding Anshar' Asteriona's starport, in over a month.

Inside the line of allreds, the landscape flattened suddenly, manicured lawn stretching as though cut with a level from the tidy edge of the carpet of fallen leaves to the fretted door. Above the bluestone lintel, carved with an abstract pattern of leaves and twining flowers, the garden room's glass wall had gone green in the afternoon sunlight. Behind it, Silence could just make out the moving shadow that was the vizier. Pacing? she thought, with a sudden feeling of dread, but

Chase Mago pushed open the fretted door before she was certain.

Another of the villa's homunculi was waiting at the foot of the back stairway, formal clothes—knee-length coats for the men, and a floor-length veil for her—draped across its stiff arms. Chase Mago absently accepted the larger of the coats, fastening its buttons all the way up to the high collar, but Balthasar waved his away, grimacing. Silence hesitated for a moment, then started up the stairs without taking the longer veil.

Halian n'Halian was standing in the middle of the garden room, staring at the central fountain without really seeing the fine haze of water. He turned at the sound of the door opening, and the sunlight streaming through the windows glittered from the tips of his forked beard.

"Sieuri."

"Vizier," Silence answered, watching his eyes. N'Halian wore his most opaque expression, but she was usually able to read some indication of his mood. She did not think he was afraid, or angry, but there was a new hesitation in his manner that troubled her.

"I am sorry to trouble you, when your servants said you were engaged," n'Halian continued smoothly, "but his Majesty wishes to speak to you."

"What about?" That was Balthasar, coming up on Silence's left. The pilot glanced sideways, and saw that the Delian's thin face was set in a truculent scowl. Before she could say anything, however, Chase Mago made his chilly, oligarch's bow.

"Vizier," the engineer said. "I hope nothing's wrong?"

N'Halian shook his head, and in spite of herself, Silence gave a sigh of relief. Balthasar's mouth twisted, but for once he said nothing.

"I'm instructed to say that his Majesty has acquired something he believes will be of use to you," n'Halian went on, with a smile that showed his gold-set teeth. "He would like to discuss it with you in person."

That's better news than I expected, Silence thought, and said aloud, "Of course, vizier. Can you give us any more details?"

N'Halian shook his head. "I'm sorry, sieura, but his Majesty hasn't told me anything more."

"I see," Silence said. She didn't quite believe him, but knew better than to press the issue. "Do we have time to change?"

"That won't be necessary," n'Halian answered. "If you'll come with me, sieuri, I have a flyer waiting."

Silence hesitated for a moment, seeing her reflection in the wall of glass behind n'Halian. She was still wearing the boys' clothes she had adopted on Solitudo Hermae, loose tunic belted over shapeless trousers, tool kit dangling from her belt—hardly the sort of thing she should wear to face the ruler of two-thirds of human-settled space, especially when it was topped off by the fraying, almost transparent shawl instead of a veil. But that was vanity, and she knew it. It wasn't the elegance of court costume—an elegance that weighed over twelve kilograms—that she missed, but the familiarity of Rusadir tunic and tights. "As his Majesty wishes," she said aloud, and wound the shawl more securely across her face.

N'Halian's flyer sat on the disused playing field beside the villa that doubled as a landing area. Its crew, a pilot, co-pilot, and a trio of soldiers in Inariman livery, lounged in the shade of its fully extended wings. Clearly, Silence thought, they'd been waiting for n'Halian for some time. At the vizier's approach, the soldiers sprang to attention, one moving to trigger the ramp, the others sliding off the wing to stiffen into a hasty salute. The two pilots stood as well, though less smartly. Silence guessed they were civilians—n'Halian's employees rather than members of the Hegemon's official household—and her wariness increased. The Hegemon usually sent his household, unless there were good reasons for secrecy. . . . Then the co-pilot dropped from the wing and began pulling off the baffle that hid the flyer's keel, and Silence suppressed a gasp of surprise. At her elbow, Balthasar whispered a curse. The ship was no ordinary flyer, but a long-range craft, its shiny keel capable of reaching the boundary between the atmospheric and celestial harmonies. She opened her mouth to ask where they were going, but Chase Mago forstalled her.

"I take it we're not going to Anshar' Asteriona?" the engineer asked, as cooly as if he were inquiring about the weather. Silence saw that Balthasar's left hand was deep in his coat pocket, and she felt sure his fingers were curled around the butt of a heylin.

"No, sieur Chase Mago," n'Halian answered, with equal courtesy. "His Majesty is at the Winter Palace."

Silence relaxed, and saw Balthasar slip his hand quietly out of his pocket. If n'Halian was willing to tell them where they were going, the secrecy couldn't be directed at them. "That's on the far side?" she asked.

N'Halian nodded once. "That's correct, sieura."

They had reached the bottom of the ramp while they were talking. The co-pilot, still stuffing the thick dura-felt baffle back into its well, stopped abruptly, staring, when he heard the title. Silence stared back, and, after a moment, the man looked away. Even so, she was aware of his interest, of the avid curiosity at her back, as she made her way up the ramp and into the flyer's passenger compartment.

"Another of your admirers, Silence?" Balthasar murmured, with a lifted eyebrow.

Silence flushed. "I doubt it," she said, tartly. She had been noticeable enough as a woman pilot—the only female pilots most star-travellers knew were from the matriarchal world of Misthia—but now she was positively notorious. Despite the Hegemon's efforts to keep her involvement secret, star-travellers' gossip whispered that she'd been a part of his victory, that she knew something about the road to Earth, that she dabbled in strange powers. . . . Having two husbands had not helped, either: three-way marriages weren't common, and the star-travellers who did not believe the wilder rumors were more than willing to speculate about her marriage. She supposed she should be pleased that she had a ready-made red herring, to take interest away from the rumors that she was—that they were—looking for Earth, but she found the whole thing rather embarrassing. The situation wasn't improved by the fact that Balthasar thought it was funny, and added his own bizarre inventions to the stories already circulating. At least Chase Mago was sympathetic, she thought—but then he, like herself, had been a citizen of one of the more conservative worlds of the Rusadir, before the Rusadir had fallen to the Hegemony. Balthasar was a Delian, and on Delos anything was permitted.

She ducked through the low hatch into the flyer's passenger cabin, ignoring the senior pilot loitering in the entrance to the control compartment. The first of the soldiers was already aboard, coiled compactly in the rearmost seat, his sonic rifle stuffed into the holster clamped to the bulkhead behind him. His face was impassive, but Silence sensed the curiosity behind his stolid gaze.

She shook away the thought, and seated herself at the front of the passenger section, choosing a place by one of the circular windows. Chase Mago dropped heavily into the seat next to her, and Balthasar, with a grimace, took his place behind her. N'Halian settled himself into the seat across the aisle, and gestured to the pilot. The man touched his forehead, and vanished into the control compartment. The rest of the soldiers trooped aboard, and the co-pilot sealed the hatch behind them. A few moments later, the flyer's tiny harmonium sounded, the low, bone-tingling base note swelling rapidly to the complex lift sequence. The flyer shuddered once, and rose. Silence leaned against the bulkhead, watching the ground drop away. This was not the dizzying upward fall of a starship's liftoff; rather, the flyer seemed almost to float upward, the harmonium's note, sounding through the half-tinctured keel, shifting slowly from Asterion's core harmony to the purer celestial tone. The note changed again and the flyer tilted sharply, the world wheeling around it, then steadied on a new course. Already, the ground below was becoming featureless, the Silvermarsh just a pale blob webbed with greyish lines. The flyer banked again, less steeply, and Silence caught a glimpse of one of Anshar' Asteriona's suburbs, a darker, more regular shape spangled with bright patches that were parks.

"Nice flying," Balthasar said, leaning forward. "You think we're on the line yet, Julie?"

Chase Mago's face wore the abstracted expression that meant he was listening with all his heart to a harmonium's seductive music, but he broke his concentration long enough to say, "Not yet. You'll hear it."

"On the line?" Silence asked.

Balthasar nodded. "You know. Whatever harmonic line will take us where we're going."

"I've never flown one of these," Silence said, with some annoyance. She bit back the rest of her thought—*I'm a star-pilot, not some planetary hack*—knowing that Balthasar had probably flown these craft at some point in his career.

"They use the envelope the way we use the system harmonies, in- and outbound," Balthasar began, but whatever he had been going to say was cut off by a sudden deep shift in the music of the flyer's harmonium. It wasn't the complex, familiar change that marked the moment a starship passed out of a planet's chaotic harmonic envelope, the affinities between the heaven, the celestial music—or its approximation—of the harmonium and the Philosopher's Tincture in the keel itself coming into resonance and steadying to a note so comparatively simple as to be almost inaudible. Rather, the harsh music, which had been wavering on the edge of dissonance, seemed almost to shift to a chord comprehensible to a human ear. It hovered heartbreakingly on the edge of completion, as though in any instant it would resolve itself into a sound so perfect that it would shatter the hearer.

Silence shook herself, seeing her own feelings—pleasure in the lovely note, despair that it was still incomplete, and the certainty of disappointment—reflected and redoubled in Chase Mago's face. For a brief moment, she wondered what more he heard, with his engineer's training, then put the thought aside. The sound was not beautiful, she told herself firmly; it was merely that the human ear perceived as beautiful those sounds which came closest to true harmonies. The harmonium was imitating, as closely as was humanly possible, some part of Asterion's core harmony, that was all.

And that, she thought abruptly, explained what Balthasar had begun to say. The little flyers worked by riding a specific note within the planet's harmonic envelope. It was only pilot's convention that said the envelope was monochromatic; like the *musica mundana*, the complex, system-filling music that resulted from the interaction of solar and planetary harmonies, the planetary envelope was actually made up of innumerable variations on the simple music of the core. It was similar enough, in its function, to make her glad she had not said anything derogatory about the art of piloting these local craft.

Outside the flyer's window, Asterion had dropped away almost completely, its rich landscape fading into broad swaths of color smeared with cloud. There were cities below, Silence knew, but they were invisible at this height. The sky itself had darkened toward the blue-black that marked the border between planetary and celestial harmony. That explained some of the perfection of the flyer's music, Silence thought. The craft was far enough above any local topographical features to avoid their distortion. Still, whatever the reasons for it, the harmonium's note was achingly beautiful, and she was glad when the sound shifted at last to the more muddled music of landing.

It was late morning at the Winter Palace. The flyer slid down an almost inaudible landing beam toward a white, featureless plain. Silence frowned out the window for a long moment before she realized it was snow. The Palace itself, multiple spires gleaming in the noon light, rose from the center of the plain like a fantastic ice sculpture. Silence remembered the Women's Palace, presented on its island like a jewel on a tray, and shivered.

"Either we're at one of the poles," Balthasar said, "or this is magi's work."

Chase Mago shrugged.

"Probably a creation," Silence said, thoughtfully. She was too far away, as yet, to feel the bending of harmonies, of reality, that marked a magus's created landscape, but she could not imagine any hegemon choosing to live at either of Asterion's poles. She glanced toward n'Halian, hoping the vizier would confirm or deny her guess, but the older man was smiling indulgently into his gilded beard, and Silence looked away. She should not have expected the vizier to betray the true location of one of the royal palaces, but he didn't have to look so smug about it. Then, reluctantly, she smiled. She and Balthasar were whistling in the dark, and sounded it. Chase Mago had the right idea: say nothing, and wait.

The flyer dropped lower still, until it was almost skimming the surface, throwing up a great cloud of snow that rattled against wings and body, completely obscuring the windows. At the same time, the noise of the harmonium changed again, showing new strain as it fought to balance the pull of the planet's core. The flyer dipped and slowed further. The harmonium cut out, and the flyer dropped neatly into an invisible cradle. Silence distinctly heard the cradle fingers clamp onto the flyer's hull, and heard, as distinctly, Balthasar's muttered comment.

"Show-off."

He meant the flyer's pilot, and Silence nodded. Before she could say anything, however, n'Halian had hauled himself to his feet. "If you'll come with me, sieuri?"

"Of course," Silence answered, with all the dignity she could muster. Ahead, she heard the thud of the hatch being thrown back, and shivered in a blast of chill air. Balthasar jammed his hands into his coat pockets, whispering a curse.

N'Halian led them forward to the hatch without showing any sign that he felt the cold, though he was no more warmly dressed than any of them. Silence hesitated in the hatchway, wondering if she could refuse to go further until she could get something warmer to wear. They were still some distance from the palace. Then she saw the gever drawn up beside the flyer, and resigned herself to a cold ride. At least, she thought, as she made her way down the cradle stairs, it's a closed car.

As they appeared at the top of the cradle, two doors popped open in the gever's side. Soldiers—members of the True Thousand this time, their splendid uniforms almost gaudy against the snow—stepped from the machine's forward compartment and stiffened into a salute. Silence shivered again, from fear this time: even if most of the True Thousand had supported Adeben's coup, she and her husbands had suffered enough at the hands of the Hegemon's elite guard. Then a slim figure, his crimson coat looped with a colonel's braid, stepped from the passenger compartment.

"Welcome to the Winter Palace, my lord vizier, sieuri."

Silence relaxed then, and sensed rather than saw the others do the same. Marcinik—a colonel now, promoted on the occasion of his marriage to the hegemon's daughter Aili—was an old acquaintance. He had been their contact in rescuing Aili from the Women's Palace; before that, he had served on the conscript transport where Silence had first discovered her powers. It was, Silence thought, an interesting relationship.

"Thank you, Colonel," n'Halian said serenely, and made his way down the cradle stairs. The bottom steps were slick with blown snow. He frowned, and picked his way delicately across. Following him, Silence suppressed a grin, and heard Balthasar mutter something behind her.

Marcinik gestured for them to enter the gever. He was a handsome man, young for a colonel, with fine aristocratic bones and almond-fair skin. Only the faint lines at the corners of his eyes and bracketing his mouth saved him from a tedious beauty.

"There are coats inside," he said, "since the vizier didn't see fit to warn you."

"I had my instructions, colonel," n'Halian answered, and ducked into the gever's wide passenger compartment.

As Marcinik had promised, there was a pile of quilted coats lying on the nearest bench-seat. Silence reached for the first one, not caring what it looked like, and realized to her surprise that the outer layer, at least, was made of silk. She shrugged it on, hugging the pillowy fabric around herself, and settled into the rear corner of the bench, stretching her feet out to the nearest heating block. The others did the same, but n'Halian waved aside the offer of a coat. A moment later, one of his own soldiers leaned into the gever, holding out a fur-lined cloak. The vizier wrapped it comfortably around his shoulders, and settled into his place. Marcinik, a slight smile on his lips, gestured for his men to close the compartment door.

"I don't suppose you can tell us what he—his Majesty—wants?" Balthasar asked. There was a note in his voice that dared the colonel to answer with more than a simple negative.

"I'm sorry." Marcinik shook his head, still smiling, but Silence thought she glimpsed a sort of annoyance behind that polite mask. She sighed, and looked away. Balthasar had had good cause to dislike the colonel—Marcinik, then a lieutenant of the Thousand, had had charge of the prisoners during the nightmare flight from Arganthonios to Sapriportus, when Balthasar had almost died—but she had thought that the two men had come to an understanding during their escape from

the Palace. She was aware of Chase Mago's eyes on her, of a
slight tightening of the engineer's lips, and knew he was
thinking the same thing.

To Silence's surprise, however, Balthasar did not pursue
the question, but leaned back against the padded seat. He
saw the pilot's glance, and made a slight shrugging movement, one shoulder moving under the heavy coat. Chase
Mago grinned, but to Silence's relief, said nothing. The gever
rose, engine whining softly, and swung around the cradled
flyer in a broad arc that would bring it up to the palace from
the east, well away from the main gate. Now that they were
moving, Silence could feel the faint, unnatural shifts in the
local harmonies—a sort of tingling, a note of almost-music,
faint as a feather's fall against her skin—that marked an artificially maintained snowfield. She smiled to herself then, staring out the tiny sideport into the plume of snow kicked up by
the gever's passage. It hardly mattered where the Winter
Palace was located on Asterion's surface; still, it was nice to
have her intuition confirmed.

The gever did not follow the well-marked track that led to
the Palace's imposing main gate, but swung off onto un-
marked snow, skirting the perimeter wall. They had travelled
almost a quarter of the way around its circle before the gever
slowed, and Silence saw one of the drivers raise a cupped
hand to his mouth. A few moments later a snowbank shivered
and split open with a shower of flakes, revealing a paved
tunnel that sloped steeply down into darkness.

"Subtle," Balthasar said, with a quick glance at Marcinik.

The colonel showed no sign of having heard him. The
gever slowed still further, engine whining fiercely to compensate, and slid off the snow onto the slick tiling of the tunnel.
The snowbank, with its hidden door, rumbled shut behind
them. The gever hung in darkness for a moment, its engine
idling, and then a light faded into existence ahead of them,
throwing a long wedge of brightness along the tunnel floor.
The gever lurched into motion again, heading toward the
light.

Silence did her best to plot the path of the tunnel, matching its twists and turns against the glimpse she'd had of the
palace and its grounds, but gave up after only the third turn.

She knew too little. . . . Carefully, she masked her impatience, and settled back in her seat, glancing as unobtrusively as she could at the chronograph slung at Balthasar's waist. It was a quarter of an hour later, by the 'graph, before the gever slowed again and made a sharp turn into a new corridor. They had to have doubled back more than once, Silence thought, glancing as casually as she could at the new surroundings, and wondered again what had prompted this unusual security. From the grim set of Balthasar's mouth, the Delian was wondering the same thing, and Chase Mago looked very thoughtful.

The new tunnel was more brightly lit than the first, and the tiles that covered the floor and the curving walls were pale blue, banded at about the height of a man's shoulder with a wide stripe of deeper blue. As they flashed past a cross-tunnel, Silence could see that its walls were marked with a double stripe, one blue, one red; the second cross-tunnel was marked in green. They had reached the palace's regular maintenance tunnels, she guessed, remembering similar arrangements from the Women's Palace, and wondered again about such roundabout dealings.

A few minutes later, the tunnel widened suddenly, and the gever slowed still further, gliding toward a shallow platform. More troops in the Thousand's bright uniforms were waiting there. They were formed up in the double line of an honor guard, but even so Silence tensed, and saw Chase Mago's mouth tighten again. Balthasar swept back the fronts of the borrowed coat and jammed both hands into the pockets of his own jacket, one thumb visibly caressing the touchplate of his heylin. Silence contrived to touch his shoulder, frowning, and the Delian moved his hand away. The pilot wrapped her coat more tightly around herself, and hoped no one had noticed Balthasar's lapse.

As the gever drew to a halt in front of the platform, the officer in command—a major, Silence noticed, an older man with battle ribbons banding his sleeves and trailing hood—snapped into a salute, then came forward to unlatch the gever door himself. Behind him, a voice high-pitched with strain barked a command. The soldiers swept their ceremonial swords from their gilded scabbards, holding them overhead to form a steel canopy from the gever to an arched doorway at the far side of the platform. Marcinik nodded and stepped from the gever, turning to offer his hand first to n'Halian and then to Silence. The pilot let him steady her as she stepped from the craft, and followed the vizier toward the distant archway. She felt the scarf, never intended to serve as a veil, slip slightly, but she ignored it, disdaining to adjust it or to glance at the men following at her back. She took a certain grim pleasure in the disciplined stir she created.

As she approached the arch, she became aware of Watchers, the created beings that could serve as a magus's eyes and ears. In the same instant, something moved in the carvings above the arch. She glanced up, breaking stride, and saw one of the carvings detach itself from the stone tree that made up the sides of the arch and launch itself, with a raptor's screech, into space. A second statue, another gold-taloned bird of prey, freed itself an instant later, screeching angrily. Balthasar's heylin, she thought, they've sensed it. Without conscious decision, she lifted her hands and spoke a single Word. The sound, hard and flat and as sharp as the crack of stone against stone, seemed to explode in the confined space, cutting through the sudden commotion behind her. The statues froze, then seemed to contract, drawing into themselves, and were sucked toward the arch as though they were metal drawn by a powerful magnet. They snapped back into their places with a noise that struck complex echoes from the walls.

Silence turned slowly—Isambard had taught her how to take advantage of the shock her powers always brought—and hid a smile at seeing them all frozen in surprise. Predictably enough, it was one of the sergeants who recovered first, glancing rapidly from Marcinik to the open-mouthed major.

"Sir, Colonel, he's got a weapon—"

The major shut his mouth as though he'd just realized it was open. Marcinik lifted a placating hand. "Take it easy," he began, and Silence cleared her throat.

"Denis?"

Balthasar made a complex grimace and straightened, slowly drawing the heylin from his pocket. Before the troopers could react, he reversed it, presenting the heavy butt to Marcinik. "I—" The Delian hesitated, then continued with more grace than Silence had expected, "—apologize for the trouble. We were not expecting the invitation."

Marcinik accepted the heylin warily, running his thumb absently across the touchplate. It was hot, signalling that the heylin was fully charged, and he lifted an eyebrow. "No more were you," he said, with a quelling glance at the indignant major. "I accept the responsibility."

The major saluted, reluctantly, and Marcinik slipped the heylin into his own pocket. "Sieur Chase Mago—" he began, but the engineer was already shaking his head.

"I'm unarmed, colonel."

"Then let's continue," Marcinik said, and gestured for the star-travellers to precede him. This time, the Watchers remained where they belonged, frozen among the stone branches. N'Halian, waiting on the far side of the archway, gave them an impatient nod. A trio of chamberlains, greying men in the long blue coats of their office, were waiting with him, leaning on their staffs of office.

Silence frowned slightly, seeing them. Always before, the Hegemon had gone out of his way to keep their meetings informal; this time he seemed to be doing everything he could to make certain the proper members of the household witnessed their arrival. "Why the publicity, my lord vizier?" she asked softly, using the coinë of the space lanes rather than the High Speech of the court, as she took her place at n'Halian's elbow.

The vizier gave her a quick, sideways glance before answering. "His most serene Majesty would honor you according to your rank."

He had used the High Speech, Silence noted, as though he'd intended to be overheard. "And what rank's that?" she asked, still in coinë. "I—we—have no offical position here."

N'Halian slipped into coinë at last, this time with a rather annoyed glance at the nearest of the chamberlains. "You are a subject of his Majesty's, and a magus. That confers rank."

It does that, Silence thought, but not sufficient rank to account for all of this. She had better sense than to say that, however, and dropped back a half-step, so that she was no longer walking at n'Halian's side. The reception they'd had, after the secrecy of the flight that had brought them to the

Palace, worried her; she couldn't think of a good reason for this sudden reversal.

The chamberlains led them down a long corridor that fed abruptly into a huge, high-ceilinged hall. The floor was covered with a thick, snow-white carpet, and the walls and massive support pillars were hung with more carpets, these woven in subtle, muted shades of grey. Strange bluish shadows flickered briefly across the carpets. Silence glanced up, not wanting to seem too obviously ignorant, and saw, high in the vaulted ceiling, a miniature skyscape. Clouds flicked across the scene, swelling and changing, then vanishing without releasing their burden of rain.

"You better hope it doesn't rain in here," Balthasar murmured, and Silence heard Chase Mago's choked snort of laughter in response. She smiled herself, tardily recognizing a magus's illusion, and followed the vizier down the length of the hall. The layers of carpet swallowed any sound of footsteps. They moved in an unnatural quiet, broken only by the hiss of the silk coats and the heavier rustling of the vizier's furs.

At the end of the hall, one of the chamberlains used his staff to touch a plate set above the gold-studded door. Chimes sounded somewhere inside, muffled like everything else by the carpets, and then, very slowly, the door was drawn back. A second chamberlain said, "The vizier Halian n'Halian, Colonel Marcinik, the doctor Leigh. Her husbands."

The figure in the doorway was also familiar: the Hegemon's favorite page. The boy bowed deeply, almost double, and answered, "His Majesty expects them."

The first chamberlain returned the bow, and stepped back from the door. The second chamberlain bowed, too, not as deeply as the others, and said, "I commit them to your care."

The page bowed again, and opened the door fully. Silence caught a brief glimpse of a warmly lit room, walls alternately paneled and hung with woven gold, and men in the elaborate robes of the Thousand and the Ten Thousand gathered in little groups beneath branching lamps that held globes and eggs and rounded polygons filled with fixed fire. Then the page gestured, with yet another bow, for n'Halian to precede him down a path market by a crimson carpet, and the vizier hissed, "Bow to the Throne as you pass it, all of you. And for God's sake, say nothing."

The intensity of his voice was enough to make even Balthasar obey. Silence drew herself up to her full height, wishing for only the second time in her life for the protection of the court regalia, with its floor-length veil, and did as she was told. From pictures and descriptions she recognized the Hall of Audience, the place where the Hegemon heard the formal requests and petitions of his nobles, but she still could not guess why she—why they—had been brought here. There could be no more public way of announcing both her presence and the Hegemon's patronage of their group. Already, she could hear the whispers beginning, and did her best to shut out the surprised disapproval.

"Bow," n'Halian hissed again, and Silence did so, automatically. She caught a dizzying glimpse of the Hegemonic throne—a massive construction of gold and precious minerals and the wood-ivory that was the bone of the semi-sentient reef-dwellers of Alonae, a display of wealth that transcended any question of taste—but then the page opened the small door that stood to the left of the throne.

"Your Majesty, the persons you sent for."

N'Halian swept through the narrow doorway without disdaining to acknowledge the page, and the others followed. The page closed the door gently behind them. Silence realized then that they had been admitted to one of the Hegemon's private meeting rooms, a privilege that at least some of the nobles waiting in the Hall would never achieve. The realization was at once flattering and frightening; to calm herself, she glanced quickly around the room, concentrating on her surroundings. The place was instantly familiar, from the shielded computer cabinet and the locked book-presses to the massive desk and the immense inverted pyramid with its light-bearing homunculissima, to the cluster of tabourets and the black-robed magus sitting in the central place. The Hegemon had brought his private office with him from Inarime, furniture, books, and all. For a moment, seeing Isambard sitting so calmly among the scattered papers, Silence could almost imagine herself back on Inarmine, a half-trained fugitive.

"Thank you, Halian. Sieuri, welcome." Adeben Kibbe

pushed aside the last of the papers that filled his desk, and leaned back in his chair. It alone was new, a tall, carved thing that strongly resembled a throne. The Hegemon, not a tall man by anyone's reckoning, should have been dwarfed by it; Silence was not surprised to see that he dominated it and the entire room.

"Thank you, your Majesty," she said, and was a little surprised at her own presumption. "May I ask what's prompted so—" She hesitated delicately and deliberately over the next word. "—flattering a welcome?"

The Hegemon smiled. Silence was aware as well of the vizier's amusement, like the sudden warmth of a fire, and of Isambard's more measured approval. "I have a present for you, sieura—for all of you." The Hegemon gestured gracefully toward Isambard's hunched figure. "Thus I summoned Doctor Isambard as well."

"A present?" Chase Mago said, softly, but the Hegemon heard him.

"A present—a gift," he amended, switching to coinë with a bland smile. Silence heard Chase Mago gasp affrontedly, and Balthasar's stifled snicker.

She suppressed her own annoyance. The Hegemon was deliberately baiting them, first with his mention of a gift and then with the insulting shift from the courtiers' High Speech to the common coinë.

The Hegemon continued. "My agents have been fortunate enough to acquire . . . something that should be very useful to you in your search." He paused, clearly expecting a question, but Silence met his gaze with a blank stare. The quiet lengthened.

Isambard said, with some asperity, "Your Majesty, I have been waiting for an hour to hear about this mysterious gift. If it will please you to hear me ask, very well, I am asking: what is it?"

Silence winced at the bluntness of the magus's words, but Adeben did not seem to be offended. "It's very gracious of you to indulge me, Isambard. I trust you'll indulge me further, and allow me to begin at the beginning." He reached for the papers he had pushed aside at their arrival, and swept on without waiting for an answer. "Three weeks ago, on

Enkomi, the local satrap's guards were called out to deal with a disturbance in the Pale."

Balthasar snorted at that, and Silence hid a grin. Enkomi's Pale was notoriously rowdy, and the satrap's forces equally notorious for their inefficiency. The Hegemon continued unheeding. "When the guard-captain and his men arrived at the bar in question, they found a fight in progress among the crew of a Rose-Worlder merchantman. One man, the ship's captain, was already dead; the others were apparently trying to take the killer into custody themselves. The satrap's men arrested both parties, and the killer threw herself onto his— the satrap's—mercy." Adeben looked up, allowing himself a faint smile. "I believe the Rose Worlds' legal code considers homicide to be an extremely serious matter." He referred to his papers again, theatrically. "Her plea was accepted, over the Rose-Worlders' protests. I might add that the woman was the merchantman's record-keeper—"

"Supercargo," Balthasar murmured, but there was a new, approving note in his voice.

The Hegemon lifted his eyebrow. "As you say. In any case, she is more than willing to trade everything she knows about the Rose Worlds and the star roads that lead between them— and about the engines that block the Earth-road—for her life."

Chase Mago said, "May I ask, your Majesty, how you got her to admit she knew about the Earth-road? From all I've heard, they put a geas on their people."

"Any geas can be broken," Adeben answered, "as you well know. And in this case, our knowing that the engines were there helped make it easy." He glanced at Silence. "I'd expected those questions from you, sieura."

The pilot hesitated. There were half a dozen things she needed to know before she could analyze this "gift," but one thing was more important than all the others. "I was wondering more about the price."

The Hegemon smiled. "I thought it was good merchant practice to examine the goods first, and then inquire the price." He held up his hand, forestalling Chase Mago's immediate response. "Frankly, sieuri, I wish you would— interview—the supercargo first, and decide for yourselves if her information will be of any use to you. Then we can talk about the thing that I want."

Silence glanced at the men to either side, and saw her own suspicions reflected in their faces. Before she could say anything, however, Isambard said, "That seems reasonable, your Majesty. Thank you."

Silence bit back her anger, recognizing from the magus's tone that no argument of hers would sway him. At least, she thought bitterly, the Hegemon didn't quite have the gall to try to pass off this supercargo's information as payment of the debt he owed her for destroying the enemy fleet at the Battle of Niminx. No, this was just the bait for some political favor, and probably an unpleasant one.

"Certainly." The Hegemon gestured to Marcinik, still waiting by the door. "Colonel, if you'd escort them to the cell block? You may use the private way."

"Very good, your Majesty," Marcinik answered.

The page rose from the corner where he'd been sitting, and crossed the room to place his palm against one of the diamond-shaped tiles that formed a band along three of the room's four walls. There was a dull pop, and a narrow door sagged open in the wall to the left of the massive desk. Marcinik bowed to the Hegemon, and stepped forward to pull the door fully open. Isambard stood slowly, gathering his robes around him, and beckoned for the others to join him. Reluctantly, Silence followed him through the narrow opening, and the page shut the door behind them.

The latch had barely clicked shut before Balthasar murmured, "Doesn't it figure they'd have a jail here?"

"Yes, it does," Chase Mago said, grimly. "Marcinik, where exactly are we going?"

There was a note in his voice that made Silence take a quick step forward and catch hastily at his sleeve. This was no time for the engineer to come to the end of his prodigious patience. "Hang on a minute, Julie, take it easy." To Marcinik, she added, "Could we have a few more details, Marcinik?"

"Of course, I'm sorry." The colonel looked genuinely chagrined, and Silence felt Chase Mago's muscles relax under her touch.

"They brought her—the supercargo—here for privacy, and

so you could talk to her more easily," Marcinik continued. "This isn't really a jail. Of course there are secure sections; they were built for things like this. You should be flattered: this is part of the private passage."

Silence glanced around the tiny, beige-walled cubicle, and had to stifle a slightly hysterical laugh. After the opulence of the rest of the Winter Palace, the undecorated room and the equally plain staircase that spiralled down from one corner seemed almost to belong to some other place entirely. Her eyes met Balthasar's, and the Delian gave her a mocking grin before stepping forward to murmur something in Chase Mago's ear. The engineer shrugged him away, but managed a reluctant smile.

"If you'll follow me?" Marcinik went on.

Silence stood back to let Isambard precede her down the curving staircase, grateful it was a closed spiral. She counted twenty complete turns before they reached the bottom, and guessed that they had come down at least two levels, were now below ground level. "Secure section" this might be, she thought, but it was beginning to look very much like a conventional jail.

The stairway ended in another beige-walled cubicle, this one with its door directly opposite the last step. The jamb was painted red—the first mark of color Silence had seen since they'd left the audience chamber—and the flat silver panel of a two-stage lock replaced any visible latchplate.

"Tell me, Colonel," Isambard said abruptly, "what sort of restraint is this woman under?"

Marcinik hesitated for an instant, then set his palm against the silver plate. "Restraint?" He did not glance at the star-travellers behind him.

Isambard, Silence thought savagely, had no such delicacy. The magus said, a touch of impatience in his voice, "Is she under geas, or trance-bound, or—which?"

"Trance-bound, I believe," Marcinik answered, with some distaste. A chime sounded then, and the door swung open, sparing him the necessity of a more detailed answer. "Sieuri, we're entering the secure section of the palace. I'll ask you to bear that in mind."

He had not looked at Balthasar, Silence thought, but his

meaning couldn't've been clearer. Chase Mago said, with some relish, "That's one for you, Denis."

The Delian grimaced, but said nothing.

The secure section had wider corridors, with walls that were painted a white tinged with the faintest admixture of blue. Every ten meters or so, a shallow alcove was set into the wall. As they passed the first one, Silence glanced sideways, into the red-glowing eyes of a guard-homunculus. It took every ounce of her control not to jump back in surprise. She made herself walk stiffly away instead, matching the others' pace, telling herself the creature was passive now, would not harm them. . . . Only if they somehow lost their authorization—was Marcinik himself their passport, she wondered suddenly?—would the homunculus become active. Balthasar touched her shoulder, making her start, but when she glanced up, the Delian's face showed only a sort of sympathetic encouragement. Chase Mago, too, had slowed his steps a little, so that her shoulder was almost rubbing against his arm. His massive presence was calming, and Silence made herself look into each alcove until she was certain the guard-homunculi could no longer surprise her.

The corridor ended abruptly, at another door that carried a two-stage lock. Marcinik put his palm to the plate, but this time the door slid open to reveal another man in the uniform of the True Thousand.

"Colonel," the stranger said. His tone was polite enough, but his eyes were wary, and his right hand wasn't far from the butt of his slung heylin.

"Captain Drieu," Marcinik answered. "These are the persons his Majesty wished you to admit."

Drieu's eyes flickered over the group, pausing briefly and unhappily on Balthasar, but then he seemed to relax slightly.

"Very good, colonel." As he spoke, he gestured unobtrusively with his left hand, and Silence was suddenly aware of the fading of a tension so all-pervasive that she hadn't noticed it until it was gone. She frowned—it was something she should have noticed, if she was going to call herself a magus—but then Drieu was motioning for them to enter.

"This way, sieuri, if you please."

They emerged into an odd, curved room, its walls banded

with multi-colored tubes of fixed fire—less a room, Silence thought suddenly, than a corridor, a circular corridor ringing some hidden core. More doors like the one through which they'd entered seemed to feed into the ring, and each was sealed with one of the complex two-stage locks. A pair of troopers in the Thousand's battle dress paced slowly along the curve, sonic rifles cradled in their arms. Another half-dozen troopers were seated on a set of benches between two doors, their rifles stowed neatly beneath their feet, but instead of playing cards or talking, their eyes were fixed on the newcomers. Silence shivered and looked away, but she was still aware of that measuring stare.

Drieu led them along the curve of the corridor, following the pair of troopers, until they came to a door set into the inner wall. Seeing it, Isambard's head lifted sharply, and, a moment later, Silence felt the same cold harmony frozen in the metal. She frowned, and studied the door more closely. It seemed to be a rather ordinary door, an elongated hexagon like a starship's hatch, ribs running from each corner to meet in a central boss. . . . Her eyes narrowed then. Six was a stable figure, more complex than solid, simple four, not as involved as busy eight; six was complex enough to carry a stasis field, and simple enough to add its own considerable strength to whatever formulae a magus chose to superimpose on it. She held her breath, and thought she could almost see the lines of the field, a faint, bluish haze clinging to the edge of the door, and running down the ribs to flare into a white-hot spark in the center of the boss itself. She blinked, and the perception faded.

"Your token, please, colonel?" Drieu said, and Silence shook herself back to reality.

Marcinik reached carefully into the inner pocket of his coat and pulled out a small cloth pouch. Its cords were knotted together at the top, and the knot had been covered with a skin of bright red wax. Drieu took the bag, wrapping his hand completely around it, then touched the door's boss lightly with his knuckles. There was a flash of heat, and a subliminal snapping sound, and then an almost invisible panel slid back, revealing a tiny keyboard. Drieu fingered that with his left hand, careful to stand so that his body blocked everyone's sight of the keys, and, with a groaning sound, the boss sank into the main part of the door and the whole thing split along the line of the ribs, each segment drawing back into the frame.

Isambard nodded almost proprietorially. "Angelos-lock," he murmured.

Silence nodded back, hiding a sudden surge of resentment—she had guessed that herself—and was saved from having to make a polite answer by Drieu's next words.

"I'm sorry, colonel, I'm only authorized to allow you and the magi into the chamber. The sieuri will have to wait outside."

Silence tensed, waiting for the explosion from Balthasar, but to her surprise, the Delian made no answer. Chase Mago said, "That's no trouble to us, colonel."

"Very well," Marcinik said. "You'll wait here, then. Doctor Isambard, sieura—Doctor Leigh, will you come with me?"

"Of course," Isambard answered, with a touch of annoyance.

Marcinik smiled, and gestured for the magus to precede him into the inner room. Silence braced herself—she disliked the idea of trance-binding almost as much as she disliked the idea of a geas, but would not show her unease—and followed, Marcinik at her elbow.

The inner room was much smaller than she had expected, as though the walls were very thick, and there was a still, dead quality to the air that set her teeth on edge. The space itself was cylindrical, divided into two semicircular sections by a transparent wall that seemed to be made of lumpy purple glass. A balding man in the red-trimmed robes of a Master in Fire was sitting in a pillow-chair on their side of the glass, a complicated meditation-pattern sketched with colored sand on the floor in front of him. Beyond the glass lay a woman, brown-skinned, fair-haired, arms folded across her bared breasts. A light blanket covered the rest of her body. From her own experiences, Silence guessed that when the magi had prepared the trance, they had not noticed the supercargo's gender, rather than sought to exploit it.

"Master?" Marcinik said quietly, and the balding man's shoulder twitched beneath the red-trimmed robe.

"Colonel," he said, without turning, and without taking his

eyes from the colored sand on the floor at his feet. "And Doctor—Isambard, is it?"

"And Doctor Leigh," Marcinik answered. He glanced at the older magus, his expression unreadable. "I leave the rest to you, sieuri." He stepped away, setting his back against the door, without waiting for a response.

Isambard nodded absently. "How is the girl held, master—?"

"Maedon Bee, doctor." The balding man's head shifted slightly, and one hand rose to indicate the complex pattern in front of him. "She's trance-bound—the trance of Giduarius."

Silence frowned. She had never made a close study of the arts of binding, and was not familiar with the schema for that particular trance—after her experiences on the troopship, she had a srong aversion to any kind of compulsive bond—but she had encountered references to the Giduarian trance in other literature. It was one of the strongest bonds, and among the most dangerous, though if properly set it would hold even the strongest of magi immobile and impotent, his thoughts accessible to any half-trained apprentice, until the maker of the bond chose to release him. But if the bond-maker made the slightest error at any stage in the long and complicated process, or if the victim struggled unduly, or any one of dozens of variables had not been calculated perfectly, the victim would die, or, worse still, go mad, his disordered mind a deadly snare for the bond-maker. Silence found herself staring at the supercargo's plain brown face with something approaching loathing, and made herself look away. Isambard was frowning, too, and Bee seemed to sense their unease.

"The trance was made by my own teacher, Rassiy, who is leader of the Alasset school on Enkomi. The woman has been questioned once, superficially, and no harm came of it." Bee glanced again at his hands, closing his eyes, and the hint of emotion drained out of his voice, leaving it as thick and toneless as the air in the little room. "I brought her from the depths to the lightless plain as soon as I was informed you would be coming. She is ready for your questions."

Isambard grunted and took a step forward, staring over the Master in Fire's shoulder at the meditation-pattern. "This is the schema?"

"The sketch of it, Doctor," Bee answered.

Isambard lifted an eyebrow, but said only, "Come here, Silence."

His tone brooked no refusal. Reluctantly, the pilot stepped forward herself, so that she stood at Bee's left, and turned her attention to the pattern on the floor. The usual linear formulae had been laid out in a mantric frame, presumably to reinforce the self-perpetuating bond, and it took her a moment to pick out the normal shape of the equation. Most of the symbols were familiar—ordinary, simple signs that, in conjunction with each other, took on a new and terrible meaning. Silence shivered, catching an echo of the trance-bond's cold power.

"Well?" Isambard demanded. "What is your analysis?"

"A most—impressive structure," Silence answered, and knew she had not fully hidden her fear.

At the sound of her voice, Bee started, and for the first time took his eyes from the meditation-pattern. "A woman—?" he began, glancing quickly from Isambard to Silence to the supercargo. "Then it's true—"

"I wouldn't indulge in unprofitable speculation," Marcinik said softly from his place by the door.

"Mind your work, Master," Isambard snapped, almost in the same moment.

Quelled, Bee dropped his eyes to the meditation-pattern, murmuring an incoherent apology. Isambard smiled thinly, but Silence was aware of Bee's continued curiosity, and of his sidelong glances, hastily concealed.

"Impressive, certainly," Isambard continued, as though there had been no interruption. "And very powerful. A well-considered piece of work." He stepped forward again, carefully avoiding the strewn sand, and placed one hand against the lumpy glass that separated their room from the supercargo. "Come, Silence."

"I'd rather not," the pilot answered, and almost instinctively folded her hands behind her back.

Isambard gave her an annoyed look. "Don't be squeamish, girl. I'll need your assessment as well, if this is to be of use."

"I'd rather not," Silence said again, and put all her strength into that refusal. She would not, could not, bear to question that still form, to invade the other woman's bound mind. "You know what's needed as well as I do."

Isambard frowned, but, as Silence had hoped, did not pursue the issue in Bee's presence. "As you wish," he said, and closed his eyes. Silence saw his hand contract slightly, then flatten against the lumpy glass.

She was never sure how long they stood there, unspeaking, barely daring to breathe, before the phantoms began to appear. At first, she thought that somehow Isambard had been careless, that the tantalizing shapes were as much emotion as image, but then, glancing hastily toward Bee and then toward Marcinik, still standing motionless against the locked door, she knew that Isambard was doing it deliberately, and that the display was for her alone. She looked away hurriedly, searching for something that would let her break the fascination being woven for her, but everything in the little room was intended to hold the supercargo in her trance. Each object led the eye back to the still figure beyond the purple glass.

Silence shook herself, hard, trying to think of something—anything—that would distract her, but the tantalizing images broke through her guard. For a fleeting instant, it seemed as though she stood on a balcony in a strange city, where the air smelled of foreign spices and the dim stars were arranged in unfamiliar patterns. She gasped, and a flat lagoon stretched before her, violet water under a metallic, cloud-streaked sky. Then she was bombarded with a rain of images, voidmarks from a dozen different star roads, each more tempting than the last. Almost in spite of herself, she stepped forward, and laid her hand against the glass. Isambard's power caught and held her, guiding her entry into the trance-bound mind.

The supercargo's mind was like a frozen garden, images curled in on themselves like ferns caught by frost. Silence cringed, afraid that she would somehow touch one of the fragile, ice-colored images and damage it beyond saving. She could not help remembering the troopship again, and how she had fought just such a geas, and overcome it for herself and for her husbands, and she was bitterly ashamed. The emotion whirled within her, threatening to break free; she gasped and heard, or thought she heard, Isambard's angry voice.

Control yourself, girl. This is no place for that.

With an effort, Silence fought down the memory, concentrating instead on the First Principles, until those stern words had caged her unruly thoughts.

Better, Isambard said dryly. *Now see what we've gained.*

Reluctantly, Silence turned her attention outward again, trying not to see the frozen images. Isambard's presence—he seemed little more than a black robe, so deeply had he submerged himself in his studies—seemed to float ahead of her. She followed the ghostly form, half afraid of what she'd find. At last he paused, and seemed to gesture; the shapes around them seemed to spring into unnatural life. Silence winced, overwhelmed by the rush of knowledge—knowledge of the star roads, knowledge of the ways of the Rose Worlds and of the Rose Worlders' ships, knowledge even of great engines that stood along a forbidden road. . . . The pilot drew back then, dazed by the rush of information, pushing forward her own knowledge and strength to dim the flaring images. Seen through that screen, it seemed odd that a supercargo should know so much. Of course, she told herself, a supercargo would have to know a little about every aspect of ship handling, but still, the indefinable strangeness remained. Cautiously, she reached out to probe the supercargo's mind, delicately searching for the knowledge that lay behind the superficial images.

Almost at once she met resistance, like a wall of glass rather than the ice that filled the rest of the supercargo's mind. Silence hesitated, not wanting to push too hard, and then the wall seemed to shatter, the sound of the falling shards blending into a note that struck an answering chord in her own memory. The voidmarks of the Earth-road itself rose in her mind—not the maimed, broken symbols she herself had seen through the distorting music of the Rose Worlders' engines, but the true marks in all their glory. It was too much to stumble over, unprepared; Silence thrust herself away from the seductive music.

She was herself again, standing at Bee's left hand, her own right hand braced against the glass wall. The sudden shift in perception, of reality, was sickening; she swallowed hard, closing her eyes against the quaking world. After perhaps a dozen heartbeats, she had mastered herself enough to step back, away from the wall, but the sickness stayed in the pit of her stomach. She could not quite bring herself to look at the supercargo's still figure, the colors of skin and hair dulled by the colored glass. Instead, she stared at the floor, doing her best to avoid the bright sands of the meditation-pattern. How could you do it? she demanded of herself. After everything, after you yourself were under geas, how could you let yourself be tricked into doing this?

"Yes, that was most enlightening." Isambard's voice was almost painfully self-satisfied, and Silence felt her stomach heave. Somehow, she made a neutral answer, but the older magus continued, unheeding, "I think we will be able to learn a great deal from her."

Silence stood mute, unable to think of any suitable reply. Marcinik cleared his throat. "I beg your pardon, sieuri, but his Majesty asked me, if you found the information useful, to bring you back to him at once, so that you might discuss the—price."

Silence looked up sharply. She had been so caught up in her own feelings that she had almost forgotten about the Hegemon's bargain. She glanced at Isambard, and saw the magus's face set in its most unreadable expression.

"Very well," Isambard said, after a pause that was fractionally too long. "Since his Majesty wishes it so."

"He does," Marcinik said, and touched a signal plate on the wall behind him.

CHAPTER 2

They returned to the Hegemon's chamber the same way they'd come, Marcinik hurrying them through the maze of corridors as though there were some unstated deadline. Silence, her thoughts still whirling from what she had done and from the vision of the Earth-road, was grateful for the haste that kept the others from asking awkward questions. Even so, she was aware of Chase Mago's eyes on her, and knew that both her husbands recognized that something had happened. At the top of the last stairway, Marcinik touched a hidden signal button, and stood back to wait. For a long moment nothing happened, and Balthasar's mouth curved slowly into a smile.

"Don't tell me he's forgotten us."

Silence shuddered, her nerves still raw, and barely stopped herself from snapping angrily at him. She knew Chase Mago had seen her convulsive movement, and glanced up, meeting the engineer's eyes in mute appeal. Chase Mago gave her a reassuring smile, and said, "Denis."

Balthasar turned, his rather startled expression fading to one of annoyance and then of understanding. As the door scraped open at last, he said, "Pull yourself together, woman, there's work to do."

Silence nodded, unexpectedly heartened by the Delian's words. Chase Mago frowned, but any response either could have made was cut off by the page's censorious, "Sieuri, his Majesty is waiting."

The lights had been lowered in the Hegemon's private chamber, the fixed fire burning low at the tips of the quasi-candles. In the dimmer light, the monkeylike homunculissimae looked even more grotesque than before, but Silence barely glanced at them. A gold-chased coffee service had been set on a low table in front of the row of tabourets, four fragile cups arranged in a formal square beside the urn. Silence wondered who would not be invited to drink, then realized that Marcinik had once again stepped aside, to take his place by the outer door.

"Sieuri." The Hegemon's great chair had been moved to the head of the line of tabourets, far enough away from the table to make it clear that Adeben would not take coffee with them. It was not a deliberate insult, Silence knew, but an attempt to make things more comfortable—the etiquette involved in actually sharing food or drink with the reigning Hegemon was complex beyond imagining—but even so she could not help feeling a touch of anger.

"Please be seated," the Hegemon continued. "You'll take coffee with me?" Without waiting for an answer, the page slipped forward, and filled each of the fragile cups. Silence accepted hers politely—there was nothing else she could do—but shook her head at the proffered spices. She cradled the cup in her hands, glad of its heat, feeling the chased-silver flowers that coiled around it, using that warmth and solidity to chase away the lingering sickness. Her recovery wouldn't last, she knew, but she hoped it would be enough to get her through this meeting.

Isambard tasted his coffee ceremoniously and nodded, murmuring some proper compliment. The Hegemon smiled austerely, and Silence hoped he wouldn't prolong the amenities out of sheer mischief. Then Adeben seemed to shake himself, and said, "Does my—gift meet with your approval, Doctor Isambard?"

Isambard took his time answering, straining Silence's equanimity almost to the breaking point. She stared into her coffee, not daring to speak for fear she would betray how much the encounter with the supercargo had shaken her, and willed Isambard to answer. At last, just as Silence was ready to speak herself, the older magus said, "It is a most generous present, your Majesty. I am able to read almost everything we will need to know in her mind."

Silence saw her husbands exchange a wary look, and frowned warningly at them. Balthasar grinned, but said nothing.

"Then you'll agree my help is worth quite a bit," Adeben continued smoothly.

But just how much do you want? Silence thought. She felt her shoulders stiffen painfully, and set her cup carefully aside. Before Isambard could answer, she said, "Indeed, what the supercargo can tell us will help, but of course your Majesty has already promised all his assistance."

A pair of tiny lines appeared between Isambard's eyebrows, and Silence wondered if she had gone too far. If all else failed, she had the Hegemon's assurance—in writing—that he was personally in her debt, but that was a promise she had hoped to use for more important things. The Hegemon smiled.

"I do acknowledge that, Sieura Doctor, as of course I must. But this additional help, I should think, would be worth additional cooperation from you."

Isambard said, "As your Majesty says. But it would help if we knew what your Majesty wants from us."

Adeben leaned forward slightly. From such a controlled man, it was as startling as if he'd suddenly stood up and started to pace the length of the room. Silence felt a chill go down her spine, and saw both her husbands set their cups aside. Only Isambard seemed unaffected.

"Sieuri," Adeben said. "You are aware, of course, of the political situation here. I am newly come to the throne—" He managed a rather wry smile. "—and I hold power only by right of conquest."

He paused and, after a moment, Chase Mago said slowly, "With respect, your Majesty, the majority of your subjects seem to prefer you to your predecessor."

The Hegemon nodded. "I won't pretend they don't. That will hold me safe against rebellion, for now—that and the fact that I control the True Thousand, and the True Thousand controls the army. But, as you, sieura doctor, are only too well aware, my legitimate child, the child of my First Wife, is a daughter. I have no legal sons."

So it comes to that, Silence thought. An old bitterness rose in her, and she fought it back with an effort. Let the shazadi—the Princess Royal—look after her own rights, she thought. It's no longer a concern of mine. All that matters is how this affects us.

"As I remember," she said aloud, "you've one son older than her Serenity—he's in your navy, I think—and at least two others who're officially of your household." She let the unspoken question hang in the air between them.

The Hegemon nodded. "That's true," he said, "and I intend Azarian to inherit. But—" He smiled again, with even less humor than before. "—he is not legitimate, and there are too many families among the Hundred—those families that can claim kinship with the ruling house, Captain Balthasar—who have legal sons. One of my oldest friends has already hinted that his son would make a worthy successor. He would have had the boy marry Aili, but he scotched that plan." He nodded toward Marcinik, standing expressionless by the door.

"And how, your Majesty, can we prevent it?" Silence asked.

"You stand a good chance of reaching Earth." The Hegemon fixed his eyes on her, and Silence shivered a little under that unblinking stare. "You have come very close to succeeding twice already. The Hegemony's interest in that search is quite well known; I've already hinted that I am as interested in it as was my predecessor. In fact, I've gone so far as to say to those who have pressed me to name an heir that I will leave this kingdom to whichever son of the Hundred discovers—or sponsors an expedition to discover—the true road to Earth. I intend for Azarian to meet those conditions."

No one said anything for a long moment, but then Isambard said mildly, "You can't seriously mean to do this, your Majesty."

Adeben lifted an eyebrow, but showed no other sign of displeasure. "And why not? I grant you, the men I've spoken to now think that I'm evading the issue, but there's nothing in law or custom to prevent me."

Silence hesitated, trying to think of something she could say that might stop him. The trouble is, she thought, in the bizarre world of the Thousand and the Hundred, where every gesture, every common daily act was filled with special meaning, it could well work. The only thing that could go wrong is if we fail. She opened her mouth to say as much, but Balthasar spoke first.

"That's for fairy tales; this is real."

Adeben looked down his nose at the Delian. "Yes, it is real, Captain. And I intend for my son to inherit."

Silence cut in hastily, afraid of what else Balthasar might say. "And what if we don't reach Earth, your Majesty?"

The Hegemon turned to face her, the tight lines of temper easing from the corners of his mouth. "Sieura Doctor, you have every incentive of your own to reach Earth, and I have no doubt that you will do it. If you fail, I'll think of some other way. But for now, will you take my—my son's charter?"

"Will you give us a little time to discuss this?" Silence asked, and Adeben shook his head.

"I'm sorry, Sieura Doctor, but I must have your answer now."

Silence sighed. They had little choice in the matter—but then, she told herself, it hardly made any difference. They would make the attempt to reach Earth regardless of any political capital that might be made of the trip later. A mere piece of paper couldn't hurt them, and in the long run it would only put the Hegemon more deeply in their debt. Glancing at the others, she saw the same knowledge reflected in their faces. She raised an eyebrow in wordless question, and Chase Mago gave a fractional nod. Balthasar scowled, but Silence stared at him until he shrugged and nodded.

"We're agreed, then," she said, and looked to Isambard.

"Very well," the older magus said. "It shall be as his Majesty wishes."

Adeben motioned to the page, who crossed to the desk and returned a moment later with a ribboned binder. "This is the charter," the Hegemon said. "Will you sign?"

"Pretty damned confident," Balthasar muttered, but nodded.

Silence said, "We'll sign."

In the end, all four signed their names beneath the Hegemon's seal, and Marcinik and the page witnessed that and the young prince's scrawled signature at the top of the charter. When they had finished, Adeben sighed softly. "It's done," he said, almost in disbelief, then shook himself. "Colonel. Escort the sieuri back to the villa, and see that they have every facility they need—see to it personally, Marcinik, if you please."

"Of course, your Majesty," Marcinik said, bowing, and gestured for the others to precede him from the room.

The flight back around the planet to the villa outside Anshar' Asteriona seemed even longer than it had before. Silence, her nerves already stretched taut, was only too aware of Balthasar's leashed anger. Her brief recovery was wearing off, too; at last, she leaned back against the cushioned seat and pretended to sleep.

They arrived at the villa in the fading darkness of a cloudy morning. Marcinik, who had quarters in the main palace complex in Anshar' Asteriona itself, excused himself at once, and vanished in the flyer. Silence hurried ahead of the others into the villa's main hall, murmuring something disjointed about getting some sleep.

"At this point, we might as well stay up," Balthasar growled. There was a note in his voice that stopped the pilot in her tracks.

"What's eating you, Denis?" Chase Mago said.

Balthasar didn't answer at once, shouting instead for a serving homunculus. When the creature appeared, its sculpted features oblivious to the hour, he ordered it to have a breakfast laid in the dining room, and turned away from its bowing acknowledgement. "Are you particularly happy with all this, Julie?"

"Reasonably," Chase Mago answered, and for the first time, there was a hint of anger in his voice. "You know as well as I do that the weak point in our plan was what to do once we got to Earth. Now we have information that will help us, and the Hegemon's even deeper in our debt. Why shouldn't I be happy? Why shouldn't you?"

"I'm not," Balthasar snapped back. "You're the one who always said we should steer clear of politics, not me. And I'm not wild about the way we're getting this 'help.'"

Silence lifted both hands to her face, unwinding her veil and then pressing her palms against her eyes. The nausea had vanished, but it had been replaced by a slowly worsening ache behind her temples. The pressure brought an instant's relief, but the pain returned almost immediately.

"Neither am I," Chase Mago said. His voice was barely under control now. "But we need it."

"We'd manage—" Balthasar began, and Silence said desperately, "Will you both shut up?"

"How the hell could you do it?" Balthasar demanded. "Silence, you know what it's like. You were bound too."

"I didn't have any choice," Silence snapped, and to her horror her voice broke in a sob. She turned her back on both men, but not before Chase Mago saw, and took a step forward.

"Silence?" he asked.

"Leave me alone, Julie, ignore it," Silence said, furious with them and with herself. "It's just that my head hurts. I'll fight fair."

The engineer froze, waiting. Silence dug her knuckles into the corners of her eyes, fighting to control herself. After a few moments, Balthasar said, sullenly, "I'm listening."

"Thank you," Silence said. "It's so gracious of you." She knew she was only making things worse, but she was past caring, goaded by the pain in her head and her own sense of guilt. She heard Balthasar draw breath for an angry answer, but Chase Mago spoke first.

"Let it go, both of you." He held out his hand, but Silence shook her head. She had said she would fight fair; she would not speak from the shelter of the engineer's arms.

"I told you," she said, with difficulty, "I didn't have much choice. The place—the whole room was set up to draw you in, to make it easy to read her, and then, when I said I didn't want to, Isambard let me see little bits, projected what he saw, until I couldn't help looking for myself." Her voice trailed off in defeat. There was no way Balthasar could understand, she thought greyly; he distrusted the magi's power too much already. "I can't explain. I wish—I know I shouldn't've done it."

The hall was very quiet for a long time—so quiet that Silence could hear the clatter of dishes in the dining room as the homunculi laid out the breakfast. Beyond the treated glass that framed the door the sun was rising, turning the clouds white. Finally, Balthasar said softly, "I'm sorry."

Silence nodded, but didn't turn, not knowing quite what

the Delian meant, and a moment later felt his hand on her shoulder.

"Forgive me?" he said again, and this time she turned into his embrace.

"It's all right," Balthasar said. "It's all right."

Silence didn't know how long she stood there, her head resting against Balthasar's shoulder, before Chase Mago cleared his throat gently. "If anyone wants it," he said, "there's breakfast waiting."

Silence pushed herself away, and even managed a smile at the engineer's indulgent tone. Balthasar laughed aloud, and gestured for the other man to lead the way.

The breaking of the emotional tension had eased Silence's headache, and the sight of food was almost welcome. She accepted a plate from the steaming sideboard, and settled herself at the table beneath the single long window. The sun was well up now; she touched the control board to darken the glass against the glare.

"Still," Chase Mago said, as he seated himself at the pilot's right, "I would like to know just what it is we're getting."

Balthasar grunted agreement, and came to join them, his plate heaped high. Silence sighed, recognizing that the brief respite had ended, and set her cup aside. "Apparently, this woman—she was a round-ship's supercargo—knows at least a little bit about everything. There's a whole lot of data on general shipping procedures, and she seems to know names of roads and even some voidmarks—"

Balthasar looked up at that. "How'd she learn those? That's the pilot's business."

Silence shrugged. "I don't know, yet. We'll find out." She shuddered in spite of herself, and added, "Or Isambard'll find out, anyway." She managed a smile. "Don't worry, I don't intend to trust any of that kind of knowledge unless I've verified it myself."

"She could've picked it up subconsciously while the ship was in purgatory," Chase Mago said, frowning thoughtfully. "At least, I've heard that's possible."

Silence nodded. "Theoretically it is, anyway, and a trance-bond's deep enough to reach that kind of buried knowledge. This was just a preliminary survey, anyway. The best thing is, she does seem to know something about the engines blocking the Earth-road, and that means she may actually have been to Earth herself."

Balthasar whistled softly. "Now, that would be useful."

"If," Chase Mago said. "Pass the coffee, Denis, would you?"

Balthasar did as he was told, saying, "So how do we handle getting this information? I assume you don't want to do it, Silence."

"No," Silence said, flatly. She controlled herself with an effort, and went on, "Isambard will do it, and I'll tell him to have it transcribed."

"Our very own guidebook," Balthasar said. "Can we trust him to find out everything we need to know?"

We have to, Silence thought. I can't—I won't touch that woman's mind again. Aloud, she said, "He knows enough about star travel. I think we can."

Chase Mago nodded. "I agree. It should be all right." He put his cup aside and stood, stretching. "I wonder if they'll send out our pipes today?"

To Silence's disappointment—she had hoped for another day of rest—the new pipes arrived some hours before noon, and Chase Mago decided to begin the difficult installation procedure at once. The next two days were spent damping the harmonium, foam-packing the parts of the array that would not be changed, and wrapping the pipes nearest to the ones that would be replaced in dura-felt sleeves. Only then could the new pipes be fitted into their place in the main array. It was dull, delicate work, complicated by the fact that the smallest pipe, a thin, ice-blue cylinder of dolor-crystal barely longer than Silence's hand, proved to be flawed and had to be replaced from the yard. Finally, however, all the pipes were in place and the last of the damping was cleared from the harmonium, and Chase Mago began the millimetric adjustments that would bring the new pipes into perfect harmony with the rest of the array. Silence had neither the ear nor the patience for the work, and was almost relieved when one of the household homunculi appeared in the workshed to announce that Isambard had returned from the Winter Palace.

Chase Mago, crouched beside the tuning studs, merely grunted an acknowledgement, and Silence said quickly, "I'll go."

It took a moment for the words to register, but then the engineer looked up and nodded. "Yes, do that, would you?"

"Right," Silence said, and set the audirim monitor she had been using on the deckplates to Chase Mago's left. The engineer nodded again, but his attention was already back on his work. Silence nodded back, and turned to follow the homunculus from the engine room. At the main hatch the intercom buzzed, and Balthasar's voice crackled from the speaker.

"Silence? What's up?"

The pilot paused by the intercom panel. "Where's Isambard?" she asked.

"Doctor Isambard is in the study," the homunculus answered, in its emotionless voice.

"Then you can go. Tell him I'll be there in a moment," Silence said, and touched the intercom's answer button. "Isambard's back, Denis. He sent to say he wanted to see me."

"Have fun," Balthasar answered, and laughed.

"Thanks," Silence said, rather sourly, and broke the connection.

The villa did not have a study, in the usual sense of the owner's private library; instead, Isambard had ordered the household homunculi to bring broad tables and comfortable chairs into a room that had originally been intended as a chance room, and had personally augmented the fixed-fire lamps so that it was possible to work for long periods at the tables. Silence paused just inside the doorway, blinking a little in spite of the heavy curtains pulled tight across the windows.

"You wanted to see me?" she asked, and frowned at the empty table caught in the cone of light. Its surface was covered with papers, but there was no sign of Isambard.

"Yes." The voice came from the shadowed corner to her left. Silence's frown deepened, and then she saw the magus. He was stooped over an ancient portfolio, his black robe effectively hiding him. "I have work for you." Isambard came forward as he spoke, and placed another sheaf of papers on the table.

"Oh?" Silence picked up the first sheet, and scanned Isambard's crabbed writing. It was part of the transcription of Isambard's "interview" with the Rose Worlder supercargo. The pilot shivered in spite of herself, and put the paper aside.

"This is the rough data," Isambard went on, as if he hadn't noticed the other's sudden revulsion. "If you won't help me collect it, at least you can set it into order for me. You know your husbands' training better than I; choose whatever system you think best." He stooped to pick up a final crumpled piece of paper, and set it on top of the rest. "I will be back here in two days with the rest."

"Wait," Silence said. "What's all this about—what are the topics?"

"Everything," Isambard answered, from the doorway. "I told you, this is the raw data. I leave its arrangement to you."

With that, he was gone. Silence stood for a moment, staring after him, then shook herself and sat down at the table. The drifts of paper were intimidating, but one thing that both her pilot's training and the course of study on Solitudo Hermae had stressed was the technique of ordering information. Years before, long before the Millennial Wars had shattered the Earth-road and Earth's hold on human-settled space, before the art of star travel had been fully understood, that sort of work had been done by artificial minds—and in truth, she thought, the old computers were more suited to it. But computers, because they parodied human thought, gave off a parody of the magi's powers—a sort of anti-thought that disrupted every function of the art; human minds could sort as well, and, once the mnemonic science had been fully developed, almost as efficiently as any machine. One sacrifices convenience for real power: that was the first lesson dinned into every apprentice of every art.

Silence sighed, and reached for the nearest sheet of paper. There were literally dozens of mnemonic systems, each one designed for a particular purpose; there was no point in trying to decide which one to use until she had made a survey of the data. At least she could rely on both Balthasar and Chase Mago to know the simple Guilian and the more complicated Grand memory Theaters, as well as the Chanfro exercises that made learning such quantities of information possible in a limited time. Balthasar, too, had been trained as a pilot by the Cor Tauri guild's method, and would certainly know the hexagram system, but it was less likely that Chase Mago would know that highly visual method. . . .

Silence shook herself, and forced herself to look at the paper in front of her. She could not decide—could not begin to decide now, before she had seen any of the information, without running the risk of choosing the wrong system, and forcing the data into a framework that it would not fit, or, worse still, that would distort the information it contained. She blanked her mind, putting aside all thoughts of any system, and began to read.

After perhaps an hour of reading more or less at random, she began to see patterns emerging in the data itself, and began to sort the sheets of paper into rough piles, following the pattern of the Grand Theater. Isambard had done his best to keep from putting more than one topic on each page, but, working without a system, he had been unable to be fully consistent in that. Looking at the mountain of paper in front of her, and knowing that there was more to come, Silence cursed softly, but then, grimly, set herself to copying out the older magus's notes so that they could be sorted more easily.

In the end, it took her almost two weeks to reduce the data Isambard had gathered to a manageable text that could be carefully transcribed by one of the homunculi. Looking at her own flash-printed copy, she had to admit that she was rather pleased by the results. For a first attempt, she thought, she'd done rather well. Still, she found herself glancing anxiously from her husbands to Isambard as she waited for them to finish skimming through the text. She could not quite read the emotions behind the abstracted expressions; she could only hope that she had done the right things.

Predictably, it was Balthasar who finished first, and set aside his copy with a wry smile. "As good as Valman's any day."

"It had better be," Silence answered, a little grimly. "Or better." Valman's Guide was the standard planetary almanac for the Hegemony and the Rusadir; it was also notoriously incomplete.

"I didn't mean it like that," Balthasar began, but before he could complete the sentence, Chase Mago looked up from his own copy of the text.

"There's an awful lot here on the siege engines. Are you going to try to break through after all?"

Silence sighed, and darted a quick glance toward Isambard. The older magus was still absorbed in his book, and the pilot let herself relax a little. "That's one of the things we need to talk about," she said. "I don't think we should risk it—"

"And I disagree," Isambard said calmly, without looking up from his book. He turned the final two pages, then closed the book and set it on the table in front of him. "We have the information we need now, either to break the engines, or at the very least, make an excellent attempt at circumventing them—"

"Did the woman know the passwords?" Balthasar broke in, frowning.

Silence shook her head. "No."

Isambard said, "But I believe I understand how the passwords are chosen, and how the responsors work. I believe I can convince the system to let us through."

"It sounds like a risk we don't have to take," Chase Mago said.

Silence gave a sigh of relief. She had been arguing with Isambard for the past few days over whether or not they should use the portolan she had won as her fee for freeing the Princess Royal, but she had not known for sure where the other two star-travellers would stand on the question. "I agree," she said, and Isambard said, "But this portolan method of yours is equally risky. This is too important to trust to some archaic theory, a theory that you admit you don't completely understand."

"And if we do it your way, and you can't unlock the engines," Silence retorted, "we'd have no choice except to break the engines—which would at the very least tell the Rose Worlders we were on the way."

"You've got a point there," Chase Mago murmured, with a

smile. Then his smile faded slightly. "On the other hand, if we could sneak through, posing as a Rose Worlder ship. . . ."

"We could do that anyway," Silence said. "We'll have to. I don't like the idea of my having to control the ship while we're hung up in the Earth-road waiting for you to figure out the engines."

"You did manage to change roads once before," Chase Mago said, thoughtfully. "You could always do that again, if things get bad."

"I did it once," Silence answered. "There's no guarantee I could do it again." The excuse was feeble, and she knew it. If she had been able to switch star roads once, under difficult conditions, manipulating two sets of voidmarks that reflected related harmonics and similar objects in the mundane universe, she could do it again.

Isambard smiled, but mastered himself almost at once. "If we use your portolan, Silence, you yourself said that we have to spend a great deal of time in mundane space. Isn't that so? Time in which the Rose Worlders can search for us with impunity. We—and particularly you, Silence—went to a good deal of trouble to obtain the portolan, but I don't think that should force us to use such a primitive method when a better one is available." He looked directly at Balthasar. "What do you say, Captain Balthasar?"

Balthasar sighed, staring at nothing, and seemed to weigh his words before answering. Silence held her breath, hoping the Delian wouldn't side against her. Isambard was determined to try breaking the engines, she knew; it would take all three star-travellers together to overrule the magus.

"I'm with you, Silence," Balthasar said at last. "I just don't trust the Rose Worlders—I never have. I'd rather not have any contact with them at all until we hit the Earth approach, and I don't want to be dependent on any of them, no matter how trustworthy she is. I see your point, Julie," he added, "but I don't think it's worth it."

How like Balthasar, Silence thought remotely, to blame the engineer for Isambard's suggestion. Aloud, she said, "It's three to one, Isambard, and I'm the one who's piloting. We'll do it by the portolan."

"I don't believe Sieur Chase Mago was in agreement with you," Isambard said sharply, and Silence held her breath.

The engineer lifted an eyebrow. "I hadn't agreed with anyone," he said, with deceptive mildness. "This is the pilot's choice."

Isambard took a deep breath, and Silence braced herself to continue the argument. But then, quite suddenly, the older magus gave a very human sigh, and shook his head. "Very well. I accept that you know more about these matters than I." He picked up his copy of the text again. "So. If we're to use the portolan method, how do we hide the fact that we haven't come the usual road? And what will be our story when we do reach Earth?"

"We should be able to sort of ease into the usual arrival point," Balthasar said, and Silence nodded.

"An entrance point to an approach road is pretty big, Isambard," she said. "Given that space within the Rose Worlds is so complexly interlinked, there shouldn't be any problem getting to it."

"As for a story," Balthasar said, and grinned, "leave that to me."

"God help us all," Chase Mago said.

The next weeks were spent in the final preparations for their departure. With the installation of the new pipes, Chase Mago proclaimed *Recusante* ready for loading, and he and Balthasar promptly vanished into Anshar' Asteriona's Pale. The engineer returned to the villa at regular intervals, each time bringing another airsled full of provisions and fuels, but Balthasar seemed to have disappeared completely. Silence, busy plotting first their ostensible course off-world, and then the passage through the dead roads into the Rose Worlders' sphere, was only peripherally aware of the Delian's absence. It was only when he finally reappeared, unshaven and disheveled, but carrying Rose Worlder papers for *Recusante* and her crew, that she realized he had been gone for some time.

"Where the hell did you get those?" she asked. "And why'd it take so long?"

They were sitting in the villa's dining room, beneath the long window, but still Balthasar looked over his shoulder. "From an old acquaintance," he said, lowering his voice almost to a whisper. "You don't know him—but you do, Julie."

Chase Mago, who had been sitting sprawled in the room's most comfortable chair, sat up abruptly. "You don't mean Morwen Daso," he said, in the flat tone of someone who expects contradiction.

Balthasar grinned. "Of course."

Chase Mago growled a curse, and Silence said, "Who's Morwen Daso?"

"An old acquaintance," Balthasar said again, with the same maddening smile on his lips.

I thought we'd broken you of this, Silence thought. Can't you for once give a straight answer? She scowled, and Chase Mago said, "He used to work for Wrath-of-God, but he sold out three years ago."

"That's before Arganthonios," Silence said, in spite of herself, and the engineer nodded.

"That's right." He stared at Balthasar for a long moment, then said, in a tone that suggested immense patience wearing very thin, "Why him, Denis?"

"He's the best there is," Balthasar answered simply. "He's the only person I can think of who could forge papers good enough to get us through Rose Worlder security."

"But he's a talker," Chase Mago objected. "Leaving aside the fact that he sold an entire network, he always had a name for talking too much."

Balthasar smiled again, the self-satisfied smile of a successful gambler. With difficulty, Silence suppressed the desire to kick him.

"Not this time," the Delian said. "Morwen's back in the business—"

"I heard he went legal," Chase Mago interjected, frowning.

"He got bored." Balthasar spread his hands. "He's got a new name, new network, he's up-and-coming—so he gives me the papers, and he keeps his mouth shut, and I don't tell the darksiders that he used to be Morwen Daso." He smiled directly at Silence this time. "Honor among thieves and all that. Most darksiders frown on selling your own men to the local cops."

Silence made a skeptical noise. In her limited experience,

darksiders—smugglers, fences, thieves, petty pirates too small to work for Wrath-of-God—were perfectly willing to ignore any treachery not directed at themselves, and to make a profit off it if at all possible.

"How're you going to enforce that?" Chase Mago asked. His tone was still disapproving, but the frown had eased a little.

"The Wrath still has an ear on Asterion," Balthasar answered. "I spoke to him."

"Who?" the engineer asked, still frowning.

"Kalle."

"Ah." Chase Mago nodded, clearly satisfied.

"I take it this Kalle's reliable?" Silence asked. In spite of herself, a note of asperity crept into her voice. It didn't happen often, but every now and then the two men's shared years with Wrath-of-God became a wall, excluding her.

"Very." Chase Mago, always more sensitive to tone, made a face. "He runs a bar in the Pale, everybody goes there. The Wrath finances him—or used to, at any rate—so anybody who has anything, any information to sell, always goes to him."

Silence nodded, grateful and still a little resentful, and Balthasar pulled himself upright in his chair.

"So," he said, "that means we're ready."

Silence blinked, startled. Somehow, despite the frantic preparations of the past weeks, she hadn't really realized how close they were to leaving Asterion. Chase Mago nodded slowly, and Silence saw the same mild surprise reflected in his expression.

"There's just the charter to deal with," Balthasar said, and there was an odd note in his voice that made Silence look warily at him.

"What do you mean, deal with?" she asked. "It's in the ship's arms locker, sealed in."

"I don't suppose we could leave without it," the Delian murmured, giving the words an odd, almost quizzical twist.

"Why?" she asked, and in the same moment Chase Mago said, "No, we couldn't. We can't afford to get any further entangled in politics, whatever you're up to."

Balthasar raised both hands in mock surrender. "All right. I just don't like playing the hegemon's little game."

There was more to it than that, Silence thought, but then Chase Mago leaned forward to pick up the flat case that held the new papers, and the moment was gone.

"So what exactly is our story?" the engineer asked.

"Routine trade run," Balthasar answered promptly. "Under special license."

"'Special license' doesn't sound exactly routine to me," Chase Mago objected, and Silence shook her head.

"There aren't any regularly scheduled runs, remember," she said. "Anything going through the engines has to have a special license."

The engineer nodded, satisfied, and slid one of the golden disks into the reader on the outside of the case, snapping the machine on as he did so. Silence watched him, wishing she felt as confident as she sounded. The Rose Worlder supercargo had known any number of scattered facts—that there were engines on a semi-forbidden star road; that a starship passing those engines needed a special pass, the sort of pass she had seen once, and remembered because of its complexity; the star-travellers reaching that blocked world were restricted to Pale and port—but so much of their plan rested on Isambard's interpretation of those facts. But of course, Silence told herself, Isambard's worked in the Rose Worlds before; he knows a lot more about them than we do. We can trust him to do his best, if only because he wants to reach Earth even more than we do. Still, the lingering sense of unease persisted.

"Mersaa Maia," Chase Mago said, half to himself. "That's good."

"It's the one Rose World we've all been on," Balthasar said, shrugging.

Silence glanced over the engineer's shoulder, and saw that both *Recusante*—the ship was keeping its own name, for once—and her crew were listed as registrants of Mersaa Maia. It was a good idea, she thought, though less because of their one brief and unpleasant visit than because Mersaa was the Rose Worlds' single open port. Of necessity, Mersaa's natives would have had more contact with the inhabitants of the Hegemony and the Fringe, and any oddities in their own behavior would—she hoped—be explained that way. "So I'm the supercargo?" she asked.

Balthasar nodded. "I figured that was easiest. And that way Morwen could copy that woman's papers for you."

Silence made a face—somehow, she didn't like the idea of carrying papers stolen from the bound supercargo—but nodded back.

"And I've lined up the cargo for us," Balthasar continued. "Our hold will contain just what the manifest says it does."

"It sounds good," Chase Mago said, and slid the last disk back into its case. "So when do we lift?"

"Marcinik said we'll take priority whenever we want to go," Balthasar answered, and looked at Silence.

The pilot hesitated, still strangely unprepared for the idea of leaving Asterion. "If Isambard's ready," she began, then shook herself, almost angrily. The older magus was ready, and had been ready for several days. It was up to her to set the time. "You're fueled and stocked, Julie?"

The engineer nodded.

"Then we'll go the day after tomorrow," Silence said.

The relative planetary harmonies gave them a choice of a predawn lift or one during the main traffic period in the middle of the local afternoon. Rather than attract undue attention, they opted for the earlier place, and Silence turned her attention to the last-minute preparations. Her course plot, the first leg from Asterion to Meng that would set them up for an easy entrance to the dead roads, had been ready for weeks; even so, she spent several more hours reviewing the unfamiliar voidmarks. Between that study, and Balthasar's unexpected demands for her help in setting up the departure course, she had less time to pack her own few belongings than she had expected, and found herself dragging her last carryall aboard less than two hours before liftoff. I think I've acquired more things than ever before, she thought, frantically trying to find secure places for the bag and its contents, though I'll be damned if I know where it all came from. Finally, however, she had crammed the last clean shirt into a latched drawer, and reached for the shipsuit she had left hanging on its peg beside the door. She worked her way into the tight, clinging fabric and jammed her discarded clothes into another of the latched drawers. Carefully, she ran her fingers along each of the seven seam-seals, making sure they'd caught, then stood for a moment staring around the little cabin.

The carryall itself lay on the tidied bunk, just waiting, she thought, for the pseudo-animation of purgatory. There was a tiny amount of the supermaterial in everything; in purgatory, stimulated by the harmonium's effects, that supermaterial substance could—and often did—cause objects to wander about the ship, seeking to return to their proper place. She smiled, and stuffed the carryall into the least crowded wall locker. The last thing she needed was for the carryall to appear on the bridge, and try to climb onto her shoulder. Nor did she need the teasing that that sort of carelessness would inevitably bring.

She glanced around again, satisfied that everything was either in its proper place or safely under lock and key, and left the cabin, locking the door behind her. The ship seemed oddly quiet, and she paused for a moment in the main corridor, listening. Very distantly, she could hear the usual noises as Chase Mago moved about the engine room, but the harmonium's notes seemed more muted than they should be. It was almost as though someone had set up an aphonic ring, she thought, or at least a damper field. Perhaps Isambard had decided to shield his cabin from the noises of lift-off? She closed her eyes, concentrating, but the strange soundlessness refused to take form. Whatever it was, she thought, it didn't seem to be coming from Isambard's cabin. If anything, it seemed to center on the empty passenger cabins. . . . Frowning, she moved farther down the corridor, toward the common room door.

"Silence!" Balthasar was halfway down the ladder that led to the twin bridges, hawk face set into a scowl. "Where the hell are you going? I need you topside."

And what's the matter with you? Silence thought, but said nothing. The past few days hadn't been particularly easy for the Delian; he was entitled to a certain amount of ill temper. Still, she thought, *I wish he wouldn't take it out on me.*

"Coming," she said, and followed Balthasar up the ladder to the lower bridge.

The bridge had changed almost as much as the rest of the ship, with larger and more powerful equipment crammed into a very limited space. Silence had to turn sideways to get past the musonar console, and practically fell into the second pilot's couch. Balthasar was already strapped into the captain's couch, his fingers dancing busily across his keyboards. The triple viewscreens showed only the walls of the improvised docking shed; the left-hand screen showed the waiting tow, crouched on its double treads. Through the dock's open door, Silence could see a slice of the grasslands surrounding the villa, the ground very dark in the pre-dawn light.

"Who's driving the tow?" she asked.

"Julie," Balthasar answered, his eyes still glued to the banks of checklights above the secondary console. Most glowed standby blue, but here and there an orange light showed a waking system.

Silence frowned. The engineer had enough to do preparing for liftoff without having to manage the tow as well. "I thought we were hiring someone from the port."

"It didn't work out," Balthasar said, as he touched a series of buttons, and studied the resulting readout intently.

"Do you want me to take it?" Silence asked, still frowning. "I can drive a tow."

Balthasar shook his head. "No, I need you here."

Silence hesitated—the second pilot's job didn't really begin until the ship reached the twelfth of heaven—then shrugged. The worst that could happen was for Chase Mago's countdown to be delayed and, since Marcinik had promised them a priority lift, there was no need to worry about delay causing them to miss their place in the departure queue. She adjusted her couch to its most comfortable position and began flipping the switches that lit her own instruments. Musonar, Ficinan model, the camera controls, the environmental boards. . . . She paused then, frowning, and rocked the switch back and forth a second time.

"Denis, I'm not getting a response from the passive internal monitor."

"Damn." Balthasar glanced over his shoulder, saw the unlit

telltales, and touched a switch on the intercom panel. "Attention, people, I'm testing the environmental alarms." With that, he flipped off the intercom and leaned back to punch a set of keys on a secondary control board. Silence winced as lights flashed across the warning screens and audio alarms began sounding throughout the ship. Balthasar let it run through two cycles, then cut the test. "Everything looks green here. It's probably just a fuse or something."

That was an awfully quick decision, Silence thought. Aloud, she said, "Do you want me to warn Julie? If it's something simple, it shouldn't take long."

"I don't want to miss the lift," Balthasar answered. "It'll wait."

"I could do it," Silence began, and Balthasar cut her off.

"Let it go. It's not important."

Silence darted a quick glance at the Delian. It wasn't like him to ignore even minor repairs without good reason. "Is anything wrong?" she began. Her voice trailed off as she noticed Balthasar's hands were shaking.

The captain saw the direction of her gaze and forced a smile. "I'm just a little nervous, I guess. It's a tricky business."

Something in that didn't quite ring true, but before Silence could pursue the issue, the intercom buzzed.

"I'm in the tow now," Chase Mago's voice announced. "Are you ready in control?"

"Ready here," Balthasar answered, and there was a distinct note of relief in his voice.

Silence glanced down at her board, now showing multiple rows of orange lights, and touched the buttons that would secure the ship's systems against the inevitable jolting of the tow. "All secure."

"You can begin the tow, Julie," Balthasar said.

There was no answer, but a moment later the left-hand screen showed the tow creeping forward on its double tracks. As the tow hook came taut, the ship's cradle jerked hard, but then settled under the engineer's cautious handling to a gentle swaying. Very slowly, cradle and tow moved toward the huge entrance, and then out onto the soft ground. Silence held her breath—the homunculi had spent some hours hard-foaming the improvised taxiway—but the cradle showed no inclination to stick. It was strange to see trees and grass in the screens, rather than the familiar buildings of the port complex, but Silence was only vaguely aware of the anomaly. Instead, she kept an eye on Balthasar, who was scowling nervously at his readouts, wondering just what the Delian was up to.

The cradle's swaying stopped abruptly, and Chase Mago's voice interrupted her thoughts. "We're in position. I'm un-hitching the tow."

Balthasar did not answer, still staring at his controls, and after a moment Silence reached across to touch the outside button on the communications board. "All right. Let us know when you're back inside."

"I'll do that," the engineer answered, and broke the con-nection. A minute later, the tow's top hatch lifted, and Chase Mago levered himself out of the cramped interior. Silence watched the viewscreen until the engineer vanished under the high nose of the cradle, out of range of *Recusante*'s cameras. A light flashed from red to green, indicating that Chase Mago had released the tow hook, and then the tow itself began to move slowly away under control of its own tiny brain. Silence caught a brief glimpse of the engineer as he crossed the left-wing camera's field of vision, but then he was gone again, only the flicker of the hatch light, from green to orange to green, marking the moment he came aboard.

Balthasar saw the flicker too, and managed a ghostly grin. He reached across the empty Ficinan model to touch keys on the communications board. "Anshar' Asteriona Control, this is DRV *Recusante*. I understand you're holding a place for us in the lift queue."

Anshar' Asteriona answered promptly—so promptly that Silence wondered if a special technician had been detailed to handle their liftoff.

"That's correct, *Recusante*. Please stand by to confirm the lift-line."

"Standing by," Balthasar answered, and Silence keyed the Ficinan display. The little globe darkened perceptibly, the planets of Asterion's system fading into existence in its depths. Each pinpoint was surrounded by a slowly deepening flush of color, a reflection of the planetary harmonies, the *musica mundana*, that surrounded each world. The outer planets, Niminx and Mim Seras, were in conjunction, and sparks flared where the harmonic envelopes touched. *Recusante*'s course line curved well away from that dissonance. "Ready for your figures."

"Transmitting," Anshar' Asteriona answered.

A moment later, a second course line appeared in the Ficinan display, hovered for an instant, and then melted into the original line. Silence glanced quickly at the numerical display to confirm it, and said, "I show a match."

"Good enough," Balthasar said. "We show a match, Asteriona Control."

"Very good," Anshar' Asteriona responded. "Please confirm your bearing."

Silence glanced to her right, reading off the numbers on the astrolabe set into the console just in front of the Ficinan globe. Balthasar repeated them into his microphone, and waited.

"The tower astrologers confirm the bearing," Anshar' Asteriona said, after a brief pause. "Traffic has been put on hold. You may lift when ready, *Recusante*."

Silence whistled softly to herself. To hold traffic on a busy world like Asterion was almost unheard of, an honor reserved for satraps and other planetary powers, not for private starships. Balthasar gave a sigh—almost of relief, Silence thought, and her suspicion deepened.

"Ready to lift," the Delian responded, and cut the outside transmitter. He touched a second button on the intercom console, saying, "All set below, Julie?"

"Everything's green," the engineer answered.

Balthasar took a deep breath, and Silence saw that his hands were trembling again. "First sequence."

"First sequence," Chase Mago answered, and an instant later the harmonium sounded. This was the first time Silence had heard the full diapason since the worn pipes had been replaced. The new sound—bone-deep, without human harmonies—woke echoes in brain and body. She shivered at the beauty of it. The note that she had heard each time they attempted the Earth-road, the note that was as close as human perception could come to the note of heaven, hung within it, implicit in that sound. *Recusante* shivered in her cradle, and leaped upward. The harmonic envelope formed almost before Silence was aware of the usual sensation of crushing weight.

"My God," she said aloud.

Balthasar nodded, his fingers busy on his keyboard. The sound eased a little, then steadied as Chase Mago made his own corrections.

"Sorry, Denis." Even through the intercom's distortion, the engineer sounded faintly shaken. "I didn't expect that."

"Shows you what money will buy," Balthasar answered, but his tone was less flippant than his words.

"*Recusante*, we show that you are steady on your departure line," Anshar' Asteriona announced. "Good voyage."

"We confirm that," Silence answered, when Balthasar showed no signs of responding. "Thank you, Control."

She switched off the transmitter, and leaned back in her couch. Already, the harmonium's music was fading as *Recusante* passed the edges of Asterion's harmonic envelope. A few moments later, the last of the core-based notes cut out, leaving only the pure, sweet chord that would take them up to the twelfth of heaven.

"On course and in the groove," Balthasar announced, with some satisfaction. He glanced at the readouts on the astrogation board. "Not long to the twelfth, Silence. You might want to go on up."

The pilot raised her eyebrows. It would be at least an hour, and more probably two, even with the power provided by the new pipes, before *Recusante* could reach a point at which the systemic harmonies were sufficiently deadened by the celestial harmonies—the delicate background note of deep space—for the ship to cross the border into purgatory. Still, she thought, there was no point in arguing, especially since Balthasar was already in a bad humor. She nodded, and released the catches on her safety webbing.

To her surprise, the minor effects of purgatory—the faint stickiness of the decking, the odd sense of a world askew—were already beginning to make themselves felt as she pulled herself up the ladder to the upper bridge. The dome, which, unlike the rest of the ship's bulkheads, was made of a special tinctureless metal, was already beginning to show translucence, the nearest stars shining faintly in its depths. Silence frowned, checking the readouts set in the hub and spokes of her control wheel, but the numbers still showed *Recusante* to be well below the twelfth of heaven. Still frowning, she fitted her headphone jack into its socket, and keyed the intercom.

"Denis, I'm getting some very strange responses up here."

"Yeah, I know," Balthasar answered. "Here, too."

Chase Mago's chuckle sounded in their ears, and Silence hastily adjusted the volume. "This is the way it's supposed to be, people," the engineer said. "This is a freshly tuned ship and mostly new pipes, remember?"

Silence nodded to herself, leaving the intercom channel open. The engineer's explanation made sense: star travel depended on the interaction between the harmonium and a starship's massive sounding keel, and if both were in perfect tune, or even close to perfection, naturally the ship would see the effects of purgatory more quickly. The harmonium produced a note as close as humanly possible to the celestial harmony, the note of the supermaterial state beyond the mundane universe, the source of the Forms on which much of the magi's Art was based. A sounding keel was made of base metal impregnated with the Philosopher's Tincture, the only celestial substance that could exist in a mundane state. The Tincture sought always to return to its proper, celestial state, but was confined by the mundane materials around it. Only under the influence of the harmonium could the Tincture approach its original state, carrying with it and being restrained by the mundane nature of the rest of the ship and its crew. The ship would never reach heaven, but it could reach the twelfth of heaven that was purgatory, and that was enough. In purgatory, so the metaphysicists said, time and space became potentially identical; the pilots manipulated the visible symbols of those potentials—the voidmarks—to move from star system to star system.

Overhead, the dome was fading toward full transparence, and Silence shook herself. Through the untinctured metal, little more than shadow now, she could see the starscape, each sun ringed by the garish corona that marked the twelfth of heaven. She took a deep breath, recalling the voidmarks she had so carefully memorized, and stepped onto the low platform before the wheel, wriggling her feet into the cling-foam covering. They were travelling by the Road of the Harmonious Spheres, one of a class of roads known generally as rolling roads. If she closed her eyes, she could almost see the illustration in her *New Aquarius*. A crowned figure, young, male, wearing an old-fashioned version of the usual Hege-monic loose coat and trousers under an even more archaic breastplate, balanced on the top of a massive sphere that seemed to contain the shadowy image of an orrery. The figure's breastplate was badged with a living eye; he held in his right hand a short, splindle-shaped wand, and in his left an open book from which rose drops of fire. Behind the central figure was a city wall and a cluster of figures in magi's robes, all of whom pointed in amazement to a sky that, though filled with clouds, showed sun and moon and stars.

Remembering the image, Silence smiled, but her smile faded quickly. The Harmonious Spheres was a crowded road—that was one of the meanings of the impossible sky—and the symbols involved were very powerful ones. The pilot's Art was essentially a passive skill, manipulating already related symbols; a magus's training made it very difficult to concen-trate on the voidmarks, without drawing in all the other symbols and Forms that existed in potential in purgatory. If she were to become distracted on a rolling road, where the wand and the book and the eye all warned of the need for precise control. . . .

Silence shook herself. She had met and dealt with the multiple symbols crowding the Earth-road, and there were no more seductive images in either the pilots' or the magi's hieroglypicae. She would not allow herself to become dis-tracted. The control yoke moved gently under her hands, and she realized abruptly that the stars had vanished, leaving only their brilliant coronae scattered across the sky. She glanced down, and saw her bones gleaming through suddenly translu-cent flesh, caught in a ruby web of blood vessels.

"We're almost at the twelfth," Balthasar's voice said in her ears.

"I'm ready to take control," Silence answered automatically.

"Switching to the upper register," Balthasar said. "Now, Julie."

"Switching," Chase Mago answered, but the word was swallowed in the sudden surge of music. The keelsong split and broadened, individual tones momentarily audible, cascading up and down the scale until they merged into a new and greater song.

Silence gasped, the sound vibrating in her bones, and then that sensation merged into a new, less pleasant feeling. *Recusante* seemed suddenly to be rushing forward at an impossible speed, as though the pilot and the ship and everything in it were balancing on the rim of a moving wheel, running at breakneck speed without ever moving forward. Silence swore, remembering tardily that this was a rolling road, and sought her voidmarks.

For the first instant, as she had feared, a cloud of symbols blocked her vision, crowding out the true signs. She forced herself to look down at the tincture-treated decking, murmuring the first cantrips. She could hear the keelsong changing, sliding out of true, but ignored it for the moment, forcing herself to recover the pilot's disciplined vision. Then, at last, she looked up.

The last coronae had vanished, and she was surrounded by the images of purgatory. On all sides, the cloudy sky of the *New Aquarius*'s drawing surrounded them, spangled with its impossible sun and stars and multiphased moon, but she barely noticed those minor marks. Ahead and slightly above swung the central image, only vaguely like an orrery, seven huge rings swinging in self-contradictory orbits around a single gleaming axis. *Recusante* was falling toward one of those whizzing rings, and the sensation of movement, of unbalanced speed, increased as they came closer to it.

Silence swallowed hard, fighting back the impulse to swerve away from the ring. She touched the control yoke gently, easing *Recusante* onto a course that would bring her keel down onto that speeding ring. The dissonance eased perceptibly, but the speeding sensation increased. It was unreal, Silence knew, as unreal as the apparent increase in speed she felt when a ship left purgatory, but still unsettling. *Recusante* settled toward the approaching ring, her movement relative to the image disorientingly slow, completely unrelated to the sense of rapid movement. The discontinuity made it very hard to judge the approach, and Silence could feel her palms growing sweaty on the control yoke. If she missed—and wasn't thrown off into the dissonances that flanked every star road, marked here by the astronomical bodies hovering in the clouds—she could probably meet the next ring. . . . But it would still be an unbearably amateurish mistake.

The ring swung closer, and Silence swung the ship so that the keel would intersect the image first. She could no longer see the image, now lying underfoot, but she was tuned to its movements. She held her breath, waiting. Now, she thought, just . . . now.

Even as she thought the word, the sense of movement stopped. In the same moment the keelsong changed, a new note sounding in its music, and the clouds to either side began to move, swirling in a great vortex around the suddenly stationary starship. Silence let out her breath with a great sigh of relief. The first part of the road had been successfully negotiated; the rest would be easy.

This was the stable part of the Road of the Harmonious Spheres; a starship could lie here, static, carried around and around by the vortex that was represented by the revolving ring, until the elemental water that powered its harmonium was exhausted and the ship fell from purgatory. The ship still had to travel "up" the ring to the axis itself, and then down the axis to its midpoint, before it could leave purgatory. Carefully, Silence pulled back on the control yoke, lifting *Recusante* from its stable place at the heart of the ring. The keelsong changed, protesting, but the sensation of movement returned. Slowly, very slowly, the ship began to move along the ring, heading toward the axis.

Silence wasn't sure how long she'd stood there, the clouds and stars spinning dizzily around her, when Balthasar appeared on the bridge.

"Shall I spell you?" he asked. "Clock's changed twice, but I think we've still got some time before you make the shift."

Silence glanced along the ring ahead of them, suddenly aware of cramped muscles and an urgent pressure in her bladder. Real time passed irregularly in purgatory, but subjective time remained constant, and demanding. They were perhaps halfway to the axis. "We should have," she said aloud. "Thanks, Denis, it's all yours."

Balthasar stepped onto the platform behind her, so close that his body was pressed against her back, and reached around her to set his hands on the control yoke. The bones and arteries showed clearly beneath his transparent skin, the knob of an old break starkly visible in the bones just above his left wrist. She avoided looking at his face, knowing what she would see.

"I've got it," the Delian said.

"All yours," Silence said again, and released the wheel, ducking under the other's arms. Balthasar was a good pilot; she did not glance back as she let herself slide down the ladders to the ship's main deck. She went into her own cabin to relieve herself, then returned to the main corridor, carefully latching the door behind her. She stood for a moment, working her shoulders, trying to shrug away some of the stiffness. I'm out of shape, she thought. The Road of the Harmonious Spheres wasn't a particularly long one—a little more than nine minutes, real time, but only four subjective hours—but it had been some months since she'd flown. She laced her fingers together and pushed them straight out in front of her, feeling the tightness in her arms and shoulders. At least by the time this trip is over I'll be back in shape, she thought. I'll have done enough piloting for that, if nothing else.

The corridor was very quiet, Chase Mago cloistered in the engine room, Isambard locked in his cabin, dreaming through the passage. Silence glanced down the corridor toward the orange safety light ringing the engine room hatch, and felt again the strange, oppressive quiet. She frowned, but knew this was not the time to investigate. Instead, she pulled herself back up the ladders, pausing momentarily on the lower bridge to check the chronometer. It had ticked once since she had left the bridge: plenty of time.

She swung herself off the ladder on the upper bridge, hurriedly scanning the voidmarks. They were closer to the end of the ring and the turn down the axis, but there was still plenty of time to make the changeover. She said, "Did

Isambard bring any equipment that needed special shielding, or anything like that?"

Balthasar did not turn, but Silence thought his shoulders tightened under the clinging shipsuit. "Not that I know of," the Delian said. "Why?"

"There's—well, a funny feeling down on the main deck," Silence answered. "Nothing serious, but it feels like a damper, or something like that."

This time Balthasar did shrug. "I don't know," he said, and his tone made it clear that he didn't particularly care. "You want to take her again?"

So much for that, Silence thought. If the Delian didn't think her feeling was important, she would let it go, at least for now. Though it did seem odd, given Balthasar's usual near paranoia. . . . She pushed the thought aside, and said, "If you're ready."

Without waiting for Balthasar's nod, she stepped onto the platform behind him, reaching around to take the wheel in her right hand. "I've got it," she said.

Balthasar nodded, and slipped aside. Silence put her other hand on the yoke, working her feet back into the clingfoam.

"I wouldn't worry about it," Balthasar said. From his voice, he was already on the ladder, but Silence did not look back. "It's probably not anything important."

"Thanks," Silence said, but the Delian was gone. Sighing, Silence put aside the minor problem, and turned her attention to the voidmarks.

Recusante was almost up to the axis, its silvery column almost twice as wide as the ship's extended stabilizers. The point at which the ring met the axis gleamed brilliantly, throwing off clouds of sparks. Silence made a face at that, but she could see that the real point of intersection was clear of interference. The starship inched its way up the ring, seeming to slow as it approached the axis. That, too, was deception, but for once it worked in the pilot's favor. Silence took her time studying the approach, letting her hands rest loosely on the wheel. Almost, she thought. And . . . now.

She swung the yoke hard, pulling *Recusante* down and to the right. The keelsong rose, a stressed note at its core, and then abruptly steadied. *Recusante* rode in a tube of silver, its cylindrical walls reflecting the glow of the starship's keel. Silence gave a sigh of relief. They were almost through. Already, she could see the black disk that marked the end of the road, could feel the false acceleration that meant the ship was falling away from purgatory.

And then they were through, the keelsong shifting pitch again, back to the normal register. Silence locked the control yoke without waiting for Balthasar's order—she could tell from the way the ship handled that the Delian had it fully under control—then let herself slide down the ladder to the lower bridge.

The displays were busy already, Meng Approach flashing multiple audio and visual instructions, and Silence dropped quickly into her couch, reaching for the communications keyboard. Balthasar, still busy fine-tuning the harmonium, gave her a grateful glance.

"We want a parking orbit, right?" Silence said, her fingers already busy filtering out the unnecessary input. "Meng, or the Anskazeion?"

"The Anaskazeion," Balthasar answered.

Silence nodded, and keyed in the commands for the proper displays. The image in the Ficinan model swam momentarily, planets shifting fractionally in relation to each other, then steadied. An instant later, the projected course appeared, a blue line running along the edge of the system, just skirting the flaring dissonance that followed a massive gas giant. A light was flashing on the communications board, indicating that someone was querying their automatic identification, but she ignored it. It was nice not to have to worry about hitting the override in time.

"DRV *Recusante*, this is Anaskazeion Approach Control," a deep voice said a moment later. "You are presently inbound for the Anaskazeion Ring. Do you wish dock or orbit facilities?"

"Anaskazeion Approach, this is *Recusante*," Silence answered. "We acknowledge we're in your lane, and would like to request orbit facilities."

There was a pause—time/distance lag more than anything else, Silence guessed—before Anaskazeion answered. "Very good, *Recusante*. There are free spaces in sector 246.29. Please stand by to receive precise coordinates."

"Standing by," Silence answered, and keyed the recorder. There was a whine, and numbers flashed across the right-hand viewscreen. Balthasar reached across hastily to freeze the output, then touched a second set of keys to transfer the information to the musonar and the Ficinan model.

"Not bad," he said, and nodded toward the musonar display.

"Anaskazeion Approach, we acknowledge receipt of the coordinates," Silence said automatically, and barely heard the deep-voiced response. She was staring at the musonar, en-thralled. Like all star-travellers, she had heard of the Anaskazeion ring, but the stories had not prepared her for the reality. Meng was a predominantly agricultural world, every meter of its amazingly fertile soil given over to growing something. Rather than waste valuable ground on a true starport and all its facilities, Meng's governors had built the Anaskazeion in what had once been an asteroid belt. That subplanetary debris was long gone, transformed into the hulls of permanent stations. In its place, a network of stations and fixpoints circled the planet, providing the star-travellers with every conceivable comfort while lighters ferried cargo to and from the planet's surface.

"Stop down to half power, Julie," Balthasar said. "Local regulations."

"Stopping down to half power," Chase Mago repeated, and the harmonium's sound faded.

Silence stared into the musonar display. She could see why the local authorities wanted ships to mute their harmonia: already the screen was flecked with the dull bronze dots that indicated active keels, interspersed with the brighter lights of the parking beacons.

"That's where we're headed," Balthasar said, and lifted one hand from his keyboards to touch one of the left-hand buoys.

Silence nodded and leaned back in her couch, watching the Delian bring the little ship in through the crowded lanes. Balthasar was a good systems pilot, she thought idly, much better than she herself was, though she was the better starpilot. At last the Delian brought them alongside the fixpoint, and cut the harmonium. He touched keys on the communications board, and the fixpoint's anchor nodes glowed, creating a newtonian field that drew *Recusante* gently in toward the fixpoint and held it steady. At the same time a power cable unfurled, probing awkwardly for the ship's intake jack. There was a sharp click, more felt than heard, and a new set of lights sprang to life on the environmental display.

"DRV *Recusante*, we show that you have docked," Anaskazeion Approach said cheerfully. "Welcome to the ring."

"We are docked," Silence agreed. "Thanks, Approach." She cut the channel and glanced at Balthasar, who looked away.

"Shall we go below?" he said, without waiting for her to speak. "There's some things we need to talk about."

Oh, really? Silence thought, all the vague suspicions of the past few days crystallizing into the conviction that Balthasar was up to something, probably no good. "Sure," she said aloud, and unfastened the safety webbing. Before she could push herself out of the couch, the intercom buzzed.

"Denis," Chase Mago began, his voice dangerously quiet, and Balthasar cut him off hastily.

"Don't panic, Julie, I'll be right down."

"What the hell are you up to?" Silence demanded, but Balthasar was already sliding down the ladder, and pretended not to hear. The pilot cursed him, and followed.

Chase Mago was standing in the doorway of the common room, his face thunderous. "I hope to hell you have a good explanation, Denis," he said, and Balthasar spread his hands nervously.

"Of course," he began, but his voice faded under the engineer's furious glare.

Silence took a deep breath, wondering just what the Delian had done this time, and pushed past Chase Mago into the common room. Three people were waiting there, one in a magus's black. Silence barely noticed Isambard's familiar figure, her attention going instead to the other two. Marcinik, as striking as ever in the Thousand's undress black, stood at attention behind the room's tallest oilchair. In that chair sat a small, veiled figure: Aili, the Princess Royal.

CHAPTER 3

Silence turned slowly, until she was facing Balthasar. "You stupid son of a bitch. What the hell are you playing at?"

Balthasar spread his hands again, grinning uneasily. Chase Mago eyed him dubiously, one fist clenched as though he was restraining himself from hitting the smaller man. "It's like this," the Delian began, and Silence cut him off.

"Don't give me any of your bullshit stories, Denis, or I'll take you apart."

"I'll help," Chase Mago said.

"Silence." Aili's cool voice cut through Balthasar's stammering answer. "This isn't entirely Captain Balthasar's doing."

Silence turned, goaded, but bit back her angry answer at the last possible moment. "You wouldn't be here without him."

"That's true." Aili rose gracefully from her chair, and came to stand between the combatants. Marcinik, with an obvious effort, remained where he was. Out of the corner of her eye, Silence could see Isambard watching with detached interest, and his very detachment steadied her.

"So why are you here, your Serenity?" the pilot asked.

"Because of my father's proclamation," Aili answered simply.

Silence frowned, and Chase Mago said, "Proclamation?"

"And, of course, the charter," Aili said. She turned her veiled head so that she was looking directly at Silence. "My half-brother is merely competent: I am both more capable than he, and the more legitimate heir." The veil hid her expression completely, but there was a note of humor in her voice. "I had thought you would sympathize with me, Silence. After all, if you can become a magus, why should I be denied mere political power?"

Silence looked away. There was some justice in the Princess Royal's words—but that, Silence thought, *is not my affair*. We only just managed to get the Hegemon on our side; we can't afford to antagonize him, not now. And won't all the authorities be looking for a runaway princess? She opened her mouth to ask, but Chase Mago spoke first, a wealth of bitterness in his voice.

"I thought you hated politics, Denis."

Balthasar shrugged, obviously torn between his habitual reticence and the desire to brag about his cleverness.

Silence said, "He just likes to make trouble." She turned back to Aili. "Proclamation or not, your Serenity, we're already under charter to your brother."

"Half-brother," Aili corrected. "And the terms of the proclamation give precedence to persons who make the search themselves."

"Why would anyone do that?" Chase Mago asked, apparently distracted by the odd condition.

Marcinik's mouth twisted into a wry smile. "His most serene Majesty was trying to get rid of a rival known for his adventurous spirit."

"Oh." The engineer nodded thoughtfully. "It makes a perverse sort of sense."

"Be that as it may," Silence said, "I don't want anything to do with this."

"They're already aboard," Balthasar said, with another nervous grin. "You can hardly put them off."

"Oh, can't I?" Silence said grimly.

The Delian's smile vanished. "Now wait just a goddamn minute," he said. "Silence, you can't."

"Why not?" Silence retorted. "Look, aside from the fact that helping them is going to get us into serious trouble with this hegemon—trouble we can't afford—they'll be nothing but a liability once we reach Earth. We don't have papers for them—" She broke off, seeing Balthasar's almost embarrassed gesture, and continued, controlling her temper with an effort, "All right, you got them papers. Still, they're not star-travellers, not even Marcinit; they'll give us away the minute they set foot in the Pale. Especially Aili. She's a woman of the Thousand—a princess of the royal blood, for God's sake. She'll be nothing but a liability. We can't do it, Denis."

"You sound just like Nils Og," Balthasar said, and Silence suppressed the urge to hit him. Og had been the most vocal critic of female pilots, even Misthians. "Take a good look at her. Does she look like a liability?"

Silence glanced at the Princess Royal, sobered in spite of herself by the Delian's words. For the first time, Aili's clothes registered properly. The Princess Royal was wearing the shapeless coat and trousers favored by the poorer citizens of the Hegemony, and her face was covered, as Hegemonic law required. However, instead of a veil, she wore the turban and draped facecloth of a member of the Bethlemites. Silence raised an eyebrow, but had to admit it was a good choice. The Bethlemite sect held, among other odd beliefs, that star travel, and especially the passage through purgatory, revealed a man's essential nakedness too clearly, and therefore kept all parts of their bodies hidden beneath tinctured clothing. It was also a small sect, and one whose members kept very much to themselves. Glancing back at Aili, Silence saw the Princess Royal had even acquired the form-fitted gloves.

"All right," the pilot said, more calmly, to Balthasar, "you found her a good disguise."

"No." For the first time, Aili's voice held a hint of anger. "I chose the disguise, Silence. I planned this. Don't insult me that way again."

Silence hesitated, unwillingly remembering a similar conversation she had had with Aili in the Women's Palace. Aili had accused her of believing that women—or at least other women—really were inferior. It wasn't true then, Silence thought, and it isn't true now. We just can't afford to help her. It wasn't much of an excuse, and she knew it. Aili's first words rang in her ears: *If you can become a magus, why should I be denied mere political power?*

Balthasar said, "It's true. They approached me with the idea."

"That must've been something to see," Silence said bitterly, then shook her head, gesturing to brush the words away. "I'm sorry, Denis, I didn't mean it." She took a deep breath, and turned to face Aili. "And I apologize to you. I was upset, I didn't mean any insult."

Aili nodded back, her tone easing somewhat. "We should have consulted you first, but there was no safe opportunity."

And you probably knew I'd react this way, too, Silence thought, already ashamed of herself. She said aloud, "Are you sure his Majesty's proclamation will really give you precedence?"

"Almost completely," Aili answered, and once again the note of humor was in her voice. "I can think of only one jurist who could break it, and I think I can pay him well enough to support me."

"In any case," Marcinik said, "that doesn't have to affect you. You will have done your duty to his Majesty and to the Princess Royal; you can argue with some justice that conflicts of precedence aren't your affair."

I doubt it will be that simple, Silence thought, but nodded. "All right, I know how you vote, Denis. Julie?"

The big engineer shrugged, a rather bemused expression on his face. "Unless you want to put them off by force—and I wouldn't want to try it with one of the True Thousand—I don't think we have any choice."

"Isambard?" Silence asked.

"The political question is immaterial," the older magus answered. His voice rose abruptly, infused with more passion than any of the others had heard from him. "But I will see Earth."

The unexpected vehemence of his words left the others speechless. When Silence finally spoke, her voice held a new seriousness. "So be it. We—all of us—go to Earth."

Recusante spent three days in the Anaskazeion, a day longer than they had originally intended. Silence threw herself into the business of plotting a course from Meng into the dead roads, star roads that once had led to worlds destroyed in the Millennial Wars. They were dangerous, their voidmarks distorted by the destruction of all or part of the end system, but Wrath-of-God had made use of them on a regular basis, and Balthasar knew them well. On their previous attempts to reach Earth, they had used the broken Decelea system as a staging point, but Decelea offered no easy road to Limyre, the point at which they had chosen to switch to the portolan system. Two other broken systems, Sebethos and Atrax, offered decent departure roads, but Balthasar vetoed Atrax on the grounds that its system was too unstable. After some searching, putting together the information in Silence's ancient—pre-War—copy of the starbook *The Gilded Stairs* with Balthasar's knowledge of the dead roads, they settled on Sebethos, by means of the road listed in *The Gilded Stairs* as the Eagle's Flight.

Balthasar snorted. "We called it the Ganymede Run."

Silence glanced again at the book lying on the common room table in front of her, and the delicate miniature filling half the page. Like all *The Gilded Stairs'* illustrations, it was a beautiful drawing, yet strangely disturbing. It showed a fiery river, flames leaping and flowing like water over a rocky bed. Lean, feral animals prowled along the riverbanks, seemingly kept in check only by the lapping fires. A bird of prey—an eagle, by the road's name, Silence thought—soared away from that fire, a naked youth caught in its claws. Looking more closely, Silence could see more naked figures, all male, all young, formed by the river's flames. Trust Balthasar and the rest of Wrath-of-God to see that, she thought, and to find the reference. Aloud, she said, "How much have the marks changed?" On most of the dead roads, the printed voidmarks were no longer accurate, distorted by the broken harmonies of the shattered systems.

Balthasar gave a twisted smile. "The marks haven't really changed, it's the emotional—hell, sexual—effect that's the problem. Something in the systemic music really touches a nerve."

Silence nodded, still studying the illustration. Fire was one of the most common symbols for desire, sexual and otherwise. From the flaming river, she guessed that the erotic potential had always been implicit in the voidmarks, though the soaring eagle—it was rising, not stooping, she was fairly certain—suggested that the eroticism had originally been harnessed and channeled to the control of the starship. She nodded again. It made sense that the destruction of the

object, the road's higher goal, would allow the unleashed
sexuality of the images full play. It was perhaps a pity that
she and Balthasar were the only trained pilots aboard, she
thought. They were both of a nature vulnerable to the
voidmarks' appeal. She shook the thought away irritably.
There was not a star-traveller alive who didn't know the
dangers of uncontrolled passions, hadn't had the horror stories dinned into him from the first days of his apprenticeship.
It might be an upsetting ride, but hardly an impossible one.

"And then, when we get to Limyre, we switch systems,"
she said, and reached for the locked carryall that sat beside
her chair. She touched the lockplate, and lifted the lid,
drawing out the battered portolan.

Balthasar nodded. "That strikes me as the tricky part." He
searched among the papers littering the table until he found
the oversized printout from the astrogation console, a two-
dimensional drawing of the Ficinan model of the Limyre
system. "Counting in all factors, we should come out of
purgatory here." One long finger touched a point just outside
the orbit of Limyre's most distant sister, an unnamed gas
giant. The Rose Worlders had probably named it, Silence
thought, irrelevantly, but that information had never made it
to the rest of human-settled space.

"We really need Julie for this," Balthasar said fretfully, and
Silence shrugged.

"He's got the final adjustments to make, you know that.
We'll have time to go over it again with him, don't worry."

"I know," Balthasar muttered, then shook himself, returning his attention to the system map. "So, as soon as we hit
the twelfth, Julie lets the harmonium stop down naturally—"

"Thus hopefully making us look like a normal flare," Silence finished impatiently. "Limyre system's supposed to be
full of them."

"I hope that damn supercargo was right about that," Balthasar
said. He sighed, and looked up. "After that, it's all yours."

Silence nodded, not entirely happily, staring at the uno-
pened portolan. No one had used the portolan system since
the third century of star travel; between that time and her
own lay both centuries and the destruction of the Millennial
Wars. She herself had never heard of the portolan system

until she had stumbled across a photoflashed copy of an ancient pamphlet, bound in with half a dozen like it, which the magi had collected as a curiosity without recognizing what it contained. No, to be fair, Silence thought, they simply didn't have the knowledge to give it context. Even being a pilot might not have been enough for me to see it could take us to Earth. But she owned a copy of a pre-War starbook, one that contained both the Earth-road and the closely guarded roads that led among the Rose Worlds. The three things together had been enough to show her a new road to Earth.

Sighing, she opened the portolan, turning the pages one by one until she found the drawing she was looking for. The portolan system was totally unlike the normal method of star travel, using the voidmarks only as signposts, rather than the potent symbols they had later become. In normal star travel, the pilot actually manipulated the voidmarks; there was a true interaction between pilot, ship, and symbol. Using a portolan. . . . Silence forced herself to look again at the double-page drawing spread out before her. It showed Limyre and environs, the planet and its sun at the center, lines—called landlines for some unknown reason—radiating out in all directions from that central point. Marks, some familiar as parts of the more complex images that made up the voidmarks, others completely unknown, lay scattered across the page as well. Each mark had its own smaller halo of landlines, and each line was carefully labelled with its harmonic bearing. Silence traced her planned course, along one line from Limyre to a mark shaped like a triple rose, then along a second line to a walled city, along a third to the goose-necked man, and so on, until at last they reached Earth. Following those lines would depend at least as much on matching the listed harmonic bearings as it would on her steering from one mark to the next; that was the reason Chase Mago was making final adjustments to the harmonium, to be sure its music was pure to the full nine places.

She sighed, still staring at the map. Theoretically, this should all work as planned, but she could not forget that most of her assumptions were no more than that, guesses based on the pamphlet she had read and the structure of the portolan itself. If she were wrong. . . . She put the image of disaster from her mind with an effort. If I'm wrong, she told herself, we will have to resort to Isambard's plan, and try to force the engines. That's all.

"Well, now." That was Chase Mago's voice, tired but triumphant. Silence looked up to find the engineer smiling down at her and Balthasar.

"Everything's finished," Chase Mago went on. "It's all done, and we're ready to go."

They left the Anaskazeion the morning of the next day, ship's time, wanting to be sure everyone was well rested before attempting the passage into the Rose Worlds. Ostensibly, they were outbound for Caire, a Fringe World noted for its resorts, and Departure Control's final "good voyage" was so wistful that Silence felt vaguely guilty for disappointing him. It was only a short run-up to the twelfth of heaven, but Silence took her place on the upper bridge early, remembering what Balthasar had said about the Eagle's Flight.

"Standing by to switch to the upper register," Balthasar's voice announced in her headset, and Silence rested both hands on the control yoke, her thumb poised over the lock. All around, the dome was fading, the stars' coronae shining through its metallic shadow.

"Ready above," she said.

"Engine room ready," Chase Mago said.

There was a momentary pause—Silence could almost see Balthasar watching his readouts—and then the Delian said, "Now."

If the engineer acknowledged the order, his words were lost in the sudden surge of music. The last wisps of the dome went transparent, as though blown away by the wave of sound. Silence smiled, caught in spite of herself by the soaring harmonies. Then she shook herself, almost angrily, and sought her voidmarks.

The feeling hit her first, a wave of absolute lust stronger than anything she had ever felt before. She gasped, body tingling, but forced herself to ignore the sensations. The voidmarks whirled around her, refused to steady into any familiar image. She swore, then cursed again as she realized she'd used a sexual image. The flaming river of *The Gilded*

Stairs' drawing took shaky form ahead of her, but she could not seem to concentrate on it enough to make it come clear. Bodies swirled up from its shadow like leaping flames, momentarily distinct, inviting, then spun away into the fire. A single figure swam before her, young, male, its muscles sharply molded. It reached for her, laughing, even as it dissolved in a shower of liquid flame. Its face had been vaguely familiar, but it vanished before she could capture the memory.

A second plume of flame rose from the fire, shaped itself into a new figure, instantly recognizable. It was the form of her first lover, the fire sharply outlining every curve and hollow of that familiar body, gleaming on the flat planes of chest and belly. There had been nothing between them except sex—he had not believed she was a star pilot, and she had not bothered to enlighten him, leaving him willingly when *Black Dolphin* left the planet—but she still remembered with aching precision the explosive delights of their lovemaking. He beckoned, smiling; Silence shivered, but looked away.

This is unreal, she told herself, it is illusion. He was—he is nothing to you. The words were powerless against the remembered passion. More shapes crowded up behind the smiling figure, familiar faces forming in the flames. Every man she had ever seen and desired was there, each one perfected, polished and completed, by years of daydream, fantasy embellishing experience. I never slept with you, with any of you but one, she thought, but the wordless challenge rang hollow in her mind. It did not matter; it was not experience but imagination that betrayed her now.

The keelsong changed, the spreading dissonance cutting through the haze of emotion. The voidmarks cleared, the eagle hovering above the flaming river, but there was barely time for that vison to register: *Recusante* was falling toward the river, its apparent speed increasing with every second. Silence's mouth set in a grim line, and she pulled up sharply on the control yoke, fixing her attention on the keelsong. She would allow no one—nothing—to distract her from the ship. The dissonance eased, but as it eased the memories returned, the figures even more desirable than before.

Something more was needed, something stronger than the

generalized protections of the pilots' cantrips and her professional instincts—something intrinsic to the road itself. Holding her breath, Silence fixed her eyes on the tinctured decking and eased the control yoke forward again, steering by the keelsong alone. The dissonance rose slightly, and Silence levelled the ship again, knowing the keel could not endure the dissonance for long without going out of tune. There was a voice in her headset, Chase Mago's voice, but she could not spare the concentration to untangle the words.

"I need time," she said, and was never afterwards certain that she had spoken aloud. The voice in the headset ceased, and she lifted her head cautiously, looking at the voidmarks.

The dissonance gave her something real to cling to, to use against the haze of memory that threatened to overwhelm her. The destruction of Sebethos had distorted the central figure, so that the eagle no longer rose, but stooped toward the flames, a naked youth dropping from slack claws as it sought new prey. On the false horizon, a tori gate still spanned the river, its once pure colors faded into greys. She took a deep breath, calming herself, putting aside the twin pressures of desire and memory. This was the Eagle's Flight—but that symbolism, of mastered passion, of royalty and freedom and conquest, provided little help now. Or Ganymede's Run. . . . That name triggered a memory from her studies on Solitudo Hermae. First the shepherd, the seducing male, and then its related symbols: the rainbow-clad shepherdess, its feminine equivalent; the huntress, its feminine antithesis; the empress, its opposite and its opposition; and finally the seeress, personified wisdom, absolute negation of everything for which the Ganymede-figure stood. She was conventionally shown armored, armed with the sickle of the moon and the flaming disk of the sun.

Without conscious thought, Silence reached for that image, abandoning a pilot's detachment to shape the symbol out of the potentiality of purgatory. She drew it to herself, surrounding herself with the symbol and its meanings, clothing heself in the seeress's armor. The compelling desire faded, but she was surrounded by too many symbols, each one triggering an explosion of related images. She controlled that with an effort, banishing all but the necessary images of the star road and the seeress who was her talisman, balancing herself between the power of a magus and the art of a pilot.

The dissonance wailed around her, and she knew she could wait no longer. Cautiously, afraid of losing her precarious balance, she pulled back on the yoke, lifting *Recusante* back into the proper road. The dissonance faded, and she braced herself for the resurgence of the memory-figures. The first one rose, scar-faced, feral, a pilot she had worshipped during her apprenticeship and for years after. He was exactly as she remembered him from her daydreams, the cruel mouth relaxed into a smile of welcome, yet the memory lacked the demanding sexuality of the other figures, was nothing more than a memory. Silence lifted her eyes to the tori gate.

It was very close now, and already Silence could feel the first subtle increase in *Recusante*'s apparent speed as the ship began to fall away from the twelfth of heaven. More figures rose from the flames, the same familiar shapes, but this time they held no power over her. *Recusante*'s speed increased still further, and then they were through, the note of the harmonium dropping perceptibly. Silence glanced over her shoulder, and saw the seeress's armored figure framed in the afterimage of the tori gate. In the instant before the image vanished altogether, the pilot thought she saw her own face beneath the shadowing helmet.

"I have control," Balthasar's voice said in her ears.

"You have it," Silence answered, and heard how flat her own voice sounded. She locked her wheel, but instead of climbing down the ladder to the lower bridge, she seated herself at the base of the yoke, drawing herself into a huddled ball. The passion created by the star road had gone sour, leaving her stale and bitter. She closed her eyes and took a deep breath, trying to put aside the feeling. It was all unreal, she told herself again, all illusion and therefore unimportant. It did not feel unimportant, and she was profoundly grateful that the others had not seen the road's images. Aili and Marcinik and Isambard were still in their cabins, locked in drugged, dreamless sleep; both Balthasar and Chase Mago would see their own desires in the fiery river. I wonder why I didn't see them among all the rest, Silence thought, but the question answered itself almost at once. The Eagle's Flight showed purposeless passion, desire unmoderated by any other influence; her marriage had become passionate, but it was founded on far more complex needs and desires.

"Silence?" Balthasar's voice held the same dulled quality as her own, and the pilot wondered momentarily just what the Delian had seen. She put the thought firmly aside: she did not want to know, any more than she wanted her own fantasies to be known.

"Oh my way," she answered, and pushed herself up off the clinging platform.

Balthasar was leaning back in his couch, one hand resting lightly on the keyboard that gave the pilot limited control of the harmonium, the other fiddling with the controls of the Ficinan model. He looked up as Silence took her place beside him, but glanced away before she met his eyes. Silence thought she recognized her own embarrassed guilt in his somber expression.

"How're we doing?" Silence asked. For both their sakes, she kept her voice businesslike, focusing all her attention on the readouts and the triple screen. There was a momentary pause before Balthasar answered, and the pilot hoped she was doing the right thing.

"So far, everything's according to plan," the Delian answered at last, and gestured to the musonar. "Nothing's stirring."

Silence nodded, careful to watch the screens instead of the other. The main pitch indicator was slipping down the lower quarter of the scale, the harmonium's note already well below human hearing, matching the music emanating from the system's outer planet. At this scale the Ficinan model showed only the wash of music from the inner planets. The musonar, set at its greatest range, showed a few tiny flecks of bronze, the reflections of starships' keels, but all of them were well within Limyre's envelope. "That's good."

Balthasar nodded back, then darted another glance in her direction. "I—" He made a face then, as though he couldn't find the words, and settled for, "It's a bad road, that one."

Silence shrugged uncomfortably, not certain quite how she should respond, but knowing something needed to be said. "You gave me fair warning," she said, and held out her hand, not quite daring to look at him. After a moment, Balthasar grasped it tightly, but said nothing. Silence glanced sideways, and saw the other's face shut against her, as it had been on Wrath-of-God, and on the transport. She said, slowly, "It's a road, Denis."

Balthasar didn't move for a long moment, but then one corner of his mouth twitched upward in a grimace that was something less than a smile. Still, from him that was enough. Silence relaxed a little, but did not release his hand, grateful for the chaste warmth. They sat unmoving, linked hands resting lightly on the globe of the Ficinan display. The pitch indicator crept toward the base line.

Chase Mago's voice finally broke the quiet. "I show that we're there."

Balthasar pulled his hand away without the smallest expression of apology and reached for the intercom.

Silence leaned sideways to get a better look at the pitch indicators. The main indicator line hovered at the base; the numerical readings below, each covering a quarter of the scale, showed three rows of zeros and a single number. "I show a match to four places," she said, and Balthasar nodded.

"Our readout shows correct to four," he said into his headset microphone.

"Five, now," Silence interrupted.

"To five places," Balthasar corrected. "There's no traffic out here. Do you want to wait for the full nine?"

There was a long pause. Silence stared at the pitch indicators. A nine-point match would be almost perfect, but it had taken them almost an hour to reach the acceptable five places, and the indicator showed no desire to move again. The longer they stayed in mundane space, the more chance there was that a Rose Worlder ship would see them. . . .

"I wouldn't risk it," Chase Mago said abruptly. "It's going to take us another two hours or better to run up to heaven Silence's way. I'd rather go now, and take my time matching the landline."

"Good enough," Balthasar said. "We'll go now." He glanced at Silence, the familiar nervous grin on his face. "Well, what's the first line, pilot?"

Silence lifted the portolan onto the arms of the couch,

opening it to the marked pages that showed the Limyre system. She had laid out the course a dozen times already, but even so, she traced the chosen line with her finger, from the system edge to the first mark, before replying. "The setting is rho five, sol seven over five, mi octavo, tau six-three-one."

"Rho five, sol seven-fifths, mi octavo, and tau six-three-one," Chase Mago repeated. In the background, Silence could hear clicking noises as the engineer adjusted the harmonium's limiting stops. "Rise?"

Silence glanced again at the chain of symbols, looking for a single number printed in red. "Eight-zero slash seven."

"Eight-zero over seven," Chase Mago said. He took a deep breath, the noise of it clearly audible in the headsets. "We're ready to go, bridge."

Balthasar looked toward Silence, still with that nervous smile on his face. The pilot nodded, holding her breath, and Balthasar said, "Go."

For a long moment, it seemed as though nothing had happened, and Silence clasped her hands tightly in her lap. To be wrong now, after everything, would be more than she could stand. Then, very faintly, she felt the first note of the adjusted keelsong, a note so deep it trembled just at the edge of hearing. She sighed, and heard Balthasar let out his breath in an explosive gasp.

"Well, at least the tuning works," he said aloud.

Silence nodded, still listening to the unfamiliar song. This was a new method to her, to all of them, even though it dated in actuality from the very earliest days of star travel. It had been the great star-faring guilds, the Leading Star, the Adventurine, and later the Cor Tauri and Num Sessa, who had developed the modern harmonia with their multiple, multi-throated pipes, and the flexible tuning systems that let a ship go directly from the lifting sequence, the harmony that countered the music of the planetary core, to the music that would take them to the edge of the systemic envelope and finally beyond the twelfth of heaven. Originally, the harmonium had been a crude instrument, with single pipes and only a few stops with which to control them; star travel had been a long, multi-stage process. The ship left the planet, then paused in orbit to retune to the systemic notes; it reached the edge of the system, and stopped to retune to the celestial harmony. Reaching purgatory had been a matter of copying the natural pattern of a harmonic flare, not creating and controlling an artificially determined music. At least that should work to our advantage, Silence thought. Limyre's musonar shouldn't be able to tell us from a normal flare.

She sighed, and glanced again at the portolan. So much depended on her having correctly deduced its workings, the workings of a system no one had used in generations. At least the tuning was given in a notation that hadn't changed over the years, but the rest of it. . . . She shook herself, hard. She had been right about the first part; she would be right about the rest, as well.

The keelsong strengthened around her, rough music after the complex notes of the normal tuning. The pitch indicators shifted, moving away from the systemic harmonies, and Balthasar leaned across to punch a new target into the console. The upper bank of numbers blurred and shifted, steadying on the new readings. Silence studied them closely, nodding to herself. There hadn't been much change, but it was moving in the right direction.

"Julie said it would be at least a couple of hours before we reached the twelfth," Balthasar said. "Why don't you go below for a while, get some rest?"

"I'm not tired," Silence said, automatically.

"Take a break, then," the Delian answered, in a voice that brooked no argument. "Get something to eat. I want you fit for purgatory."

Silence made a face, but had to admit the other was right. "Can I get you anything?"

Balthasar hesitated, then nodded. "Bring me up some daybread, please. And coffee."

"Right," Silence answered, unfastening the safety webbing, and let herself slide down the last ladder to *Recusante*'s main deck.

To her surprise, the common room door was already unlatched and someone was moving about inside. She pushed through the door, and Aili turned to face her, one hand holding her loosened veil across her face. Seeing who it was, she let the veil fall again, murmuring a greeting.

"I didn't expect to see you awake yet," Silence said, and felt instantly rather foolish. Of course the elixer would have worn off by now, she thought. It had been over an hour since the ship left purgatory.

To her surprise, however, Aili looked away, and the pilot thought she saw a blush coloring the other woman's cheeks. "We were hungry," Aili said, and the blush deepened.

Silence stared for a moment, completely confused, then understood. Evidently the star road had produced its effects even through the elixer's influence. She looked away, keeping face and voice carefully neutral. "There's plenty in the cells. I came down to get something for Denis and me." She crossed the room to the intercom panel. "And to see if Julie wanted anything." Without waiting for an answer, she punched the engine room button. "Julie? I'm in the commons. Do you want anything to eat?"

There was a moment's pause before the engineer answered. "Concentrate bar?"

"What about a sandwich?" Silence said.

"That would be better," Chase Mago acknowledged. "Thanks."

"May I help?" Aili asked.

Silence hesitated, the instant refusal dying on her tongue. Like all the women of the Thousand, Aili had been trained to keep household, knew how to manage common kitchen equipment and prepare a simple meal. It was one of the few skills women of rank were able to acquire. "Sure," she said, and then, belatedly, "Thanks."

The two women worked side by side, almost without conversation, slicing the heavy, faintly sweet daybread and covering it with mounds of the salty, protein-rich isawra spread. They finished five sandwiches before Silence glanced at the remaining bread, shrugging.

"Might as well finish it," she said.

Aili noded, handling the serrated knife as deftly as a soldier. They made seven more, piling them into a keepbox. Silence filled two of the covered mugs from the wallboard's coffee unit, and reached for a tray to carry it all, but Aili caught her hand.

"Let me," she said again, wrapping the veil back across her face in a single deft movement. "You should rest."

Silence shook her head—what was life becoming, that the Princess Royal should wait on a pair of star-travellers?—but said, "All right."

"Thank you," Aili said, and there was a note in her voice that hinted she was smiling. "I'll feed Isambard too, if he's awake." She lifted the full tray, and was gone.

Left to herself, Silence drew a third mug of coffee from the wallboard, and took it and a sandwich across to the table, suddenly weary. The Eagle's Flight had taken more out of her than she had expected, though the drain was more emotional than physical; still, she could feel the sluggishness in her very bones. She closed her eyes for a moment, resting her head in her hands, then reached for the sandwich and began, methodically, to eat, washing the food down with the scalding coffee. It was a star-travellers' maxim that when you can't sleep, you eat, and Silence had long ago learned the truth of that. Aili returned, carrying the emptied tray, but seemed to sense Silence's mood and left again without speaking. When the Princess Royal had gone, Silence finished a second sandwich, and then a third, before the intercom buzzed.

The pilot frowned, but pushed herself up out of her chair, and crossed the room to push the answer button. "Commons."

"Silence," Balthasar's voice said. "You might want to come up now."

Silence's frown deepened, and she asked, "Trouble?"

"Not exactly," Balthasar began, and Silence could almost see the wary grimace. "Not yet, anyway."

"I'm on my way," Silence said, and flicked off the intercom. Hurriedly, she shoved the remaining sandwiches into one of the refrigerated cells, and jammed the dishes into the cleaning slot—if there was no emergency, there was no excuse for letting things wander about unsecured—then left the commons, latching the door behind her. She pulled herself up the ladder to the lower bridge, craning her neck to see the readouts even before she'd stepped off the rungs onto the decking. Nothing seemed out of the ordinary at first glance, and she frowned again as she slipped into the second pilot's couch.

"What's wrong?" she asked. Even on a closer examination, the readouts looked normal, nothing showing on musonar except the distant haze of the last planetary envelope. The Ficinan model was still clear, and the rows of status lights showed monotonously green. The pitch was lower than usual, but that had been expected.

Balthasar looked up from his keyboard, worry lines sharp between his eyebrows. "Listen."

Silence did as she was told, closing her eyes to concentrate on the keelsong. For a moment, the unfamiliar music made everything seem out of place, but then, as she became accustomed to the music, she began to hear something else beneath the eerie harmonics. There was a note of strain—no, not strain in the usual sense of unresolved dissonance, but a laboring sound, as though the harmonium were being pushed beyond its limits to maintain the new song. She looked up, and Balthasar nodded grimly.

"You hear?"

"I hear something," Silence answered, and reached for her headset, lying discarded over the arm of the couch. She settled it into place, and keyed the intercom. "Julie, what's going on?"

"I'm not entirely sure," the engineer answered, almost too promptly. "We're not developing a clear harmony at this setting—I've tried increasing my input power, but that just creates more intereference in the damped pipes."

Silence made a face, trying to understand just what this would mean. She had known—they had all known—that the given setting was intended for an old-style harmonium, using only a quarter of the pipes in *Recusante*'s harmonium. They had not expected that this would be a problem. After all, Silence thought, don't we only use part of the array at any one time? "I don't understand," she said aloud.

"I'm not sure we're going to make the twelfth," Chase Mago said.

"Not make—" Silence bit off the rest of her horrified echo, furious at her self-betrayal.

Balthasar nodded, glaring at the screens.

"Even if we make it, we won't go much above it," the engineer continued. "There won't be much for you to work with."

Silence took a deep breath, trying to order her thoughts. "That isn't so much of a problem," she said, slowly. "We don't want to manipulate the marks—and I doubt the old ships went very deep into purgatory anyway."

"But they did get there," Balthasar murmured. "Do you really think we're not going to make it, Julie?"

"Would I say it if I didn't?" Chase Mago retorted, with some asperity. "If we don't get more power, clean up the song, we're going to peak just below the twelfth." He paused, then continued, "I want to cut in the upper register."

There was a momentary pause. Balthasar covered his microphone with one hand and glanced toward the other pilot. "Silence? You know more about this than I do."

Silence hesitated. Cutting in the upper register would take them well beyond the twelfth of heaven—and probably too deep into purgatory for her to be able to use the portolan. Damn it, she thought, they used this setting, they got to purgatory on it. . . . The laboring note of the keelsong sounded in her ears; she could hear, at its heart, the imperfections that would keep it from matching the celestial harmony closely enough to take them into purgatory. God, it couldn't be that the tuning was damaged going through the Eagle's Flight, she thought suddenly. Could it? But no, that would have showed itself at once. This has to be something else.

"If the old ships got to purgatory this way," she said, half to herself, "so can we."

She had not intended to speak aloud, but Chase Mago answered anyway. "Their harmonia—their whole engine setup was very different. We may just carry too many pipes."

Silence did not answer at once. Something was tugging at her memory, something the engineer had said back on Asterion, during the weeks they had spent planning the flight. Something about the differences between *Recusante* and other modern ships and the ships that had originally used the portolan system, something about power as well as pipes and stops and settings. . . . "You said," she began slowly, "you said the old ships didn't carry the power we do, right? That we develop half again as much?"

"About a quarter more, I think," Balthasar said, when Chase Mago didn't answer immediately.

"That's about right," the engineer said, after a moment. "Why?"

"What are we carrying now?" Silence asked.

"Seven-eighths of normal capacity," Chase Mago answered, promptly this time. "Why—" His voice died away abruptly. "I think I see. If we cut back to their maximum, or even a little below, that might purify the song."

"We're using the same harmonic setting, so we should duplicate the power level as well," Silence said.

"That means spending more time in mundane space," Balthasar objected automatically.

Silence nodded toward the empty musonar display. "I think we can afford it."

Balthasar gave a reluctant nod. "All right. Do what you think's best, Julie."

"I'll power down," Chase Mago answered, and moved away without switching off the intercom. Silence could hear him moving around the engine room, could hear, on the quiet bridge, the faint clicks as the engineer adjusted his equipment. Slowly, almost imperceptibly, the keelsong changed, the sense of strain—a tension more felt than heard—easing away. The change was too slight to register on the bridge instrumentation, but Chase Mago gave an exclamation of delight.

"I think—yes, that's done it." His voice grew clearer as he returned to the intercom panel. "We'll reach purgatory in a little more than an hour."

Balthasar made a face, but said, "Good enough, Julie." Glancing sideways, he added, "Thanks, Silence."

"Good thought," the engineer agreed, then cut the circuit.

Silence leaned back in her couch, smiling a little at the unexpected compliments. She had worked with men—notably her maternal uncle—who had resented any and all of her suggestions, particularly when she turned out to be right. It was pleasant to be valued fairly.

"Do you want to go below?" Balthasar asked, and gave her a rather whimsical smile. "Sorry to have got you up here, when this turned out to be so minor."

Silence shook her head, returning the smile. "I'll stay, see if I can catch some sleep up here"

Balthasar nodded, and Silence adjusted her couch, tilting it until it formed a reasonably comfortable bunk. She slipped off her headset, and hung it over the arm of the couch, turning so that her face was to a bank of telltales. As always, she didn't mean to sleep, but the steady drone of the harmonium, purified now of the note of strain, was almost hypnotic. She dozed, waking now and then from dreams that slipped away the instant she reached full awareness. They were not unpleasant—in fact, they left no emotional residue at all—but that very blandness made her uneasy, and she shook herself fully awake well before they reached the twelfth. Balthasar lifted an eyebrow as she pulled her couch upright.

"You could get another quarter hour at least."

Silence shook her head. "I'm not really tired." She picked up her portolan, cutting off any response. The first mark was unmistakable—a triple rose, white and black and red—but she couldn't help wondering, not for the first time, exactly how it would appear. If she had understood the system correctly, the symbol should appear on a false horizon, conjured by the similitudes of landline and keelsong; *Recusante* would seem to travel up to and then through that image. The next image after that was a walled city, its representation in the portolan incredibly detailed. Silence frowned at it, suddenly convinced that a magnifier would show even more detail, impossible detail, behind the painted walls. Why should the printer do that? she wondered. What possible purpose can it serve?

She put the book aside, pushing that problem to the back of her mind. Whatever the reason—magi's obsessive concern with accurate representation, or just old-fashioned precision—it could have nothing to do with the road itself. In the screens, the stars were beginning to show faint coronae, and she glanced instinctively toward the pitch indicators. Not far to the twelfth now, she thought, and loosened her safety netting. "I'm going up."

Balthasar nodded, too much a pilot himself to question her even though it was still some minutes to purgatory, and turned his attention back to his control consoles. Silence pulled herself up to the upper bridge, the ladder oddly slick, unstable underfoot. She frowned, then realized that purgatory's secondary effects were only just beginning to be felt. The usual stickiness of deck and ladders was almost completely missing.

She shook herself, annoyed at having wasted even that much thought on such an unimportant thing, and came to stand in front of the wheel, her hands not quite touching the control yoke. The dome had begun to fade a little, but she could barely see the bodies of the stars. The coronae were completely obscured by the hazy metal.

Her headset clicked, and Balthasar's voice said, "I'll give you a countdown."

"All right." Silence stared at the still-solid dome. "How far off are we?"

"Half a step, still, but who knows how long that means?" Balthasar's voice was irritable with nervousness. "No, here we go. Three-quarters. . . . Seven-eighths. . . . Now."

There was no familiar roar of music, no sudden burst of song to lift *Recusante* out of the mundane universe. Instead, the dome simply faded a little more, and the keelsong seemed suddenly lighter. Silence took a deep breath, and sought her triple rose.

The dome had not vanished completely. Its shadow enclosed the bridge, transparent but definitely there, and Silence shook herself, momentarily disoriented. Then, through the thin veil of fog that was the dome, she saw the triple rose, blood red petals enclosing ebony enclosing a central flower as white as sunlit snow. It gleamed with a light of its own, but somehow it lacked the weird vitality of the usual voidmarks. Seeing it hovering in the distance, Silence felt suddenly like an insect, bearing down on the most tremendous source of pollen ever discovered. She laughed, but then put away the image.

"Bearing, please?" she asked.

Chase Mago's response was reassuringly quick. "Exactly in

the groove. Do you want me to give you a check every five minutes, or wait until we go off the line?"

Silence hesitated, then shrugged. "Every five minutes, at least for starters. If you don't mind."

"Every five minutes," Chase Mago repeated. "No problem."

Very slowly, *Recusante* crept toward the massive rose. Once, twice, a third time the ship slipped from the proper bearing, but each time Chase Mago reported the deviation, and Silence corrected it within minutes. The mark did not alter, or change its apparent position on the false horizon. The early pilots couldn't have steered by it, Silence decided, and shook her head at the thought.

She tensed suddenly, very aware of the immense, unchanging image, filling half the apparent sky ahead of the ship. If it did not show a deviation from the proper bearing, would it show any of the changes that marked the end of a normal star road? And if it didn't, how did this road end? She bit her lip, conquering her fear with an effort. Surely there would be some change, she thought, some signal to let a pilot know he's reached the end of a bearing—unless that's supposed to be relayed from the engineer's sensors? Damn, I didn't count on this at all.

"Julie," she said aloud. "We're getting close to the end. give me a continuous reading, please."

Chase Mago's voice sounded faintly surprised, but for a mercy he didn't argue. "Continuous readings. Very well." A moment later, the numbers began sounding in Silence's headset, a comforting drone. *Recusante* was cleanly on the bearing, correct to the last points.

The rose swelled ahead of her, filling most of the apparent sky, its lower petals hidden by the decking. The whole image seemed to curve inward slightly, as though the cupped flower would engulf the ship. Silence thought she saw faint stars reflected in the black petals. The center of the innermost flower was directly ahead, its parts—stamen, pistil, grains of pollen—gleaming as though they were made of solid gold. The engineer's voice sounded in her ear: *Recusante* was still on course, still perfectly on the bearing.

Still, Silence thought, trying to control her own nervousness, you almost always pass through a mark, leaving a normal star road. It's only logical for us to go through this one. She had no proof of that, however—there had been nothing in either the portolan itself or in the pamphlet she had read back on Solitudo Hermae. She could feel herself beginning to shake, as much from tension as from fear, and self-consciously worked her shoulder, trying to relax tight muscles. It did little good; she could feel herself trembling as *Recusante* slid past the last petals into the flower's golden center.

Instantly, the bridge was suffused with an eerie yellow light, as though the golden pistils and the gold-lined petals themselves were transparent, a strong light shining through them. Silence glanced over her shoulder, and saw only a tiny black disk to mark their point of entrance, as though the flower itself had folded shut over them. The bearing remained constant in her ears.

Cautiously, Silence guided the ship past the towering stamens, past grains of pollen almost as large as *Recusante* itself, into the very heart of the rose. It loomed ahead, a golden wall faintly shadowed where the petals met and overlapped, a tiny black dot visible at its very center. Silence smiled, certain she saw the way out of the mark, but her smile faded as the ship drew closer. The black dot wasn't the mark of an opening into the mundane universe; rather, it was a shadow, a stain on the gilded perfection of the flower. Still, the bearing remained constant, pointing *Recusante* directly at the spot. Experimentally, Silence pulled back on the control yoke, lifting the ship toward the nearest stamen. The droning numbers faltered and shifted: that way lay certain destruction. She let the ship slide back onto its original course, and the bearing steadied.

Then, quite abruptly, the numbers changed, shifting wildly as though somehow threefold space itself was in flux. At the same moment, the keelsong howled, reflecting sudden dissonance. Silence swore, clinging to the bucking control yoke, but could find no visible sign of that disharmony.

"Three point eight, four, four point five, four-nine, five point three," Chase Mago chanted. "God, Silence, I think the line's gone. Six-five, six point seven, point nine—"

Silence shut out his words with an effort, hauling back on the control yoke. It refused to respond, the sympathetic linkages distorted by the rising dissonance. She cursed again, seeing the black spot looming ever nearer.

"Eight point one," Chase Mago said, "eight point four, eight point six, point seven—"

"Get us out, Julie," Balthasar snapped, and in the same instant, Silence said, "Stop down—power down now."

The engineer obeyed without question, and the noise of the harmonium sank, bringing with it the deceptive increase in their apparent speed. Silence cringed, seeing the black spot rush closer, but the rest of the image was already fading, the golden walls irregularly shadowed, stars shining through sudden holes in the gilded fabric. Then *Recusante* burst through the shreds of the image sending a last wave of dissonance through the ship. Silence screamed, knocked backward by the explosion of sound, but her voice was drowned in the sudden wail of the keel. And then they were through, the dissonance dropping to a whisper and then vanishing entirely.

"What the hell?" Balthasar demanded. "Silence, are you all right?"

Silence pulled herself upright, and managed to spare a wry smile for her bruises. She had taken ships through dissonances before, but never yet had one been strong enough to knock her off the pilot's platform. "I'm not hurt," she said, and was instantly annoyed at how shaken she sounded. She cleared her throat and tried again. "A couple of bruises, that's all. Did we make it?"

Balthasar did not answer for a long moment, and when he spoke again, it was to the engineer. "Julie, how's the tuning?"

"All right," Chase Mago answered. "Not even shaken." He paused himself, then asked, falsely casual, "Do I retune to the new bearing?"

There was another, longer pause before Balthasar finally answered. "No. I can't find the line."

Silence swore, her bruises forgotten, and scrambled for the ladder. As she slid down it, she asked, "What do you mean, you can't find it?"

"Just what I said," Balthasar snapped. He was staring at the three viewscreens, two of which showed a musonar display, while the third flashed strings of numbers in response to the Delian's touch on his keyboard. "I can't find it."

There was a note of controlled hysteria in his voice that terrified Silence. She fought back the urge to panic, and slid into the second pilot's couch, reaching for her own keyboard. The musonar displays showed the almost-black of true interstellar space, the distant stars no more than pale dots with only the faintest harmonic envelopes. The display was set to its largest scale, Silence realized; nothing smaller would show anything at all. She shivered, awed by the immensity of space. Every pilot had heard tales of missing a voidmark, of failing to control the forces of purgatory—how ships had fallen to mundane space in unfamiliar places, unable to reenter purgatory without the correct voidmarks, doomed to wander between the stars until the crew starved, until at last the elemental water that powered the harmonium was exhausted, and the ship was drawn inevitably into some distant star.

Silence shook herself, angry at her own imaginings. "We can't be that far off," she said aloud. "We were right on course, right on the line up to the end."

"Yeah," Balthasar said, "but who knows how far off course we came when we lost the line—" He bit off whatever else he had been going to say, and punched a new set of numbers into his keyboard, watching the figures shift and reform on the central viewscreen. When he spoke again, he was almost calm. "What happened then, anyway?"

"I'm not sure," Silence answered honestly. "I'm still learning the damn method—" She broke off, angrily aware that Balthasar had stopped listening after her first answer. With an effort, she controlled her anger, and said, "What can I do to help?"

"I'm trying to find the landline; it should show up on the musonar," Balthasar answered. He shook his head. "I don't know, keep an eye on the figures. Maybe you'll see something I've missed."

Silence nodded, too glad of something to occupy her thoughts to protest being given such an unimportant job, and fixed her eyes on the screen. The numbers shifted and reformed as Balthasar tilted the musonar horn this way and that, but nothing matched the listed harmony. Where did we—I—go wrong? Silence wondered, still watching the screen. It should have worked. I don't understand why it didn't. . . . Unless, somehow, the ship isn't supposed to leave the mark? But I couldn't find the next landline if the ship stayed in purgatory.

"Got it," Balthasar exclaimed, and pointed to a red dot flashing on the screen. "That's it." Silence gave a sigh of relief, but Balthasar ignored her, still talking excitedly. "Julie, retune to the numbers Silence gave you, but don't put in the riser yet. We should reach the line in, oh, two or three hours; you can adjust it then."

"Right," Chase Mago answered, and Silence could hear the relief in his voice as well.

Slowly, very slowly, the keelsong changed, one note replacing another, others blending into new and subtle harmonies. Silence barely heard it, still staring at the screen. After a moment, frowning, she punched in a second set of numbers, and saw the same point of light flare on the visual screens. Balthasar gave her a curious glance, but said nothing. So, Silence thought, the first landline seems to end in the same place that our second line begins. Therefore, since the portolans deal more with physical correspondences than the voidmark system, that must be the "place" that's roughly equivalent to the rose. Which means that we have to leave purgatory before we leave the mark—but that still doesn't tell me when.

Balthasar asked softly, "Found something?"

"Maybe," Silence answered. Quickly, she outlined what she had guessed, but ended, "Unfortunately, that doesn't tell me when to leave purgatory. I'd imagine leaving too soon would be as bad as leaving too late. Or maybe not." She frowned, hardly seeing the control room around her. "Maybe not. If we stopped down early, the resemblances should still carry us along to the natural departure point, and even if they don't, we'd still be on that line, not in uncharted space. Denis, I think that's it."

Balthasar was nodding. "That makes sense."

"So when we reach purgatory on this second road," Chase Mago said slowly, "I start stopping down and trust that the resemblance will carry us through?" His voice made his distrust of that plan perfectly clear.

"No," Silence answered, "you stop down as soon as we enter the mark. I'll tell you when."

"I see," the engineer said, and there was a long pause. Silence held her breath, wondering if she should say more, and was very grateful that Balthasar said nothing. Then Chase Mago sighed. "All right, pilot, the next ride can't be worse than this one."

"Thanks," Silence said, rather sourly. She waited for an answer, but the engineer did not reply.

Balthasar cleared his throat. "We've got four, five hours before you have to take the next leg, Silence. You should get some rest."

"I'm not tired," the pilot answered automatically, but even as she spoke she knew it for a lie.

"You look like death," Balthasar said frankly. "Go on, get below."

Silence managed a wry smile, and pushed herself up out of the couch. A lot of her weariness was emotional, she knew, the result of fear and tension, but it was no less real for that. She made her way cautiously down the ladder, suddenly aware of pain in her wrists. *Probably from being knocked backward while I was trying to hold onto the wheel,* she thought, and pushed open the door of her cabin. The tidy bunk looked so inviting that she almost cried, but she turned away from its softness, leaning on the back of her chair instead. She stood there for a long moment, gathering strength, then doggedly began to strip off the tight-fitting shipsuit. She pulled off sleeves and bodice, then began working the clinging fabric down over her hips. A purple bruise the size of her hand was already visible on her left leg just below the point of her hip. She touched it lightly, experimentally, and winced at the pain. *I must've landed on it when I fell,* she thought, then put the discovery aside. After a moment's hesitation, she pulled on an outsized sleepshirt and crawled into her bunk, leaving the shipsuit crumpled on the floor. She was asleep almost before her head hit the pillow.

She woke to a hand on her shoulder and a familiar voice in her ear, riding over the rising note of the keelsong. "Julie?" she said, still half asleep, and pushed herself upright.

"I brought you coffee," the engineer said. "It's about half an hour to the twelfth."

"Half an hour?" Silence echoed, then shook herself fully awake. "You should've waked me sooner."

Chase Mago shrugged, and held out a closed mug. Silence took it automatically, murmuring her thanks.

"Denis figured he'd let you sleep now, and then he could take a break while you ran us through purgatory," the engineer continued.

Silence nodded and took a sip of the coffee, studying the other. Chase Mago looked almost as tired as she had felt, circles clearly visible under his eyes, his dark hair falling lank across his collar. "When are you going to get a break?" she asked, with some concern.

To her surprise, the engineer managed a tired smile. "As soon as we hit purgatory, I'll curl up in a corner. I've waked your magus. He can at least read the numbers, and I've rigged you a buzzer. You get a steady tone when you're on the line; the pitch will rise or fall if you get off it."

"Good idea," Silence said. "Thanks." We should've hired another engineer, she thought. Julie won't be able to keep this up for too long—but then, we didn't know how this was going to work, and anyway, who is there we could've trusted to hire? She stretched, feeling the bruises on her hips and back and the sore muscles in her wrists and forearms. "How're Aili and Marcinik doing?" she asked, idly.

"All right. Fretting a little because there's nothing they can do to help." Chase Mago smiled. "Except carry sandwiches. I've never been waited on by a princess before. Speaking of which, I brought you a sandwich, too."

Silence smiled back. "Thanks."

The engineer pushed himself to his feet and stretched slowly. "I'll leave you—I've got to get back to work. Remember, we hit the twelfth in half an hour."

"I'm not likely to forget," Silence said to his retreating back, and levered herself out of the bunk as the door closed behind him. She took a quick shower, then dressed, snatching a few bites of the sandwich as she did so. She ran her fingers through her short hair—it was still damp, and would be an unruly mess when it dried, but there was no time to do more—then tested the last seal, and started for the upper bridge.

Balthasar swung around in his couch as she reached the lower bridge, managed a nod and a smile. He looked dreadful, Silence thought, unshaven and disheveled, great circles under his eyes, but his voice was cheerful enough. "Almost there."

Silence nodded. "You should get some rest, Denis."

"I will," Balthasar answered. "Once you've taken over, and we're in purgatory."

Silence shook her head, but there was nothing to say. She pulled herself up the rest of the ladder—the rungs still felt strange without the clinging effect of deep purgatory—and took up her position in front of the wheel, hands resting easily on the control yoke. The dome had faded considerably already, star-coronae showing clearly through its shadow. Even as she watched, it faded further, to the strange translucence of the twelfth of heaven, and the stars vanished completely, leaving only their coronae blazing against a flat black sky.

"At the twelfth," Chase Mago announced.

"I have control," Silence responded, and flipped off the lock.

"You have it," Balthasar said.

"Get some sleep, Denis," the engineer said, and Silence could hear Balthasar's soft laughter.

"I will, I promise. Good night."

With an effort, Silence banished both of them from her thoughts, staring instead out into the starless night. The next mark, a massive walled city, rode an imaginary horizon. Its towers—Silence counted seven, and suspected that others were hidden behind the red-tiled roofs—were topped with gaudy banners; its walls seemed to end in stony fringes, trailing off into nothingness like the roots of a tree.

"I'm putting on the buzzer now," Chase Mago's voice said in her ears.

"Go ahead," Silence answered, and a moment later a low, pleasant tone sounded in her headset. Experimentally, she moved the control yoke forward, and then back. The tone changed, dropping and then rising in response to the ship's movements. Silence nodded, satisfied, and pressed the transmitter button, momentarily overriding the signal. "It sounds good, Julie. Why don't you take a break now, if Isambard can spell you?"

She wasn't particularly happy about working with the magus in purgatory—piloting was her own special skill, her first Art, and one she wasn't eager to share with Isambard—and she gave a sigh of relief when the engineer answered, "I'm going to. Don't worry, Isambard will wake me if there's any sign of trouble—of anything at all unusual," he amended fiercely, and Silence grinned, picturing the magus's restrained annoyance.

"Thanks, Julie," she said. Chase Mago did not answer, but an instant later the tone sounded again in her ears.

The passage along the landline to the mark itself was remarkably uneventful, so uneventful that in the end Silence had deliberately to tip Recusante off the proper course to keep herself from falling asleep at the wheel. Progress seemed impossibly slow, but at last the city wall loomed ahead, filling the apparent sky. Twin towers guarded an open gate set a little to the left of Recusante's course. Silence eased the control yoke over, tilting the starship toward the opening. The warning tone wavered momentarily, then settled again. "Isambard," she said aloud. "Wake Julie."

"I'm awake," the engineer answered.

"We're coming up on the mark," Silence said, and damned herself for having left things so late. "Denis, do you hear?" There was no answer from the Delian. "Damn. Julie, send Isambard forward to wake him, if you would—and tell him to check in as soon as he's in?"

"Right," Chase Mago answered, and there was a momentary pause while he passed her request to the magus. "He's going forward now," the engineer reported. "How close are we?"

"It's hard to tell," Silence answered. "It looks like a hundred meters or so to the gate, but you can't tell how long it's going to take to cover it."

Chase Mago grunted his agreement, and Silence turned her attention back to the mark ahead. Through the open gate, she could see a wall of buildings, each one elaborately decorated with columns and grotesques and fancifully carved cornices, each one with shutters pulled tight across its windows. With a detached corner of her mind, Silence wondered what the symbolism of that was. Infuriatingly, *Recusante* seemed to hang almost motionless, barely creeping toward the gate.

There was a rattling noise in her headset, just audible under the warning tone, and Balthasar announced, "I'm on, Silence." He still sounded tired, Silence thought, but more alert than before.

"Thanks," she said, and kept her eyes on the mark.

Recusante crawled on toward the gate. As the ship came closer and closer to the massive towers, Silence tensed, waiting for some change in the tone. Nothing happened, and she forced herself to relax, to keep her hands loose on the control yoke. At last, *Recusante* slid between the towers, under the shadow of the gate.

"Begin stopping down, Julie," Silence said, and held her breath.

"Stopping down," Chase Mago answered, and for once there was a genuine note of nervousness in his voice. The keelsong changed subtly, thinning out, but the mark stayed clear, showed no signs of deterioration.

Silence sighed hard. So far, she was right—or at least she hadn't done anything terribly wrong. Now all she could do was hope that she'd guessed right, and that the altered song would carry them out of purgatory as soon as the landline faded.

Recusante floated through the wide gate, the apparent pace maddeningly sedate. As they emerged from the wall's shadow, Silence glanced quickly to her left, only to find the way blocked by yet another wall of shuttered houses. Instinctively, she swung the yoke to the right, and found herself sailing down a wide avenue between palatial buildings. At the same moment, the warning tone began to drop.

She pulled back on the yoke, lifting the ship until the tone steadied on its proper note. *Recusante* floated now just above the level of the housetops, well above the illusory pavement. From this perspective, Silence could see that *Recusante* was following the single street, which spiraled inward from the gate to the town's central tower. Its walls were ivory-colored, its scattered windows sealed with crimson shutters, and a vine, its leaves as red as blood, coiled three times around the tower's base before spiralling up toward the gold-tiled roof. There seemed to be a wealth of symbolism in the image, but Silence had no time to contemplate it. Already, *Recusante*'s apparent speed was increasing, the ship careening along above the street as though carried by a rising wind.

Silence tightened her grip on the control yoke as the ship began to slip sideways, sliding toward the red-tiled roofs to either side. She held the course, though it took all her strength to do it, and leaned hard against the wheel as the curve of the spiral sharpened. *Recusante* was moving even faster now, whipping around the final circles with dizzying speed. As they swung into the final curve, Silence caught a glimpse of the tower base. A gate had opened just above the triple-wrapped vine, the portcullis drawn up just far enough to admit a starship. Do we go in after all? she wondered. And what will I find if we do? Then *Recusante* swept past the gate, circling the tower for the final time, and Silence realized with a shock that the city was fading around her. The bright colors dimmed, went misty, the shuttered windows cleared, though the interior of the tower remained maddeningly dark. They would not enter the tower, despite the open doorway, and Silence bit back a cry of frustration. It had promised such a wealth of secrets. . . .

And then they were through, the last shadows vanishing just as *Recusante* started to circle the base of the tower itself. Silence swore softly and locked her wheel, tasting disappointment. Only a little farther, she thought, just a little farther and I could at least have seen into it. That would have told me something.

"I have control," Balthasar's voice said in her ears. He sounded dead tired still, Silence realized, belatedly—and no wonder, she thought, considering how little sleep he's had. That was enough to drive the thoughts of the tower from her mind.

"On my way," she said, and dropped down the ladder to the lower bridge. Balthasar nodded a greeting as she took her place in the second pilot's couch, but said nothing. Once again, the triple viewscreen was slaved to the musonar, one showing the distant starscape only faintly touched with music, the other showing a maze of multicolored lines. The central screen was filled with numbers, changing in response to promptings from Balthasar's keyboard.

"How're we doing?" Silence asked, readjusting her headset.

"As I just told Julie, I'm looking for it," Balthasar answered. He made a face then, and glanced apologetically in her direction. "Sorry. I think it's worked this time, but it just takes a while to be sure."

Silence nodded, trying not to feel hurt, and fixed her attention on the right-hand screen. The display showed the harmonic lines that crossed and recrossed in the local volume, some stronger and brighter than the rest, most shown in a dull blue that was barely visible against the black background. The brighter ones formed a pattern that seemed somehow familiar. Silence reached again for the portolan, opening it to the marked pages. The pattern didn't seem to match the halo of lines surrounding the city-mark, but it was hard to tell among the confusion of markings. Certainly there seemed to be a correspondence. "Denis," she said slowly, "would you block out the lesser lines, everything that shows blue?"

Balthasar gave her a rather irritated glance, but did as she'd asked. The blue lines faded, leaving only pale yellow ones, crisscrossing the screen like counters in a giant game of pick-up sticks. Still, it didn't match the pattern in the portolan. Silence stared at it for a moment longer, then covered two-thirds of the mark. The remaining lines matched the pattern in the screen. "There," she said aloud, and held the book out so that Balthasar could see.

The Delian grunted, and punched numbers into his keyboard. A moment later, lights flashed green across the monitors, and all but one of the lines vanished from the screen. Balthasar nodded, and said, reluctantly, "Thanks." He straightened almost painfully, stretching against the stiff cushions of the couch, then reached across to flip the intercom switch. "We're right on the line, Julie. You can retune now."

"Retuning," Chase Mago answered distantly, and the Delian cut the connection.

Silence said carefully, not looking at the other, "Why don't you let me handle the run-up, and you get some proper sleep?" Balthasar made a sort of growling noise, and Silence braced herself for a blistering rejoinder. Then the Delian sighed, and relaxed perceptibly.

"That'll leave you wiped out for purgatory."

"If I'm too tired, I'll let you handle it," Silence said. "You've seen how it works."

Balthasar hesitated a moment longer, then nodded, reaching for the clasp of the safety webbing. "All right. I'll hold you to that."

"You can trust me," Silence said, but the Delian had vanished. She sighed, already feeling the strain of the trip through purgatory, then unclasped her own safety webbing to slide across to the first pilot's couch. It felt odd to sit there, in Balthasar's place, for all that she had handled a first pilot's duties a hundred times before. She hesitated before fastening the webbing firmly around herself. She couldn't control the ship as easily from her own couch; it was necessary to switch. She made herself check each of the display boards and readouts, running through the changeover list, immersing herself in her pilot's duties, before reaching for the intercom switch.

"Julie? I'm taking the con for now."

"Good idea," Chase Mago answered. "I'm going to hand over to Isambard as soon as I've got us on line."

"All right," Silence said, and did her best to hide her sudden feeling of disappointment.

A few minutes later, the engineer's voice sounded in her ears again. "I show us on the line, Silence. Do you confirm?"

"I confirm it, Silence said.

"Then I'll let Imsabard watch things from here," Chase Mago said, a faint note of satisfaction in his voice. "He'll wake me if there's anything unusual."

"All right," Silence said again, and cut the connection. She could almost feel the moment when the engineer put aside his responsibilities, and then damned herself for an overimaginative idiot. She felt strangely lonely without either Chase Mago or the Delian to share the watch, even though she knew perfectly well that any emergency would bring them instantly to their posts. It had been a very long time since she'd stood a watch without one of them—the last time had been when *Recusante* was still *Black Dolphin*, before her grandfather's death. She shivered, suddenly chilled. Even on Asterion, in the Women's Palace, she had not felt quite so alone. No, she corrected herself, this wasn't precisely loneliness, but a sense of wrongness, of time and place askew.

She shook herself then, annoyed that she had let her emotions get the better of her. This is a part of the pilot's Art, she told herself, the pilot's Art that was your first love. There's nothing wrong aboard, just a new method that requires some adjustment. That's all. She scowled down at the monitor, forcing herself to be aware of every single point in the rows of green lights, submerging her uneasiness in the routine of her work.

CHAPTER 4

Balthasar returned to the bridge a little more than half an hour before *Recusante* reached purgatory, and Silence was glad to leave the passage up to and through the next mark to him. It was not so much that the portolan's system was physically exhausting, she decided, but that it demanded the pilot's attention for such long periods of time. The engineer had it even worse, she knew. Even with Isambard's help—and occasional unskilled number-watching from Marcinik and Aili—Chase Mago was having to handle all the transitions himself, and they could all hear the rising exhaustion in his voice.

"Do we hang here and rest for a few hours?" Silence wondered aloud, staring at the musonar readings displayed in the viewscreens without really seeing them. They were past the fifth mark, well over halfway there, and the strain was beginning to tell on the big engineer.

Balthasar shrugged, his fingers moving on his keyboard as he tilted the musonar horn, looking for the next landline. "I'd rather not," he said, and nodded toward the left-hand screen. Instead of the blank starscape visible between the other points, this one showed a nearby sun, its music spreading out in fading shades of red to cover nearly half the screen. "You never know when someone'll show up, so close to a system. Maybe between six and seven."

Silence nodded reluctantly. They were too close to the sun, even if they were too far away for the musonar to pick

105

out the contrasting music of any daughter planets. For a moment, she wondered if any human being had ever seen this star before, if it held planets too alien to be reached by more conventional methods—if in fact the portolan method might somehow offer a key to reaching truly alien worlds—but then the enthusiasm was drowned by the encompassing weariness. Alien worlds seemed unimportant, even as reaching Earth was beginning to seem trivial, compared to the importance of pushing through one more mark. With an effort, Silence dragged her mind back to the conversation at hand. "We ought to rest then anyway. It's my turn, I'll take number six."

Balthasar nodded, saying, "You hear, Julie? One more." He glanced at Silence. "You get below and rest."

Silence did as she was told, stopping in the common room only long enough to bolt down one of the sandwiches left in the hotbox by Aili. The Princess Royal, recognizing her lack of technical skills, had taken over food preparation as the one thing she could do, and had done it with, in Silence's opinion, a commendable lack of fanfare. I wouldn't exactly want to be in Aili's shoes, Silence thought, as she settled herself once again into her unmade bunk. It can't be easy for her, not being able to help—Marcinik is an officer at least, he knows how to read the simple instruments, but Aili hasn't had any of that. There was a lesson in that somewhere, the pilot knew, but she fell asleep before it could penetrate.

Aili appeared to wake her half an hour before the transition to purgatory. Silence hauled herself out of the bunk, groaning, and found herself halfway dressed before she was fully aware of what she was doing. She swore, rubbing at her forehead. This wasn't the first time she'd caught herself doing things by rote. It was something about the portolan method, a method she was rapidly growing to hate passionately. The ship never seemed to get far from purgatory, or to go far enough into it; she was surrounded by a perpetual unresolved, unresolvable tension that was ultimately far more enervating than the piloting itself. They all felt it, she knew, though after the first complaints the three star-travellers had conspired to ignore it in the hopes that the feeling would eventually go away. It had not, and Silence found herself wondering more and more often if they wouldn't have been better off trying to break the siege engines after all.

She was wondering it again as she climbed to her station, barely pausing on the lower bridge long enough to exchange monosyllables with Balthasar. The routine of changeover proceeded properly, the faint change in the keelsong, the dimming of the dome, and then the warning tone in her headset, giving its monotonous assurance that *Recusante* was on course. First Balthasar and then Chase Mago announced that they were taking a rest, and Silence was left alone, watching the new mark take shape on the false horizon.

This one was an arched gate, rather like the triumphs on Asterion, but its triple columns were carved with cabalistic symbols rather than with political insignias. Silence regarded the symbols without affection, knowing that the ship would not come close enough for her to read them clearly. That was one more thing she hated about the portolan: its symbols promised much, but in the end proved as sterile as the rest of the method.

Very slowly, *Recusante* crept up to the triumph, Chase Mago stopping down as soon as the ship came under the shadow of the gate. As Silence had more than half expected, the image began to fade at once, the symbols blurring into nothingness. *Recusante* slid out of purgatory as she passed through the gate. Silence sighed, locked her wheel, and headed back down to the lower bridge.

Balthasar managed a crooked smile of welcome, the familiar crisscross pattern dancing across the screens. "You're getting better at this, Silence. We're practically on the line now."

"Do we take a rest now?" Chase Mago's voice asked from the intercom.

Balthasar looked up at the musonar display, then back at Silence. "What do you think?"

The pilot studied the left-hand screen, trying to focus her attention on its information. To her surprise, the screen was almost black, only a few pale dots showing to indicate very distant stars. It was a disconcerting picture, almost a frightening one, an emptiness few star-travellers ever experienced. She looked away quickly. "It looks—good for what we want."

"Yeah." Balthasar grimaced, not looking at the left-hand screen. "I think we chance it. I doubt there's much traffic out here."

Wearily, they began the job of preparing *Recusante* to float free in mundane space, held only by its affinity to the local harmonies. Chase Mago stopped down the harmonium to the lowest setting that would maintain ship's power, while the two pilots locked the bridge controls into positions that would match local conditions, and set the deadman alarms that would trigger a warning if the ship drifted too far off course. When they had finished, Balthasar sighed, and reached for the intercom switch. "Marcinik? I'm ready to show you what I've done."

"I'm here," Marcinik said from the bridge ladder.

Silence gasped in spite of herself, and saw Balthasar jerk in his couch.

"Damn it, don't do that to me," the Delian snapped, then got himself under control. "Come here."

The colonel came to stand at Balthasar's elbow, and Silence saw the Princess Royal pull herself up onto the bridge behind him.

"I hope you don't mind," Aili said softly, to Silence.

Before the pilot could answer, Balthasar interrupted his quick explanation of the deadman system to say, "Not at all. Why don't you listen, then, so you can be useful, too?"

Silence glared at the Delian, but Aili nodded quite seriously, and moved to join the colonel. The pilot shrugged to herself, biting back her first answer. If Aili wasn't offended, so much the better.

Balthasar finished his instructions, and levered himself up out of the couch. "You know where the intercom is," he said, as Marcinik took his place at the first pilot's station. "Call if there's anything at all unusual."

"We will," Marcinik said, the ghost of a chuckle in his voice, and Aili echoed. "Of course."

Balthasar gave them both a dubious look, but nodded and let himself down the ladder to the main deck. Silence followed him, hiding her laughter.

Chase Mago was waiting in the corridor just outside the

common room door, one hand on the latch. "I've left Isambard to watch things," he said. "Are either of you hungry?"

"Not particularly," Balthasar said.

Silence shook her head, the laughter fading from her thoughts. She was suddenly aware of the vast quiet that filled the ship, of the absence of the familiar keelsong and the little noises from a dozen other systems, all shut down now as nonessentials. She shivered, remembering the uncannily empty starscape, and could see from the others' faces that they were thinking of the same thing. She did not want to leave either of them, to sleep alone with the unnatural quiet, but Marcinik and Aili occupied the spare cabin, she told herself roughly, and there was no room in any of the others for all three of them. Still, she could not bring herself to turn away. They stood unspeaking for a long moment, and then Chase Mago said, awkwardly, "I think my bunk's the biggest."

"That's not saying a lot," Balthasar murmured, but nodded. "We might just fit."

In the end, they did fit, but only just. Silence lay wedged between the two men, too tired to feel any discomfort, sleepily grateful that their presence warded off the emptiness that surrounded the ship. She was vaguely aware that they were arguing about setting an alarm, but couldn't bring herself awake enough to express an opinion. She fell asleep before the question was settled.

She woke to the realization that someone was missing. She stirred, opening her eyes, and saw Balthasar standing by the monitor console, one hand resting on the alarm switch. He had deactivated it before it could ring, she realized, and felt Chase Mago stir behind her.

"Damn it, Denis," the engineer said, "we agreed on eight hours."

Balthasar shrugged, unabashed. "I thought you might as well sleep while you could."

"I'm awake now," Chase Mago said grimly, but he was smiling.

"What's been happening?" Silence asked, and levered herself out of the bunk.

"I assume nothing, since we weren't called," Balthasar

said. He touched the intercom button. "Bridge? How're things?"

"Everything is still as you left it," Marcinik answered promptly. "The ship's drifted a little, but it's well within the limits you set."

Silence nodded, satisfied, and pushed open the cabin door, ignoring Chase Mago's protest of, "And what about my engines?" She made her way back to her own cabin, showered, then dressed quickly, pulling on a clean shipsuit. It was the last one, she realized, and smiled. It was just as well this was the last stage of the road.

The others were already in the common room, Balthasar sawing awkwardly at a loaf of daybread under the engineer's critical eye. As Silence entered, Chase Mago shook his head. "There's no doubt about it, Denis, her highness is a better cook than you are."

Balthasar glared at him, and slid the plate of sliced bread across the table with more force than was necessary. The engineer caught it, grinning, and Balthasar reluctantly smiled back. "Coffee, Silence?" he asked, still smiling.

"Thanks." Silence took her place at the table, wondering what had brought on the sudden high spirits. She could feel it herself, though, a pleasant apprehension that bordered on fear. For a moment she frowned, puzzled, then froze in understanding, the coffee mug forgotten in her hand. In a few short hours—five, six, ten at the most—they would be on Earth, or dead. One way or another, all their work would be over, and, with luck, something entirely new would have begun.

"Silence?" That was Chase Mago, one eyebrow raised in question.

The pilot shook herself. "Sorry. I guess—I can't quite believe it, that's all."

Balthasar nodded, a crooked smile on his gaunt face. Chase Mago said, "I know. It's strange, isn't it?"

"It is that," Silence agreed. They sat for a long moment, no one saying anything, and then, with a decisive gesture, Balthasar put his cup aside.

"I'm going to collect our papers and ID tapes now, cue them up properly. We'll leave in, say, fifteen minutes?"

Silence nodded, suddenly unable to speak, excitement choking her. Chase Mago said, the same excitement in his voice, "In fifteen minutes."

Once the Delian had left, Silence busied herself tidying the common room, making sure that everything was stowed away for the passage into purgatory. Aili could have done it, she knew, or at worst, they could simply have locked the common room door, but she needed something to occupy her hands for the moment. Chase Mago grinned, pushing himself away from the table.

"I'm going on to the engine room," he announced. "Might as well get started."

Balthasar had been gone less than two minutes by the common room clock. Silence laughed, and pushed the last mug into the cleaning slot, saying, "I know. I think I'll head up to the bridge myself."

"It is hard to imagine, isn't it?" Chase Mago said again, and disappeared.

Silence gave the common room a final glance. Everything was in place, dishes and food stowed in the appropriate cells, furniture securely dogged to the decking. She nodded to herself and left the room, latching the door behind her.

Balthasar was already on the bridge, perched on the arm of the first pilot's couch to get at the communications console's automatic-identification unit. The access panel was folded back, and two stacks of disks lay on the console beside the opening. Silence recognized one set as *Recusante*'s legal—or at least quasi-legal—Delian papers, the disks showing opalescent blue under the bridge lights, and knew the others had to be the disks forged on Asterion. They didn't show the same convincing wash of color, and the pilot couldn't help wondering if Balthasar's mysterious contact had done his job properly. She shook the thought away—it was too late to worry about that now—and took her place in the second pilot's couch, glancing automatically at the console displays. The checklights showed green and standby blue across her boards. Nodding to herself, she reached for the portolan.

By now, the book opened to the proper pages almost by itself. Silence sat for a moment, staring at the bizarre map, with its patchwork of symbols linked by the overlapping rays of the landlines. It was hard to believe, even now, that this archaic system—this infuriating, exhausting, archaic method— would actually lead them past the Rose Worlders' engines to Earth. And yet it had brought them this far, deeper into the ring of the Rose Worlds than any uninvited foreigner had ever come. Murmuring the first cantrip, she turned her attention to the final mark.

The tiny drawing, impossibly detailed like all of the illustrations on the map, showed four women dancing in a ring on a grassy hill, their right hands lifted toward a child dressed only in a wreath of bright flowers who floated just above their fingertips. Each wore a long gown cut to an unfamiliar pattern, and each carried something in her left hand. Silence leaned closer, concentrating on each of the figures in turn. The nearest one, a golden-haired woman in a flowing gown that seemed to shift in color from white to a tawny shade so dark as to be almost red, held a slender wand; her long sleeves were caught up to her shoulders by pins shaped like salamanders. To her left was a dark woman in rich russet patterned with bunches of grapes, a square crown confining her jet-black hair. She carried a dull bronze disk in her free hand, but held it so loosely that she seemed almost about to toss it into the air like a juggler. Next to her, half hidden by the golden woman, danced a woman in a turquoise gown. Her trailing sleeves were lined in a paler blue, and the great cloak that streamed back from her shoulders seemed to flow from a black blue-green in the shadows to a strange almost-color like thickly flawed glass. Her hair was hidden by a silver coronet from which fell a draped curtain made of strands of pearls, and she carried a closed silver cup in her left hand. The fourth woman, at the golden woman's right, was dressed all in greys. Her gown was more severely cut than the others', tight in the cloud-colored bodice, and then swirling out into an immensely full skirt that darkened from the cloudy grey of the bodice to a rich blue-purple at the flaring hem. She alone carried a sword, but held it so easily it seemed to have no weight at all.

Those were the old symbols of the four elements, Silence realized abruptly, symbols taken from a system even older than the portolan itself. The sword stood for elemental air, the cup for water, the bronze disk for earth, and the little wand for fire. Four dancers, four suits of the tarot, four elements—the last four symbols of the Earth-road. The portolan's symbols were not that different from the voidmarks given in *The Gilded Stairs*, Silence thought, but while the original image used the alchemical marriage, the active union of the king and queen, the portolan, true to its passive nature, showed the result of that union, the Child that symbolized the end of every quest. It was an auspicious image with which to end their own journey.

She looked away, deliberately breaking the mark's spell, and realized that Balthasar was watching her, a wry smile on his face.

"I was looking at the mark earlier," the Delian said. "It's—beautiful, but do you think the siege engines will have affected it, too?"

Silence made a face. Until now, she had assumed that, since the pilot did not manipulate the portolan's marks in any way, the engines would not be able to distort what she saw in purgatory. But if the symbols of the mark were the same as the last four symbols of the Earth-road, there was at least a chance that they, too, would be affected. On the other hand, the engines could not distort the symbolism too thoroughly, or the Rose Worlders' own ships could not pass the barrier their own magi had created. . . . "I don't know," she said, slowly. "All things considered, I don't think they will."

"I hope not," Balthasar said, and turned back to his keyboards. He touched a button on the intercom panel, and looked back at Silence, a quirky smile on his face. "Ready?"

"I'm ready," Silence answered.

"Julie?" Balthasar asked, and the engineer answered promptly.

"Ready when you are, Denis."

"Then let's go," Balthasar said.

For a long moment, nothing seemed to happen, and then Silence heard the first note of the new keelsong, rising very slowly and by a deliberate progression toward the twelfth of heaven. She shivered, fighting back her excitement, and settled herself to wait.

As always, it seemed to take forever to reach the twelfth.

Silence leaned back in her couch, doing her best to wait patiently, and not lose the unexpected pleasure she had found in the final image. It was a losing battle. By the time *Recusante* came within fifteen minutes of purgatory, the excitement had been drowned by the tedium of the run along the landline.

Sighing, she unfastened the safety webbing, and pushed herself out of her couch. Balthasar glanced over his shoulder, a crooked smile on his face.

"Enjoy yourself, Silence."

"Thanks," the pilot said, sourly, and climbed onto the upper bridge. The dome had begun to thin out already, but she ignored it as she plugged in her headset and checked the line of status lights running across the hub of the control yoke. Everything was in order, all the lights showing green.

"Five minutes," Chase Mago's voice announced.

"Five minutes," Silence acknowledged absently, resting her hands on the wheel. Her thumb hovered over the lock. She moved it aside, grimacing—it was much too early—but put it back a moment later.

"Three minutes," Chase Mago said.

Silence repeated the engineer's words, her attention on the dome around her. It was fading more rapidly than it had on the other stages of the voyage, but in patches, like ice melting. Some sections were almost clear, or as clear as they ever became following the portolan's lines, while others were still almost opaque. Silence frowned, wondering if this was an indication of trouble to come, but then the last solid patches abruptly vanished.

"You have control, Silence," Balthasar said. "Everything looks good here."

"I have control," Silence answered, and unlocked her wheel. For the first time since she'd begun to follow the portolan, the yoke moved stiffly, with the slight hint of resistance she associated with normal star travel.

"We're on the line," Chase Mago said. "Everything looks good. I'm switching on the warning."

"Go ahead," Silence answered, and a moment later the familiar tone sounded in her ears, sweet and true. Ahead, a green knoll rose from nothing, its roots trailing off into shadows. The four figures were frozen in midstep, circling its crown. Above their outstretched hands floated the Child on its wreath of roses and lilies, apparently asleep, serenely unconscious of its position. Silence smiled in spite of herself, and let *Recusante* follow the landline toward the dancing figures.

As *Recusante* drew closer to the mark, Silence became aware of a change in the image, a faint haziness circling the little hill just below the dancers' feet. It was less than shadow, a sort of fuzziness above the grass, distorting the shapes only slightly, but it was something that should not be there. It had not been a part of the portolan's drawing, that much was certain, but she could not make it take any clear shape. Silence kept *Recusante* on course, frowning, and felt her shoulders tighten in spite of herself, ready to pull the ship out of possible danger.

The ship came closer, but the weird circle still refused to take on concrete form, wavering almost like heat-shadow on a sun-baked road. Silence deliberately looked away, the way she looked away from the faintest lights in a darkened room, but the image stayed obstinately vague. Whatever it is, she thought, I don't like it. She pulled back gently on the control yoke, lifting *Recusante* until the warning tone began to rise in pitch. She levelled off then, shaking her head. The maneuver had gained her a little altitude relative to the circle, but not enough. If the line ran true, *Recusante* would have to pass through the upper edges of that shimmering disturbance.

Of course, a magus's skills might be able to determine what it is, she thought, but hesitated. She wasn't sure what the effects of a pilot's semi-active power would be on the delicate balance of the landlines and the simple mark, had refused to let Chase Mago call in the upper register on the first stage of the journey and had been proven right. A magus's power was even more active, so much so that its use might completely destroy her ability to perceive the portolan's images. Maybe if I asked Isambard to do it? she thought, but rejected the idea almost at once. The effect would be the same, no matter who wielded the active power. There was nothing to do but wait. The tone was steady in her headset, indicating that the ship was still solidly on the line; even so, she touched the intercom button to override it.

"Julie, Denis, are either of you picking up anything unusual?"

Balthasar answered first, as usual. "Not a thing. Is anything wrong?"

"Everything looks fine here," Chase Mago said, almost in the same instant. "Why?"

"I'm not sure," Silence said. "There's something funny about the mark. . . ." She let her voice trail off, not quite sure even how she should describe it.

Balthasar's voice sharpened. "Trouble?"

"Maybe," Silence said, staring at the strangely blurred line. It was closer now, but no clearer. She had never seen or heard of anything like it, and she could hear the frustration in her own voice. "I can't see it well enough to tell."

Recusante was almost at the foot of the little hill, and Silence broke off the conversation. There were formulae that could be used to test the substance of an immaterial object; the magi used them to investigate the nature of Forms. Maybe, she thought, one of them would be good enough to test this—whatever it is. Very cautiously, she murmured one of Jabir's cantrips, putting only a fraction of her strength into the probing formula. She felt the faint tingling that meant she had called on her power correctly, and in the same instant the universe seemed to stagger, a sickening, earthquake sensation. She broke off the cantrip instantly, hoping she had been able to hold it long enough to get a result. Nothing happened: either she had succeeded and the wavering circle was harmless, or, more likely, she had not had time to complete the cantrip. She grimaced, but kept the ship on course, knowing there was nothing else she could do.

And then *Recusante* had reached the edge of the mark. "Julie, stop down now," Silence said. There was no acknowledgement, but the keelsong thinned slightly. The warning tone began to drop as well, and Silence pulled back on the yoke, lifting the ship farther above the illusory grasses. The dancing figures loomed overhead, but the pilot barely saw them, fixing her eyes instead on the odd band of haze. This close, it had a sort of shape, like a wall of invisible flame, the upper edges of the circle pulsing very slowly, as though in time to some distant heartbeat.

Then, too late, she knew what it was, and damned herself for a fool. Balthasar had guessed it, for all he wasn't a magus, had warned her, and she'd been too stupid to listen. The shadow was the reflection of the siege engines that had corrupted the elemental symbols each time she had tried to force the Earth-road. They weren't able to affect this passive perception of the symbols, but they did exist, and they did block her path into the mark. Swearing, she pulled up on the control yoke, lifting *Recusante* as far off the landline as she dared. The warning note changed, protesting, and was swallowed in an explosion of pure noise as the ship's keel touched the top of the invisible wall. Silence winced, cringing under the sheer force of the sound, and ripped off her headset. The sound eased a little, but seemed to take almost solid form, rising like mist, like static, to destroy her vision of the mark. She swore again, twisting the control yoke from side to side to find the landline, but she had lost the warning tone when she pulled off the headset. Cursing, she brought the ship back to what she hoped was the proper course, fighting down panic. She could not hear the keelsong through the smothering roar; she thought the ship trembled underfoot, but could not longer trust her own perceptions.

With a tremendous effort, she controlled her fear, forcing herself to think logically. If Isambard were here, he would know how to break the engines—had always known, and here where the engines' force was weaker, he might actually succeed. . . . But the magus wasn't there, and there was no way—and no time—to send for him. Silence groped frantically for the memory of how Isambard had attempted to break the engines. He had invoked the Forms of the elements, she remembered that much; she remembered the words themselves, but not the formulae that bound those Forms to his bidding. She sobbed aloud, feeling the deck shake beneath her. *Recusante* was tearing herself apart, disrupted by the noise that was the ultimate dissonance. The stolen mailship, *Bruja*, had almost gone the same way, shattered by the engines' music.

The thought of *Bruja* sparked a vague memory. Silence

fought back panic, knowing she had no time to waste, and focussed her thoughts inward, forcing herself into a state of awareness. It had been on *Bruja* that she'd learned she had a magus's power, first by breaking the Hegemonic geas and then, when she had tried to fly the Earth-road. . . . The memory came rushing back, and with it came the ghost of the Earth-road's music, the note that once before had taken *Recusante* to the eighth of heaven. She reached for the memory of that music without conscious plan, knowing only that it had saved *Bruja* so many months before. She twisted it, turning it outward, forcing it to take on a Form, and then forced that Form to become reality. The note sang in her and around her, driving back the engines' noise.

The deck steadied underfoot, though she could still feel it trembling, and the blurring static faded slightly. A line appeared in the haze ahead of the ship, faint at first, then growing solid. Colors ran along its length, black to white to peacock-blue to royal purple, strobing away from her in great waves of light that also carried the sound of heaven to blend with the keelsong in glorious diapason.

Blindly, Silence turned *Recusante* onto that brilliant pathway, feeling the ship's trembling ease further. Then, quite suddenly, the static was gone, though the path remained, stretching away up the hill to twist in and out of the feet of the unmoving dancers. Shaking, Silence glanced back over her shoulder, and saw the hazy wall behind her: she had passed through the engines' influence without destroying it, or them.

Now that the engines' noise was gone, she could hear faint voices calling from her headset, but she could not leave the wheel to pick it up. She put the voices from her mind, concentrating on the images ahead. *Recusante* was moving very fast now, skimming along above the multicolored path. Silence leaned against the wheel, turning the ship to follow the path as it wound around the first dancer's monstrous ankle. As *Recusante* completed the loop, Silence thought she saw the dancer's other foot, lifted for the next step, tremble slightly, but the path led away from that figure, heading directly across the dance to the figure that stood for elemental water. Fire to water, Silence thought, dizzily, then earth to air?

The glowing path traced a loop around the water-dancer's foot as well. Silence leaned on the wheel, forcing *Recusante* into the sharp curve. As the ship came around again, closing the circle, she caught a glimpse of the fire-dancer. The golden woman had moved, she thought, had taken another step along the pattern—but surely that was impossible? The path twisted, whirling her away before she could be sure.

As she had half expected, the path took her next around the earth-dancer's foot, then traced a line back through the center of the dance, crossing itself again. This time, as she passed the first two dancers, she was certain they had moved, were moving, continuing a dance suspended for too many years, and knew without looking back that the earth-dancer was stirring, too. The keelsong rose gloriously around her, and she was suddenly aware that it was the harmonium's full concord, upper and lower register both, but she did not know if she had triggered it, or if Chase Mago had guessed what was happening, and opened all the stops.

The path looped again around the final dancer's foot, almost touching the hem of her flaring skirt. Silence held her breath, but *Recusante* passed under it safely, and turned to follow the path back to the center of the dance. A moment later, she heard a whisper of sound behind her, almost blending into the swelling keelsong, and guessed the skirt had brushed the path as the air-dancer shifted into motion.

All the dancers were moving now, tracing the steps of the dance with monumental grace. The path seemed to end in the center of the turning figures—or rather, Silence realized, the path joined itself again, closing the knot. For a moment, she wondered if the ship would have to retrace that pattern, dodging the dancers' moving feet, but then *Recusante* reached the center of the pattern, and the path abruptly vanished. Silence blinked, startled, her hands freezing on the wheel. Before she could move, however, the ship began to rise, as though lifted by an invisible hand. She glanced down instinctively, but the tinctured decking blocked her view. She looked up, and saw that the Child had vanished. The wreath remained, and through its circle Silence could see the unhaloed stars of mundane space.

The dancers swung past again, serenely beautiful archetypes, and then *Recusante* had reached the wreath and was through, harmonium dropping into the lower register. Silence shook her head, completely without words for what she had done, then, stiffly, locked her wheel and bent to pick up her discarded headset.

Balthasar's voice sounded instantly in her ears. "—down. We're on the normal exit point, and I don't see any hostiles. Silence, are you there?"

"I'm here," the pilot said slowly, and her own voice sounded harsh and clumsy after the music of heaven.

"What happened?" Chase Mago demanded. "My God, I thought we'd had it that time."

Silence took a deep breath, fumbling for the words, and Balthasar said, "Let it go, Julie. She brought us through the engines, right? And that's quite enough for now." His voice sharpened. "Silence, I'm going to need your help. Their Approach Control's going to be signalling any minute."

The demand seemed doubly unfair, coming so soon after the wonders of the passage. Silence felt tears stinging in her eyes. She wanted nothing more than to sit quietly until she understood just what had happened, what she had done—but Balthasar was right. This was only the first part; if the Rose Worlders suspected them now, all her work would have been for nothing. Still, it was hard to make herself climb down the ladder, and take her place in the second pilot's couch beside Balthasar.

All three of the viewscreens showed the same image, a single sun against a sea of stars. Silence frowned, wondering why Balthasar had not switched one of them to musonar display, and the Delian leaned toward her, reaching across the Ficinan model to touch her hand.

"There it is," he said softly. "The first sun, Earth's sun."

Silence stared at the screens, not quite able to believe it even now. But it *is* Earth's sun, she told herself firmly, the words sounding more real with each repetition, and somewhere in there is Earth itself. They were still too far out for the real-light cameras to pick up planets. She turned to the

Ficinan model, suddenly desperate to prove that Earth really did exist, that it had not been destroyed like so many worlds during the Millennial War.

The globe showed a schematic image, the sun at the center surrounded by slowly pulsing waves of light, ringed by planets, each of which moved in its own circle of color, deepest at the center, fading toward invisibility at the edges. Here and there, interference showed darkly red, where two planetary envelopes overlapped. Silence counted, her breath coming more quickly: nine planets—nine planets and a pale band of blue that was certainly an asteroid belt. Nine planets. . . . She could remember only a few of the extra names—the other worlds were useless, their names meaningless and easily forgotten without the key that was Earth—but every star-traveller knew that the third world from the First Sun was Earth. The image hung in the globe, much like any other planet, a pinpoint of light surrounded by the waves of the *musica mundana*. She touched the crystal of the Ficinan globe just above the point, as though that could make it more real.

"I know," Balthasar said. "I know."

Silence nodded, and lifted her eyes to the viewscreens. The first sun looked quite ordinary, much like any other sun in human-settled space. It took a deliberate effort of will to convince herself that it was something special.

"Captain Balthasar." Isambard's voice sounded very loud in the intercom speakers. "We've arrived? May I come on the bridge?"

Silence gave the Delian an imploring glance, and Balthasar grinned. "We've made it into the system, Isambard, and we're waiting for a signal from the Approach Control. I'd rather you stayed in commons for now; I'll patch the picture onto the screen there."

Silence bent to adjust the remote-screen controls, slaving the unit in the common room to the bow camera. Isambard didn't say anything for a long moment, but finally sighed deeply.

"Very well, Captain Balthasar, I'll wait here."

"Thank you," Balthasar said, almost cheerfully, and touched another button on the intercom panel. "Marcinik? We made it to the system, anyway. I've patched our camera view into the common room screen if you and her serenity want to take a look."

"Thanks," Marcinik answered. "We shall."

Balthasar cut the connection, the smile fading from his face. "Question is," he murmured, "where's our approach contact?"

"You said we came out on the usual appearance point?" Silence asked. That had always been one of her worries—managing their emergence from purgatory so that it looked as though *Recusante* had flown the normal Earth-road.

Balthasar nodded. "According to the supercargo's information, we were close enough that even the orbital musonar couldn't tell the difference."

According to the supercargo's information. That was the sticky point, Silence thought. All their knowledge of Earth was based on what that woman had told them, and there had been no way to verify more than a few minor details. Not for the first time, she wondered if they had learned enough.

"Ah, here we go," Balthasar exclaimed, pointing to the communications console. Lights flashed orange on the automatic-identification panel, indicating an arriving signal, then turned green as the equipment recognized the inquiry and broadcast the forged papers in response. Silence held her breath, waiting for the acknowledgement, and saw without surprise that Balthasar's hands were white-knuckled on his controls. She reached across the Ficinan model to adjust the musonar, scanning the volume around them for signs of any other ships. The screen stayed clear, with only a faint reading just at the edge of their range to worry about—and if that diffuse blob was another ship, Silence thought, it would take even a navy six at least an hour to cover the distance between the two. Still, she did not relax until the external speaker crackled to life.

"Double-M vessel *Recusante*, this is Interior Approach Control. You are entering a special license area. Please transmit your permit at once."

"Interior Approach, this is *Recusante*," Balthasar answered, his voice remarkably calm. "Transmitting now." He touched a button on the communications console, and a new light flashed red. Silence held her breath again, hoping the supercargo's memory had ben accurate, and that Balthasar's forger was as good as the Delian had claimed. There was a long pause before the speaker hissed again.

"*Recusante*, this is Interior Approach Control. Your permit has been received and verified. Please set up to accept your entry course."

Silence let out the breath she had been holding in a great sigh, and hastily adjusted the astrogation console. "Ready," she said, too quietly for the microphones to pick up her voice, and Balthasar nodded.

"We're ready to accept the entry course," he said.

"Stand by," Interior Approach said severely. "Transmitting."

The astrogation console whirred briefly, then stopped. Silence checked the telltales, and said, "It's recorded and shows green."

"Course recorded and on our board," Balthasar said into his microphone.

"Please retransmit to verify," Interior Approach responded, and the Delian lifted an eyebrow.

"Wrath-of-God wasn't this sticky," he said. Silence winced, but saw his microphone was safely off. Balthasar winked, and flipped his headset on again. "Retransmitting," he announced, and Silence hit the necessary keys.

There was a brief pause, and then Interior Approach said, "We verify the course as correct, *Recusante*. Do not, I repeat, do not deviate from this line for any reason whatsoever. You will be under observation from planetary stations and from patrolcraft to make certain you obey the restrictions."

Balthasar made a face at that, but answered evenly, "Understood, Approach."

"You will be contacted again when you reach the planetary envelope," the severe voice continued. "Interior Approach Control out." The open-channel indicator winked out before the Delian could respond.

"Rude set of bastards, aren't they?" Balthasar murmured. His grim expression belied the flippant words.

"Charming," Chase Mago agreed, but his heart wasn't in it. "Patrolcraft, Denis?"

"We were warned about them," Silence said soothingly, hands already busy on her keyboards. The musonar was already set to broadscan at its longest range. She left that as it was, and adjusted the astrogation console so that the central viewscreen and the Ficinan model displayed their assigned course. The yellow line curved in toward Earth in a wide arc, threading a narrow channel of undistorted space between two worlds just past their closest approach. It was clearly a course intended to waste their time, to make sure that the Rose Worlders—or whoever it was that Interior Approach Control's stiff voice represented—had time to take a very good look at the newcomers.

Balthasar frowned. "I don't like the looks of that," he said, and tapped the little gap between edges of the planetary envelopes. "I don't like it at all."

"There's plenty of room," Silence began, and Balthasar cut her off.

"Yeah, plenty of room for those patrolcraft Approach was talking about."

Silence stared at the musonar image. To either side of the indicated course lay a wash of color, the reflection of trailing planetary harmonies. The edges nearest the course line were tinged with red: interference cast by the conflicting harmonies. "I wouldn't want to take a ship into that," she said aloud.

Balthasar snorted. "It wouldn't be that bad, provided you knew the system music pretty well, and turned accordingly. And all that underlying noise is going to play games with our musonar; that's something else they'll use."

Silence made a doubtful face, but she had to admit that the Delian, with his Wrath-of-God experience, knew more about such things than she did. "Well, so far I don't see any sign of a patrol."

"Keep looking," Balthasar said, and touched the intercom switch. "Julie, we're headed in-system. Give me half power."

"Half power it is," Chase Mago answered. "What do we do about the patrols?"

"Just what we planned," Balthasar answered. "*Recusante* looks enough like a Rose Worlder freighter—no offense, Silence—so we'll just play innocent and let them stare as much as they like."

Chase Mago made a rather skeptical noise, but said nothing else. Silence looked to her left, and saw that Balthasar was chewing thoughtfully on his lower lip. The Delian saw her glance, and smiled. "On the other hand, there's no point in being stupid," he said, and pressed another button on the intercom panel. "Marcinik? Are you there?"

The colonel answered after only a second's delay. "I'm here, Balthasar. What is it?"

"I want you to man the guns," Balthasar answered, and Silence thought she heard a murmur of surprise from Aili in the background. Whatever the Princess Royal had been about to say was cut off by Isambard.

"That would ruin everything," the magus said indignantly. "You mustn't take the chance of their seeing that you're ready to fight."

Balthasar took a deep breath, obviously fighting back his anger, and Silence said hastily, "Let me talk to him."

"He's all yours," Balthasar said, with relish.

"We discussed this back on Asterion," Silence said, not bothering to respond to the Delian's remark. "Even if they spot us now, there's a good chance we could break away, and take what we've learned back to the Hegemon."

The magus did not answer for a long moment, but at last he said, "Very well."

Balthasar did not bother to acknowledge him, saying only, "Take the guns, Marcinik."

"On my way," the colonel answered. A moment later, Silence heard the faint sound of the common room door opening and closing. To her surprise, however, the intercom sounded again.

"Is there anything Doctor Isambard and I can—should be doing?" Aili asked, her voice preternaturally calm.

"What do you think?" Balthasar growled at his closed microphone. "Damn stupid question."

"Shut up, Denis," Silence said. She could not help feeling sorry for the Princess Royal. It wasn't the easiest position to be in, sitting and waiting for disaster or success, all the while knowing that nothing one did could affect the result, and the pilot let that sympathy color her answer. "I'm afraid not, Serenity. If anything comes up, we'll call, I promise."

"Thank you," Aili answered, her voice still very much

under control. "I'll be in my cabin, and Doctor Isambard will be in his."

"Silence?" Chase Mago said. "Tell them they can be going over their stories, making absolutely sure they know them. We may need them to back us up."

Silence nodded, even though she knew the engineer couldn't see her, and repeated his words to the two in the common room. It was a good idea, even if it wasn't strictly true—they had all spent weeks learning their cover story, in learning-trance and out—and it would give Aili in particular something to occupy her mind.

"We'll do that," the Princess Royal said, and broke the connection.

Silence leaned back in her couch then, staring at the musonar. It still showed nothing but empty space and the dull wash of music from the outermost planet, and she sighed deeply. "So now we wait," she said.

"We wait," Balthasar agreed.

After a moment's thought, Silence adjusted the musonar so that the side viewscreens showed the results of short-range scanning: nothing unusual, unless you wanted to count the strange readings from the two outermost worlds. The tiny ninth world wasn't even within the plane of the system, but swung through it on a weirdly tilted orbit, trailing a cloud of pinkish interference. The next world in was surrounded by an inner envelope of a peculiar, violent blue, and that envelope in turn was enclosed in a flattened pale-blue oval. A strange, intense music sang in that world's core, and for a moment, Silence could almost remember its name. The teasing memory vanished before she could seize it, and the pilot made a disgusted face.

They still had a very long way to go, she thought, and almost said the words aloud until she glanced sideways and saw Balthasar's set face. The Delian was in no mood for conversation, that much was clear. Sighing, Silence edged back further into her couch, with an effort turning her thoughts to what they had to do once they actually landed on Earth. From the beginning, even before they had known for certain that the Rose Worlders controlled Earth as well as the Earth-road, they had known they could do nothing more than a quick survey. That had been modified only slightly since. All they intended to do—all they could do. Silence told herself firmly—was land, deliver their faked cargo, and try to guess how strongly Earth was held. Then they would lift, and return to the Hegemon with the knowledge they had gathered. I'm tempted to try the Earth-road going back, Silence thought. It would be quicker than the portolan's route, and probably a lot more pleasant—maybe even safer, if the Rose Worlders suspect anything. After all, Isambard's pretty sure he can break the engines, and once we're through that barrier, we're almost home. If we went back by portolan, we'd have to spend so much time in mundane space that the Rose Worlders would be sure to spot us.

She shook her head then, still not quite able to believe that this was really Earth's system. Maybe it isn't, she thought, a sudden rush of fear threatening to overwhelm her. Maybe somehow the Rose Worlders have tricked us—there must be other nine-planet systems, after all—maybe they're hiding in that lovely ambush spot Denis picked out, just waiting to blast us out of space. Maybe Earth really was destroyed, the way I was always sure it had been, and this is just the Rose Worlders' way of eliminating inquisitive star-travellers.

She cut off that flight of fancy abruptly. It was hardly likely—if nothing else, the Rose Worlders could not have produced the images she had seen on the last stage of the portolan-journey. Still, the feeling of unreality persisted, despite the images on the screens.

Slowly, *Recusante* crept inward along the prescribed course. A quarter of the way along the yellow line, Silence caught the first flicker of another keel on the musonar; fifteen minutes later, the musonar picked up a second ship, as big as a Navy five but even more heavily armed, moving along a course that paralleled *Recusante*'s own.

"What do you want to bet they're scanning us like crazy?" Balthasar murmured.

"Let them," Silence said, with a confidence she was far from feeling.

"And next they're bound to query the A-ID," Balthasar continued, as though he hadn't heard. "Yes, there they go."

Silence looked at the communications console. Sure enough,

the green light was on above the automatic indentification panel, and she could hear the faint whine as the console automatically broadcast the information contained on the disks in its various cells. The light blinked out, and she could hear Balthasar's quick breathing, both of them bracing against possible attack. Silence's eyes went to the chronometer. A minute ticked by, impossibly slowly, and then another, and she began to relax. In the musonar, the patrolship kept its station, neither moving off nor closing in.

"I suppose that's something to be grateful for," she murmured, and realized with some embarrassment that she had spoken aloud.

Balthasar grunted. "We'll know for certain in about half an hour," he said.

Silence frowned at the course plot, then understood. If the five kept station, its course would bring it up against and then into the *musica mundana* of the seventh planet in half an hour, where the interference would be too strong even for a ship well-tuned to the vagaries of the local system. She stared at the screens, willing the five to turn back.

"Captain Balthasar." Marcinik's voice in the headset made Silence jump. "The gunnery sensors show a target at extreme range. Do you want me to do anything about it?"

Balthasar grinned, and Silence had to suppress a slightly hysterical giggle. The idea of *Recusante*, with her tiny cannon, "doing something about" a well-armed patrolship was ludicrous. She sobered a little as she realized they might have to try.

"Not just at the moment, colonel," Balthasar said.

"Permission to power the guns?" Marcinik asked.

Balthasar hesitated. "No," he said, after a moment. "They might spot the change. Don't worry, I'll give you plenty of warning."

"Please do," Marcinik said, and broke the connection.

"Trust me, damn you," Balthasar said to his dead microphone, and shook his head. "We'll have time, if it comes to fighting."

Silence nodded, then realized he was speaking more to reassure himself.

Slowly, *Recusante* crept along the course line toward the

inner planets. As the patrolship approached the edge of the planetary envelope, Silence held her breath, then forced herself to breathe normally. For a long moment, the patrolship too, held steady, nosing a little way into the shadowy color, and the musonar picked up the faint sparks of dissonance flaring around it. Then, quite suddenly, it swung away, back toward the edge of the system, accelerating until it vanished from the musonar altogether.

Balthasar sighed noisily. "Well, that one believed us."

Let's hope the others do, too, Silence thought, but said nothing. Instead, she directed the musonar forward, throwing in as much power as she dared. They were coming up on Balthasar's ambush point, the narrow gap between the harmonic envelopes, and Silence swung the horn back and forth, scanning the areas of low interference. As the Delian had predicted, the rising harmonies of the envelopes made it difficult to pick out details from the background clamor, but she thought she saw the bronze shadow of at least one keel in the wash of color. It was too quick a sighting to determine the class of ship, but she could not delude herself into thinking it would be anything less than a warship.

"Anything?" Balthasar asked.

Silence shrugged. "I thought I saw at least one keel, but the clamor blocked it before I could get a good reading. It looks like you were right, Denis."

"Mmm." Balthasar stared at the screen as though he could force it to come clear, once again chewing on his lower lip. Then he reached for the intercom in sudden decision. "Marcinik, power the guns—low setting for now, but get the fires running."

"Certainly, Captain Balthasar," the colonel answered. A few seconds later, a row of lights blinked orange and then pale green on the status board. Silence lifted an eyebrow. Marcinik must've been sitting with his finger practically on the button to respond that quickly, she thought. And I don't blame him for it, either.

As *Recusante* edged her way into the gap between the two envelopes, the musonar cleared momentarily. Silence caught a brief glimpse of four, maybe five keels before the flaring color hid them completely. Balthasar swore softly.

"Did you get a guess on the class?"

Silence shook her head doubtfully. "I don't think any of them were any brighter than that five, but I couldn't swear to it."

"Damn," Balthasar muttered, and fixed his brooding stare on the screens.

Silence divided her attention between the musonar, the real-light cameras' tiny screen, and the chronometer. When five, and then ten minutes passed without an attack, she allowed herself to relax a little. Still, she jumped when the communications console clicked, her heart pounding painfully.

"Checking our papers again," Balthasar said, and smiled. "That should mean they still believe us."

Silence nodded, heart still beating too hard for her to speak. Still, Balthasar seemed to be right. Other than that one inquiry, the hidden patrolships gave no sign of their presence. Even so, Silence could not quite breathe easily until *Recusante* emerged from the narrow lane. The course ahead showed empty of patrolcraft. After a moment's consideration, she adjusted the musonar horn to point back along the way they'd come. There was nothing there either—and then a small bronze dot slid out of the screening music. Silence swore as the patrolcraft—it looked like another five— moved slowly forward to take up station behind them, effectively blocking any attempt to escape.

"Denis, we're being followed," she said aloud.

"I see it." Balthasar sounded surprisingly calm. Silence glanced warily in his direction and saw that he was smiling. She made a face, but there was nothing to say to that unexpected cool. Instead, she reset the musonar, leaving one of the smaller units to watch the trailing ship, and turned the main horn forward again.

As they moved deeper into the system, more traffic showed in the screens. Silence counted four more patrolcraft—smaller ships this time, the equivalents of Navy threes and fours— and perhaps half a dozen other ships moving within the orbit of the fourth planet. One of those was recognizably a roundship, another freighter similar in size and tuning to *Recusante*, but the others gave off strange, contradictory readings. It was almost as though there was no keelsong involved, Silence

thought, just the musonar's notes reflecting off bare, untinctured metal. It was more than that, she realized a moment later; there was a secondary harmony involved, one that
bore a strong resemblance to the note of elemental fire. That
sparked a memory. The primitive, chemical-fuel tugs used by
Wrath-of-God had given off a similar reading—though why
Earth would use that kind of ship is a mystery to me, Silence
thought. Aloud, she said, "Denis, I think I'm picking up
flame-throwers."

"You can't be," Balthasar said automatically, but looked to
the musonar. His frown deepened. "But that's what it looks
like, isn't it? I wonder why. . . ."

"Wrath-of-God used them at the Wrath," Silence said, and
waited.

"Yeah, but that was because we were water-poor. Earth
should have all the distilleries it needs." Balthasar shook his
head, and touched the general speaker. "Julie, Isambard, can
you think of any good reason to run flame-throwers—chemical-
fuel ships—instead of normal subcelestial keels?"

Neither the magus nor the engineer answered for a long
moment. Finally, Chase Mago said, "I can't." Silence could
almost hear the shrug.

The magus took longer to answer. "There is no reason that
I can think of, except lack of elemental water or an inability
to tincture a sounding keel correctly. Both hypotheses seem
to be ruled out a priori: we see true starships all around us."

"Thanks," Balthasar said sourly.

Silence grimaced, leaning back in her couch. The chemical-
fuel ships seemed clustered in the shadow of Earth's envelope, hovering around the single moon. Maybe they were
tugs, like Wrath-of-God's, she thought. Most moons were
barren, dead earth at their cores; if there were some sort of
station on that moon, it might be more economical to use
chemical-fuel ships than import elemental water. But why
would anyone go to the trouble of setting up a settlement on
a moon when there was a perfectly good world available?

Recusante crept inward along the curving course line, following a well-buoyed path through the ring of asteroids, then
skirting the edge of the fourth world's harmonic envelope.
After a moment's hesitation, Silence switched one of the

triple screens from musonar display to the image from the bow cameras. At the system's highest magnification, the red-orange disk showed darker lines, and bright icecaps at both poles. A pair of ragged moons circled it. Silence watched, entranced, until the image dwindled in the screen.

The intercom clicked again. "Mars," Isambard said, his voice tinged with reverence. "Captain Balthasar, we are coming up on Earth. I ask you again to allow me on the bridge."

Balthasar rolled his eyes, but answered politely enough, "I'm sorry, Isambard, there just isn't room. I'm afraid you'll have to make do with the pictures."

"Captain Balthasar—" the magus began again, and Silence cut in hastily, "Isambard, it's all the same picture."

There was a brief pause, and then Isambard sighed. "So it is. You do well to remind me."

Balthasar put his hand over his headset's microphone. "I wish to hell he'd remember it, then."

Silence nodded, but said, soothingly, "We still have an hour to go." Her eyes flickered to the chronometer to confirm the guess. Yes, she thought, it would take a little less than an hour to reach the end of the set course— She broke off then, shaking her head. In a little less than a standard hour, *Recusante* would be in Earth orbit: she could not quite make it seem real.

She adjusted the bow cameras, focusing them on the still-distant world. It was little more than a pinpoint on the screen, barely distinguishable from the stars around it—a little brighter, perhaps, its brilliance tinged with blue, but there was nothing particularly noticeable about it. Very slowly, the image swelled on the screen, from a mere dot of light to a visible disk, from a disk to the great, white-banded globe of legend, continents half hidden under the streaks of cloud. Silence's breath caught in her throat. This, then, was Earth, humankind's first home: there were no words for the moment, and she did not even try to find any, caught up in the wonder of it all.

A noise from the communications console broke the spell, and a new voice said, "MMV *Recusante*, this is Earth Traffic Control. Please transmit your manifest and supporting documents."

Balthasar touched keys on his board, frowning deeply. "Transmitting," he said, and switched off his microphone. "That's not coming from the planet."

Silence adjusted the secondary musonar, sweeping its lesser horn in short arcs. "You're right," she said, after a moment. "It's an orbital station."

"Why?" Balthasar demanded, the frustration clear in his voice. "That's all I want to know. Why make things difficult?"

Silence shrugged, and was grateful when the communications console beeped again, cutting off her reply.

"*Recusante*, this is Earth Traffic Control. Please stand by for your field assignment."

"Standing by," Balthasar said, and keyed the intercom. "Julie, be ready to record the field beam."

"Ready to record," Chase Mago answered.

"Right," the Delian answered. "Earth Traffic Control, we are ready to record."

Traffic Control answered promptly. "You will be landing at Ladysprings. Transmitting course and beam now."

"Ready," Balthasar answered, and keyed the astrogation console. It whined abruptly, and an instant later Chase Mago's voice came over the intercom.

"Field beam's recorded."

"And the course is in the box," Balthasar said, with a quick, nervous grin. "This is it, people, we're going in." He touched the transmitter for a final time. "Earth Traffic Control, we have recorded landing instructions. Ready to commence our descent."

"Very good, *Recusante*," Earth Traffic Control answered. "You may land when ready. Switch to frequency sixteen for Ladysprings Field Beacon."

"Thank you, Traffic Control," Balthasar said. "Switching now."

At his nod, Silence touched her keyboard, adjusting the console to the new frequency, but did not open the transmitter. Balthasar adjusted the astrogation display, projecting the new course onto the central screen. The bright yellow line skimmed across the edge of the atmospheric envelope, following a line almost parallel to the world's equator. It crossed into the planet's night after travelling only a few thousand kilometers, then changed to the red of beam descent above the center of a huge island.

"So that's Ladysprings," Balthasar said, half to himself. "Keep the frequency open, Silence, but we'll let them make first contact. Julie do you need a pitch reading?"

"Already in," Chase Mago answered. "Compensators set, stops at planetary maximum."

"Then we go," Balthasar said. Despite the confident words, there was a perceptible pause before he touched his own controls. *Recusante* dropped further toward the atmosphere, levelling off with its keel just skimming the line of demarcation. Silence winced as the contact set off a thin, high whining, just at the upper range of audibility. Balthasar touched keys again, and *Recusante* lifted slightly, the noise easing a little.

There was nothing to do now but wait. Silence leaned back in her couch, trying to relax, but she could feel her muscles tensing with every new sound from the keel. She could picture how *Recusante* must look from the planet's surface, a streak of light that trailed a fine line of cloud through the daylight sky, then changed to a crackling red vee of interference as they passed into night. They would be very bright against the stars—automatically, she checked the weather readings, and saw that it was indeed clear over their landing field—and she wondered just why the Rose Worlders were steering them to a darkened field. Surely it would make more sense to have them land in daylight—or would the trail of clouds be more conspicuous than the lights?

Recusante crossed the divider into darkness then, and she saw Balthasar's hands tense on his controls. "Coming up on the beam, Julie," he said.

"Ready," the engineer answered, but his words were swallowed by the sudden shrilling of the musonar.

"What the hell—" Balthasar began, and Silence cut him off, her eyes fixed on the musonar display. It was somewhat obscured by the noise from their own keel, but she could see clearly enough to know that they were in trouble.

"Aircraft, Denis, bearing one-three-five relative." She shivered reflexively, seeing a second flight of four ships rising over the curve of the planet. "Eight of them. I'm not getting a keel reading—" She broke off at Balthasar's abrupt gesture, too frightened now to be offended. Somehow the Rose Worlders had spotted them, had lured them in this far, and now the trap was sprung. . . .

"Full power to the guns—now, Marcinik," Balthasar snapped, and Silence forced herself to concentrate, waiting for orders. "Julie, we got trouble. I need everything you've got." He fixed his eyes on the triple screen. "What's the range, Silence?"

The pilot stared at the musonar for a moment without understanding, fear digging claws into her stomach. She had never flown in combat before, not really—at Arganthonios, the real fighting had happened before the little ships arrived, and then they hadn't made it to the ship before the Thousand landed. The battle off Asterion had been different, too, a space battle . . .

"Silence?" Balthasar said again, and the pilot shook herself.

"About three hundred kilometers," she answered, and somehow her voice was almost steady. "Still no reading on class or weapons. I don't think they're standard."

Balthasar made a face, and swung *Recusante* southward, away from the approaching ships. At the same time, he touched keys to lift her farther, away from the sticky atmosphere. The musonar cleared slightly, and Silence swung the secondary horn toward space, scanning the volume above and behind them. Two more dots appeared on her screen, both showing the brilliant white-bronze of subcelestial keels. She swung the horn forward, cursing, and found a third ship closing in from ahead.

"Two fours on our tail," she reported, "and it looks like a five ahead of us."

"Damn it," Balthasar muttered, and slammed his hands down on his keyboard. *Recusante*'s nose dropped sharply, and the ship dove toward the planet's distant surface. Interference sang around them, and the main musonar display dimmed perceptibly.

"Denis," Chase Mago said, warningly, and Balthasar snapped, "Compensate."

"The aircraft are still closing," Silence said, and clenched her teeth to keep from saying anything more.

"Damn it," Balthasar said again, and touched another sequence of keys. *Recusante* seemed to stagger slightly, and Silence knew that the ship was running flat out, making its top speed through the interference of the atmosphere. Starships aren't designed for this, she thought, numbly. We can't hold out, not against aircraft.

"Marcinik," the Delian said. "Fire as soon as you can, and keep firing. How long 'til they're in range?"

"Ten minutes, no more," Marcinik answered, and Silence could hear the controlled panic beneath his cultured tones. "Firing at range, affirmed."

"That's one for the soldiers," Balthasar muttered. He took one hand off his controls long enough to rub his chin, and Silence could see the fingers shaking. "Damn, Julie, give me more power."

"I'm sorry, Denis," Chase Mago answered, and for once Silence could hear the fear in the big man's voice. "You've got everything I can give you."

Balthasar didn't answer, staring at the triple screens as though he could force them to change by sheer strength of will. In the central screen, Silence could see the double flight of aircraft closing in, a flashing red dot marking the projected interception point. They were much faster than *Recusante*, and more maneuverable—any aircraft would be, as sluggish as a starship was in atmosphere. Balthasar could only delay a meeting, not avoid it. Without much hope, the pilot glanced at the left-hand screen. The three starships had slowed their approach—letting the aircraft take care of us, Silence thought bitterly—but they still blocked any attempt to return to space.

Something flashed in the center screen, and a trio of tiny dots, almost too small to be visible to the musonar, detached themselves from the leading aircraft. Silence frowned, not recognizing them, and Marcinik said, incredulously, "Missiles."

"Oh, fuck," Balthasar said. His hands moved convulsively on the keyboards, and then he had himself under control, his hands dancing across the keys. *Recusante* staggered sideways, throwing itself into a ponderous series of evasive maneuvers. Too slow, Silence thought, watching the musonar, oh, too slow. The ship shuddered down its length: Marcinik was finally returning the aircrafts' fire. No, she realized an instant later, he was shooting at the missiles instead. He fired again, and a third time, the fixed-fire shells bracketing and then falling behind the little dots. He missed them all, but one of the dots wavered and vanished, its turning apparently disrupted by the concussion.

"One missile gone," Silence announced, and was remotely surprised at how calm she still sounded. Marcinik fired again twice, in rapid succession, and a second dot disappeared. "Two gone. Third missile still closing."

Balthasar whispered a curse, hands busy on his controls. *Recusante* wove a drunken course through the air, keel wailing in protest, interference keening around them. Marcinik fired again, but the missile was inside the cannon's optimum range.

"Still closing," Silence said. "God, it intercepts in two minutes."

Balthasar wrenched the ship sideways, turning it practically onto the tips of its stubby wings, and pointed its nose at the planet's surface. The keel shrieked as Chase Mago failed to compensate for the unexpected maneuver, its chorded notes of air and earth suddenly sounding only against air. The ship fell, reeling down toward the water suddenly not so far below. Silence, biting back a cry of utter panic, saw the missile slide past above them. An instant later, an explosion rocked the ship, and she heard and felt a rattle of metal along *Recusante*'s sides.

Swearing steadily, Balthasar swung the ship, easing it back into a more normal position, keel pointed again toward the planetary surface. The shrieking eased a little, but there was a definite note of strain, a raggedness in the roaring music.

"Shit," Chase Mago said, and Silence felt herself grow suddenly cold. She could not remember having heard the engineer swear. "Denis, we're out of tune."

"Damn, damn, damn," Balthasar whispered. He swung the ship into a series of tight, irregular turns, and said at the same time, "Silence, where are the fucking aircraft?"

Silence swallowed hard, staring at the musonar. "One hundred fifty kilometers," she whispered. She took a deep breath, and tried again. "Still closing. Oh, damn it all, missiles." She clenched her hands together, trying to control her shaking, to remember what she had to do, what information had to be passed along. "Two, three targets, intercept in eight minutes."

"I see them," Marcinik said. A moment later, the twin cannons began firing. He was trying something different, Silence realized, laying down a barrier of shells, of disturbed, distorted air, between *Recusante* and the approaching missiles. The missiles entered that barrier and abruptly vanished. Silence gave a cry of triumph, abruptly cut off as she caught a glimpse of the cannons' status lights. They had paled from healthy green to yellow, would have to build up again before Marcinik could repeat his tactics.

"Nice shooting," Balthasar said, grimly.

Recusante had fallen deep into the atmosphere in their attempt to avoid the missiles, Silence saw, but to her surprise the Delian made no attempt to regain the lost altitude. Instead, he brought the ship lower still, until the already stressed keel was almost sobbing, the sound discordant enough to bring tears of pain to her crew's eyes. The pitch shifted, wavered as Chase Mago attempted to compensate for the strong core harmonies, but there was little he could do without a field beam to help him cheat the shattering dissonances.

A flicker of change in the main musonar display caught Silence's eye, but she had to look twice before she could believe what she had seen. "Denis! The aircraft, four of them are turning back!"

Balthasar grunted, and for an instant Silence felt almost hurt. Then she saw the second set of blotches rising, ahead and to the right of *Recusante*'s course, and wanted to sob with the disappointment. "No, four more taking their place," she said instead.

"Where are they coming from?" Balthasar asked.

"Ahead—about three thousand kilometers? Bearing about two-thirty," Silence answered. They were coming up on the end of the ocean, she realized remotely. The astrogation console showed a large landmass ahead, linked to a second continent by a narrow hook of land.

"Find me a storm system," Balthasar said. "The biggest you can."

Obediently, Silence adjusted the musonar. There were a few minor storm cells to the south, toward the approaching aircraft and the hook of land that curved away toward the planet's southeast, but nothing big enough to hide the ship.

She turned the horn toward the north, sweeping across the bulging coastline. There were clouds just at the ocean's edge, and those clouds thickened inland into a swirling storm that trailed a long curve of disturbed air back toward the sea. "There," she said aloud, and touched keys to display the image on Balthasar's screen.

"Good enough," Balthasar said, "but will we get there first?"

Silence touched more keys, calculating relative speeds. "Yes! If we can hold this speed," she amended quickly, and cleared Balthasar's screen of everything except the medium-range musonar display.

"We'll hold it," Chase Mago said, and somehow the Delian smiled.

"I knew you could," he murmured, and swung the ship planetary north onto her new course.

Silence held her breath as the seconds ticked by. She could see Balthasar's plan clearly enough. Within the disturbed air of the storms, *Recusante*'s keelsong would be less noticeable, might even, if the storm were strong enough, be drowned out altogether in the general clamor of the roiling air. They were moving steadily toward the cloaking clouds, but the aircraft were moving equally steadily toward a point of interception just north of the storm's first major cell.

"Come on," Balthasar muttered. "Come on. Julie, can't you give me anything more?"

The engineer did not answer, but a moment later the intercept numbers flickered and changed, the point of interception moving deeper into the storm. Balthasar grinned.

"I knew you'd have something in reserve," he said. His voice sharpened instantly. "Silence, how're the aircraft doing?"

The pilot was already watching the musonar intently. So far, there was no movement, no change on the numbers, but she let another minute tick by before she answered. "No change."

"Then we know their top speed," Balthasar said. "By God, we might just make it."

Silence watched as *Recusante* crept slowly over the land-mass, moving up the coast toward the storm's trailing edges. The aircraft followed inexorably, gaining seemingly by centimeters. They would be in missile range in less than five minutes, the pilot realized, and felt the same cold fear in the pit of her stomach. They were back in daylight now, had been since they crossed the coastline; as the first clouds swallowed them, the light dimmed visibly, went chill and milky. Balthasar pushed the ship lower still, evoking more protest from the already stressed keel. Silence winced, but knew better than to protest. The ship rocked beneath her as the first winds hit her, and Balthasar controlled it with an effort.

The musonar display faded further, and Silence fiddled with the controls until she found a setting that seemed to override some of the storm's music. "The aircraft will be in missile range in three minutes," she announced, and glanced at the cannon-status display. The lights showed green again, and she gave a sigh of relief. At least that much was going well.

The first aircraft fired before it was actually in range; the others fired a few moments later. "Missiles fired," she reported, glancing quickly at Balthasar. The Delian was very pale, sweat standing out on his forehead, but his hands still moved across his keyboard with sure grace. *Recusante* rolled sideways into her ponderous evasive maneuvers, and Silence held her breath, waiting for the cannons' blast to rock the ship. Marcinik held his fire for a long moment, so long that Silence wanted to scream at him, order him to fire. Then, seemingly in the last second, he fired rapidly, once again laying down a pattern of bursting shells between the ship and the approaching missiles. Three vanished at once from the screen. The fourth came on, but it was wobbling, its tracking devices clearly disrupted. It exploded well above and to the left of *Recusante*, the blast rocking the ship, but doing no other damage. The musonar image dimmed further as Balthasar flew them deeper into the storm, the blips that were the pursuing aircraft flickering in and out of the rising wash of color.

"I've lost the aircraft," Silence said, and reached forward to adjust the musonar again. Nothing happened, and she allowed herself to relax a little.

"Let's hope they've lost us," Balthasar said. "What about the starships overhead?"

Silence checked the musonar again. The storm distorted the view above the ship as well, but the music of the warships' keels was strong enough to cut through that dissonance. The bronze dots flickered through the clouds of bluish static, still blocking any escape to the safety of space. "Still there," she said at last.

"How's the contact?" Balthasar said, and grimaced as a gust of wind hit the ship, sending it lurching across the sky.

"Intermittent, at best," Silence answered.

Balthasar grunted. "Let's hope their sighting isn't any better."

Silence nodded. The starships would have to look down into the worst of the storm—and they would be looking for a ship whose keelsong was far quieter than their own. With any luck, she thought, they won't be able to find us at all.

"Aircraft?" the Delian continued.

"I've lost them," Silence answered.

"So they should've lost us," Balthasar murmured, then said, more loudly, "Keep alert, Marcinik, just in case."

"I'm watching closely," the colonel answered.

Balthasar took a deep breath, and Silence saw his shoulders move slightly, relaxing.

"Now what?" she said aloud, and the Delian grimaced.

"I don't know," he said, almost too softly for her to hear. "We can't make space, not with that lot watching for us, but I don't want to set down—"

"Denis." Chase Mago's voice was flat calm, but there was a note in it that sent Silence's heart into her mouth. "Denis, we've got real trouble. The keel's losing tuning. That last missile must've been the last straw—"

"How bad is it?" Balthasar interrupted.

"We've got an hour's flying time," Chase Mago answered.

"Then you'll have to put her down."

"Shit!" After that first explosive response, Balthasar's voice went calm again. "All right. We've got an hour. Silence, what do maps and musonar say?"

Silence stared at the twin consoles, trying to control her own panic. A southerly course was out; that would only bring them back into the paths of the pursuing aircraft. The storm stretched northeast, curving up across the continent. Most of the land beyond its eastern edges was heavily populated—if they could rely on anything the supercargo said, she thought, bitterly. Some of her information had obviously been unreliable—if the whole thing, the woman's plea for asylum and her offer of information, hadn't just been an elaborate trap. It was too late now to worry about that, she told herself, and put the thought aside. They had no other choice now; they would have to rely on the only maps they had.

If *Recusante* followed the concealing storm northward, forty minutes' travel would bring them out of the storm a hundred kilometers or so to the north of the heavily populated area on the continent's eastern coast. They could set the ship down there, conceal it in the thick forest that was supposed to dominate that area. And if the supercargo had lied, and the area wasn't unpopulated forest, they would still have twenty minutes in which to turn back into the storm and find another place to land. She turned one of the secondary horns groundward, trying to pick out the terrain details through the double distortion of untuned keel and the storm itself. The land below seemed very flat, unpopulated, but without any topographical features that would help hide the downed ship.

"Fly local northeast along the storm track," she said at last. "When we reach the edge of the storm, we should be within a few minutes of a very large woodland. We can set the ship down there, and hide it until we figure out what to do."

Balthasar nodded. "Sounds good to me."

For the next half hour, Balthasar nursed the crippled ship northward through the storm, easing it lower, and lower still, until it was wallowing through the atmosphere at an altitude no higher than that of an ordinary flyer. Chase Mago babied the keel, making constant minute adjustments to the harmonium in hopes of easing the strain on the tuning, but even Silence, no engineer, could hear how badly the ship was laboring. She focussed her attention on the musonar, sweeping the clouds behind and above them for further aircraft. The warships remained in orbit, but there was no sign of pursuit from atmospheric craft, and she began to hope that the warships had lost sight of them as well.

Then *Recusante* broke out of the storm's cover. It lurched

sharply, the keel no longer fighting the storm as well as the pull of Earth's core, and Chase Mago adjusted the harmonium, swearing. The ship steadied, but it was clear from the grating keelsong that it would not last much longer.

"Well, Silence?" Balthasar demanded.

Silence adjusted the musonar for what she hoped was the final time, sweeping the horn in a slow arc across the bow of the ship. To the south, confused harmonies flared: the populated area the supercargo had spoken of. Beyond that lay another ocean. But directly ahead, long fingers of woodland stretching toward them as if in welcome, lay the promised forest. Silence sighed deeply, and heard the relief in her own voice as she said, "The forest is coming up. You can let us down in two minutes, Denis."

Balthasar smiled again, fingers moving delicately on his keys. *Recusante* staggered forward, dropping lower still, keelsong fading in and out of true. Now the forest was visible in the cameras' images, rolling land covered in trees whose leaves were so dark a green as to be almost black.

"Do you see a clearing?" Balthasar panted.

Silence shook her head. "Not yet."

"There has to be one," Balthasar muttered. "There has to be. . . ." He brought the ship lower still, until the tortured keel was almost skimming the treetops. Silence watched the branches thrashing beneath her, a detached part of her mind admiring the Delian's skill.

And then, quite suddenly, the keelsong died. Balthasar cursed, pulling *Recusante*'s nose up sharply, but the starship had never been designed to glide in atmosphere. It fell like a stone, crashing into and through the trees, keel skidding along branches and dirt with a noise like a cry of pain. Silence swore as she was thrown against her safety netting, swore again as *Recusante* ground to a halt at last, the bow nosing gently up onto some unseen object. She reached shakily for the camera controls, but the bow cameras had been ripped away. At her side, Balthasar managed a rather hysterical laugh.

"Welcome to Earth," he said.

CHAPTER 5

Silence laughed with him, but brought herself under control before she gave way to the tears that threatened to overwhelm her. Instead, she reached across for the intercom controls, hoping that the system was still intact, and said, "Julie? Are you all right?"

Balthasar interrupted her. "Everybody, check in. Status, please."

"I'm all right," Chase Mago said, breathlessly, and with grim emphasis, "but I don't know about the keel."

Marcinik answered next, panic tinging his voice. "Nothing serious here, just cuts, but Aili doesn't answer."

"Hang on, colonel," Balthasar said, "it may just be systems failure." Without waiting for Marcinik's answer, he cut the connection, and touched the button that connected him directly with the Princess Royal's cabin. "Your Serenity? Check in, please."

There was no answer, and Silence loosened the safety webbing, wincing at the bruises it had left. The crew positions were well protected against a crash, as of course they had to be, but the cabins were less well shielded. Unless both Aili and the magus had strapped themselves into their bunks at the first sign of trouble, there was a good chance that they had been badly hurt. There wasn't time to warn them, Silence thought, trying to suppress the sudden feeling of guilt; there just wasn't time. Damn, this was why I didn't want Aili along in the first place. . . .

The intercom clicked then, and Aili's voice said, weakly, "Captain Balthasar? I'm—all right, I think. Oh, my head!"

"Marcinik—?" Balthasar began, and the colonel cut in quickly.

"I'm on my way. I'll take care of her."

Balthasar nodded, not bothering to reply. "Silence? Better check on the magus."

Silence paused, her hands already on the ladder leading to the main deck, suddenly aware that Balthasar hadn't moved from his position in front of the first pilot's consoles. "And you? Are you hurt?"

Balthasar managed a wry smile. "No more than you are. But it's daylight out there, Silence, and I bet we left one hell of a trail. Someone needs to monitor the musonar, just in case we have visitors."

Silence hesitated at the top of the ladder, torn between conflicting needs. Balthasar was right. *Recusante*'s crash would have torn a huge gash in the virgin woodland, a raw clearing that would be only too visible from the air. She could create an illusion to cover that gap—but Isambard and probably the Princess Royal as well needed her help.

As if he'd read her thoughts, Balthasar said, "Musonar doesn't show anything yet. I think maybe we lost them in the storm." He nodded encouragingly. "See if you can help Marcinik first."

Silence nodded back and slid down the ladder, wincing as she discovered still more bruised muscles. Of course Marcinik would know rudimentary medicine—he was an officer of the Thousand, after all—and, with luck, that would be all they'd need.

The door to Aili's cabin was already open, and Silence could hear voices talking softly inside. She gave a sigh of relief—at least the Princess Royal was alive, and not too badly hurt—and tapped gently on the doorframe, glancing quickly inside. "Is there anything I can do?"

Marcinik was sitting on the bunk at Aili's side, supporting her with one hand while the other pressed a bloody cloth to the Princess Royal's temple just above her left ear. "It's all right," the colonel said quickly, and Aili managed a weak smile. "It looks worse than it is. But the magus?"

"I don't know," Silence said, and pushed herself away from the door. Isambard's cabin was at the far end of the corridor, opposite the engineer's. Its door was still tightly closed, and she felt a stab of fear as she reached for the latchplate. Before she could punch out the master combination, however, the door sung open under her hand. Isambard stood there, leaning heavily against the frame. His lined face was very pale, and his wide-open eyes were strangely unfocused. Frightened again, Silence caught at his shoulders and staggered as the magus fell toward her. He was surprisingly light, even for an old man. She held his weight, glancing over her shoulder toward the lights of the engine room.

"Julie? Marcinik?"

"No." Isambard's voice was little better than a whisper. "Earth—I must *see*. . . ."

"We've landed," Silence said. "There's plenty of time—"

"I must see it," Isambard said again, and pushed feebly at her hands, trying to shove her away. She blocked him awkwardly, not wanting to hurt him further, and the magus stood still, breathing heavily. A measure of awareness seemed to come into his eyes, and he said, "We did not land at the port, I think. A crash?"

Silence nodded, wishing one of the others would appear to help. "They knew who we were, attacked us. We lost them, but the tuning went and we had to land." To her relief, Chase Mago's massive figure loomed behind the glare of the warning lights ringing the engine room hatch, and she loosed her hold on the magus long enough to beckon to him. "Julie? I need you."

Chase Mago stepped over the coaming and came to join her, one hand still pressed to his bloody nose. Silence eyed him anxiously as he approached, but could see no other sign of damage.

"Let me see, Isambard," the engineer said gently, but the magus waved him off.

"There are things—I must cast—" He broke off with a gasp of pain, one hand going to his forehead. For the first time, Silence saw the ugly cuts running across the back of his hand.

"Get Marcinik," she said softly, to Chase Mago. The engineer nodded and ducked away, leaving her supporting the old man's weight. "Isambard, tell me what has to be done. I can do it for you."

The magus looked up at her, struggling to focus his eyes and thoughts. "We crashed," he managed, after a moment, "did we not? I remember—" He broke off, frowning. "No matter. There will be traces. I must hide them—"

Silence interrupted him firmly, trying to project more confidence than she felt. "Tell me what schema to use, and I'll do it. I'd already thought of it, truth."

Isambard nodded, slowly. "The Maids' Breath would be easiest," he said, his voice fading again to a whisper. "Silence, let me go. I must see Earth!"

"In a few hours, maybe," Marcinik said firmly. At his nod, Silence stepped back, letting him slip his arm around the magus's shoulders, easing him back into the cabin.

"No!" Isambard cried, pushing the colonel away. "I want to see, before I die—"

Silence glanced at Marcinik, and saw her own sudden panic reflected in his eyes. "Marcinik, he isn't—" she began, and the colonel shrugged roughly.

"How can I know, if he won't let me look at him?" Marcinik took a deep breath, obviously fighting for calm. "All right, Isambard," he said, after a moment. "You win. I'll take you to the main hatch, but let me look at you there, all right?"

The magus sagged slightly in the colonel's grip, but then pulled himself upright again. "Very well," he said. "Very well."

"I have to go," Silence said hastily. "I'll send Julie to help." Marcinik nodded, his attention fully occupied with the task of easing the magus toward the hatch. Silence turned and ran back up the corridor toward the ship's main hatch, almost colliding with the engineer as he emerged from the common room, wiping his face with a damp towel.

"Julie, Marcinik needs you to help with Isambard," the pilot gasped, but Chase Mago caught her arm. Silence winced as his fingers touched a bruise, and the engineer hastily eased his hold, murmuring an apology.

"Denis—is he all right?"

Silence nodded. "He says so. He's watching the musonar, I've got to see what I can do about our trail."

Chase Mago nodded. "Go on, then, and good luck."

Silence turned away before he'd finished, hurrying toward the hatch. There was no need to go through the elaborate routine of test and counter-test. This was Earth, humankind's first world: despite the number of generations that had passed since her ancestors left the planet, she had still been bred to breathe this atmosphere, to walk under this sun. She fumbled with the controls, swearing as the handwheel that controlled the hatch itself refused to turn. Surely, oh, *surely* the mechanism wasn't damaged in the crash, she thought, and in the same instant felt the stubborn wheel give way. The hatch swung outward, and there was a flurry of air as the pressures equalized themselves. Silence stood frozen, staring out at Earth.

Recusante had landed lucky, she thought, when she could think at all. The ship had come down in the valley between two steep hills, where rocks sprouted from the ground between the tangle of trees, and had slid to a stop just as the land began to rise steeply again. A few hundred meters farther on, and the ship would probably have hit the hillside nose-first, killing them all. Silence shuddered, and reached for the crank that extended the rampway. She turned it stiffly, hoping the mechanism would work. After a couple of turns, the gears caught, and the ramp began to extend itself, clanking, toward the ground below. The tip touched the dirt at last, but Silence gave the handle a few more turns, jamming the ramp hard into the soil, before trusting herself to it. It sagged a little under her weight, but held. After a moment's thought, she reached for the charged heylin that Balthasar insisted on hanging just inside the hatch, and started down the ramp.

The air smelled strange, sweet and cool with an odd, almost tangy undertone. She stood for a moment, fascinated, but unable to work out where she had smelled that scent before. Then, with an effort, she shook herself back to reality. There was work to be done, she told herself sternly. Jamming the heylin into her belt, she began to walk back along the length of the ship, heading toward the stern.

She did not have to go far before finding the first evidences of damage. Halfway back from the ramp, she was forced to climb over a broken tree, its splintered wood poking out from under the dulled keel. The broken parts were very white, and covered with a strange, sticky liquid. The tangy scent was much stronger here, and she sniffed curiously at her hands: it was the tree sap that gave the air its peculiar smell.

There were more broken trees astern of the ship, some snapped completely, others—farther away, the ones *Recusante* had struck first in the headlong descent—with huge branches snapped and dangling. It was all as conspicuous as they had feared, and Silence shook her head, wondering what to do. *An illusion is what's needed,* she thought, *but an illusion needs a model, and I don't have any idea what all these things looked like before. . . .* She glanced to either side, up the valley's sides. The trees there seemed to be of the same species, tall, rough-barked, trunks rising for meters before branching out into clusters of branches. The leaves were very dark green, like long spines. *I could use them as a model,* she thought, chewing on her underlip, *but whatever I do, I'd better do it soon. Damn, what was it Isambard said?* She frowned, and then remembered. *The Maids' Breath,* he'd said, *that would be the easiest. . . .*

He was right, too, she thought, and for the first time since landing, her mouth curved into a real smile. The technique known as the Maids' Breath wasn't really an illusion; rather, it was a way of seeing the proper state of a thing. Usually, the magi used it to read palimpsests, or to decipher manuscripts too faded to be legible, but it would serve to give her a guide. She took a deep breath and turned slowly, scanning the valley. She let herself absorb the quiet of the place, the sunlight, the brilliant blue of the sky above her, unbroken now by clouds, the smell of the trees and the faint sighing of wind through their uppermost branches. Only then did she murmur the First Cantation, the words bending reality around her, ready to receive the imprint of a new Form. She spoke the schema of the Maids' Breath; the words were no sooner spoken than they lost audibility and rolled off into the supermaterial, seeking what had been. Shadows moved and shifted first, the valley dimming as though trees once again shaded it, and then ghostly images appeared. The hanging branches wavered, then seemed to swing back up into place;

an entire tree rose from where it lay shattered by *Recusante*'s passage. Silence studied the images for a long moment, then spoke a final Word. The images steadied, solidified into something approaching reality. Ghost-trees filled the valley, rising from their broken remains. Silence turned back toward the ship, and saw a shadowy trunk apparently thrusting through *Recusante*'s spine. Another was half-swallowed by the hull near the bow, and a third sprang up from a point just astern of the far wing.

Shaking her head, she made her way back toward the ramp, suddenly exhausted. Isambard was sitting at the top of the ramp, bandaged hands folded in his lap. Marcinik crouched beside him. Silence tensed, afraid again, but Marcinik saw her and shook his head, smiling. She smiled back but kept a wary eye on the magus.

"How are you?" she asked, as she started up the ramp.

Isambard waved the question aside. "Well done, your illusion. I am pleased."

"Thank you," Silence said, startled, and wondered for an instant if the crash had affected the old man's brain. Praise for anything she did was rare.

"He's just shaken up," Marcinik said.

Before she could answer, Balthasar's voice rose indignantly from inside the hatch. "There's a fucking *tree* in here!"

Silence began to laugh helplessly, and called back, "It's an illusion, Denis, don't worry."

A moment later, Balthasar appeared in the hatch, Chase Mago looming behind him. The engineer's hand was at his mouth as if to hide a smile.

"You got us covered, then?" the Delian asked.

Silence nodded. "The question is, will it hold up under a real scanning?"

Balthasar nodded back, pressing the back of his hand against his mouth. The lower lip was swelling and bloody—probably he'd bitten it in the landing, Silence thought, and suppressed the desire to laugh again. "How is everyone, anyway?" the Delian went on. "Where's her Serenity?"

"I'm here."

Aili still sounded rather shaken, Silence thought, and then the other star-travellers edged aside to let the younger woman past. The Princess Royal had resumed her Bethlemite turban and veil, but it was pushed askew by the lump of bandages that covered the left side of her head, revealing one dark eye and a narrow expanse of cheek and forehead.

Marcinik said, frowning, "I thought you were going to rest."

"I'm much better," Aili answered, and lowered herself carefully to the ramp at the colonel's side. "I need to know what's going on," she said, in a softer voice, and Marcinik nodded.

Balthasar said, "So we're all here. What about this illusion, then? Will it hold?"

Silence spread her hands, glancing at Isambard, but before either magus could answer, Chase Mago said slowly, "I've been thinking about that, Denis. We got some damn strange readings coming in-system—those chemical-fuel ships, the aircraft. I'm wondering if they've got anything that'll see through it."

Isambard said, "Properly created, an illusion will be tangible and effective to musonar and other sensors. This one is properly created."

"Thanks," Silence said again, and saw Balthasar grin.

"But what if they're using some other system?" Chase Mago persisted. "The readings were just too weird to ignore." He shook his head, still frowning. "It was almost like they were using mechanics."

"They couldn't be," Balthasar said. "It wouldn't make sense."

"If for some obscure reason the Earth-natives are using mechanics," Isambard said, "the illusion should be sufficient. After all, it produces a facsimile of reality, correct in outward similitudes. But they will not be using the Mechanical Arts. Not on Earth."

There was nothing anyone could say to that pronouncement, though Chase Mago still looked troubled. Watching the engineer's unhappy face, Silence couldn't help wondering if he were right after all. The chemical-fuel ships were mechanical in nature, after all; the musonar had treated the aircraft as though they were bare metal, without the treated keels that lifted most ships away from a planet's core—in other words, as though they, too, were mechanical. But there her imagination stuck, unable to conceive of a world that chose to use machines instead of the creations of the Art. Maybe there were restrictions of some kind that made machines more practical for some things—such as the crowding on Delos, which made mechanical systems an absolute necessity.

"How does the ship look, Julie?" she said aloud.

Chase Mago shrugged, his expression bleak. "Not good at all, I'm afraid. But I want to take a close look before I do anything." He glanced at Balthasar. "I'd better get started."

"Yeah," Balthasar said. "Do you need a hand?"

The engineer shook his head. "Not really."

"It's the keel?" Silence asked.

"Yes." Chase Mago sighed. "We lost tuning completely. I have to see how deep it goes."

Silence shivered despite the warmth of the sunlight on her back. It was almost unheard of for a keel fully to lose its tuning. The sort of stress that could so disrupt the tinctured metal usually destroyed or at least damaged the rest of the ship beyond repair. The resonances were set at the molecular level, worked deep into the structure of the tinctured metal itself; while the surface might shift slightly—would shift slightly under even the best conditions—that shifting never affected the true tuning at the heart of the keel itself. Or almost never, she thought, and glanced warily at the keel. Most of it was buried in the soft earth, little waves of dirt and scattered rock thrown back along its length, but the visible portions looked sickly, without the usual oily sheen. She shivered again, and looked away.

"Let us know if we can help," Balthasar said. Chase Mago nodded, and started down the ramp.

"What I would like to know," Aili said, breaking the sudden quiet, "is where we are." Marcinik nodded in thoughtful agreement.

Balthasar sighed, and gave the empty sky a final wary glance. "I guess you're right. Let me get the tapes, and I'll meet you all in the commons."

"Right," Silence answered. She started up the ramp to assist Isambard, but Marcinik was already helping the magus to his feet. She paused at the top of the ramp to offer her hand to Aili, glancing back over her shoulder at the forest as she did so. For an instant, as the breeze freshened and swirled around them, Silence thought she smelled burning, but the scent was gone before she could be sure. She scanned the sky above the tree-tops, but saw no rising plume of smoke, and turned away, shrugging to herself.

"This is very bad, isn't it?" Aili said, as they moved toward the common room.

Silence hesitated, torn between the desire to reassure and the need to confide in someone. "It isn't good," she said at last. "At the very least, we're untuned, and that usually means a dockyard job. If it isn't too bad, Julie might be able to rig something off the harmonium, force-tune it here—but if it goes very deep, we'll have to take it into a dock. And if the keel itself is damaged—if it cracked, or one of those rocks took a chunk out of it, say—we'll need a new keel before we can lift."

"And at that point," Aili said, "we might as well get a new ship." The crooked veil still hid most of her expression, but Silence could hear the uneasiness in her voice. "But a keel is very strong."

"Yes," Silence said. "It's tinctured metal; it should take a lot of abuse. That's really the worst-case scenario."

Aili nodded, but said nothing more.

The shadow of a tree trunk thrust through the corridor just outside the common room. Silence stopped with an exclamation of dismay, then put out her hand to test the illusion. Her fingers moved easily into and out of the grey bark, and she nerved herself to step quickly through. As she passed through the image, she heard a faint sighing, a breath of dissonance, but it vanished before she could fix its origin for certain. A little dissonance was only to be expected, she told herself, and beckoned for Aili to follow. After all, an illusion wasn't meant to be walked through.

The others were already in the common room, Isambard seated at his usual place at the main table, Marcinik busy at the kitchen console. Aili moved hastily to join him, but the colonel waved her away.

"Sit, please," he said. "You're the injured one."

After a moment's hesitation, Aili did as she was told, sighing softly in spite of herself.

"How is your head?" Silence asked, and crossed the room to collect tea for all of them.

"It hurts," Aili said, and the pilot thought she heard a ghost of a smile in the other woman's voice. "But I'll be all right."

At that moment, Balthasar appeared in the doorway, a sheaf of rough-printed papers tucked under one arm. "I'm not fond of wildlife on the ship, Silence," he said, with a grin.

The pilot glared back at him, suddenly too tired to respond in kind. Balthasar took his place at the table, spreading the papers out in front of him. "I set the musonar to warn us if anything comes near the ship—a full-volume warning, fifty kilometers' diameter." He accepted the mug of tea Marcinik handed him, but winced as the hot plastic touched his swollen lip, and set it aside. "I also ran a quick scan. It doesn't look like we're in a settled area at all—no sign of open land, much less human habitation, at least not on my preliminary look— which I guess is good news."

Silence grinned at the Delian's rather dubious tone. Balthasar had been born and raised on Delos, where every centimeter of available land had become part of the city that covered most of the planet's surface. He was not fond of wilderness. She picked up her cup of tea and started, almost spilling it, as Marcinik touched her arm.

"Sorry," he said, and slid a small packet across the table in front of her. "I thought you might want these."

Silence picked the packet up curiously, recognized the mark of one of the Hegemony's more famous pharmaceutical companies.

"Hamma," Marcinik said. "It'll ease the soreness, and help heal wrenched muscles."

"Thanks," Silence said, tearing open the packet, and swallowed the capsules gratefully.

Balthasar accepted his own share from the colonel and bolted them with a grimace. "This is the rough map we had," he said, spreading papers across the table, "supplemented by observations along the first part of the descent." His finger traced a curved line from the smaller of the two main oceans toward a large island, then across a much larger ocean toward the northernmost of two linked continents. "That's about

what our course was. We came down here." On the map, the
northern continent's eastern coastline swelled out into a huge
horn, a smaller horn protruding beneath it. Balthasar's finger
rested on the center of the smaller horn.

Silence nodded thoughtfully. "Most of that's forest, if I
remember right," she said, and was pleased at how casual—
how normal—her voice sounded. Privately, she doubted she
would ever forget the pattern of the storm, and the forest that
lay beyond its edges.

"Yeah, that's right," Balthasar answered. "And hills. And,
like I said, my first survey didn't pick up any sign of
settlement."

"Do you have any idea where the nearest settlements are?"
Marcinik asked.

"South, I think," Balthasar said, and Silence nodded.

"I picked them up on the musonar as we came in."

"How far?" the colonel asked.

Balthasar rustled his maps again until he found an enlarge-
ment of the area where they'd landed. It didn't show much
detail, and Marcinik eyed it warily.

"About three hundred kilometers," the Delian answered,
after a moment. He touched a point where the coastline
began to curve outward again.

Silence frowned, studying the image more closely. Something was tugging at her memory—something the supercargo
had said, something that was in the text she had so carefully
structured. . . . She closed her eyes, calling up the structures
of the Grand Theater, letting the errant thought find its own
place in that pattern. "One of the big centers is on this
coast," she said, after a moment. "A place called Man's Island."

Isambard gave a little exclamation of surprise. "Yes, that is
so. A—continental control point, the woman said."

"I'm not at all sure we ought to trust any of the information
she gave us," Balthasar said sourly. He shook his head. "She
sure suckered us in—all of us."

Isambard drew himself up indignantly, and Silence said,
"Some of the information is good—we were able to check at
least some of it, remember? That's probably true."

The older magus relaxed slowly. "I admit that I was deceived," he said, after a moment. "I apologize, Captain Balthasar."

The Delian's mouth fell open in shock. Silence stared hard at him, willing him to understand just what he was being offered. The magi did not admit to making errors, much less apologize for them—and certainly never to mere star-travellers. Balthasar closed his mouth abruptly, and said, with unexpected grace, "It could've happened to anyone."

Isambard nodded gravely, and said nothing more. No one said anything for a long moment, all of them staring at the maps spread out on the table in front of them. Silence barely saw the lines and spaces, thinking instead of the little room at the center of Asterion's Winter Palace. Should I have helped Isambard question her? she wondered. Could I have seen that it was a trap, if he didn't? I am a star-traveller; I have that advantage. . . . All too clearly, she remembered the faint note of strangeness she'd sensed in the supercargo's mind, the one time she'd been forced to enter it. That had to have been the mark of a second, deeper geas, she thought—and I felt it, I knew something was there, but I didn't have the knowledge to identify it. I could have stopped this, if only I'd realized. . . . She looked up in relief as Chase Mago stepped into the room, grateful for the distraction even of bad news.

"What's the word?" Balthasar said, softly.

The big engineer shrugged, exhaustion written on his bearded face. "It could be worse," he said. "The keel's intact, at least—we were lucky there, the ground's very rocky." He sighed, the momentary animation fading from his voice. "However, the first eighty-one centimeters are completely untuned, and it's pretty random almost to the center line. That's still true, but. . . ." He let the words trail off in defeat.

Silence could hear her own heart pounding, could feel a spreading chill in the pit of her stomach. She saw her own fear reflected in the engineer's face, in Balthasar's narrowed eyes.

"I don't understand," Aili said, tentatively. Marcinik shook his head, but Chase Mago roused himself to answer, and even managed a humorless smile.

"What it means is, we have to do a full retuning before we can lift, your Serenity, and I don't have the facilities for the operation. Sometimes you can force-tune, using the harmonium itself to realign the resonances, but that only works when the harmonies're just a little out of true. I need a dockyard's equipment."

There was another long pause, broken at last by Marcinik's quiet voice. "Wouldn't it be easier just to—acquire—another ship?"

"No," Silence said, in instinctive, indignant protest, but the others ignored her.

"It might be," Balthasar said, "but just how easy do you think it is to 'acquire' a starship?"

"You acquired this one," Marcinik said.

"*Recusante* was mine," Silence said, "and is mine, my ship. I don't intend to abandon her." She paused, fighting down her anger, and tried to bolster emotion with logic. "Besides, when we took her, back on Mersaa Maia—well, it was a very different situation."

"That's true," Chase Mago said unexpectedly, and Silence threw him a grateful look. "Besides," the engineer went on, with a stubborn glance at Isambard, "I still say we've seen too many mechanical things around for me to feel comfortable finding a starship anywhere close at hand."

"Could you retune, if we could get into a tuning shed?" Silence asked, and held her breath, hoping for the answer she wanted.

"Of course I could," Chase Mago said, and Marcinik cut in, "Forgive me, but I can't see how you could get permission to use any field facilities."

Balthasar said, "You'd be surprised at what I can come up with, colonel." There was a light in his eyes that made Silence frown, remembering some of the Delian's other plans.

"Hold it," Chase Mago said, cutting off an acid rejoinder from Marcinik. "Just wait. I don't need the whole shed, people; I just need a tone generator."

"Oh, well," Balthasar said, after a moment. "That makes it easy." Silence eyed him warily, unable to decide if he was being sarcastic or not.

"Easier, anyway," Chase Mago said. He glanced at the non-star-travellers, and said, "The tone generator's the most important thing a tuner has. It produces really pure notes, purer than a harmonium can provide, since its pipes are adjusted to the idiosyncracies of the ship. It creates a sort of Form, and you force the keel to follow it." He looked back at Balthasar, and added, "Hell, if I could get the right components, I could build one for myself."

The Delian nodded slowly. "So," he said, almost cheerfully, "all we have to do now is get a tone generator."

Silence gave him a jaundiced look, but refused to be drawn. Chase Mago looked at the maps in front of him, not meeting anyone's eyes.

"And just how, Captain Balthasar, do you propose to do that?" Marcinik said. "We're at least three hundred kilometers away from the nearest settlement, and I doubt this ship carries an all-terrain vehicle."

"We have a runabout, actually," Silence muttered, unable to ignore the slur on her ship. The little three-wheeled cart was only good on paved roads, however, and she was just as glad that no one responded.

"There must be other settlements closer to us," Balthasar said. "After all, we've only done a preliminary survey, and this is Earth. There'll be roads."

Silence sighed, unable fully to share the Delian's enthusiasm, but offered what little support she could. "I thought I smelled smoke earlier," she said. "That might mean someone living near here."

"The way our luck's been running, it's more likely a forest fire," Marcinik murmured, but he was smiling.

Balthasar ignored him. "Right, then," he said briskly. "Silence and I will set up a box-scan, and then we'll go watch-and-watch—I'll need your help, Marcinik, and her Serenity's—until we turn up a settlement."

"And then?" Silence asked, rather skeptically, but it was impossible not to be infected by the other's optimism.

"We'll see how big it is, and then decide," Balthasar answered. "Come on."

Silence sighed, but hauled herself to her feet, and followed the Delian back onto the lower bridge. The musonar system was intact—they'd been lucky there, too, Balthasar said, more soberly—but it still took them several hours to transfer everything to back-up power and then to set up the search pattern.

Balthasar insisted on keeping a secondary horn pointed skyward, and Silence did not argue. Even if they had shaken off the pursuing aircraft, there was no harm in staying alert for other searchers. They set the search grid in motion, and then drew straws to see who'd take the first watch. Silence, to her secret relief, drew the long straw, and headed gratefully for her cabin.

She stripped off her shipsuit, wincing at the bruises dotting her body, and forced herself to take a hot shower before dropping exhausted into her bunk. She had not thought she would be able to relax after the tension of the pursuit and then the crash itself, but to her surprise she slept almost as soon as her head touched the pillow.

The persistent shrilling of the intercom woke her at last. Silence pulled herself upright, swearing at her sore muscles, then reached across the bunk to slap at the answer plate. She hit it on the second try, and said, "What the hell is it?"

Balthasar answered. "We've spotted a settlement, we think."

"I'll be right up," Silence said.

"In the commons," Balthasar added hastily, and the pilot cut the connection.

Dressing was a painful process, but by the time she'd fastened her shirt and pulled a loose tunic over her head, Silence had to admit she was in better shape than she had expected. She made her way to the common room, ducking through the illusory tree trunk, feeling almost confident.

The others were there ahead of her, clustered around the main table. A number of sheets of rough-printed paper were spread out in front of them, some held together with strips of tape. Balthasar looked up as she entered, and smiled. "We're in luck again," he called. "Come and see."

Silence came to look over the Delian's shoulder. The papers showed a rough contour map of the area surrounding the ship, the lines spilling out from the blank spot that was the valley. To the north and west, the forest continued unbroken; to the northeast, several rivers and one higher mountain showed through the cloaking woods. Due east lay water—the edge of the smaller ocean, Silence thought—and more forest.

"There," Balthasar said, and pointed.

His finger was touching a small break in the forest, barely

more than a thin wedge of cleared ground on the slope of a steeply rising hill. There were marks in the center of the clearing, but the symbols meant nothing to Silence. She looked up inquiringly, and Marcinik said, "We picked up a single large metallic structure first, something tall but narrow—I couldn't really tell any more closely. I think there are buildings around it, but they're made of stone or wood, hard to pick out. The shaded square marks the metal structure; the other marks are for the other buildings."

"It looks like some kind of farm to me," Aili said slowly. She leaned forward, holding her veil in place with one hand. "You see? That would be a main building, and those the barns and a greenhouse, and then the metal thing would be a pump, or a power vane. And before you say it," she added, lifting her head to stare directly at Balthasar, "I would know better than you how a farm is laid out. There are enough of them on Inarime."

Balthasar lifted both hands in surrender. "It sounds reasonable to me."

Silence nodded. "All right," she said, "so what do we do?"

"That's the question," Chase Mago said. He sighed, staring at the crude map. "How far is it?"

"A little under twenty kilometers," Marcinik answered. "That's a full day's hike."

"What if we started before sunrise?" Balthasar asked, and the colonel shook his head.

"I wouldn't want to risk it. This may be Earth, but there is still a certain amount of hostile wildlife to consider. Not to mention the risk of getting lost in the dark."

Balthasar shrugged, but nodded.

"That's all very well," Silence said, "but what are we going to say once we get there?"

"Perhaps we could tell a part of the truth," Aili suggested. "We could say we'd been stranded by an air crash."

"That could work," Silence said, doubtfully, "but wouldn't they already have searchers out, if that were true?"

Balthasar shrugged again. "I say we play it by ear."

Chase Mago cleared his throat, drawing all eyes. "Forgive me for saying it, but I don't think her Serenity should come with us. Nor should Doctor Isambard," he added hastily, as Silence gave him an incredulous look.

Aili's expression was hidden by her veil, but her voice was dangerously quiet. "And why not, sieur Chase Mago?"

"Three reasons," the engineer answered. To give him credit, Silence thought, he didn't flinch under the Princess Royal's stare. "First, someone should stay with the ship. Second, both you and Isambard have been injured; and third, because of that, you're the ones we can spare to watch the ship."

Marcinik's chin lifted dangerously. "And if anything happens to us, who will protect Aili?" he demanded. "The magus isn't a star-traveller, he couldn't take her off-planet."

Silence intervened hastily, watching the Princess Royal. "Julie's right," she said, "if we just make a quick reconnaissance, and don't try to contact anybody unless we're positive it's safe to do so."

"I think I should stay with the ship," Marcinik murmured.

Silence shook her head. "You're the only real soldier we have aboard. We need you."

After a moment, Aili sighed deeply. "You're right, damn you for it. I'll stay—and you'll go, Marcinik."

There was a note in her voice that brooked no argument. The colonel bowed. "As you wish."

Once that decision had been made, it didn't take long to settle the rest of the plan. At Marcinik's insistence, they left the ship just at sunrise, each one carrying a light pack made up from the ship's survival kit and a fully charged heylin. They carried extra charges as well, and Silence had a smaller version of a magus's kit slung from her belt. Chase Mago, unarguably the strongest of the four, carried the communications unit.

For the first hour, they trudged in silence up the valley's eastern side, steering by Marcinik's compass. The morning air was very cool under the trees, cool enough that Silence found herself shivering a little despite the exertion. Then, quite abruptly, they reached the top of the ridge, and emerged into a narrow clearing. Silence slowed her steps a little, soaking up the sunlight, and saw that the other star-travellers were doing the same. Marcinik paused at the edge of the clearing, laughing.

"Come on," he called, "you'll warm up soon enough."

The colonel had spoken only the truth, Silence discovered all too soon. By midmorning she was sweating, and stopped to slip off her overtunic, knotting it around her waist by the sleeves. As she tugged it into place, pulling the heylin forward a little so that the draw wasn't impeded by the bundled fabric, she heard a shout from her right. She tensed, but in the same instant recognized Chase Mago's voice.

"Hey! I've found a wall!"

Obediently, Silence made her way across the carpet of brown, dead spines fallen from the towering trees. There was little undergrowth, for which she was grateful, and the wall was clearly visible. It was made of piled stone, the smallest the size of her own head, the largest that she could see a massive boulder almost a meter across. It seemed to start from nowhere, running off into the trees to the right of their original path. Chase Mago was standing at its end, frowning down at it.

"I think it turned a corner here," he said, almost to himself.

Silence nodded. A little cascade of stone fell off from the side of the wall, and there were more stones trailing away in odd heaps and jumbled piles at a right angle to the part that was still standing. A field wall? she wondered. A boundary marker? It couldn't ever have been high enough to provide real protection. . . .

Balthasar said, "It's a wall. So?"

"So someone lived here once," Silence said impatiently, and stepped around a pile of rock to examine the land the wall had once enclosed. It was as overgrown as the rest of the forest, showing no signs of recent growth—though who can tell what recent growth might look like here? Silence thought.

"Interesting," Marcinik said, coming up to join them. "So maybe this was more populated once?"

"At least there was something here," Silence said. Chase Mago dug a booted foot into the dirt, then squinted down the length of the standing wall.

"There might be foundations in there," he offered.

Marcinik hesitated, then shook his head. "No. We don't have the time to waste. Come on."

Chase Mago grimaced, but made no other protest as the

colonel led them away from the crumbling wall. They walked almost a kilometer before he spoke again.

"I wonder why the site was abandoned."

Balthasar snorted. "Would you live here if you had any other choice?" he demanded.

The engineer laughed, and slapped the other man lightly on the back of the head. Silence laughed with them, but sobered quickly. Why would anyone abandon what must have been a fairly large estate—especially when land, real property, was always a source of prestige and power? Or was that always true? she wondered suddenly. Certainly it was the case in the Hegemony and on the worlds of the Rusadir and the Fringe, but that didn't mean it would be true on Earth. Hostile wildlife? Certainly they'd seen nothing larger than the occasional climbing mammal, and the only predator seemed to be some sort of large black bird—and in any case, Silence thought, all accounts said Earth had controlled its animal life fairly closely. They would never have allowed dangerous animals to remain in a populated area. Then they reached a narrow, swift-running stream, and she put aside her musings to concentrate on the treacherous stones that spanned it.

They came to a second stream two kilometers farther, and Marcinik paused on its bank, staring dubiously at the rushing water. It was bigger than the first one, wider and deeper both, but the water flowed as quickly. Silence eyed it uneasily, and was grateful when the colonel said, "We'll ford it farther down."

"It's not that deep," Balthasar objected.

Marcinik didn't answer directly, but stooped to pick up a handful of the tree spines that still littered the ground. Unspeaking, he tossed them into the water. Light as they were, they didn't reach the center of the stream, but the current still whirled them away at a frightening speed. "And it's damn cold," Marcinik said.

"I take the point," Balthasar said, but he was smiling.

They had to follow the stream for almost two kilometers before it finally slowed and widened, waters rippling over a wide stretch of sand and pebbles. It looked like a perfect ford, but Marcinik still checked it carefully, tossing grass and tree spines into the water, then tossing fist-sized rocks into the sand to scare off any lurking predators, before he nodded and sat down on the bank to unlace his knee-length boots. The others followed his example, but hung back as the colonel waded out into the stream. He gasped a little at the cold, and walked out to the middle of the ford, splashing noisily, before he beckoned for the others to follow. Silence stepped gingerly into the water, and barely stopped herself from shrieking aloud. She had expected chill, but not this numbing cold. It took every gram of self-control she possessed to keep walking. Behind her, she heard Balthasar swear loudly, but did not look back.

The far bank was in sunlight, the grass pleasantly warm. Silence rubbed her feet dry with the hem of her tunic, but couldn't seem to force warmth back into them. She looked up, and saw that even Marcinik seemed to be having the same difficulty. He met her glance with a smile.

"Break for lunch?" he suggested, and the pilot laughed.

"You won't get any argument from me."

The colonel didn't let them rest for long, however. As soon as they had finished the thick bars of nutrient concentrate, Marcinik was on his feet, boots laced and ready. "Come on," he said, and the others groaned and followed.

As the afternoon wore on, they passed more broken walls, and once a rusted hunk of metal that Chase Mago admitted might once have been some sort of engine. He could not identify it, and Silence could feel no harmful energies lurking in it, but nevertheless they gave it a wide berth. The pilot was glad when it was swallowed in the forest.

The shadows had lengthened perceptibly, and the sun no longer reached to the bottoms of the deeper valleys when Marcinik called a halt.

"The settlement should be over the next rise," he said, unconsciously lowering his voice. "About a kilometer."

Silence shivered again, though the air was not cold, then unfastened the tunic's knotted sleeves and slipped the garment over her head. The dark green material had dried nicely, was still a little warm from the sun, and she hugged it to herself, suddenly afraid. She could not quite bring herself to contemplate what they might do if this turned out to be a

Rose Worlder settlement. Where there are people, there are vehicles, she told herself firmly. We can always steal one. Then Marcinik was speaking again, and she forced herself to listen.

"—heavier growth to the north," the colonel said. "We'll go through that, stop on the ridge line, and lie up there for a while. That'll give us a good chance to get a look at the place."

The others nodded, Chase Mago swinging the communications unit forward to type out a quick report for the ship, and Silence saw her own fear reflected in their sober faces. Almost without conscious thought, she drew her heylin, running her thumb across the touchplate. It was comfortingly hot, the weapon fully charged. Marcinik saw the movement and smiled.

"Let's hope we don't need them," he said, but Silence was very aware of the fact that he had not ordered her to put it away. She kept the heylin in her hand as she followed the others up the last ridge.

It took them almost an hour to cover the last five hundred meters, and Silence was made depressingly aware of her own inadequacies as a woodsman. Despite all her efforts, she knew she had left a trail of broken vegetation behind her. The only consolation, she thought, is that the others aren't any better.

And then, at last, they reached the ridge. Marcinik covered the final meters on his hands and knees, easing himself into position behind a screening clump of bushes. Silence watched enviously, knowing she would never be able to do it so quietly, and heard the leaves stir faintly behind her as Chase Mago shook his head in admiration. After a moment, the colonel beckoned for them to join him, and Silence scrambled awkwardly up after him, wincing at the noise she made. She dropped to her belly beside Marcinik, screened by the same line of bushes, and a few minutes later the others joined them.

"Look," Marcinik whispered.

Cautiously, Silence peered through the bushes' lowest branches. As Aili had predicted, the place had once been a farm. The charred skeletons of half a dozen outbuildings clustered around a central building whose stone walls still carried black stains of smoke. For an instant, Silence felt close to tears, sure the place had been abandoned, and then she saw the signs of repairs, the raw yellow wood shoring up the central building, and forming the sides and roof of the single remaining shanty. The metal structure that had showed up on the musonar was clearly visible, and clearly still in working order: a windmill tower stood to one side of the crude compound, its metal-film vanes turning lazily in the light air. Beyond the windmill lay newly plowed fields. From one of the outbuildings came a low animal cry, a plaintive, moaning noise; a moment later, a door opened in the side of the central building and a boy emerged, a metal bucket swinging in one hand.

"Feeding time?" Balthasar whispered, unable to keep quiet any longer.

Silence shrugged, and kept her eyes on the scene below. The boy crossed to the remaining shanty—almost, Silence thought, you can hear him whistling—and vanished inside. Nothing else moved within the compound. After some time, the boy reappeared, pulled sideways a little now by the weight of the bucket. He returned to the central building, and shut the door carefully behind him.

"Do I call the ship?" Chase Mago murmured, and Marcinik shook his head.

"Not yet. Wait until we have something to report."

The pilot frowned, wondering what they should do. All their plans had depended on finding transport here, but so far she had seen no signs of any such device, and the condition of the buildings argued there'd been a serious fire. Still, the windmill's still running, she thought, frowning down at the settlement. Surely that argues that people are still here.

"All right," a harsh voice said from behind her. "Stand up slowly, all of you, and keep your hands where I can see them."

Silence did as she was told, her heart pounding in her throat. She caught a brief glimpse of Marcinik's face, chagrin and resignation mingling in his expression, and then she had pushed herself to her feet, carefully holding her hands away from her body.

"Put it down, girl," the harsh voice said. Silence hesitated, unable to locate the source of the voice—somewhere in the shadowed ground to her left, she thought—and Marcinik said softly, "Do as she says, Silence."

The pilot stooped slowly, still scanning the woods to either side, and laid the heylin gently on the carpet of tree spines at her feet.

"All right." The harsh voice was definitely coming from the trees to their left, Silence thought, and then the branches rustled over a meter from the spot she'd chosen and a brown-clad figure edged out from among the trees. It was a woman, an older woman, grey hair bound back with a dirty rag, who leaned heavily on a metal crutch. One leg was roughly splinted, trouser leg ripped almost to the waist to accommodate the bandages, but the injury didn't seem to affect her steady grip on her lowered weapon. It looked rather like a sonic rifle, but no resonance chamber ringed the slim barrel just beyond the stock. Still, Silence had no doubt that it was just as deadly.

"What the fuck do you want here?" the woman demanded. "Haven't you done enough?"

Silence forced herself to think calmly. The woman spoke a form of the star-travellers' coinë, heavily accented, but entirely understandable; she should be equally able to understand her captives.

"Whatever's happened," the pilot said carefully, "we had nothing to do with it." The woman's expression did not change, but at least she made no pretense of not understanding. Emboldened, Silence went on. "Our ship—we crashed, up in the hills. Yours was the nearest settlement."

"We're not on the maps," the woman said flatly. "And don't try to tell me you're from around here."

"No, we're not," Silence agreed, desperate to keep the conversation going. "And you weren't on our maps, no, but your tower showed up on musonar. It was the closest, so we came here."

The woman shook her head, her grim expression unchanging. "It won't do, girl," she said, and steadied the weapon against her body.

"Wait!" Silence cried. Out of the corner of her eye, she could see Marcinik shift slightly, readying himself for a hopeless attempt to seize the woman's rifle, could sense the same subtle tension in the other two men. "You're making a mistake; we're not involved. We're from off-world—" She broke off abruptly as the other woman's mouth twitched downward into a frown.

"Off-world," the woman repeated. Silence held her breath, hoping that somehow she'd hit upon the right words. At last, very slowly, the older woman shook her head.

"Goddamn mystics," she growled. "Javerry's dead, no thanks to you."

Despite the words, she sounded less hostile than before. To Silence's left, Balthasar slid his foot forward in the carpeting tree spines. When the woman did not seem to notice, he eased the rest of his body forward as well. He'd gained only a few centimeters, Silence knew, but every little bit would help, if it came to a fight. Hardly daring to breathe, she groped for the words that would consolidate her slim gains. "I— We don't know any Javerry, I'm sorry. We're strangers here ourselves, from off-world like I said. Our ship—" She broke off abruptly, not wanting to reveal anything more about *Recusante* until she had to.

Leaves rustled sharply, this time to Silence's right, and a new voice said, "They could be telling the truth, Mama."

Balthasar whispered a curse, and Silence saw Marcinik's shoulders twitch. She could feel the despair sour in her stomach, tasted fear. Two of them, she thought crazily, there's nothing we can do if they don't believe us, nothing we can do but die. . . .

"Easy, now," the older woman said sharply, her hands tightening again on the weapon's stock.

"Mama," the voice said from the woods, and in the same moment, Chase Mago said, "Sieura, please. We mean you no harm."

"You're as bad as your damn father," the older woman snapped, without looking at the source of the new voice. "You, what'd you call me?"

The leaves rustled again, then parted as a man stepped out to join her. He was blond, as his mother might once have been, with a high forehead and a straggling beard, and very thin. His left sleeve was empty, the cuff pinned neatly to the shoulder seam, but he held his short twin-barrelled weapon securely in his remaining hand, bracing it against his side.

"Shotgun," Balthasar hissed, almost in spite of himself.

"Be quiet," Silence said, and tightened all her muscles in a vain attempt to stop her shaking. A shotgun was—mostly—a Delian weapon, meant for use against crowds, and generally restricted to that world because of its mechanical nature. It broadcast a cloud of solid pellets that would rip through anyone stupid enough to get in its way—and the worst of it was there was nothing even a magus could do to stop the random blast of metal.

"Well?" the woman said again. "You with the beard, answer me."

Chase Mago shook his head, glancing uncertainly at Silence. She shrugged, not daring to do more, and the engineer looked away again. "Sieura?" he said, carefully, and the young man gave an exclamation of pleasure.

"You see, Mama?"

"There's proof and there's proof," the older woman said, her hands steady on the strange rifle. "And if they really are off-worlders—" She smiled suddenly, bitterly, showing a missing tooth. "We'll take them back, let them prove it there."

"Mama—" the young man began, warningly, but his mother cut him off.

"You four, put your hands on your heads and walk real slow toward me. There's a path through here. Get on it and follow it down to the farm. One wrong move, and we'll blast you."

Silence laced her shaking fingers together and rested her hands on the top of her head, then followed Balthasar and Chase Mago down the ridge. Despite the crutch, the older woman skipped nimbly out of their reach, keeping her weapons levelled on them at all times. Silence glanced over her shoulder, almost falling over a tree stump, and saw the son bringing up the rear, shotgun steady.

As the woman had promised, they thrashed through thick growth for a few meters, then emerged onto a narrow path. Balthasar hesitated, his shoulders working slightly as though he was looking for a chance to run. Silence tensed, willing him not to do anything stupid, and the woman growled, "Don't even think it, bright boy."

The trail curved gently to the left as it rose over the ridge line, but too gently to provide any sort of cover. As they came out of the woods into the cleared land of the compound, the door of the main building burst open and a dog rushed out, barking wildly. It stopped short, brought up by its chain, and Silence saw the boy they had seen earlier peering warily around the doorframe. The young man saw him too, and his voice cracked in a shout.

"Get back inside, Cass!"

The boy tugged at the dog's chain, and managed to pull the reluctant animal back inside. He slammed the door, but Silence could still hear the barking.

"Keep going," the older woman said. "Around the back."

"Mama?" the son asked. "What're you—"

"Shut up," the woman said. "You lot, keep going."

Silence could feel her arms shaking as they rounded the corner of the house, partly from the strain of keeping them on her head, but mostly from fear. The same fear was sour in her stomach. Somehow, she had lost the brief advantage she'd gained by saying they were out-worlders, and she didn't know how or why—or why it had gained them anything in the first place. She heard Chase Mago gasp, and Balthasar curse softly, and looked up. They were facing the charred ruins of one of the outbuildings, but beyond that, just outside the line of the plowed field, was the unmistakable mound of a new-dug grave. There were three more beside the first, one much smaller than the others, and she bit back a whimper of sheer terror. They could not have come so far just to die here. . . . She pushed away the thought, and was aware that both her husbands had edged closer, trying to put themselves between her and the natives' weapons. The last rays of sunlight glinted from the tuning wheel on the communications unit slung over Chase Mago's shoulder, and Silence stared at it, wishing she could control it from a distance. There was nothing *Recusante* could do for them, but Aili and the magus deserved to be warned, to know that they'd failed. . . . She closed her eyes, struggling to think of something—anything—

that might help them now, but the other woman's harsh voice cut through her concentration.

"Stop there."

"Mama, what the hell are you doing?" the young man demanded again, but the woman ignored him.

"All my life," she said, "they've been telling me the off-worlders're going to come for us, going to come work miracles and save us all. All right. You say you're off-worlders, so work me my miracle. Give me back what I've lost. Give me back my Javerry, and Ardis, and the babies. I've lost too damn much waiting for you not to get something back."

The sudden fury in her voice snapped something deep in Silence. The levelled weapons seemed to vanish from her perceptions; instead, she saw, with stark clarity, the way the harmonies of Earth's core rose into and through the land around her, vibrating in the air to all sides. She lowered her hands, reaching out with them and with her new-trained powers to grasp that dark music, twisting it to match a new and unexpected Form. Wind howled, rising from still air, and she heard her own voice shouting in it.

"I don't have any miracles, woman, and I can't raise the dead, but I have power!" Flames sprang from her hands, and from the ground beneath her hands, fountained up to fall back in a rain of fire that vanished the instant before it touched the earth. Faintly, she heard a cry of fear, and then a voice shouting her name. Chase Mago's voice, she thought, and the recognition shocked her back to reality. Carefully, she loosed her hold on the elemental harmonies, letting them ease back into their proper places. The firefall dwindled to a swirl of sparks, then vanished altogether as the wind ceased.

"Good God almighty," the woman was saying quietly, in a voice queerly torn between despair and awe. "My God almighty."

Her son was very pale, the shotgun dangling forgotten in his hand. "It's true then, Mama. It's the Empress, here, just like Pap said."

The woman shook her head, her own weapon on the dirt at her feet, but did not answer.

"Empress?" Silence said. The sudden upswelling of power and emotion had left her drained, unable quite to comprehend the emotions she felt around her. She clung to the simple question as though to a lifeline. "What do you mean?"

The young man turned to face her. "It's what we've always said, like Mama told you, that the off-worlders would come for us, teach us their secrets. And when we came up here, Pap—my father," he corrected himself, with sudden formality, "cast the cards, and he said you'd come. He saw your card, the Empress, and he told us all you'd be here before summer."

"A bit late for him," the woman growled, but the worst of the anger was gone. There was even a hint of exasperated pride in the glance she gave the nearest grave. "So. You've really come." She shook herself then, and reached for the weapon lying at her feet. Silence tensed in spite of herself, and saw the others ready to jump, but the woman shouldered it easily, juggling it and the crutch with practiced ease. "I'm Emma Javerry," she said, "and you're on what's left of my farm." She jerked her head toward the one-armed man. "My son, Quin."

Silence hesitated, still wary, and said, "My name's Leigh, Silence Leigh. My husbands, Denis Balthasar and Julian Chase Mago, and Colonel Yles Marcinik, of the True Thousand."

Quin hissed softly through his teeth, and the woman's eyes widened.

"More proof, Mama," the young man murmured.

Emma Javerry nodded. "Will you accept our hospitality, gentlefolk?" she asked, with awkward formality.

"Sieuri," Quin added, the foreign word clumsy on his tongue.

Silence hesitated again, but could think of no good reason to distrust them any longer. "Thank you," she said slowly. "We're—grateful for it."

Emma Javerry gave a brusque nod, and swung herself around, leaning heavily on her crutch. "This way," she said, and started toward the main building without waiting for an answer. Quin made an odd, embarrassed movement, ducking his head and shrugging slightly, and gestured for the others to follow. Silence exchanged glances with her fellow star-travellers, seeing her own residual wariness reflected in their faces, and saw Marcinik shrug, his shoulders lifting only a few millime-

ters. The message was clear: *what have we got to lose now?*
Silence smiled almost in spite of herself, and followed the
older woman toward the house.

It was unexpectedly warm inside the stone-walled building, and the light was very dim. Silence stood, blinking, in
the doorway, and Emma Javerry, herself no more than a
clumsy shadow in the darkness, said, "You can open the
shutters now, Cass."

There was no answer except a murmur, but then there was
a rattle of metal from the distant wall, and the waning sunlight streamed in. The boy she'd seen earlier moved on to the
next window, folding back those shutters as well.

"Where's the dog?" Javerry asked.

The boy paused, one hand still on the shutters' latch. "Out
back. I put him there when I saw you coming in."

"And what have I told you about peeking out when we've
told you to stay in?" Javerry asked, but her tone was fairly
mild. "All right, leave him there for now."

"Yes, Grandma," the boy said, dutifully enough, and moved
on to the next window.

"Have a seat, all of you." Javerry lowered herself into the
largest of the room's battered chairs, and lifted her splinted
leg onto a footstool, grimacing a little. She set the crutch
beside her on the floor, and Silence realized she had already
discarded the strange rifle. The pilot moved toward the nearest chair, glancing around covertly as she did so, and saw
that Javerry had placed the rifle in a rack that stood just to
the left of a side door.

"Thanks," Silence said again, and seated herself opposite
the other woman. She was shaking a little—reaction, she
thought—and hoped no one would see.

"That's my grandson Cass," Javerry went on, jerking her
head toward the boy. "Quin's son." She looked up at the rest
of the star-travellers, still hanging back by the door, and
scowled. "Sit down, damn you, we're not going to eat you."

"Sieura, I wasn't sure," Balthasar retorted, and Silence bit
back a laugh, watching the older woman's face. The scowl
deepened, and then, quite suddenly, eased into a fleeting
smile.

"And so you weren't," Javerry said. "Now sit."

This time, the star-travellers did as they were told, arranging themselves on the couch and one of the two remaining chairs. Quin, following them in, set his shotgun in the rack by the far door, and crossed the room to join them.

"Would you be hungry?" he asked. "We can offer a meal, soup and bread and cheese—or just bread and cheese, if you don't eat meat."

"Food would be good," Silence said, suddenly aware that she was very hungry. "The soup would be fine." The other star-travellers nodded, and she saw Quin's eyebrows lift slightly.

"Of course, sieura," he said, and turned toward an inner door.

"How come you can eat meat?" the boy said suddenly, ignoring his father's admonitory frown. "Grandpa couldn't."

Silence frowned back, genuinely puzzled. "There's no reason I know of that I shouldn't," she said at last. "It's hard enough to deal with allergies and the like, travelling, without adding trouble. . . ." Her voice trailed off as she realized she was babbling. Javerry gave her a rather skeptical glance, but said nothing, easing her bandaged leg on the uncomfortable footstool.

The sunlight was fading fast now, and the boy Cass moved without being told to light the twin lamps that stood on a sort of sideboard beside the inner doorway through which Quin had disappeared. Silence watched idly, but the boy's body hid the movements of his hands. Javerry said something too low-voiced for the star-travellers to hear, and the boy brought one of the lamps forward, setting it on the low table that stood by his grandmother's chair. With a shock, Silence realized that the glass globe held real fire, an ordinary flame dancing above a pool of some dark fuel. Then Cass brought the second lamp, placing it so that they sat at the heart of two overlapping circles of golden light.

Javerry made a face, the expression almost hidden in the shadows. "We used to have electricity—still do, for the important things, now that Quin has the mill working again—but I don't like using it unless we have to. I swear that's how they hunted us down."

"Now, Mama," Quin said, appearing in the doorway with a

tray balanced in his hands. His tone suggested they'd had the argument before.

"Why who hunted you down, sieura?" Marcinik asked.

Javerry didn't answer at once. "Go help your daddy, Cass," she said, after a moment. The boy made a face, but pushed himself up off the floor.

"Get the bread, please," Quin said, and the boy vanished into the kitchen. Quin continued into the room, setting the tray on the low table beside the lamp, and ceremoniously handed out the steaming bowls of soup. Silence accepted hers warily, but the aroma of the alien spices was so enticing that she put aside her caution. She dipped her spoon into the cloudy liquid, and tasted it. The only familiar thing was salt; the rest—shreds of some pale, sweetish meat, chunks of multicolored vegetables, odd flecks of spice—was strange, but so good that she forgot Marcinik's unanswered question, concentrating on the exotic flavors.

"Bread, m— sieura?" Cass asked shyly.

Silence looked up to find the boy standing at her elbow, holding out a basket filled with slices of thick brown bread. She took one with a smile, and a murmur of thanks, and glanced to the side to see the other star-travellers bent over their bowls, each wearing the same expression of absolute absorption in the tastes and smells. Her smile widened to a grin, and in the same moment Chase Mago looked up, meeting her gaze with a rather rueful smile.

"It's very good," he said. "Thank you."

Marcinik nodded his agreement, but before he could repeat his question, Emma Javerry said, "Now, then, offworlders, what brings you to Earth?"

Silence paused, and knew the others were looking at her again. Why me? she thought, with sudden, irrational anger, but shoved away the response. She was to answer because she was the magus, and because in the end it was she who had gotten them into this situation. Unfortunately, none of their plans had included telling even a part of the truth, and she was unprepared. She chewed the rest of her bread methodically, mind racing, and swallowed without having found a good answer. "We've come to Earth," she began, slowly, "because—well, because it's here."

"Hell, we weren't entirely sure of that," Balthasar cut in, with a lopsided grin, and Silence threw him a grateful glance.

"That's true, too," she said. "The thing is, the records of the Earth-road were lost during the Millennial Wars, at least to the Fringe, and the Hegemony and Rusadir. People have been trying to rediscover it ever since, and—" She stopped there, not knowing quite how to explain the sequence of events that had brought her and the others into the search for Earth. Hell, I never wanted to look for Earth, she thought; that was my Uncle Otto's obsession—and do I want to tell this fierce old woman that somebody's keeping Earth blocked off from the rest of human-settled space? Javerry was staring at her, and Silence finished lamely, "We were able to find an old starbook, an old method, and so we got through."

Javerry and her son exchanged looks, and then Quin said, "Did you have any—difficulty—getting through?"

So they do know, Silence thought, and barely stopped herself from glancing at the other star-travellers. Or at the very least they suspect—but do I tell them about it? She said, cautiously, "Yes, we had some difficulties."

Balthasar smothered a half-hysterical laugh. "You could call it that, yeah. Difficulties!"

Silence looked at him with some annoyance, and the Delian mouthed, *tell them*. The pilot hesitated a second longer, then shrugged to herself, saying, "The leadership of the Rose Worlds—the worlds that used to be called the Ring—has built siege engines that block the Earth-road, distort the harmonies that a pilot should follow. We got through them, but their people attacked while we were landing, and shot us down."

Javerry nodded, an expression of dour satisfaction on her face. "Typical Unionists."

Silence started. "Unionists?"

Javerry nodded again, impatiently this time. "Them—the government down on Man's Island, and all the rest of them."

Silence said nothing, not quite certain what she could say to that. "Unionist" surely meant the pre-War Union of the Human Sphere, but she had never heard the word spoken with such disgust before. All the accounts she had studied on Solitudo Hermae had praised the Earth-centered, Earth-founded

Union; star-travellers' legend said much the same things, and mourned it as a lost golden age.

"These Unionists," Marcinik said, and Silence heard the same disorientation in his voice. "Were they the ones who attacked here, sieura?"

"Who else?" Javerry said bitterly.

Quin said, "Are you telling us they're off-worlders, too?"

"I don't know," Silence said. "Some probably are—the Rose Worlders have to be involved in this somehow." She looked back at Javerry. "But why did they attack you, sieura?"

Javerry grunted, her eyes going to her son. Quin made a face, and looked away. "Hah," the older woman said, "so you'll let me tell it now?" She looked back at the star-travellers, fierce eyes sweeping across them all. "The Unionists, they don't like people living in the exurb—they don't even like the suburbs much, but not everyone'll fit in the mainurb no matter how hard they try." Her face changed then, softened and saddened. "I remember, when I was a girl, when they closed the texurb. I saw it on the newsband, bringing out the last people on the jet-hoppers. They none of them had anything more than what they could grab up when the hoppers landed, because they didn't believe—nobody really believed—the government would do it."

Silence frowned, not quite understanding, and Javerry elaborated, "That the government'd make them move. They wanted to clear out all the people, bring them into the mainurb so they could use the land for farming, or so they said. I think they just don't like anybody living outside the urban net— and I say that's why they came down on us, because we're outside the net and happy out of it." She turned to her son with one of her fleeting smiles. "Quin disagrees."

The younger man shrugged, embarrassed. "Well, I do," he said. "The texurb was a special case, and you know it. There were a lot of small-holders there, and they were organized, most of them, and they'd been trouble for generations. It was entirely different." He stopped, seeing the other's blank looks, and flushed slightly. "But that's beside the point. What I think is, it was because of my father and his experiments. He was working on a lot of things—and getting somewhere with it, too. Look how he predicted the Empress, and here she is."

The last was for his mother, Silence realized belatedly. Clearly Emma Javerry hadn't shared either her husband's or her son's interest in the experiments, whatever those experiments were. From Quin's words—and I must ask him to explain just what it was his father did, Silence thought, "casting the cards"—it sounded as though his father had been involved in the Art. Then Quin was speaking again, and the pilot hastily dragged her attention back to him.

"Pap knew a lot of people in the mainurbs, and all over the world," Quin said. "And he kept in pretty close touch with them, so it wouldn't've been hard to find out both what he was doing and that things were beginning to work. They wanted to stop him; that's why they attacked us."

"Just what was he doing that the Unionists felt they had to stop him?" Marcinik asked slowly.

Quin gave him a blank look. "He was trying to get off-world power, like she has." He nodded toward Silence. "Magic."

Silence realized her mouth had fallen open in shock, and closed it hastily, trying to think of an answer to that. Before she could say anything, however, Balthasar said indignantly, "It's not magic, it's the Art, the magi's Art."

"If you say so," Quin said, doubtfully. Javerry gave a snort of laughter, but said nothing.

"If you don't use the Art," Silence said, "what do you use?" Seeing their uncomprehending expressions, she added, "For—for farming, or heavy labor—for things human beings can't do."

Javerry and her son stared at the younger woman—looking, Silence thought irritably, as though I've lost my mind. When neither of his elders answered, Cass piped up, "Machines, of course. We use machines."

Machines. Silence let the word roll through her mind. *Mechanics.* An entire world that used machines. She shook her head, unable quite to comprehend it. Delos, of all the worlds she'd ever visited, had used mechanics more than most, but even there the individual units were banned from the ports, kept small and isolated and carefully shielded. But an entire world—and Earth, of all worlds—

"Aren't they restricted?" That was Chase Mago, the bowl of soup forgotten in his hands.

"No," Quin said slowly. "Why should they be?"

"They must be," Balthasar said. "You can't lift a starship when there are machines around the port—"

"There aren't any starports," Javerry said. "Or are there?"

"There are," Silence said grimly. "There are." She looked at her husbands and then at Marcinik, her mind racing. "We know there are at least two, Ladysprings and S'haar, because we were going to land there. And we know that their rules restrict star-travellers to port and Pale—I think we can believe that much of what the woman told us." She turned to Javerry. "Who farms all that land that was taken from those people—the texurb?"

"Robots," Javerry said. "AFMs—automatic farm machines."

Silence nodded, looking back at the other star-travellers. "So we know two more things. They use machines for everything, for things we'd never dream of, and they don't know much about the Art. If they did," she added, forestalling a question from Marcinik, "his father wouldn't've been wasting his time on predictions, he'd've been working on something useful, like harmonics—or symbology and manipulation." Too late, she saw Quin's stricken expression, and winced. "I'm sorry, I didn't mean. . . ." She shook her head helplessly. "Prediction is a wild-card talent, not really a part of the Art. It can't be taught, and it can't be refined much beyond the basic stages. It sounds as though your father had the talent, all right—I'm here, and you say he did foretell it—but it's ultimately a dead end."

"Very much so, for him," Javerry said, dryly.

"I'm sorry," Silence said again, and the older woman shrugged.

"It doesn't matter. Go on with what you were saying; I'm interested."

Silence grimaced, trying to recover her train of thought. "So it looks to me as though the Rose Worlders are trying to keep you from finding out about the Art," she said at last, knowing how flat the conclusion sounded.

No one said anything for a long moment. Glancing to her left, Silence could see the other star-travellers struggling to absorb the idea and all its implications. To her surprise, however, it was Cass who spoke first.

"But of course they are. They pretend to laugh at it, but every time anyone gets serious, the Unionists crack down."

Javerry cleared her throat. "Be that as it may," she said, "our guests look like they're about ready to drop. I assume you'll be staying the night, gentlefolk?"

"Sieuri," Quin murmured, and was ignored.

"Thank you, sieura," Marcinik said, "you're most kind. We'd planned to sleep out, but—" He smiled. "We would not say no to a roof and a bed."

"It'll be air mattresses in the storeroom," Javerry warned, but she didn't seem displeased with his compliments. "But you will be warm—and dry, if it comes on to rain. See to it, Quin, will you?"

"Of course, Mama." The blond man pushed himself up out of his chair, and motioned to his son. "Cass, why don't you take people's plates, if they're done with them."

Silence handed her bowl to the boy, suddenly aware of just how tired she was. Much of it was reaction, she knew, first to being spotted and then to the use of her powers, and finally to the Javerrys' description of life on Earth, but it was none-theless real. She leaned back in her chair, trying to decide just what they should do next. They had been lucky so far, she knew, finding a household that was sympathetic to them, but it didn't look as though the Javerrys would be able to provide much more than sympathy and, possibly, informa-tion. Nor, if what she guessed were true, would any other Earth natives, trapped as they were within their mechanical society; the tools of the Art would have to come from the Rose Worlders.

Chase Mago cleared his throat suddenly. "I better check in," he said to Marcinik, and the colonel nodded.

Emma Javerry stiffened. "There's more of you?"

The engineer hesitated, but answered honestly. "Yes."

"We said our ship was wrecked," Marcinik said. "There're still some people aboard."

"How many?" Javerry demanded.

"Two more," Marcinik answered promptly. Silence winced, but then realized it was a cheap concession: the Javerrys would still have to find the ship. "Another magus, Silence's teacher, and her Serenity the Princess Royal Aili Kibbe, eldest daughter—eldest child—of his most serene majesty the Hegemon of Asterion and its allied worlds." The titles rolled sonorously from his tongue, and Silence saw his head lift proudly. "And also my wife."

Javerry's eyebrows rose, her mouth twitching into a sardonic smile, and Chase Mago cut in hastily, "With your permission, sieura?" He gestured to the communications unit slung at his belt.

"Sure," Javerry answered. "If you need to be private, you can step out into the yard. The dog's inside."

"It's not privacy I'm worried about," the engineer said frankly, "it's your machines." He gave Silence a questioning glance, and the pilot shrugged.

"I don't know. I've never dealt with this many machines before."

Balthasar said, "It'd probably be better outside."

Chase Mago nodded, and rose ponderously to his feet. "If you'll excuse me, sieura?" he said again.

"Of course," Javerry answered. "You'll excuse my not getting up. Get the door, Cass, would you?"

The boy scrambled to obey, staring up at the big engineer with something approaching awe. Recognizing the reaction, Silence smiled. She had felt much the same way about Chase Mago when she'd first met him.

The engineer returned quickly. Almost too quickly, Silence thought, and sat up, frowning.

"Problems, Julie?" Balthasar asked.

The engineer shook his head. "Nothing to speak of; a little distortion. I got through, told them we were all right, and signed off." He looked at Javerry. "I didn't want to take any chance of someone getting a fix on my signal."

"Thank you for that," Javerry retorted. She lifted her voice to a shout. "How're you doing in there, Quin?"

"Just finished, Mama." A moment later, Quin appeared at the inner door, saying shyly, "If you'd come with me, sieuri?"

Silence pulled herself to her feet, surprised again at how

exhausted she was, and Balthasar caught her arm, steadying her. Together, they followed Quin through the door into the huge, well-scrubbed kitchen, and out into the storeroom. Quin had done his best to make it comfortable, pushing aside the crates and barrels to clear a fairly large stretch of floor, and there was a pile of dust in one corner where he'd left his broom. He had brought in another of the ordinary-fire lamps as well, and it stood with an earthenware pitcher on an upturned metal crate. The four air mattresses lay in a neat row in the middle of the cleared space, and Quin shrugged a little uncomfortably.

"I thought you'd want to make your own arrangements."

"This is fine, thank you," Silence said.

"I brought some extra blankets," Quin went on, gesturing to a pile of dark cloth that lay on top of the nearest barrel. "They're not much to look at, but they are clean. The bathroom's back through the kitchen; the first door on your right takes you into the hall, and then it's the last door on the left. Is there anything else I can get you?"

Silence shook her head, and the others murmured vague answers.

"Then I'll say good night," Quin said, and backed away, closing the door firmly behind him.

"Well," Balthasar said, after a moment. He crossed the room on tiptoe and turned the door handle cautiously. It moved easily. He nodded to himself, and pushed the door gently open. "So we're not locked in," he said, and closed the door as quietly as he'd opened it.

"No," Marcinik said, and there was something in his voice that made Silence look up quickly. The colonel was standing by the storeroom's single window, staring out into the darkened yard. "But the dog's loose out there."

"They probably turn it loose every night," Chase Mago said, and seated himself, sighing, on the nearest mattress. It creaked, but held his weight.

Marcinik nodded reluctantly, and settled himself on the end mattress, tugging off his heavy boots. "Probably," he said.

"What do you think, Silence?" Balthasar asked.

"About what?" the pilot returned, yawning, and bent to unlace her own boots.

"Can we trust these people?" The Delian stretched, then began methodically loosening the clasps of his shirt. Silence watched idly, too tired to take any particular interest, but Marcinik politely turned his back.

"I'd trust them," Chase Mago said. "Look what's happened to them already."

"That's what worries me," Marcinik said.

Balthasar grinned. "Silence?" he said again.

The pilot sighed. "I don't know," she said at last. "I think—I feel that they can be trusted, but I haven't got any reasons for it, just a feeling."

"Your feelings, sieura doctor," Marcinik began, and bit off the rest of the sentence. He finished in a slightly stifled voice. "—should be good enough for anyone."

CHAPTER 6

Silence woke to the sound of rain, familiar even on this alien world, and a strange, damp smell. She sat up in her cocoon of blankets, nose wrinkling. It was not exactly unpleasant, she decided, but it was very strange.

"I think it's the vegetation," Balthasar said, rather doubtfully, and reached for the shirt Silence had discarded the night before. The pilot took it from him, shrugging it over her shoulders just as the Delian said, "And now what?"

Silence scowled, and concentrated on the shirt's clasps. Why ask me? she thought, but before she could think of a better answer, Marcinik said from the doorway, "I suggest we bring her Serenity and the magus here, and discuss it with them." He closed the door gently behind him, and leaned against it, a ragged towel dangling from one hand.

"Discuss what with who?" Chase Mago sat up, his mattress groaning, and rubbed at his eyes and beard.

"What we're going to do," Balthasar said.

Silence glanced quickly at him, but the Delian didn't seem inclined to continue. "Aili should be here," she said, "and so should Isambard." She lifted her hand as Balthasar frowned, cutting off his automatic retort. "Look, we're going to have to stay here a while, if the Javerrys will have us, don't you see? They know Earth, which we don't, and we're going to need their help if we're going to get off-world again. And we're going to need everybody's knowledge—especially Isambard's, but Aili's, too—if we're going to come up with a plan that stands even half a chance of working."

"You're right," Chase Mago said, yawning. Balthasar nodded, and made no further protest.

"Then I'll bring them," Marcinik said. "Assuming Sieura Javerry permits."

To Silence's surprise, Emma Javerry raised no serious objection to the idea of bringing the other off-worlders to her farm, suggesting only that they wait until the rain stopped. The star-travellers agreed to that readily enough, and Silence set herself the task of persuading Quin to tell her about his father's researches. It was not particularly difficult work—Quin was proud of his father's discoveries—but Silence found the whole experience unexpectedly depressing. The senior Javerry had been, from Quin's description, at least potentially a fairly skillful practitioner, but without a coherent paradigm to shape his work, he had drifted away from his earlier, successful symbolic experiments into attempts at prediction. He had been better at those than most, as he had the wild-card talent for it, but Silence found it even more frustrating that the father had just resumed his symbolic work a month before the attack that killed him. *That tends to support Quin's theory that the farm was attacked because of the elder Javerry's work,* Silence thought, *but I'd better not take sides in that argument.* Instead, she questioned Quin further about his father's predictions, and particularly the empress he'd seen.

Quin shrugged uncomfortably, searching for the right words. He was afraid of offending her, Silence realized, afraid of offending both because of the images his father had seen and because of the rituals involved.

"Pap—he set up the circle, and the table," Quin began, and darted a quick glance, appeal and apology combined, toward the pilot.

Silence nodded, strictly controlling her automatic reaction. That would be the neo-Apollonarian ritual, long ago rejected in the human-settled worlds, mentioned in the magi's curriculum only as an example—*the* example—of a deceitful symbolic connection. In actuality, of course, the connections were there—the symbols did not, could not, lie—but led nowhere real. The ritual would enhance whatever native

talent that practitioner had for prediction, would even enhance the practitioner's sensitivity to the subliminal clues
visible in even the most skeptical querant's posture and movements, but, unlike the most other operations of the Art, it
could go no further. "The ritual of Apollonius," she said. "I
know it."

Quin nodded. "Well, he set it up, at the right time and in
the right conjunctions, following all the preparations, and at
just the right moment—I was timing it, I know that part was
done absolutely correctly—he cut the cards and the Empress
came up. Pap put away the rest of the cards then, and set the
Empress in the place he'd made ready, and waited." Quin's
voice faltered. "I suppose he was meditating. Anyway, it
seemed like forever, and then he said, 'The empress is coming.' He said that again, and then he said, 'She will have the
twelve-star crown, and she will be the one of three. But she's
coming, Quin she'll be here.'" Quin stopped abruptly, as
though embarrassed, and shrugged again. "That was what
happened, Silence—what he saw, anyway."

The pilot nodded slowly. "He had the talent for the Art,"
she said, and closed her mouth firmly over the rest of the
thought. Quin did not need to be told again that his father
had wasted his skills, that his life's work—the work for which
he had died—was a blind alley.

"We looked some of it up afterward," Quin said. There was
an odd note in his voice, almost defiant, and Silence gave him
a questioning glance. The young man looked away, blushing
hotly.

"Well, I did, anyway," he muttered.

"You have a hieroglyphica?" the pilot asked.

Quin shook his head. "No, but you can find the meanings
of things in other books."

If you work hard enough at it, Silence thought dryly. She
said, "So what did you find out?"

"Not a whole lot," Quin admitted. He looked away again,
embarrassed. "The Empress—the card, that is—is supposed
to be an Earth-mother symbol. You're not quite what I'd
expected."

Silence laughed, but smothered the response as Quin
blushed even more hotly than before. "That's one of the

meanings, yes, but not the only one." In spite of herself, her voice took on the precision drilled into her on Solitudo Hermae. "On a higher level, it simply means creativity, creativity specifically of the mundane world—the magus as operator within the mundane universe. The twelve-star crown means control of those forces—the twelve stars are the twelve operations of the Great Transformation. The association of the number three—among its other meanings, the number of synthesis and the basis of harmony—with the symbol of the empress is fairly obvious."

"I thought that meant there would be three of you," Quin said, rather dryly.

Silence flushed. It was annoying at her age, to be caught showing off. . . . She controlled herself instantly, and said, "There's that, too, though the Empress is the third card, and the number/symbol link's always been there. It could be either."

The rain had stopped by noon of the third day, but Marcinik waited until the next morning to return to *Recusante*. Quin offered the use of the farm's drag-cat, and the colonel accepted, taking Balthasar with him to manage the machine. Even with its assistance, however, they did not return to the farm until late in the afternoon of the next day. Silence, watching from the doorway of the farmhouse, saw Javerry's eyes narrow at the sight of Aili's Bethlemite disguise, and braced herself to meet the Earth-woman's disapproval. To her surprise, however, Javerry's tone was merely thoughtful.

"Now I wonder, did that fashion come from off-world?"

"Fashion?" Silence said.

Javerry nodded. "Started when I was a girl, among the rich folks, the real Unionists. Girls—and some of the boys, for that matter—wearing veils or little masks, or just brushing their hair half over their faces. Still popular in the mainurbs, Quin tells me, for fancy dress." She looked directly at Silence. "Did this come from off-world, too?"

"I don't know," Silence said. Javerry frowned, and the younger woman added hastily, "In the Hegemony—that's one of the associations of worlds—the laws say a woman has to keep her face covered in public, and it's become common practice all over human-settled space. But I don't know if it ever was a Rose Worlder practice, and it's the Rose Worlders who're in charge here."

Javerry grunted. "And you say she's a princess?"

"Yes."

The older woman shook her head, apparently disconcerted by the baldness of the answer. Silence bit her tongue to keep from saying anything more. Let Aili deal with this, she thought; let her win Javerry over. The Princess Royal was more than capable of that.

"And the old man," Javerry continued. "You say he's a wizard, like you?"

"He's my teacher," Silence said. She made herself add, "He's far more experienced than I am."

Javerry nodded, half to herself. "We'll see," she said. "We'll see."

Silence hid her smile as Aili swung herself easily out of the drag-cat's short bed, barely touching Marcinik's steadying hand. Her eyes flickered above the veil as she favored Javerry with a single, searching glance. From that instant, she treated Javerry precisely as she would treat a noble landholder, without arrogance, but with due awareness of her own worth. It was the right approach, Silence thought: Javerry was not the woman to admire a pretense of weakness.

In the end, they spent almost two weeks at the Javerrys' farm, and most of that time was spent picking the Javerrys' brains for information about the urban net to the south. Quin, it appeared, had contacts—friends—in the nearest suburb, and through them was able to obtain local maps and a copy of the regulations-book for the mainurb farther to the south. He was also able to barter for Earth-style clothes, including a loose coat large enough for Chase Mago. Silence protested, afraid the younger Javerry would put himself in danger, but Quin shook his head.

"Everyone knows there're a few people living in the exurb," he said, "but nobody, except maybe the real highest-ups, cares a whole lot. I mean, the people down in Diesmon know me—know I live outside, though I've made damn sure they don't know where. And they don't really care, as long as I don't try to persuade anyone to join me. They figure the suburb'll catch up with me sooner or later." A shadow seemed to pass over his face then. "That was why we figured we weren't in any danger, when Pap started his work. But those were the real Unionists, not the local authority."

He shook the memory away, and Silence hastily changed the subject, turning her attention instead to the maps and regulations-book he had brought. Over the next few days, she and the other star-travellers studied these closely, questioning the Javerrys, and particularly Quin, about everything they could think of, until they had built up a picture of the conditions inside the urban net. As they worked, it became clear that neither Aili nor Isambard could pass for Earth natives—it was impossible to meet the legal requirement of the veil, or for Isambard to hide his knowledge of the Art— and it was decided that they would remain with the ship. Marcinik, with some reluctance, agreed to stay with them.

Once that decision had been made, Silence turned her attention back to the books, and spent several days reducing all the accumulated information to a pattern that would fit into the framework of the Grand Memory Theater. Despite all her work, however, she knew there were entirely too many gaps in their knowledge. She knew, too, that they were gaps she could not fill from the Javerrys' farm.

She said as much that evening, when she and the other star-travellers had gathered around the low table in the farmhouse's central room. Balthasar nodded in thoughtful agreement, both hands wrapped around a mug of the herbal tea Javerry brewed nightly.

"I think it's amazing how much you've gathered—and how efficiently you've ordered it," Quin said, with just a hint of reproach in his tone.

"Hah." Javerry spoke from the kitchen doorway, her hands wrapped in a tattered towel. Isambard had examined her injured leg, and despite her protests, had performed a simple operation to speed its healing. She was able to walk without her crutch now, though she still limped a little, favoring the mending leg. "At least she has the sense to recognize her limitations." She came in to join them, seating herself in her favorite chair beneath the suspended lantern.

Aili said softly, "Silence is right, of course."

Chase Mago looked up sharply, glancing from the Princess

Royal to Silence. "Surely you don't mean for us to go into the mainurb now. . . ." His voice trailed off as Silence nodded.

"The longer we delay, the more chance there is that the ship will be traced, despite all the wards we set on it. We can't learn much more here, and I'm afraid we'll put the Javerrys in danger. I think we ought to go now, or at least very soon, within the next few days." She glanced around the circle, and saw Marcinik nod thoughtfully. Balthasar smiled at her, but said nothing.

"I see your point," Chase Mago said, "and I admit it's a good one. But the nearest star port we know of is on the next landmass. I don't know if this mainurb/suburb mess will have what I need to repair the ship—and even if it does, how're we going to get hold of it?"

Silence sighed, wishing the engineer would not make things so difficult. "Man's Island's a major government center. From everything Quin's told us, there's a sort of Pale around it, and a black market in curiosities."

"My father used to buy things there," Quin put in.

"Exactly." Silence glanced again around the circle of faces, softened and made strange by the golden light from the lamps. She had grown comfortable on the Javerry farm, she realized; it would be painful to leave it. Or perhaps it was less the farm itself than the settled routine of its daily life, so different in its specifics from the routine of star travel, but oddly familiar in its ordered complexity. She shook the thought away and said, "I think we can deal with a black market. We should be able to get what you need, Julie."

The big engineer shrugged, unconvinced. Balthasar said, "Come on, Julie, it's no different from the Wrath."

"It's very different," Chase Mago snapped. "There're too damn many machines." He glanced to his left then, toward Javerry. "I beg your pardon, sieura. Your serenity."

Javerry laughed softly. Aili said, as if he hadn't spoken, "I think it has to be now."

Chase Mago sighed, and looked at Silence. "All right." He still did not sound convinced, but the pilot knew she could ignore his doubts for the moment. "This Pale—the black market you mentioned, Quin. It's around Man's Island itself?"

The younger Javerry nodded, reaching for the largest of

the maps lying on the low table. "The island itself is here," he said, pointing. "It's off-limits, as you can see. It's the areas on the shore, here, where they say you can buy—things."

"Man's Island's a long way south of here," Balthasar said. "How do we get there?"

"There's a high-speed transit line that runs from Diesmon all the way into the mainurb," Quin offered, but the Delian shook his head.

"Transit lines mean tickets, and that means money. Probably ID, too, and we don't have either."

Isambard stirred then. "Identification is not a problem," he said. "If Sieura Javerry will allow me to view her papers, you and I, Silence, can copy them easily enough."

Balthasar nodded, but said, "Money?"

Javerry said, "I have money, credit and such. You're welcome to it." Silence glanced at her, startled, and the older woman said, "This was what Javerry wanted; he said you'd be here. It's the least I can do."

"Thank you," Silence said, after a moment. "We—this is very generous of you. We're truly grateful."

Isambard cleared his throat, frowning slightly. "Indeed, sieura, the offer is most generous, but we need not presume so far. We—Silence and I—should be able to create as much cash as we need, if you will only provide us with a sample."

"Cash?" Javerry said, and laughed.

The older magus's frown deepened, and Quin said hastily, "Most people are tied into the net's credit lines. But, Mama, you haven't used those numbers in years."

"They're still good," Javerry said.

"Still, we don't want to put you in any danger," Silence cut in, forestalling any further comment from Isambard. "I think it'd be better if we used cash, even if it does look a little odd." The other star-travellers nodded, and Javerry shrugged.

"Whatever you want, then. There are bills in the kitchen—you can fetch them, Cass—that you can copy."

"Thank you," Silence said again. If the truth were to be told, she was just as glad not to have to try to deal with the complex workings of the urban net's financial systems. Quin had tried to explain them to her, and to the other star-travellers, but the idea of a system in which no tokens of value ever changed hands was completely alien to all of them. "May we see your papers, too?"

"I'll get them," Quin said, and vanished into the farm's back rooms.

Silence leaned back in her chair, suddenly afraid. Once the copying was done—and that was a simple, almost mechanical task—they would have to go south, into the immense city Quin had described, a city full of machines, and hostile to her Art. . . . She pulled away from that line of thought, angry at herself for letting her fears run away with her. They would manage somehow—after all, this could not be that different from Delos itself. And, in any case, they had no choice.

Silence spent most of the next three days closeted in the remaining outbuilding with the older magus, producing first the raw copies of the papers and bills that the Javerrys provided, and then making the minute changes, cosmetic and structural, that made them usable. Balthasar watched nervously, unable to stay away.

"They must have ways to check for created money," he said, for the fifth time.

Silence put aside the bills she had been working on, and turned to face him, framing a blistering retort. Before she could speak, however, Isambard said, "Captain Balthasar, such means are certainly available in the rest of human-settled space, and were we dealing with Rose Worlders alone I would not risk it. However, to detect such counterfeits requires the Art, and the Art is clearly not much known on this world. Does this resolve your difficulties?"

It was the first time the magus had ever spoken with such annoyance, and Silence hid her smile. Balthasar made a face, but nodded.

"Then have the kindness to go away and let us work." Isambard turned back to his improvised equipment without waiting for an answer.

Balthasar frowned, and Silence said, "Do it, Denis."

"All right." The Delian turned on his heel and stalked away, but paused in the doorway. "Sorry," he muttered, and was gone.

Silence smiled to herself, unaccountably cheered, and turned back to her own work. There wasn't very much to be done,

she realized suddenly, just a few more serial numbers to be
changed, and then they would be ready to leave. She looked
up, and Isambard said, "Yes. When you've finished, you
might want to begin packing."

There wasn't that much to pack, Silence thought that evening, staring at the single satchel that held her and her
husbands' belongings. She had left her starbooks with the
ship, for fear their off-world information would betray her;
without them, even with the Earth-style clothes Quin had
provided, the satchel was barely full. She shook herself,
unable to shrug off her sudden depression, and crawled into
bed between her husbands.

The next morning dawned clear and cool. Silence picked at
the breakfast Javerry had prepared for them, and seized the
first chance she could find to make her escape. I don't think
it's true that you get used to being afraid, she thought, as she
made her way toward the outbuilding where Isambard slept.
At least I haven't—and I didn't notice Denis or Julie eating
too heartily, either. The thought was perversely encouraging,
and she felt a little more confident as she tapped on the
window.

"Come in," Isambard called.

Silence reached for the latch, and felt the lock that held it
fade under her hand. She turned the handle as though she
had noticed nothing, and stepped into the musty room.
Isambard was standing behind the table that had served as
his workbench over the past few days, staring thoughtfully at
the few pieces of improvised equipment that remained. An
old-fashioned carryall of woven plastic lay at his feet, and
there were several odd, paper-wrapped packets on the table
as well.

"Good morning, Silence," the magus said, without looking
up. "The papers and the money are here, a package for each
of you, and such materials as I can spare have been packed
for your use. I think that is all."

"Thanks," Silence said, and reached for the packet that
bore her own name. She broke it open, even though she
knew what it contained, and checked the papers before tucking the leather ID folder into one pocket and the money-

wallet into another. She picked up the other packets, and shouldered the carryall as well. "What about the rest of this?"

"I thought it could be left for the young sieur Javerry," Isambard answered. "He seemed interested in pursuing his father's researches."

"I just hope he's more careful than his father was," Silence muttered.

"He has had an object lesson," Isambard said dryly, and motioned for her to precede him into the farmyard.

The drag-cat sat idly in front of the house, Quin leaning against the steering tackle. Balthasar was already sprawled in its bed. He lifted a hand in greeting as the magi approached, then reached down to help Silence aboard. "Julie's getting our stuff," he said, "and Sieura Javerry's packed us a travelling-lunch."

"Picnic," Quin corrected, rather diffidently.

"Picnic," Balthasar repeated, shrugging. "So we're off."

We certainly are, Silence thought, and handed him his papers. In the same moment, the door of the house opened and Chase Mago appeared, the clothes-satchel balanced on his shoulder. Marcinik and Aili followed, the Princess Royal fidgeting with the draperies that concealed her face. Balthasar lifted an eyebrow, and Silence kicked him, not gently. It was hard enough for Aili to stay behind—especially when her presence was keeping Marcinik out of the action—without Balthasar making comments.

"Keep your mouth shut, Denis, do you hear me?" she whispered.

Balthasar sighed. Silence glared at him, and the Delian shrugged. "I hear," he said. For once, Silence thought, I think he means it. She nodded at him, and took the satchel Chase Mago passed to her, shoving it out of the way against the side walls.

"Is everything set?" Quin asked, from the driver's perch.

Silence nodded, unwilling to delay any longer. "I think so. Yes, we're ready."

"Wait a minute." The farmhouse door had opened again. Javerry herself stood beside the drag-cat, a covered basket in one hand. Cass hovered at her side, his expression at once excited and afraid. "You'll want your lunch," the older woman

said. Without waiting for an answer, she hoisted the basket
into the drag-cat. Balthasar took it from her, sliding it toward
the other carryalls at the front of the car.

"Good luck," Aili said, and Marcinik echoed her.

Isambard gave his student a long, appraising glance. "Be
careful, Silence. Use the Art as I have taught you."

The pilot nodded, wishing they would start.

"So." Javerry's harsh voice was deliberately cheerful. "Be
off with you, Quin, or you won't get to the station in time."

"We'll get there" Quin said. "Don't worry so much, Mama."
He slipped the drag-cat into gear, drowning out any answer
Javerry might have made. Silence grabbed for the nearest
handhold as the machine lurched into motion, tracks digging
into the loose ground. They were off at last.

The path that the drag-cat followed through the woods was
very rough, the ground still muddy from the rains, but the
machine's tracks handled it without too much difficulty. After
perhaps an hour's travelling, the path—it was little more than
twin ruts cutting through the worst of the underbrush, Silence thought—joined a wider track, and Quin swung the
drag-cat onto it. More vehicles obviously used this road: the
ground was flattened in less regular patterns, the mud showing the tracks of several different types of machine, and
something heavy had been dragged down the very center of
the trail, cutting a shallow ditch now almost filled with stag-
nant water. Quin was careful to keep the drag-cat out of that
depression, choosing instead to let the machine wallow over
the rocks that studded the rest of the trail.

The jolting made that part of the trip seem interminable,
but it was actually only two hours by Chase Mago's chronometer before they reached the point at which the trail joined a
semi-paved road. Silence gave a sigh of relief as the drag-cat
hauled itself up onto the cracked surface, and and saw her
emotion reflected in the other's faces. Quin glanced over his
shoulder, grinning.

"Not too bad, eh? All downhill from here."

He meant that literally as well as figuratively, Silence
realized after a moment. The new road twisted and turned,
the drag-cat veering from side to side to avoid the worst of
the breaks in the paving, but it was indeed sloping always

gently downward. She closed her eyes, trying to picture the maps she had studied back on *Recusante*. If they were going downhill, she decided at last, they must be moving south and east, toward the flat land of the coast, and toward the mainurb that covered it.

"How much farther?" Balthasar asked, after a while.

"About another ten kilometers," Quin answered, without turning. "Then we hit the station road—it rings the Diesmon suburb—and take it on in to the terminus."

Balthasar nodded, and settled back into the bed of the drag-cat, closing his eyes, seemingly oblivious to the jolting. Silence eyed him enviously, then, sighing, resigned herself to the discomfort. This was the easy part of the trip, after all; things would be different at the Diesmon Terminus. Quin had promised that they wouldn't be conspicuous there, that enough squatters moved in and out of the exurb for their presence to attract little notice, but the pilot could not feel as confident about it as the younger Javerry apparently did. Still, she told herself, he knew this world, and she did not. They would have to trust him.

The battered road got better as they approached the larger station road, and the junction itself had actually been repaired so recently that the black patches had barely begun to crumble. There was even a stamped metal sign to mark the junction, but it displayed only a single, south-pointing arrow, despite the fact that the station road ran north as well. Silence frowned, curious, but Balthasar spoke first.

"What's up that way?"

"Squatters' town." Quin spoke brusquely, wrestling the drag-cat onto the new surface. After a moment, as the cat steadied, he spoke again, his voice calmer. "It isn't really a town yet, just a collection of houses and a lady who runs a sort of store, but they'll probably attach it in the next census. They might even run a spur out there, if there's enough people."

"What do they consider to be enough people?" Silence asked.

Quin shrugged. "Anything over a dozen adults."

Chase Mago whistled, but Silence nodded. "It makes sense," she said, as much to herself as to the engineer. "If the point

is to keep control of people, what better way to do it than to
tie them into the rest of the mainurb?" Still, it was interesting that the Rose Worlders found it worth their while to
control as few as a dozen people.

The station road was in much better shape than the other
tracks they had been using, but just as empty. They did not
encounter any other vehicles until they were almost within
sight of the station itself, and then it was only another drag-
cat, this one driven by a scrawny adolescent. Its bed was full
of oddly shaped bundles, piled around a central crate. Quin
nodded a greeting as the two machines edged past each
other, calling, "Did you get the parts, Mattie?"

"Just came yesterday," the other driver—it was a girl,
Silence realized, with some surprise—called back, and let her
drag-cat grind to a stop. "Going in town?"

Quin geared down his own machine until it was moving at
a snail's pace. "That's right. Said I'd give these folks a ride,
too." He nodded over his shoulder toward the star-travellers
crouching in the back of the cat.

Silence held her breath, but the girl nodded, and gave
them a friendly smile.

"Settling?" she asked.

Silence felt the words catch in her throat, almost strangling
her. Chase Mago returned the girl's smile. "We think, maybe,"
he said, with a passable imitation of the local accent.

The girl nodded again, her interest apparently satisfied.
She adjusted her gear lever, setting her drag-cat in motion.
"Good luck to you, then," she called, over the sudden noise
of the engine, and let the machine make its way down the
road.

Silence realized she had been holding her breath, and let it
out with a gasp. Quin smiled. "You see?" he said. "I told you
no one would think about it."

Balthasar grunted. "Let's just hope the station folk are as
easygoing."

The station itself was a bizarre sight, a long, low building
made of the metal-and-poured-stone that Silence always associated with pre-War construction. This one, however, was
obviously new and spotlessly kept, doubly weird against the
massive trees that rose above its polished roof. Even when

the drag-cat swung onto the narrow approach road, and she could see the ramshackle buildings—mostly wood frame, occasionally stacked stone, never the stuff of which the station was made—that were the Diesmon suburb, the station retained its incongruity.

Quin turned the drag-cat into a barren square of packed earth, let it grind its way to the edge, and cut the engine. Silence, stretching, levered herself out of the cat's bed and turned to take her carryall from the engineer. A moment later the others had joined her, and then Quin straightened from under the nose of the cat, wiping his hand on his trousers.

"All set," he said, in answer to their questioning glances. "The fluid has to be checked occasionally, that's all. Are you ready?"

Silence took a deep breath, but nodded. "We're ready."

"I'll wish you luck now, then." Quin led them back over the packed dirt, then across the narrow approach road and up a short row of steps into the terminus itself. Inside, the building was cool, and very damp, as though years of rain had seeped into the poured-stone walls and never been released. Silence shivered, hugging her thin jacket against herself. Overhead, polished metal arches defined the distant ceiling; a flickering notice board hung from the intersection of the arches, constantly changing menus displaying the departure and arrival schedules, and the ways in which the Diesmon line joined the wider network. The pilot paused beneath that board, staring up at the palm-sized letters, even though they had chosen their time before they left the Javerrys' farm. At least the Earth natives used a simplified form of the usual coinë, she thought, watching the familiar letters dissolve and reform. The Rose Worlders didn't take that away from them. . . . No, she realized suddenly, it works the other way. Earth used this language first, invented these symbols to encode it. We're the ones who changed it, not them. The thought was dizzying, as though she'd suddenly looked down from a very great height. She was glad when Balthasar caught her arm.

"At least the trans is on time," he said, a little too loudly, his eyes fixed on a point somewhere beyond her shoulder.

Silence froze, then turned as nonchalantly as she could to face whatever it was that had frightened the Delian. A pair of men in the saffron-colored jackets that Quin had described as Transit livery were watching them from beside a massive, box-shaped machine. Lights flashed across its dull surface and from its various offices; a sign above its central panel read *Tickets/Inbound.* "We'd better get the tickets, then," she said aloud, through stiff lips.

Balthasar nodded, unspeaking.

"Don't worry," Quin said, and, unbelievably, smiled. Without further ado, he set off toward the Transport men, lifting his hand in greeting. The smaller of the two waved back, and came to meet him, though their conversation was too quiet for the star-travellers to hear more than the pitch of the voices. After a moment, the Transport man nodded, gesturing toward a distant door. Quin thanked him, and walked on; the Transport man walked with him, still talking idly. The second Transport man took a few steps away from the box-like machine, watching them.

Silence took a deep breath. Quin had done his best for them; now it was their turn to act. "Let's go," she said again, and forced her stiff body into motion. The others followed at her back.

The walk across the station's plastic-tiled floor seemed interminable—Silence was remotely amazed at how long it seemed to take her to cover the dozen meters—but at last they'd reached the machine. The Transport man was less than two meters away, to her left. Carefully, she did not look at him, fixing her eyes on the banks of controls that covered the machine's face. For a moment, the coinë lettering swam before her eyes, refusing to focus; she took a deep breath, forcing herself to concentrate. One slot was for the plastic cards that served for credit on Earth; another eventually produced the tickets, but she could not seem to find the place to insert the sheaf of bills she had ready in her pocket, or even a way of finding out the precise fare. There was a single-pad keyboard below the machine's display screen, but the screen itself was blank. Experimentally, she touched what she thought should be the inquiry key, but nothing happened.

"Silence," Balthasar hissed. "For God's sake, do something."

The pilot glanced up, and saw the Transport man watching them, a light frown on his long-jawed face. She looked away again hastily, but not before the Transport man had seen the movement.

"Damn it," Chase Mago said, very softly. "He's coming over here." There was note of suppressed panic in his voice.

Silence bit back a curse of her own, and turned to face the approaching stranger. She knew she could not manage a convincing smile, and fought only to keep from looking too hunted. The Transport man stopped just out of reach—though not out of range of Balthasar's heylin, Silence thought. But that would betray them before they began.

"Can I help you folks?" The Transport man's voice was perfectly neutral, touched with the same flat accent as the Javerrys'. He glanced at the ticket machine, and the neutrality seemed to ease a little. "Going inbound?"

Silence nodded, hardly daring to speak. "That's right."

The Transport man gestured toward a sort of drawer set into one side of the machine, just to the left of the keyboard. "You've got to pay first—new rules."

"Oh?" Silence fumbled with the wad of bills in her pocket, pulled out one almost at random, and slid it blindly toward the slot. As the edge of the bill entered the machine, something seized it, drawing it fully into the slot. A chime sounded, and the keyboard sprang to life. Silence gave a sigh of relief, and turned her attention to the letters forming on the screen, trying to ignore the hovering presence of the Transport man. The codes were listed by exchanges rather than by final destination; she studied the system for a few moments, letting the words scroll by, until she could guess at the overall pattern.

"Giving up the exurb?" the Transport man asked.

Silence hesitated, unable to answer safely while most of her mind was focussed on the unfolding system, and Balthasar said, "Yeah. We've had about enough of it."

"Going anywhere in particular?" There was no particular interest in the Transport man's voice, Silence thought, but any wrong answer—any odd answer—would certainly turn his idle curiosity into distrust. She touched a set of keys, praying it would call the menu she'd intended, and was rewarded with the codes that controlled access to the longer distance lines. She pretended to study them for a second, listening for the Delian's answer.

Balthasar shrugged, the movement painfully casual. "South," he said, and somehow managed a quick grin. "Just about anywhere'll do."

The Transport man nodded, leaning to look over the pilot's shoulder. Silence hesitated for an instant, and then, when it was obvious that the man wasn't going to leave, reluctantly touched the key sequence that called up all possible runs to Man's Island. The Transport man whistled.

"You're brave."

Silence managed what she hoped would be an embarrassed smile. "We may not go there," she began, and Chase Mago cut in quickly, "We haven't entirely decided."

The Transport man shook his head, but before he could continue the conversation, something on the far side of the lobby caught his eye. "Well, good luck," he said, and strode away.

Silence took a deep breath, feeling some of the tension drain from her body. After a moment, she bent her head to scan the listing, looking for the next departure.

"It's all right," Chase Mago said, after a moment. "He's talking to Quin."

"Let's hope that's good," Balthasar growled. "Come on, Silence, let's get the tickets."

"Give me a minute," Silence snapped. "I'm still not sure I understand the system—ah, there." The screen showed the trans they wanted, leaving Diesmon in less than a local hour, then linking onto a larger trans at the Sayl'm suburb, which then continued along the coast, picking up other, smaller trans until it reached its end point at Man's Island. It was a long ride, almost twenty hours, with a lot of stops along the way—but at least, Silence thought, as she keyed in the code that passed the full schedule in review across the little screen, they didn't have to worry about making connections anywhere along the way.

"It looks right," Chase Mago said. "How do we pay?"

"I'm not sure," Silence began, but at that moment the

display loop reached its end, and a new message, which gave prices and instructions, was fed onto the screen. Silence typed in the codes it listed for three round-trip tickets, and fed the required bills into the cash slot. The screen blanked itself, and then a thin pad of paper was extruded from the ticket slot. She took it, handing it automatically to Chase Mago, and the slot spat a second booklet, and then a third.

Balthasar took his warily, flipping through the stiff pages. "You use these to unlock the car doors, right?"

"That's what Quin said," Silence answered. She glanced over her shoulder, and saw the younger Javerry still deep in conversation with the Transit men. He saw her look, and lifted his hand in careless farewell. The pilot copied the gesture, wishing there were time for more, and turned away. To her right, a bright orange sign proclaimed "Departures"; she turned toward it, the other star-travellers following.

The sign directed them to a flight of stairs leading down into a space lit in an unnatural, blue-tinged light. Silence slowed, but made herself keep walking, following the stairs downward into a vast, barrel-vaulted space. Three walkways extended like fingers from the platform at the base of the stairs, and there were dirty, ditch-like docking spaces in between the walks. A silvery cylinder—no, Silence realized an instant later, it was a cylinder made of a dozen smooth segments, almost perfectly joined—lay beside one of the walkways. A woman was walking up and down beside it, gently bouncing the child she carried in her arms, but there was no one else in sight.

"It's a tube train," Balthasar said, and there was a note almost of indignation in his voice.

It did look something like the trains she'd seen on Delos, Silence thought, but there were differences. Instead of the massive, brown-stained wheels of a normal tube-train cast from elemental earth and tuned to the harmony of the planetary core, this train—*trans*, she corrected herself, frowning—had dozens of tiny, silvery wheels, the metal showing none of the peacock marking that might mean a magi had had a hand in its casting.

"No." Chase Mago shook his head. "No, look, no drive

wheels and no resonators—and no baffling, either. It's something else. Something mechanical."

The note of distrust was strong in his voice, and Silence found herself nodding in agreement. Whatever it was that powered this machine, it was something profoundly alien to everything she had ever learned. Her steps slowed still further. She did not want to touch any of those shiny doors, did not want to enter any of those bullet-like compartments. . . .

Balthasar grunted then, breaking the spell. "Whatever runs it, it looks like a tube train and it acts like a tube train." He glanced at Silence and added, with emphasis, "Nothing more."

Silence grimaced, annoyed at her own weakness, and reached into her pocket for the book of tickets. Flipping back the cover, she studied the cards for an instant, then tore loose the first one. "Which car?"

Balthasar shrugged. Chase Mago said, "In the middle?" He paused, staring at the train. "How do we tell which ones are occupied, anyway?"

"A green light means full," Balthasar said, impatiently. He stalked forward along the walkway, and jammed his ticket into the meter of the first unoccupied car. The door popped open a few centimeters; he caught the handle and pulled it back against its stops. At his gesture, Silence stepped up into the car, tossing her carryall ahead of her. As soon as her weight was fully inside the trans, a buzzer sounded, and the door jerked itself out of Balthasar's hand, slamming shut behind her. Silence choked back a startled cry, reaching for her carryall and the heylin concealed in its lining. A moment later, the door opened again, and Balthasar gave her a sheepish grin.

"I guess they want to make sure everybody's got a ticket," he said. Behind him, Chase Mago shook his head, and fed his ticket into the machine. The only apparent result was a faint click, but the door did not close as the engineer climbed into the car. Balthasar tossed the last carryall in after the others, then handed in Javerry's food basket, and climbed in himself. The buzzer sounded, and the door sealed itself behind them. Overhead, a ventilator fan began to whine, and a mechanical female voice said, "This is Trans East number 627 south. You are in a coastal-route car. This is Trans East number 627 south. You are in a coastal-route car. If you wish to change cars, or are in the wrong Trans, please touch the alarm button located beneath the speaker, and a Transport worker will be with you momentarily. We will be departing in twenty minutes. Thank you."

"That's ours?" Chase Mago asked.

Silence nodded, looking around the confined space. The little car seemed comfortable enough, at least for now, though she had her doubts about how comfortable it would seem at the end of the twenty-hour trip. There were broad, heavily padded benches at each end of the closed space, and storage nets hung above each one. Balthasar, following the direction of her glance, nodded, and began securing the carryalls, tightening the netting carefully around them. The cubicle in the corner was marked with an unfamiliar symbol, but could only be one thing; Silence unlatched the door anyway, and was glad to find the sanitary facilities.

"I've found the environmental box," Balthasar announced, and turned out the car lights to prove it. Chase Mago swore at him. When the lights returned, the Delian looked somewhat chastened. "I was looking for—ah, there."

Overhead, the speaker crackled to life, tinny music pouring into the car. Silence winced, and Balthasar hastily adjusted the volume, until the sound was barely audible.

"Do we have to listen to that?" Chase Mago asked.

"Quin said the line keeps passengers posted on news and such," Balthasar answered. "That should be the channel."

"I'm not sure it's worth it," Chase Mago said, but shrugged.

Silence said, "It can't hurt to know what's going on."

Some time later—the repetitive music blurred her perception of time—a chime sounded, and the mechanical voice spoke again, overriding the music. "This is Trans East 627 south. Last call, please. Last call."

The voice repeated the message twice more, but Silence was no longer listening, staring instead out the car's tiny window. The station was empty now, the woman with the child presumably back in a compartment; the only sign of life was the display board on the far wall. Even as she watched, the departure listing for Trans East 627 winked out, and the trans jerked slowly into motion.

Surprisingly, the machine was very quiet, especially when compared to the tube trains on Delos. The driving engine rose from a distant whine to a dull, steady rumbling not much louder than the background hum of a stopped-down harmonium. After the first minutes, the jolting stopped, too, settling to a steady, regular swaying.

Leaving the station, the trans entered a long, unlighted tunnel. Silence thought she could feel a steady acceleration, but without visual references, she was unprepared for the moment the trans flashed out of the tunnel onto the elevated track. The trans was going very fast indeed, so fast that the treetops, rising just to the edge of the tran's windows, merged into an indistinct green blur. She edged forward on the padded bench, trying to focus on some individual object, a tree, or some part of the track itself, but the trans was moving too quickly. The effect was literally dizzying; she leaned back again, avoiding the windows until the dizziness passed.

"We are moving," Balthasar said. The pilot was maliciously pleased to see that he, too, avoided looking out the windows.

"Well, obviously they'd have to maintain a substantial speed, to make Man's Island in twenty hours with all the stops," Chase Mago said.

"Substantial," Balthasar repeated. "Yeah, you could say that."

The worst of the dizziness had vanished now. Silence glanced cautiously toward the nearer window, keeping her eyes away from the rushing vegetation at the bottom of the frame. The distant hills, and the band of settlements—shiny roofs and strangely spidery towers competing with more solid structures—in front of them were still moving rather too fast for something so far away, but the effect was not quite as disconcerting as before. Then, unexpectedly, the trans began to slow, engines whining. The tracks ducked again into a tunnel, still slowing, and finally ground to a halt against a platform that seemed to be a copy of the one at Diesmon. Silence leaned against the window, watching curiously as the few passengers on the platform selected their cars. No one got off. A few moments after the trans had pulled into the station, a buzzer sounded, and it began to move again.

The countryside flattened as the trans moved south and east, but the pattern of settlement did not change much. The knots of settled land grew larger, the buildings more complex, but the land between the suburbs remained empty, overgrown. Once, Silence thought she caught a glimpse of some broken structure in the center of one barren spot, but the trans was past before she could be sure. I wonder where they get the food to supply all the people? she wondered. Each of the suburbs they passed looked easily large enough to hold several thousand people; the station suburbs, glimpsed only briefly as the trans entered the braking tunnel, looked much larger. Quin had said that the Rose Worlders—Unionists, she corrected herself—farmed the uninhabited interior of the continent; still, the transport costs must be very high. And therefore, she added thoughtfully, there must be some compelling reason for forcing people into the mainurb. If I could just figure out what it is. . . . The connection eluded her. She leaned back against the padding, shaking her head.

The sun was setting as they reached the larger suburb of Sayl'm. This time, the trans did not duck into a tunnel, but slowed above ground. Silence frowned, unsure of what was happening, and in the same moment saw that there was a second elevated track next to theirs, running at a shallow angle toward a point of meeting. The trans slowed further as it reached the intersection, and Silence pressed herself against the window, trying to see back along the second track. For an instant, she thought she saw another trans moving toward them along it, but then her own trans had moved forward, cutting off her view. It couldn't've been, she told herself, but felt her muscles tense anyway. A moment later, there was a gentle but perceptible thump at the back of the car, and the trans began picking up speed again. Of course, Silence berated herself. This is where our trans links up with the main line—and I'd guess the link was just made.

"That was neat," Chase Mago said idly, and the pilot was glad that the dimming light hid her blushes.

They ate Javerry's picnic in the sunset light, then settled back against the padding. Balthasar adjusted the car's lights to a comfortable level, then, after a moment's thought, banished the tedious music. There was something about it—about the trans in its entirety, Silence thought, that created a strange lethargy. The star-travellers had barely spoken a dozen words to each other since leaving Diesmon, caught up in the passing scenery and the weird, noiseless travel. It was not a comfortable feeling, either. Now that night had fallen, and there was nothing outside to distract her, Silence felt a dull ache beginning behind her temples, and a strange queasiness at the pit of her stomach. She swallowed hard, wondering if she had been wise to eat at all.

"Look," Balthasar said. "We're coming up on another suburb."

Grateful for the distraction, Silence glanced out the window. At night, the suburbs turned to heaps of lights, carbon-crystals spilled out carelessly across the countryside. Trails of lights led away from the suburb—lighted roads, Silence guessed, or more of the transit line. Another suburb appeared almost before the first had been left behind, and a third was just visible in the distance, barely more than a scattering of lights on the horizon. They must be approaching the mainurb, she thought, trying not to feel the worsening headache, or whatever invisible line divided the suburbs from the sprawling, continuous settlement of the mainurb. She sighed and closed her eyes, resting her cheek against the cold wall of the car.

Chase Mago gave her a wary glance. "Are you all right?"

Silence made a face, not opening her eyes. "I've got a headache," she admitted, after a moment.

"We packed some pills." That was Balthasar. Silence hesitated, wondering just what the medicines would do to her already queasy stomach, but then nodded. A moment later, the Delian had taken her hand, and poured a couple of flat tablets into her palm. She sat up, wincing a little, but took them dutifully, washing them down with a swallow of water from the Javerry's spring. The water, kept pleasantly cool by the fields of Chase Mago's djin bottle, tasted remarkably good. She took a second swallow, letting it drive away the headache for a moment, but set the bottle aside for fear of making herself sick. She felt a little better, though, and smiled. After a moment, Chase Mago put his arm around her; she leaned into his embrace and let herself fall asleep.

When she woke again, after some hours of fitful sleep, the headache and the nausea were much worse. Outside the windows, a river of lights streamed past, throwing crazy reflections and shadows into the car. It was worse than daylight travel. She looked away, shivering, but the flickering lights pursued her. She closed her eyes, but could not shut out the play of light and shadow. She shivered again, miserably certain she was going to be sick, and pulled free of the engineer's sleep grip. Balthasar stirred at that.

"Silence?" He sat up, automatic smile turning to a worried frown. "Are you all right?"

"I don't feel good," Silence said.

"Neither," Chase Mago said deliberately, "do I."

Balthasar glanced once at the box that had held their picnic, then, as visibly, dismissed it. "I'm all right," he said, and reached for his own carryall. He rummaged through it until he found the emergency kit he'd been carrying since the star-travellers had been forced to abandon *Recusante*, and pulled out two of the kit's bulbous diffusers. Silence took hers eagerly, recognizing the symbol of the powerful anti-nausea drug on its label. It was intended for use against space sickness, but surely it would be effective against other things. She set the soft tip against the veins of her wrist, feeling the material mold itself to her skin, and pushed the dispenser button. There was a brief numbed sensation, cold pins and needles against her wrist, and then the diffuser was empty. She leaned back and closed her eyes again, waiting for the drug to take effect.

Somewhat to her surprise, the nausea began to recede, and she sat up cautiously. I haven't had motion sickness since I was eighteen and an apprentice, she thought bitterly. Why now? Or was it even motion sickness at all? She could still feel the queasiness, a strange, unbalanced—unanchored—sensation not only in her stomach, but throughout her body. The drugs had dulled the misery enough for her to analyze the feeling. No, she thought, not an ordinary sickness at all. Very carefully, she murmured Paimel's Cantrip, reaching for the harmonic lines that had to surround the trans. There was nothing there. She swallowed hard, fighting back the surge of nausea, tasted bile. There had to be something there; no

planet could exist without casting a shadow into the supermaterial, without that shadow creating the complex interaction of dissonances and harmony on which the magi depended for much of their work. She took a deep breath, and
tried again.

This time, she caught the brief echo of the nearest harmonic, faint and badly distorted by the noise of the trans,
before she was forced to give up. No, she realized almost
instantly, not by the noise, but by the mere presence of the
trans, and by the suburbs around them—by all the machines.
She had known academically, intellectually, that the Unionists' machines would interfere with her hard-learned skills,
but she had not guessed, until now, just how disturbing this
interference would be. And if she could not find some way to
overcome it, or even to overcome its effects on herself. . . .
She thrust the thought away. She would have to find some
solution; there were no other choices. She wished suddenly
and passionately that Isambard had come with them, then
put that thought aside as well.

Sighing, she opened her eyes, studying the car as though
seeing it for the first time. Balthasar had turned up the lights,
drowning out some of the outside reflections, but otherwise
nothing had changed. The river of lights still flowed past the
windows, the unnatural brilliance seeming now to mirror the
static spread across the land, cutting her off from her instinctive awareness of the core harmonies. It would not be easy to
counter the effect, especially not from the moving trans. . . .
She killed that thought, and reached for the djin bottle. It
was an ordinary thing, its walls enclosing a simple stasis field;
its touch was reassuring, a reminder of other, more modern
worlds. She sipped the cool water, trying to think of some
way out. She was aware that the other star-travellers were
watching her nervously, but did her best to ignore them.

Whatever she did would have to spring from her own
internal resources, not from the unreachable planetary harmonics. There were techniques for creating harmony with
oneself, techniques intended for magi working in deep space,
where the mundane music that bounded common transformation was almost nonexistent. She had learned the theory, at
least, on Solitudo Hermae, but the practice was a different

matter. And even in space, a magus had a starship's harmonium at hand, to keep the music true. She looked down at the djin bottle then, frowning. Its stasis field could provide a basic harmony, a set of guide-notes, but she herself would have to do the rest.

She forced herself to relax, breathing easily, then murmured the First Cantation, the djin bottle held loosely in her left hand. She could feel the stasis field through the confining metal, but did nothing yet, letting the faint music of the stasis field travel through the enclosing bottle and into her fingertips. When she was sure she had it, she summoned her own strength, the talent and knowledge that was her power, molding it into a thing receptive to the delicate tones. Then, slowly, carefully, she teased the elusive harmony into the bones of her hand, until the music filled it and, looking down, she saw her flesh glowing with the borrowed power. Already, the music had grown a little stronger, reverberating from the bones themselves as if from a starship's keel. As it grew, she let the music rise along her arm, humming deep in the twinned bones of her forearm and tingling in the hollow of her elbow. For a moment, it hung there, then surged up the thicker bone of her upper arm. It struck her shoulder like a wave, and splashed into the bones of her chest and body. The music seemed to fade then, weakening. Silence held her breath, not sure how or where to intervene, and felt the harmonies revive, altered and amplified by her own power. The music rippled through her body, crested, and seemed to vanish. The sickness, the headache, vanished with it. The pilot murmured Paimel's Cantrip and heard, faintly, the music that was now within her sound again, driving back the machine-made dissonance.

"Are you all right?" Balthasar said again.

Silence grinned. "Much better," she said, and turned to Chase Mago. "It's the machines that're doing it. Give me your hand, Julie."

The engineer extended a clammy hand, and Silence took it, wincing in sympathy with the obvious suffering on the bearded face. She could feel the machines' noise, their aching dissonance, in his touch, and quickly murmured the Words that would establish the mirrored rapport. The Words woke echoes; she felt them sing through her bones, reinforcing her new-made internal harmony. Dimly at first, and then more strongly, she felt the same music wake in Chase Mago's body.

When she was sure the harmony was fully established, she released his hand, and couldn't help laughing at his expression of distrust and relief. "I take it it worked."

Chase Mago nodded warily. "It . . . worked, thanks. You said it's the machines?"

"Yes." Silence turned to Balthasar, who shook his head.

"I'm all right, thanks."

Silence shrugged, feeling obscurely hurt, and glanced back at the engineer. "We were always taught that mechanics would interfere with the Art, but I didn't realize how bad it could be—or that it would affect people as well as operations."

"Neither did I," Chase Mago said. "This could be a problem, you know."

"Tell me about it," Silence said, grimly. She didn't really want to think about that possibility until she had to, and glanced back at Balthasar instead. "Denis, are you sure you're. . . ?"

The Delian abruptly extended his hand. "No, not really."

Silence folded her hands around his palm. The gesture reminded her painfully of their first days on the Hegemonic transport, and she knew from Balthasar's twisted grin that he was thinking of the same things. "Relax, Denis," she said.

The Delian made a face, but Silence thought she could feel the tension ease in his fingers. She murmured the proper Words, repeating the operation she had performed for Chase Mago. When it was finished, the harmony fully established, Balthasar gave her an approving smile.

"That is better—like there was a shield between you and it."

That was it exactly, Silence thought, and if I ever make it back to civilized space, I'll name the schema for it—if no one else has thought of it, of course. That was a small question, compared to the first, but she put it aside. "Where are we—how much longer to Man's Island?"

Balthasar had shrugged in answer to the first question. Chase Mago said, "Another thirteen local hours, it looks like." He stretched, awkward in the cramped space, and attempted to settle himself more comfortably against the padded bench. "I'd suggest we try to get some sleep."

Silence nodded, burrowing in against him, and Balthasar, shrugging again, turned down the lights.

They were wakened before first light by the insistent voice of the mechanical announcer. Silence pushed herself up on one elbow, struggling to understand the accented words.

"—disembark at the Havens for a rolling check. All passengers will disembark at the Havens for a rolling check. Please have your papers ready at this time. Thank you."

The announcement was repeated, but Silence wasn't listening, trying instead to remember if any of their sources had ever mentioned "rolling checks." Nothing sprang to mind, not even when she summoned up the Grand Theater; the symbolic nexus that should hold that information was completely empty. She closed her eyes in order to concentrate, searching for related concepts. Balthasar spoke before she finished.

"The Havens. That's not even a major stop, is it?" He was already eying the car doors thoughtfully, as if plotting an escape.

Hastily, Silence reviewed the maps she'd memorized back at the Javerrys' farm. "No," she said slowly. "It's just inside the official boundary of the mainurb—we were scheduled to stop there, I think—but it's not one of the big centers." The key word was border, she realized abruptly, borders and border checks. She summoned the Grand Theater again, riffling through the carefully nurtured memories, until she found the proper nexus. It was less useful than she had hoped: the supercargo had mentioned that IDs were often checked at the border between suburb and mainurb, but rarely elsewhere. So we should be all right, Silence thought—assuming that we can trust that part of her information. She said aloud, "I think this is just routine, people. We'll know more when we stop."

"There won't be much chance to run inside the station, if it turns out they're on to us," Balthasar said.

Chase Mago snorted. "And there's no chance at all to get off this thing. Not at this speed."

Balthasar made a face, but nodded. "All right."

Already the trans was slowing. Silence glanced out the
window, but saw nothing except the flickering lights. Then
the lights vanished: the trans had entered the braking tunnel.
The announcer's voice said, "All passengers, please collect
your baggage and be ready to disembark as soon as the trans
has stopped moving. Please have your papers ready when
you reach the checkpoint. Thank you."

Silence stooped to collect the remnants of Javerry's picnic,
cramming the bits and pieces back into the basket. There was
no time to be tidy about it. The trans had slowed signifi-
cantly, was slowing more with every moment. Even as she
snapped the catches closed again, light sprang up beyond the
windows. The trans had entered the Havens station.

This platform was a little different from the others they had
seen, she thought. Instead of the immense high-ceilinged,
multi-tracked stations they had seen at Diesmon and at the
other stop along the way, this one was little more than a
grey-walled tunnel with a broad ledge running along one
side. She couldn't see any doors in the curving walls. Balthasar
shook his head.

"I don't like this," he muttered. "I don't like it at all."

"This was obviously built for inspections," Silence said,
with more confidence than she felt. "I don't think they're
stopping it just because of us."

The trans ground to a halt with a final sighing of brakes,
and the car door unsealed itself. At the same time, the
mechanical voice announced, "All passengers, please disembark now. All passengers, please disembark. Thank you."

"Let's get it over with," Balthasar said, and pushed the
door fully open.

Silence stepped cautiously past him onto the narrow platform, trying not to stare too obviously. All along the length of
the trans, people were climbing out of their cars, baggage in
hand. Most were very soberly dressed, at least by Hegemonic standards, men and women alike in trousers and short
jackets of tough, grey-blue workcloth. A few—a very few—
were more colorfully dressed, long coats of brightly patterned
fabric drawn close over lighter, fuller trousers and soft tunics.
Unlike the other passengers, they seemed to take the check
in stride, their bodies revealing boredom rather than the

others' wariness. The plainly clad passengers gave them a wide berth, Silence realized, though she saw no weapons beneath the swirling coats. Frowning, she filed the information for later use.

There was a door at the end of the platform after all, and the other passengers were walking slowly toward it, forming themselves into a ragged line. Silence tucked the picnic basket under her arm and fell in behind the nearest native, a tall, heavily painted woman. I haven't yet seen a veiled woman, the pilot thought, irrelevantly, and was glad Aili had remained with the ship. Chase Mago moved up beside her, carryall slung over his shoulder. His left hand was close to the breakaway compartment that held his heylin, and Silence shivered.

"Can you see what's coming up?" she asked, softly.

"Yes." The engineer stretched to see over the crowd ahead. "There's some sort of a metal gate, and guards at a table behind that. I think they're checking papers." He had kept his voice low, barely more than a whisper, the words almost lost in the sounds of the moving crowd, but Silence glanced around nervously nonetheless. No one seemed to have heard, the other passengers busy with their own worries. Somewhere in the crowd, a baby was crying angrily. She tried to make herself relax, but her muscles remained painfully taut.

To her left, the trans's engines whined suddenly to life, and the linked cars began to move again, drawing away from the platform. "What the hell—" she began, and realized too late that none of the natives seemed concerned. Flushing, she tried to pretend she hadn't spoken, but the painted woman was already glancing back.

"Don't ride the trans much, do you, honey?" Her voice was more accented than the Javerrys' had been, harsher and flatter on the vowels. Silence shook her head mutely. The stranger didn't seem exactly unfriendly, despite the rough words, but they could not afford to attract any notice now.

"None of us do." Balthasar spoke softly enough, but there was an edge to his voice that made the native woman shrug.

"Hey, I'm not messing with you. That's their job." Her hard eyes swept over the three of them, curious now, assessing clothes and baggage. Silence swore internally, but could think of nothing that would distract her.

"You've been in the exurb," the stranger continued. It was not a question.

Balthasar hesitated, then nodded tightly. "Yeah."

The stranger eyed him speculatively. "All right," she said after a moment, her voice dropping to match the Delian's quiet tones. "This is just routine—same as at Danb'ree, they just moved it. I'll talk to you after." She turned away before Balthasar could answer, her painted face already setting into an impassive mask.

Silence frowned, wishing she knew just what was going on, and glanced at Balthasar. The Delian lifted his shoulders in a fractional shrug, but his grey eyes were thoughtful. He knew something, or guessed something, Silence recognized, and could have screamed in frustration.

They were coming up on the barrier at last, and Silence leaned sideways, glancing around the shifting bodies. As the engineer had said, an immense metal arch spanned the platform a few meters ahead, lights flashing from various parts of its dulled surface. It was a machine, and a powerful one: she could feel the bizarre dissonances—no, she corrected herself, not dissonance but worse, the very antithesis of the music with which she had lived all her life—from here. Beyond that barrier waited half a dozen men—and women—in saffron Transit livery; three more sat behind a long table piled high with more machines. As she watched, a passenger stepped beneath the arch of the machine, glancing warily to either side as he did so, then came forward to lay the plastic folder that contained his papers on the table before the nearest Transit officer. Yawning, the woman took the folder and inserted it in her machine, tapping her fingers as she waited for a readout. Silence relaxed for an instant—surely it was a good sign if the officers themselves were bored—but snapped alert again the next instant. As the woman with the crying baby stepped beneath the arch, a different pattern of lights flared. The lounging Transit men snapped to attention, leveling strange weapons that seemed to have materialized in their hands. The woman paused, looking bewildered and frightened; the nearest Transit officer beckoned her toward a second table set to one side. They kept their guns on her as she crossed to it. Another Transit officer spoke to her briefly. She nodded, and then, made awkward by the child in her arms, swung her lumpy bag onto the table. The Transit officer ripped it open, and began searching it with practiced speed.

Silence looked away, tasting fear. If the officer searched her bag, or her husbands', they couldn't help but find the magi's supplies, or the heylins in their hidden pockets. . . . And we don't even know what the machine is scanning for, she thought. It took all her will to keep from looking around frantically for an escape route. She glanced sideways once, and saw Chase Mago chewing unhappily on stray hairs of his beard.

Then they were almost at the gate. The painted woman glanced back once, with apparent unconcern, but Silence saw her give Balthasar a ghostly wink. She turned away again, and stepped through the arch when her turn came. Lights flickered, but the Transit officers did not move. Silence took a deep breath and followed her, her fingers clammy on the thin plastic of her folder. More lights rippled across the dull metal. With an effort, she kept from looking to her right, toward the Transit officer, and stepped up to the larger table, holding out her papers. The seated officer, a young man this time, took the folder from her nerveless fingers and inserted it into his machine.

Silence held her breath, watching the man's bored face for any betraying change of expression. Her hands were closed painfully tightly around the strap of the carryall; she forced herself to loosen them, hoping the officer had not noticed her tension.

"O.K." The young man pulled the folder from his machine and handed it back to her. Silence took it with trembling fingers, not daring to speak. She turned away from the table, fumbling the folder back into her pocket, heading blindly for the narrow door set into the far wall. Both Balthasar and Chase Mago were still at the table; she was aware of them, but did not dare glance back. A Transit officer, black metal weapon slung at his hip, pushed the door open for her, smiling. She smiled back, lips stiff and cold, and then she had stepped through into a small, coldly lit tunnel. It led without turning into an immense, multi-platformed station.

It was much like the one at Diesmon, only much larger. Her mind registered that fact mechanically as she took a few steps up the platform, her heart still racing. They didn't suspect me, she thought, and felt herself trembling with relief. There was a bench ahead, unoccupied except for an old man who sat mumbling to himself. Heedless of his presence, she sat down on the far end, letting her carryall fall to the stone floor between her feet. Her papers had passed the first test—she was safe, but where were the others?

She looked up, newly afraid, and saw Balthasar emerging from the passageway. Chase Mago loomed behind him, stooping beneath the low lintel. She gave a sigh of relief and started to stand, to go to meet them. Her legs were shaking too badly to support her; she sank back on the bench, swearing to herself, and let them come to her.

Balthasar dropped to a crouch beside her, a self-satisfied smile on his thin face, and touched the pocket where he kept his papers. "Nice work, Silence." His voice was too low to carry to the old man, even if the native had been capable of hearing; nevertheless, Silence winced.

"Are you all right?" Chase Mago asked.

Silence hesitated, then nodded. "Yes. Just reaction, that's all." Already, her body felt stronger, the tremors almost gone from her muscles. Chase Mago gave her a quick, encouraging smile, but the pilot hardly noticed. "Denis, that woman— what do you think she wanted?"

Balthasar raised an eyebrow. "I'm not sure," he began, and then his eyes shifted, focusing on something behind the pilot's shoulder. "Damn, here she comes."

Silence turned, to see the native woman bearing down on them. Chase Mago extended his hand, and the pilot took it, pulling herself upright. For some reason, she did not want to meet this stranger from a position of weakness.

"Hello," the stranger said. Her eyes swept over all of them, and settled on Balthasar. "I said we'd talk. You want to go somewhere?"

The Delian shook his head.

The native studied him briefly. "The trans isn't here yet,

won't be in 'til they're finished searching. . . ." She let her voice trail off, and shrugged. "Talk here?"

Balthasar hesitated only for a fraction of a second. "Yeah." He took a few steps away from the bench, out of earshot of any of the other passengers. Silence followed, very glad of Chase Mago's looming presence.

The stranger did not seem particularly intimidated. "If you're carrying," she said, "I might deal."

The words meant nothing to Silence, but Balthasar's expression shifted slightly. He was pleased, the pilot realized, but why?

"I couldn't do that," Balthasar said. "Contracts."

"We're good," the woman answered.

"So's mine." Balthasar paused, visibly considering the stranger's words. "But if I was thinking of a deal—?"

The woman smiled cynically. "You might try the Lirior. By the Kills. I might be there." She turned away without waiting for an answer, moving up the platform as though looking for someone. Balthasar nodded to himself.

"What the hell was that all about?" Silence asked.

The Delian grinned. "I don't really know," he admitted. "Drugs, I think—that's what it would be on the Fringe, anyway."

Chase Mago made a choked sound that might have been laughter. Silence's mouth fell open; she closed it with a snap. "Do you mean to tell me you went through all that without knowing what the two of you were talking about?"

"Not exactly," Balthasar said. He shrugged again, half embarrassed, half pleased with himself. "Remember, I was a courier for the Wrath for a long time—longer even than you, Julie. That's what it felt like, and that's how I played it."

Silence shook her head, incredulous. It was typical of the Delian, she thought; it was equally typical that it had somehow worked out. She started to say as much, but her voice was drowned by the sudden whine of a trans. The silvery cars droned into the station, sliding to a gentle halt beside the platform. The waiting crowd turned almost as one, heading for the doors. Silence pulled her book of tickets from her pocket and moved with them, aiming for the nearest car. Somewhat to her surprise, no one cut her off. She fed her ticket into the box, popping the door, and waited for the others to do the same. The machine acknowledged the tickets with a faint chirp. Balthasar swung the door wide, and they climbed aboard.

The rest of the trans ride into Man's Island was uneventful. The machine moved more slowly, travelling along surface tracks; to either side stretched acres of crudely painted poured-stone buildings. The sun was up now, but the light did nothing to make the mainurb seem more appealing—if anything, Silence thought, it only made the buildings look uglier. They weren't far from the Man's Island terminus, she knew, at least geographically, but the trans made maybe half a dozen stops before the mechanical voice finally announced the end of the line. Shivering again, she collected her belongings, and the three star-travellers stepped out onto the platform.

The terminus was twice as large as the Havens station, three or four times bigger than the station at Diesmon. To her right, Silence counted five more platforms; still more were hidden behind the trans. Ahead, the platform curved to join a second platform, and the merged walkway led onto a circular island filled with hurrying people. There were still more platforms beyond the island, all filled with people—so many that for a moment Silence thought she was looking into an immense mirror. Man's Island was certainly the hub of something; she just hoped it would be large enough for them to find the materials Chase Mago needed.

The engineer touched her elbow gently. "This way," he said, nodding toward the central island. Balthasar was already striding ahead.

Silence followed in a daze, overwhelmed by the crowd and the noise that echoed against the curved ceilings. Even in the time she'd spent on Asterion, the capital of the Hegemony—even in her brief time on Delos, which had a higher population than any other human-settled world—she had never seen so many people crowded into a single space. She glanced at the engineer, and saw that he was frowning darkly, watching the moving crowd.

Balthasar made his way through the mob with efficient ease, barely seeming to notice the natives, who hardly seemed aware of him. Silence did her best to copy that indifference,

but was glad of Chase Mago's presence at her side. The
Delian paused on the central island only long enough to
orient himself by the flashing signs and arrows. The others
had barely drawn even with him before he was off again,
heading down a walkway that led off to the left, rising slightly
toward a distant doorway. Silence followed, scowling, length-
ening her stride until she'd caught up with Balthasar. She
caught his sleeve, intending to demand to know where they
were going, but he frowned at her, and shook his head
slightly. There was a tension in his muscles through the worn
cloth of his jacket that kept her from speaking, a fear more
daunting than his frown. She concentrated instead on matching his pace, Chase Mago stiff-faced beside her, and, after a
moment, she recognized what the Delian had already seen.
None of the natives were talking; they hurried along the
platforms as though to linger was somehow dangerous.

Only when they finally reached the end of the walkway did
the pace slow. The massive opening, perhaps twice as wide as
it was high, gave onto a gloomy plaza, the light filtering in
through thick ceiling panes of amber glass. Or maybe there
were artificial lights set behind the ugly rectangles, Silence
thought. Whatever they were, they did little to relieve the
dimness. Most of the passengers turned sharply to right or
left, heading for air-lock doors labeled in red and blue letters,
but enough moved on into the plaza proper to keep them
from being conspicuous,. Balthasar slowed, glancing warily
from side to side, then nodded to a kiosk that stood toward
the middle of the plaza. The sign above it said, "Information."

A skinny youth—barely more than a boy, Silence thought—
stood at one face; a greying man in grey, straight-cut tunic
and trousers was consulting the other. As the star-travellers
approached, the boy turned away. Balthasar appropriated his
place, running his hand across the glowing touchplate. Somewhat to Silence's surprise—she had expected to have to pay
for the service—the screen sprang to life in front of him.

"Do you want me to make the inquiry?" she asked, low-
voiced. At the kiosk's other face, the greying man grunted to
himself, and pushed himself away. The pilot sighed her relief.

Balthasar nodded, and made room for her in front of the

keyboard. "What we want," he said, studying the display over her shoulder, "is the Kills."

Silence gave him a questioning glance, and he elaborated. "Look, that woman said to go there if we were dealing, right? Then that's a place where there won't be people asking many questions."

It makes sense, Silence thought. Still, she wasn't sure she liked the idea.

"I hope you're right, Denis," Chase Mago growled.

The Delian grinned, unrepentant. "So do I."

Wonderful, Silence thought. Just wonderful. Scowling, she triggered the inquiry mode, and waited while the screen filled up with a mix of letters and symbols. The system seemed to be organized in precisely the same way as the one she had used at Diesmon—maybe, she thought, typing further codes, it's all the same system? The screen blanked, then, more slowly, refilled. The information on the Kills was rather limited, just locator-codes and list of the various ways the neighborhood could be reached, without any of the hostel listings or other advertising that was attached to other names. If nothing else, it bore out Balthasar's guess about the nature of the area, but the pilot still wasn't sure that was a good thing. The file did contain a map, however. She called it up, meaning to memorize its listings, but one of the options displayed below its border was to print a copy. She touched the proper keys, and a concealed printer chattered, spitting out a fold of thin, pin-printed paper. Balthasar took it from her, scanning the faint lines dubiously.

"I suppose it's better than nothing. So how do we get there?"

Silence consulted the screen again. "It looks as though there are two choices—three, if you count walking. Take the tube-train—it really is a tube-train, this time—or take a taxi."

"Tube-train," Balthasar said at once, and the engineer nodded. "We don't want to draw more attention to ourselves than necessary."

Silence nodded, and turned to scan the plaza. To their left, a red arrow pointed down a flight of stairs. The sign above it read *Public Access Transportation*. "That must be it," she said, and the others nodded.

The tube-train—which wasn't a tube-train after all, but another mechanical contrivance like the trans—was very crowded, and both the platform and the long, windowless cars smelled strongly of people and machines. Silence swallowed hard, feeling an echo of her earlier sickness, but the shielding music protected her, keeping it at bay. She kept her attention on the caged display screen at the end of the car, watching the stops flash by. Balthasar was watching, too, his eyes flicking from the screen to the doors and back again. At last the symbol they had been waiting for flashed onto the screen; Silence looked at Balthasar, who nodded, a twisted smile on his face.

"This is it?" Chase Mago asked, pitching his voice to carry through the incessant rumble of the engines.

"This is it," Balthasar said.

The tube-train was slowing. Silence balanced against the changing motion, hitching the carryall to a more comfortable position on her shoulder. There didn't seem to be many others leaving the train at this point, she noticed; those who stood, gathering satchels and shapeless web-paper sacks, wore a weird mixture of the cheapest work clothes and single expensive pieces, here a richly beaded jacket, there a realstone torque, even a shawl-scarf that might be made of Akra Leuke silk. In spite of her best intentions, her expression sharpened, seeing that. The dark girl wearing it scowled back, and moved away a little. The whole picture reminded her irresistibly of the poorer parts of a Transients' Pale on any Fringe World.

"Denis," the pilot began, and Balthasar grimaced.

"I saw," he said. "But not here."

The tube-train ground to a halt, metal shrieking against metal. Silence made a face, and Chase Mago looked physically sick at the sound. Then the doors sighed open, and they stepped out onto the platform.

It was above ground, this time, and not merely on the surface but well above it. To the left, looking back along the way the train had come, an elevated trackway led across a greasy river toward a towering cliff. The tracks emerged from a tunnel halfway up that crumbling wall of stone. To the right, the trackway curved gently down to another tunnel entrance, this one almost lost among the crowding, ugly buildings. Beyond their roofs, Silence could just see the dark line of the ocean. Somewhere beyond that—and not far beyond it, either—lay the administrative complex of Man's Island. Silence stumbled, staring, and Chase Mago caught her elbow.

"Easy, now." the engineer said, and turned her gently toward a metal turnstile at the far end of the platform. Silence shook herself, and followed the men through the gate and down the rattling metal stairs to the street. Balthasar barely hesitated at the first intersection, before striking out to the left along the badly paved street. There were no other pedestrians in sight; remembering the people who had left the train with them, Silence glanced once over her shoulder, but saw no one following. The ugly, windowless buildings rose to either side, cutting off the thin sunlight. The air smelled strange, sharp; looking up, she saw the sky half obscured by a pale yellow haze that thickened to clouds above the water.

Balthasar led them across another street, turning left again at the next intersection. Silence frowned, but before she could say anything, Chase Mago asked mildly, "Do you have any particular place in mind, Denis?"

Balthasar looked back, grinning, and pointed. "There."

Silence's eyes narrowed. The Delian was pointing to a lighted sign, pale in the sunlight, that advertised rooms for rent. It hung above an unimpressive arched doorway flanked by chipped poured-stone columns; undecorated windows rose above it for five or six stories. The pilot shook her head. "No," she said, "there were no hostels listed."

"That was a search pattern," Chase Mago cut in, with some disgust.

"I found us a hostel, didn't I?" Balthasar shot back. "What are you complaining about?"

"You may have found a hotel," Silence corrected. "Let's see what it looks like on the inside."

The door beneath the arch led into a long, dimly lit room divided in half by an elaborately scrolled metal grille. It looked more functional than decorative, Silence thought, and found herself looking warily in the corners. There was no central desk, as there would be in a hostel on most other worlds. Instead, a kiosk like the one they had used in the trans station stood in the center of the worn tiling, wan lights flickering behind its screens. As they moved closer, the camera set at the top of the kiosk swivelled toward them, and the nearest screen brightened.

"—help you?" The tinny voice came from a grille somewhere beneath the camera; the speaker sounded as though he didn't really care about the answer.

"Yes." Silence stepped forward, glancing first at the camera and then at the flickering picture now visible on the screen. It showed an older man, lank grey hair fringing his bald head. The camera was set somewhere above him, and he was looking down into something—presumably a viewscreen of his own, the pilot thought. She looked up into the camera, schooling her face to remain emotionless. "We want a room."

"Rates are twenty-five for the top floors, twenty-eight with bath, thirty for the first and second floors, and thirty-five for a suite with a bath." The man recited the list in a monotone, still watching his screen. Heavy, thumping music sounded faintly behind him.

Silence darted a glance at Balthasar, who shrugged.

"Top floor?" he said.

"With bath," Chase Mago murmured.

Silence nodded. "The top floor'll do—with bath, please."

The man's hands moved off-screen. "How long you staying?"

"We haven't decided," Balthasar said silkily.

"Hah." The old man seemed unmoved by the statement. "Minimum deposit's fifty, split it how you like."

"Put us down for two weeks," Silence said, after hasty calculations. "With an option to renew."

"Fine." The man did something off-screen again, and a new panel lit up below the kiosk viewscreen. "Insert your card."

"This is cash," Silence said.

"Cash?" There was a long pause, and then the old man said, "There's a ten percent surcharge for cash."

"Surcharge?" Silence asked, and just managed to keep the outrage from her voice.

"Yeah. For the security risk." The man looked up into the camera. "You sure you don't want to use your cards?"

"That's right," Silence said. "Cash."

The old man folded his arms across his chest. "Show me."

The star-travellers exchanged glances. If someone else is watching, Silence thought, if this is just a setup for robbery, we're in trouble. Still, there are three of us, and we have heylins within reach. . . . Balthasar nodded slowly, as if he'd read her thought. Chase Mago slid his hand across the surface of his carryall, so that it was resting on the opening of the hidden pocket. Reassured by that, and by the weight of her own carryall, Silence reached into the pocket of her jacket and brought out the wad of bills she and Isambard had made. She fanned them slowly in front of the camera.

The old man grunted. "All right. I'll be down. You wait."

It took him a few minutes to emerge from his hiding place. Silence glanced nervously around, scanning the blank, white-painted walls, then schooled herself to wait with at least outward calm. At last, the old man appeared behind the heavy grille. Silence stepped forward, hand in her pocket, and he flinched back instantly.

"Hold it right there, woman. Take your hand out slow." There was no weapon in sight, but Silence had no doubt that he had one concealed somewhere in his shapeless clothing. She frowned, but did as she was told, pulling a second sheaf of bills from her jacket pocket. The old man's eyes brightened at the sight, and he beckoned her forward.

"That's three ninety-two for the room, plus the surcharge— four thirty-two all told."

Silence raised an eyebrow at that, but carefully counted out the proper fee and passed half of it through a slot in the grillwork. The old man scowled, but grudgingly unlocked the narrow door to let them into the rest of the hostel. Silence let the other star-travellers go first; only when they were safely inside did she step through herself, and hand the rest of the bills to the old man. He took them avidly, counted and recounted them, then stuffed the money into the pocket of his trousers.

"This way."

The top floor rooms were cheap, it seemed, because the ancient gravity lift was shut down after the midnight curfew. They could come and go as they liked, the old man's shrug-

ging explanation implied, but they would have to climb the
six flights of stairs. Silence listened, nodding, as the lift
carriage whined its way to the top of its shaft, and dismissed
the man as soon as they'd reached the door of the room. He
left without trying to charge them for the third keycard.

The room itself was surprisingly comfortable. The furnish-
ings—table, two chairs, the media center that filled one
corner, and the oversized bed behind a painted paper screen—
were worn but still serviceable; the thin carpet and the tiled
bath were unexpectedly clean. Chase Mago dropped at once
onto the huge bed, throwing one arm over his eyes. Seeing
him reminded Silence of just how tired she was; she slumped
into the nearest chair, her carryall forgotten by the door.

"So here we are," she said.

"Yeah." Balthasar was prowling the room, fingering the
thin curtains and warily inspecting each piece of furniture.
Checking for listeners, Silence knew, and sat quietly, waiting. The Delian finished quickly, but stood for a moment in
the center of the room, a dissatisfied expression on his face.
Then he crossed to the media center and folded back the
double doors. He studied the controls for a moment, then
flipped a set of switches. A square of carpet slid aside, almost
under his feet—he dodged, cursing, and Silence grinned—and a
strange black cube rose through the floor. A moment later, its
top began to glow, and images coalesced in the air above it.
At the same time, sound faded on, coming from the base of
the cube. It was a harsh, monotonously accented music,
overlaid by the scree and wail of some unfamiliar instrument.
Chase Mago sat up quickly, wincing, but Silence hardly
noticed the engineer's discomfort. That machine was a
holotable, something she'd only read about in ancient novels.
As she watched, the image fuzzed briefly, music fading, and
shifted to another set of musicians. She looked up, smile
fading, as Balthasar cleared his throat.

"I'm still not sure I'd know a listener if I saw one," he said,
his voice barely audible through the noise from the holotable.
"But, I tried."

"Now what?" Silence asked. She matched the pitch of her
voice to Balthasar's, but her lighter tones were swallowed in

the music. She made a face and tried again. "What do we do next?"

Balthasar made a face. "This is the area where the kid said you could buy stuff. I guess we try to make some contacts, see what we can turn up that might be of use. . . ."

His voice trailed off, and Silence sighed. In other words, she thought, you don't know either. To buy time to think of something more constructive, she said, "Wait, let me set a ring first, before we do any more planning."

The Delian nodded, and Silence pushed herself to her feet, looking around for something with which to sketch a circle. There was nothing at hand; she leaned into the bathroom, looking for soap powders, when Chase Mago said, "Look. That's it."

Silence turned back to face the engineer. He was pointing to the fuzzy image on the holotable, a new, self-satisfied grin on his face. "That's it," he said again.

"What's it?" Balthasar ran a hand through his hair, and darted a puzzled glance at the other man.

"That, the vox—the instrument he's playing." Chase Mago paused, visibly collecting his thoughts. "Look, the blond one, there. The instrument he's playing is a vox humana, and a vox humana is one of the ancestors of the harmonium. I can use that to tune—" He broke off abruptly, the excitement fading from his face. "At least, I think I can; the mechanisms shouldn't've changed too much. . . ."

Silence said, slowly, hearing the same excitement rising in her voice, "If you can retune using one of those—"

"We wouldn't have to deal with any underground," Balthasar broke in. "Yeah, that would make it easier. Can you do it, Julie?"

"I told you," Chase Mago answered, "if the mechanisms haven't been changed too much over the years, if I can get pure tones from one—yes, I think so."

"Where does one buy a vox humana?" Silence asked. She was thinking aloud, but Balthasar answered anyway.

"A store that sells musical instruments, I suppose—or, no." There was a sudden, smug grin on the Delian's face. "Pawnshops. That's the place to look."

"If they have pawnshops here," Silence said automatically, but she hardly took her own objection seriously. They would have pawnshops in the Kills, or some equivalent institution; it was almost as inevitable that musicians would be poor enough to make use of them. She nodded thoughtfully. "I'll start checking the directory."

CHAPTER 7

The room's media center contained yet another keyboard-and-screen combination, this one linked to some sort of district-wide network. That network was in turn linked to a more powerful system that served the entire mainurb. Silence eyed the access commands rather wistfully—she had had enough success in deducing the structures of the smaller systems to feel fairly confident in her ability to handle something larger—but confined herself to the local net. It was set up rather differently from the other systems she had dealt with, but the time she'd spent on Solitudo Hermae had made her adept at deciphering unfamiliar symbolic systems. By the time the district curfew shut down the network, she had found half a dozen shops that looked promising, and Balthasar had located them on the map they'd gotten back at the terminus. Chase Mago pulled the crude communicator he'd improvised from the bits and pieces of *Recusante*'s emergency system from the lining of the satchel, assembled it, then reported briefly to the ship. The media center contained a tiny kitchenette unit along with everything else, water heater and antique hotbox, and a limited supply of dried staples. Chase Mago fixed a scanty dinner from among those packages, and then they went to bed.

They breakfasted from the kitchenette as well, almost emptying the supply cabinet, and then started on the round of the pawnshops and free-brokers Silence had found in the district directory listings. After some debate, they left the carryalls and the picnic basket in the hostel, but, at Balthasar's insistence, each star-traveller carried a fully charged heylin in his or her pocket.

It was warmer in the streets than it had been the previous day, and the air was damp and sticky. Silence grimaced, loosening the clasps of her jacket, and glanced up. The band of sky visible between the building was even more tinged with yellow than it had been the day before, like a brassy, metallic dome over the city, but there were no clouds, no real signs of rain to relieve the oppressive heat.

There were more Earth natives visible than there had been the previous day, the traffic about evenly divided between the old and the very young. A few shopkeepers watched the passersby from their doorways, both men and women narrow-eyed, wary, but ready for business; their shops were well guarded, with heavy grilles across doors and tiny windows. The one or two that actually displayed their goods did so through remote-view cubes. It was not so very different in spirit from poor worlds like Cibistra or Elysium, Silence thought. Only the technology had changed.

The street turned abruptly into a broad market square, where foodstuffs—vegetables and grains in huge web-paper sacks—were stacked on trestle tables. The space was very crowded, men and women alike pawing over the piled goods. The noise of haggling was very loud, sharp voices rising in calculated anger. Silence faltered, suddenly afraid of being recognized as an outsider, and Balthasar gave her a quick, encouraging smile.

"Don't worry," he said, under his breath. "Who's going to notice us, in this mess?"

"No one, you hope," Silence said, but her voice was mild enough. The Delian seemed able to find his way in this world; she would trust him this far, at least.

Balthasar led them along the side of the square, where a line of locked storage bins formed a sort of narrow alley, mostly out of sight of the hurrying crowd. One or two of the merchants called after them, but no one else seemed to pay any attention. Even so, Silence breathed a sigh of relief as they turned out of the market onto a quiet side street.

"The first shop should be over there," Balthasar began, and grinned. "And there it is, Samson Liu's."

It was not a very imposing building, seen from a distance, just a tall, windowless rectangle—brick, this time, rather than the ubiquitous poured stone—with a white-painted grille over the door opening and several more grilles along the front where the windows should have been. It was no more attractive close up, and Silence found herself wondering if they were doing the right thing. There was no handle on the door-grille; she reached for the grille itself, and felt the warning tingle of some kind of defensive field. She drew back instantly, saying in a low voice, "Careful, don't touch it."

Chase Mago frowned. "So how do we get in? I don't see a call button—"

A clicking from the grille cut him off, and Silence, standing closest to the barred doorway, felt the defensive field fade and die. A sexless voice said, "Enter, please."

The star-travellers exchanged a wary glance, and then Silence reached cautiously for the grille, ready to snatch her hand back if the field reappeared. It did not; the metal of the grille was barely warm to the touch, and cooling rapidly. Silence took a deep breath, and pulled open the door.

The interior of the store was coldly lit, and very clean. It reminded Silence irresistibly of pictures she had seen of hospices, in the days before the Art had proved the efficacy of color-therapies. A single short counter ran the length of one wall; otherwise, the white-painted room was completely empty. Silence frowned uneasily, and glanced at the two men. Chase Mago was frowning too, but Balthasar's face was impassive, his hands tucked deep into the pockets of his trousers. Seeing her look, he shrugged, and gave her a lopsided smile.

There was a clicking sound from behind the counter, and a line appeared in the white wall. It expanded, became a door, and a small, olive-skinned woman stepped through it to take her place behind the counter.

"Can I help you?" she asked. Silence barely heard the words, all of her attention focusing on the other woman's bizarre dress. She was wearing a strange, broad-shouldered coat—or perhaps it was a gown; the counter hid her body from the waist down—that tapered drastically from the shoulderline, so that she was reduced to tiny, mincing steps, tottering as though she wore high-soled clogs as well. Great clusters of orange and blue feathers further extended the shoulder line, and rippled down the outer seams of the sleeves, suggesting gaudy wings; her face and hair were striped with the same colors, and she wore a palm-sized medallion covered with unfamiliar symbols—also orange and blue—pinned between her breasts. She put her hands on her hips then, the feathers fluttering wildly.

"What's the matter," she asked, "you Greenies or something?"

Silence shook herself, and managed a smile. "No," she said. "Sorry."

The woman grunted disbelievingly, but seemed to accept it. "So what do you want?"

Chase Mago cleared his throat. "We want to buy a musical instrument," he said. "Do you have any?"

The woman eyed him thoughtfully. "We've got a lot of them," she said. "Did you have something particular in mind?"

"I'm looking for a vox humana," the engineer answered.

The woman shook her head, frowning. "I've never heard of that. Are you sure it's an instrument?"

Silence saw the sudden flicker of panic on the engineer's face, felt the same fear stirring in her belly. They hadn't even considered that possibility, that the vox humana would be known by some other name. She closed her eyes, searching the patterns of the Grand Theater for anything that might be of use, but found nothing. She opened her eyes again, and saw the woman behind the counter staring at her, expression changing from indifference to curiosity. "It's a—keyboard," the pilot began, fumbling for a better description, and the saleswoman scowled. Silence barely managed to bite back the rest of her sentence before she betrayed herself further.

"For God's sake, why didn't you say so?" She reached beneath the counter, and brought out a squat machine topped by a cloudy glass dome. After a moment's search, she produced a pair of gold-colored disks, and slid them across the counter. "That's the catalogue," she said, pointing to one, "and that's the update."

"Thanks," Chase Mago said absently, staring at the machine.

"God." The woman leaned across the counter, twitched the disk out of his hand, and slid it into a slot in the machine's side. The glass dome fuzzed and darkened, displaying a holographic image of a glittering pin. The woman touched a knob on the machine's side, and the image shifted, became a cube of words, a marker flashing in the center of the array. "Where are you from, anyway?"

Silence tensed, weighing her answer, but Balthasar spoke first. "You ask a lot of questions."

"Hey." The saleswoman took a step backward, almost falling in her tight skirt. "No offense."

Silence smiled at her mockingly, and the other woman moved farther away. "Yell if you need me," she said, and retreated to the far end of the counter.

"Silence," Chase Mago said, softly. "Can you figure out how this is arranged?"

The pilot turned her attention away from the saleswoman, focusing on the image in the dome. The individual words were almost too small to read. She glanced at the machine's controls—a pair of buttons, a large, unlabeled dial, and a well-worn socket-ball—and touched the upper button gently. The image swelled instantly, and she snatched her hand away almost too late. The cubed image completely filled the dome, losing a few letters at the corners of the structure, but at least she could read the individual words.

The pattern that governed the cube was a completely unfamiliar one. She frowned into it, recalling the techniques of analysis she'd learned on Solitudo Hermae, and chose a line of words at random. Time faded; she opened her mind as fully as possible, letting the words trigger all possible connections in her memory. Slowly at first, and then with blinding suddenness, she understood. She looked up quickly, and saw with some shock that only a minute or two had passed. Chase Mago lifted an eyebrow in question, and she smiled reassuringly, setting her hands on the machine controls.

"I understand it," she said, softly, and added to herself, or at least I understand it well enough to find what we need. It was an interesting system, though, one that would bear remembering—something else that she might be able to sell when they returned to human-settled space, something the magi could turn into a new mnemonic device, as revolutionary as the memory theaters themselves. The data, Samson Liu's inventory, was ordered in three dimensions rather than in the usual two; in this case, the two horizontal dimensions—axes? she wondered—indicated type, while the vertical dimension was an index of value. She thought that the side-to-side axis was the indicator of general item type, while the front-to-back axis was being used for specific items within the class, but too many of the actual listings were unfamiliar to her for her to be certain of that. Still, it was a fascinating system. Her smile faded then. Of course, if it were to be used on the human-settled worlds, they'd have to come up with some inexpensive non-mechanical means of projecting a three-dimensional display. . . .

She shook herself, annoyed at having wasted even that much thought on something so distant, and flicked the socket-ball. The flashing marker shifted with it. She maneuvered it quickly to the section she wanted and paused, studying the controls. The other woman had used the dial to change images, she thought, and cautiously touched it. It seemed soft under her hand, and she pressed harder. There was a faint click, and the cube of words vanished, to be replaced by an unfamiliar array of black plastic tablets. The printing beneath the image identified it as a not particularly expensive set of drums. She frowned, considering, then shifted the dial to the left. After a few moments' maneuvering, controlling her position with it and the socket-ball, she found the part of the matrix that displayed the voces, and nodded to the engineer.

"Here you are."

"Thanks," Chase Mago said, and took her place in front of the machine, murmuring to himself as he studied each of the machines. Silence sighed, and resigned herself to waiting. She didn't know precisely what the engineer needed from the vox humana in order to be able to use it to retune, and didn't quite know what to do to help. She glanced at Balthasar, but before she could say anything, a buzzer sounded from somewhere near the outside door. Silence glanced curiously toward the saleswoman, and saw her fumble again with something beneath the counter. The buzzing changed to a tri-toned chime, and a moment later, two more people entered the shop.

They were dressed in the same colors as the woman behind the counter, the boy in flaming neon shades, the girl in more muted tones. Their gaudy coats had the same exaggerated shoulderline as the saleswoman's dress, though the girl's was slit front and back for ease of movement. The boy's coat was quite short, the hem barely falling below his buttocks, and buttoned close around slender hips. Silence glanced side-ways, sighing, and saw Balthasar's appreciative grin. She kicked him, and he looked away.

If the newcomers saw the movement, they ignored it, crossing at once to the counter in front of the saleswoman. The boy said something, low-voiced, and the girl swung a plastic-covered bundle onto the counter. Pawning—or selling—something, Silence thought, and craned her head as unobtru-sively as she could. At the saleswoman's nod, the girl loosened the wrappings, but kept the plastic tucked around whatever it was, effectively concealing the contents. The boy glanced down the length of the counter, scowling, and Silence met the look with a blank stare. He looked away then, still frown-ing, and said something to the saleswoman, who shrugged.

"Not from around here," she said, her voice fading in re-sponse to a murmur from the girl.

Silence glanced back at the domed machine, now display-ing something that looked like a control keyboard mated to a misshapen harp with crystal strings. Chase Mago considered it gravely, but looked up as Silence moved closer.

"I think this could be what we want," he said. "I need to see the internal arrangements, though."

"You don't ask for much, do you?" That was the sales-woman, moving closer. She reached under the counter for another machine, then slid it along the counter top toward the waiting couple.

Silence called after her, "Is that possible?"

The woman shrugged. "Yeah, I guess. But you'll have to wait."

"All right." The newcomers were watching them now with open curiosity, Silence saw, and steeled herself to meet their stares. After a moment, the girl said something, and they both looked away, but the pilot could still feel the heat of their interest. Then the saleswoman had taken their cards and put each one through the reader. The boy nodded, and the saleswoman swept the bundle under the counter. The boy seemed inclined to linger even then, but the girl spoke again, low-voiced, and drew him away. The buzzer sounded behind them as they left.

"You wanted to see the insides?" The saleswoman had returned to the other end of the counter, her hands poised over something just under the counter top.

Chase Mago nodded, absently, and Silence said, "That's right."

There was a momentary pause, and then the saleswoman shrugged. Her hands moved on the hidden controls; there was a distant whirring, and a faint series of clanks from behind the nearly invisible inside door. Silence's eyes narrowed in spite of herself. The noises were oddly familiar—and then she remembered a spice warehouse on Cibistra, where the shielding walls, a good meter thick, had hidden a bizarre machine like a metal lattice, from whose intersection points had hung strange, basket-like containers. Her grandfather had made his purchase—a kilo of arianhrodae, to be resold on half a dozen other worlds—and the entire structure had clattered into motion, pulleys and wires rearranging the baskets until at last the container of arianhrodae had dropped into the spice merchant's waiting hands. It would make sense for Earth's natives to use a similar system, especially when coupled with the cubic index. . . .

A door slid open in the wall beside the counter, and a shelf extended itself, servos whining under its burden. The machine they had seen pictured in the dome was waiting there, the thin crystal spines above the keyboard carefully shrouded in clingfoam.

"There it is," the saleswoman said, and reached for a section of counter top. Silence realized instantly what the other woman intended, and leaned hard against the hidden gate, effectively blocking her escape.

"We won't hurt it," she said, and kept her position. "You can get on with your other work."

For a moment, she thought the saleswoman would protest further, but then the other woman dropped her eyes and turned away, shrugging in a painful attempt at nonchalance. "All right," she said. "God, some people."

Silence held her pose for a few minutes longer, watching the saleswoman. She was aware of Chase Mago, busy with his palm-sized tool kit, and of Balthasar's leashed impatience, but she did not dare turn to see what was happening. Then Chase Mago sighed.

"No, it won't do. See there."

Silence risked a quick glance, saw only the tilted casing and the engineer's hand pointing to something at the base of the crystals. Then Chase Mago had closed it again, neatly refastening the catches.

"You mean after all that you don't want it?" The saleswoman glared at them from the far end of the counter.

Silence smiled sweetly at her. "That's right," she said. "Thank you for your help."

The saleswoman turned away disgustedly, and did not answer. Balthasar grinned and gestured for the others to precede him from the store. "After you, people, after you."

His smile faded once they were in the street, however, and Chase Mago shook his head, sighing. Silence glanced around quickly, saw no one within earshot, and said, "What was wrong?"

The engineer grimaced. "The active mechanical elements were too close to the crystal, powered them directly—in fact, I don't think they needed the crystals as resonators at all, I think they were just there for decoration." He squinted thoughtfully into the hazy sunlight. "I could maybe do something with it, but I'd have to rebuild the whole thing. . . ."

"We'll come back if we have to," Silence interrupted firmly. "For now, let's see if any of the other places have something closer to what you need." She glanced at Balthasar. "Where next?"

"A place called the Fish Pier," the Delian answered, and pointed. "That way."

The Fish Pier proved to have no musical instruments in stock, and the next stop had only a less well cared for version of the instrument they'd seen at Samson Liu's. As they made their way through the maze of streets toward the next shop—a placed listed in the directory as Rafaiel's Bulletin Board, Coffee Shop, and Small Loans Bank—Silence felt an odd chill at the nape of her neck. Almost, she thought, as though we were being followed. But she had seen no signs of that, only a few unremarkable pedestrians. She had read, somewhere, that the thing to watch for was the shoes—you could vary outer clothing easily enough, but rarely shoes—but saw nothing that looked familiar. Still, the nagging feeling persisted.

"Denis," she began. "There's something—I feel as though we're being watched."

The Delian nodded without turning his head, frowning thoughtfully. "I know, I feel it, too. But, damn it all, I can't actually see anybody."

"Do we head back to the hostel?" Chase Mago asked.

Balthasar gave a frustrated grimace. "I don't know—no. If there is anybody, let's find them out; if there isn't—" He shrugged. "We might as well keep going."

Silence nodded, and, after a moment, the engineer did the same. It isn't as though there's anything definite, the pilot thought, not as though either of us—any of us—had seen something suspicious. It could well be that the strangeness of the planet, and of all these machines, is what's making us nervous. That's probably all it is. The feeling faded as they walked further, until it was no more than a tickling at the back of her mind.

Rafaiel's Bulletin Board, Coffee Shop, and Small Loans Bank was located at the end of a suspiciously clean cul-de-sac. The building itself was almost identical to the windowless box that housed Samson Liu's, but Rafaiel, or whoever actually owned the place, had used neon tubing to sketch windows on the blank brick facade, and added fantastic neon flowers and curtains as well. The colors were pale in the sunlight, but Silence could picture the nighttime splendor. The sign over the open doorway read "Rafaiel's" in meter-high letters; beneath that were the initials BBC.

"What, he ran out of room?" Balthasar muttered.

Silence shrugged.

"Are you sure about this place?" Chase Mago asked.

"It was listed as a pawnshop," Silence said. "What do you think, Denis?"

"I say we take a look," Delian answered.

Silence nodded. "I agree."

The interior of Rafaiel's BBC was warmly lit, and smelled strongly of baking bread and grilled meats. Silence swallowed hard, suddenly aware that she hadn't eaten since breakfast, and looked around for any sign of a pawnshop. The big, wood-floored room held a dozen, perhaps two dozen small tables crowded together to either side of a central aisle marked out by a strip of well-worn carpeting leading to two curtained doorways. Only a few were occupied right now, most by men and women old enough to have retired from their work, but a couple of younger men moved along the walls, which were completely covered in crudely printed handbills. So that's the bulletin board, Silence thought, and in front of me's the coffee shop—but where's the small loans bank?

"Can I help you?" A dark-skinned woman ducked through the bright blue curtain and came down the aisle to meet them, a tray and clickpad balanced on her hip. "Food, news, or money?"

"Money, I think," Silence said, and tried a tentative smile. "Except we've come to buy?"

The dark woman did not return the smile. "Upstairs, then— through the green door." She touched a couple of buttons on her clickpad, and turned toward the nearest occupied table.

"Thanks," Silence said, to her departing back, and started down the aisle, the other star-travellers following.

The narrow, badly lit stairway led directly into a long room with candy-striped walls. More brilliant stripes outlined a set of doors and hatches at the back of the room. A round counter set toward the end of the room encircled a column of amber-tinged glass, at the center of which sat a honey-skinned man with short, greying hair. He lifted a hand in greeting as the star-travellers emerged into the cool light, and his voice crackled from a speaker set at the top of his column.

"Greetings. I'm Rafaiel. And what can I do for you?"

He knows part of it already, Silence thought, with sudden conviction, either from the woman downstairs or from the other shops we've been to. There was something in Rafaiel's slight, superior smile that hinted at hidden knowledge.

Chase Mago spoke into her hesitation. "We're looking for—we want to buy—a vox humana."

"A keyboard," Silence corrected hastily.

Rafaiel smiled. "Which is it, people, a keyboard or a vox?"

"You have a vox?" Silence allowed a polite skepticism to color her tone, and Rafaiel's smile widened.

"I have four keyboards of the type you've been examining," he said. "And the vox."

So he had been in touch with the other shop owners, Silence thought. She did not dare look over her shoulders at the other star-travellers. "If you have one," she said slowly, "we'd like to look at it."

"You're welcome to examine it fully," Rafaiel answered. His hand moved on the controls beside him. There was a distant clicking noise, like the sounds Silence had heard in Samson Liu's, and then a door slid open in the far wall. A plastic-shrouded box was waiting in the opening. Silence nodded to Rafaiel, but made no move toward it.

"If you'll permit us?" she asked.

"Of course." Rafaiel leaned back in his raised chair, obviously enjoying himself. "Make free."

Only then did Silence dare to glance at the other star-travellers. There was no expression on Balthasar's thin face, but she could read an unease that matched her own in the set of his shoulders. Chase Mago stared at the wrapped box with open curiosity; feeling her eyes on him, he smiled.

"Let's take a look," he said.

Unwrapped, the vox humana didn't look at all different from the machines they'd already examined. Silence bit back an exclamation of disappointment, and Chase Mago gave her a quick grin.

"It's too early to tell, yet," he said softly, and slipped his tool kit from his pocket. Silence deliberately maneuvered herself to block Rafaiel's view as the engineer folded back the stiff protective cover and slid out the first of his tools. Delicately, he released the minuscule screws that held the cover in place, and carefully lifted it away. Balthasar caught the opposite edge, easing it up and over the thin tubes of crystal.

The interior of the vox was a labyrinth of multicolored wires, snaking from the keyboards to a central unit that looked to Silence like a metallic honeycomb. That in turn was separated from the mouths of the crystals by a wedge of what looked like durafelt. Chase Mago made a soft, satisfied sound, and carefully lifted the wedge from its seating.

"This is it," he said, still softly. "Feel that."

Obediently, Silence put out her hand, and touched a familiar roughness. "That's durafelt," she said aloud, and the engineer nodded.

"It's also a real vox humana, and I don't know what it's doing here," he said, and eased the wedge back into its place. "I want it, Denis. This is what we need."

Balthasar nodded, and Silence was not entirely sorry to let him assume the responsibility of bargaining with Rafaiel. She might be pilot and magus, but she had never been an independent starship's captain. She remained at Chase Mago's side, helping him lower the awkwardly shaped cover back into place, then waited while the engineer tightened the tiny screws. She could hear, distantly, the rise and fall of Balthasar's voice, and Rafaiel's machine-distorted answers, but did not really listen. For once, the price truly did not matter; she could, and would, create more bills to make up for whatever they spent on this.

"—holding it as a pledge," Rafaiel was saying, "and it's only a couple of days overdue."

Silence's attention sharpened, and she glanced warily toward the central column. Balthasar said, "But it is yours to sell."

"Legally," Rafaiel answered, "but morally. . . ." He let his voice trail off suggestively.

"Surely nobody pays your morals," Balthasar said. There was a new tension in his posture, Silence saw, a controlled anger in the movements of his hands and arms. She willed him to be careful, not daring to speak.

"Look," Balthasar said, and kept his voice reasonable with an effort, "we want to buy the vox. Are you selling?"

Rafaiel managed to look coy behind the amber wall. "It's a matter of my obligations," he complained. "I owe it to my business—to my wife and children, and to my employees—to make what profit I may. But it's also my obligation not to be too hasty in turning my customers' pledges into credit, when they're only a little late. . . ."

Balthasar cut through the stream of chatter. "I'm willing to pay your asking price," he said, firmly, "and a hundred more to salve your conscience."

Rafaiel's eyes brightened—though not, Silence thought, entirely with greed. "Very well," he said, "though I must ask you to leave your name and address, so that if the original owner comes to redeem it, I can tell him where you've gone. And I would also ask that you seriously consider permitting him to buy it back from you."

"Of course," Balthasar said. "We haven't got a permanent address, though. We're staying at one of the hostels; you can reach us there. At the Blue Lion; tell him to ask for Garret Kisigi."

He lies well—he always has, Silence thought—but I don't think Rafaiel believes him. She watched, cold with fear, while Balthasar ceremoniously counted out the necessary bills and passed them one by one through a tiny slot in the amber glass. Rafaiel recounted them just as ceremoniously, and then bowed to Balthasar. "It's all yours, Kisigi."

The vox was fitted with a carrying strap and a foamfelt collar to protect the delicate crystals. Chase Mago snapped both into place, not hurrying, and lifted the vox gently to his shoulder. Silence nodded toward Rafaiel, still watching from his enclosed column, and started toward the stairs. The men followed.

No one in the coffee shop paid any attention as they made their way back down the aisle toward the main door, though Silence was aware of two more people in the bright orange and blue livery— adolescents, again, like the ones who had come into Samson Liu's—off to one side, scanning the notices pinned to the walls. The taller of the two gave the star-travellers an incurious glance, and looked away again. Silence shivered, but could not decide if she was being unreasonable. Alone, the blue and orange meant nothing—the saleswoman at Samson Liu's had worn it, too— but coupled with Rafaiel's too-great knowledge and the sense that she'd had all after-noon of being followed, it meant trouble. She held her breath until they were out on the street, but nothing happened; no one moved inside the coffee shop.

"Denis," she said quietly, and the Delian nodded.

"I saw," he said, and glanced up and down the alleyway. There were no side streets of any kind, and all the doors were set flush into the walls of the blank-faced warehouses, but he eyed them suspiciously anyway. "We get back to the hostel as quickly as we can."

"I agree," Silence said, and flushed, realizing how relieved she sounded.

"There's one thing, though," Chase Mago said. "No, don't stop, we can talk as we go—but this vox, it's a work of the Art."

Silence hesitated, the danger momentarily forgotten, and had to hurry to catch up. "How can that be?" she asked. "Earth doesn't use the Art for anything, especially not for something so trivial."

The engineer shrugged. "I don't know. But this is a real vox humana, people, and it's not pre-War, either. I'm almost willing to bet it was made in the Fringe, maybe even on Sabate."

Silence eyed the well-padded instrument with more respect. The artisans of Sabate were famous throughout human-settled space for their craftsmanship. . . . She said aloud, "That doesn't explain how it got here."

"So somebody's trading with the rest of space," Balthasar said impatiently. He paused at the corner of the next street, gnawed his lip for a moment, then pointed to the left down a wide avenue.

"From everything the Javerrys said, that's not just illegal but literally unthinkable," Silence said. "They don't know there's anything out there, so how could any of the natives trade with it?"

Balthasar grimaced again. Ahead, the road divided around a wedge-shaped building; he hesitated only for an instant before choosing the right-hand fork. "Come on, Silence, there can't be that many Rose Worlders on-planet at any one time. They have to have recruited some help from the local elites— and I bet off-world luxuries are a pretty good bribe to keep them quiet, too."

Silence made a face at the Delian's back, annoyed at her own stupidity. What Balthasar had said made perfect sense: the Rose Worlders couldn't function without some support from the local population, and those natives in Rose Worlder service couldn't be of much use unless they knew at least a part of the truth. And the taste of off-world goods—of the things only the Art could supply—would probably go a long way toward reconciling them to their inferior position. She had seen plenty of people like that in the Rusadir and on the Fringe—for some reason, they all seemed to work in Customs.

"I'm a little worried that we had to give that Rafaiel any name," Chase Mago said thoughtfully. "Even a false one."

Balthasar shrugged. "I wasn't wild about it, but what could I do? We could switch hostels, but I don't see it doing us any good."

Silence said, "We can't get out of the district before the curfew anyway, but I think we ought to catch the next trans out of here. We've got what we came for—haven't we?" She gave the engineer a sharp look.

He nodded. "Yes. This should be sufficient."

Balthasar had a discontented look on his face, and Silence frowned. "Well, Denis?"

The Delian shrugged. "It just seems a shame, to have come so far, and to see so little. . . ." His voice trailed off unhappily, and he shook himself. "No, I know you're right, Silence. But it's hard."

"Not for me," Silence said, lying only a little, and Chase Mago nodded. Balthasar managed a twisted smile.

"All right. But don't blame me if you're disappointed."

They turned onto a side street—avoiding the now-empty market, Balthasar said—and Silence stiffened abruptly. There was something wrong in the road ahead, a shadow that had no business being where it was. She reached into her pocket, fingers curling around the butt of her heylin. Its touchplate was warm under her thumb: full charge, she thought, and kept walking. Balthasar had seen it, too; she could tell it from the sudden set of his jaw and the way he'd jammed his left hand into the pocket of his jacket, but he kept walking. Chase Mago tugged the vox humana to a safer position on his shoulder, wrapping his arm protectively around the crystals.

Silence scanned the street around her, coldly afraid. She saw nothing—the warning shadow had vanished, dissolved as if it had never been—but the buildings to either side did not quite meet, leaving crooked passageways between their poured-stone walls, perfect for an ambush. The buildings themselves were old and abandoned, boards tacked across their doors and windows, and one or two bore the black scars of recent fires.

"Great choice, Denis," she muttered, and was instantly ashamed. The maps they had consulted didn't give any indication of the status of an area: Balthasar couldn't have known.

The Delian turned to face her, scowling, but his words were drowned in a sudden sliding rumble. It came from behind them, from the end of the street. Silence swung around, instinctively drawing her heylin. The entire facade of one of the fire-marked buildings had collapsed, the rubble blocking the street almost completely. No, she realized an instant later, not collapsed. It had been brought down deliberately, a neat and very effective trap. Figures in orange and blue were climbing over the piled rubble, and out of the broken building. She glanced without hope over her shoulder, and saw still more of them edging out of the alleys.

"Oh, fuck it," Balthasar said softly, his heylin cradled in both hands. Silence lifted hers as well, hoping that the advancing figures would recognize the threat. Chase Mago swept the vox protectively against his body, leveling his heylin one-handed. The figures—they were all young, mostly adolescents, Silence realized numbly—stopped when they were a few meters away, and began spreading out, trying to encircle the star-travellers.

"Oh, no, you don't," Balthasar said, and fired quite deliberately into the wall just in front of a tall boy in blue feathers. He jerked back—none of them had been expecting the heylin's fixed-fire bolts, Silence thought, with sudden hope—and the advance halted. She kept her heylin levelled anyway, pointing it at the nearest of the attackers.

"Do we try talking?" she murmured.

Balthasar shook his head, and somehow managed a strained smile. "No good. This kind don't talk."

Wonderful, Silence thought. "So what do we do?"

Balthasar didn't answer immediately, swinging slowly to face the direction they had been travelling. Very deliberately, he lowered his heylin at the closest of the figures—a young woman this time, her hair bound up with orange and blue beads—and took two steps forward. The woman hesitated, then took a slow step back. Balthasar took another step forward, saying softly, "Follow me."

The woman leaped backward, shouting, "Fitch!"

Balthasar cursed and dodged sideways, just avoiding a thrown rock. Silence fired twice, not bothering to aim, and saw one of the attackers fall. Then she saw a glint of metal in the hand of a youth at the back of the crowd, from an object she recognized only too well. The magi's usual protections were useless against it; her only defense was to use the Art before the boy could fire. She fired at him, but missed, and saw him dive behind a pile of rubble. Time slowed; she reached instinctively for the planetary harmonies, to shape the weapons she needed, but her mind rebounded from the overlying noise of the machines. It was not as bad as it had been in other parts of the city—the buildings here were empty shells, the dull brick acting almost as a baffle. She let her heylin fall to the ground at her feet, reaching again, with more care and with more focussed strength, for the harmonies surrounding her. For a fleeting moment, the world wavered, and then she had it under control, the music vibrant in the air around her.

Already, the boy hiding behind the rubble had levelled his gun, was shouting for the others to get out of his way. She could feel its distortion in the enclosing music. This was no place for subtlety, for the usual barriers and counter-Words. She spoke a single Word, and a tiny patch of hell blossomed between her cupped hands, a door into the Formless potential of the submaterial world. Hastily, she summoned Form, the first that sprang to mind, the union of fire and air that was the lightning bolt, then spoke the Words that would direct it to its target, the combination of metal and powdered fire that practically shrieked its menace aloud. There was no time to do more, to shape the bolt or to allow for displacement. She opened her hands and the lightning roared upward, air splitting away from its passage. A man's height above her hands, the bolt divided, became threefold. The three fell together, one striking at the youth Silence had seen behind the pile of rubble, the others splitting off to strike guns she had neither seen nor felt. Then the fire vanished, the air rolling back in a single long peal of thunder. Silence swallowed hard, looking at the charred corpses, but kept her hands steady before her, containing and controlling the patch of hell.

"Let us pass," she said, and her voice was very loud in the sudden quiet.

For a long moment no one moved, the figures in orange and blue standing frozen in the dirty street. Then, very slowly, one tall boy let the chain he carried slide, rattling, to the ground. The clatter and splash of metal seemed almost as loud as the thunder; Silence winced, and kept her hands steady with an effort.

"It's her," the boy said, and sank slowly to his knees.

An inarticulate murmur like a sudden wind ran through the group. Silence did not dare take her eyes from them to glance at the other star-travellers, waiting tensely at her shoulders, but in her state of heightened awareness she could sense their confusion and wary hope, feelings that matched her own.

"No. . . ." The voice, a woman's voice, came from behind Silence. The pilot turned, not daring to move too quickly, keeping the patch of hell steady before her. The opening spat and fizzed as the unFormed potential struck her hastily constructed barrier, sparks rising from and falling back into an eye-searing disk that was at once all colors and no color at all. Another awed murmur rippled through the crowd, the sound tinged with fear. Another youth dropped to his knees, and a girl followed him, stretching herself face down on the cracked paving. One by one, the others followed, until only a single woman was left standing. It was she who had spoken before, Silence knew, but she herself said nothing, waiting for the other woman to speak.

"Silence," Balthasar said, very softly. "Silence. . . ."

"Shh." Silence fixed her eyes on the standing woman, and lifted one eyebrow in imperious question. The woman hesitated a moment longer, then, grudgingly, bent her knee. Silence took a deep breath, and nodded to the men at her shoulders.

"All right, let's go," she whispered, and took a step forward.

"Lady." It was the kneeling woman who spoke, in a harsh, painful voice. "We repent our sin. Don't leave us, we beg you."

Silence froze, the words echoing in her mind. Behind her, she heard Chase Mago's startled gasp, and Balthasar whispered a curse.

"We will serve you faithfully. We've waited for you loyally all these years," the kneeling woman went on. "Punish us however you want, but don't leave us."

"Who—" Silence began, and then rephrased her question, a vague plan forming in her mind. "Who am I?"

"Herself," the kneeling woman answered. "The Empress."

Abruptly, Silence was seized with the desire to laugh. It was too much, that these crazy natives should go from trying to kill her to kneeling at her feet, that they should call her empress. She struggled to keep her face expressionless, the laughter welling up inside her.

"We'll serve you," the kneeling woman said, her voice cajoling now. "We'll do whatever you want—look." She reached into the bloused front of her bright-blue vest, and pulled out a small, glittering disk. "See, we've done what we were told; we've gathered the forbidden tools. Please, stay."

Silence's eyes narrowed, the laughter draining away. The woman was holding an old-fashioned astrolabe, the tool port astrologers had used to calculate relative planetary positions and the intersecting harmonic envelopes. Such a thing shouldn't be loose on Earth, especially not here in the Kills. . . . At her shoulder, Balthasar said softly, "This is beginning to show potential."

Chase Mago shook his head fractionally, the vox humana still hugged close to his body. "I don't like it," he said.

Silence hesitated. She had no doubt that this gang was dangerous, and the dangers of impersonating a deity were a staple of star-travellers' fiction. But the woman had an astrolabe—carried it in her pocket like any professional astrologer—and she promised other items. . . . And, almost as important, they could use this gang to protect themselves from Rafaiel. I've been with Denis entirely too long, she thought, but nodded slowly. "Very well," she said, and closed her hands over the patch of hell, whispering the Word that sealed it. "We'll stay with you for a while."

"Thank you, lady," the kneeling woman said. She looked up, questioningly, and Silence realized she was waiting for permission to rise. The pilot nodded, and the other woman pushed herself slowly to her feet, her head still lowered subserviently.

"I'm named Efelay," she said. "What—how should we call you, lady?"

The pilot hesitated in her turn, wondering if she should invent something, but then shrugged internally. "My name is Silence," she began, and was cut off by the sudden awed murmur from the crowd.

"Haven't they ever heard a virtue-name before?" Chase Mago muttered into the noise.

Silence shook her head. "Why should they have?" she answered, still watching Efelay. The native woman lifted her hands, waiting until the crowd quieted again.

"And these others?" She nodded toward Balthasar and Chase Mago.

Silence hesitated again. If she told the truth, she might be able to associate the other star-travellers with whatever odd virtue she'd acquired; a lie would be pointless, without knowing more of this group's morals, and difficult to maintain. She said slowly, "They're my husbands. Julian Chase Mago and Denis Balthasar."

Efelay nodded, an almost ritual movement. "Then will you come with us, sieuri?"

"We will," Silence answered.

At her back, Balthasar gave a choked laugh, and said, in his broadest Delian accent, "Gods-consort, are we? What next?"

CHAPTER 8

Efelay led them through the narrow, empty streets with unerring grace, the rest of the gang following at a respectful distance. Silence was very aware of their presence but was equally certain that she had cowed them, at least for now. As they passed yet another burned-out group of factories, these marked with some of the same orange-and-blue symbols worn by the gang members, Silence wondered again if she was doing the right thing. Still, they did have the astrolabe, and Efelay had promised other "forbidden items": even so, Silence kept her inner ear tuned to the surrounding harmonies, ready in an instant to summon up the powers that had over-awed the gang before.

They were coming up on another building almost covered with orange-and-blue markings, the painted symbols taller even than Chase Mago. Some were completely unfamiliar, names and slogans written in a mixture of coinë and local orthography; others were distortions of the magi's symbols. Silence's eyes narrowed, seeing those. One was a symbol of simple conjuration, and the double lines of alchemical multiplication were repeated above and to either side of a boarded-over doorway; beyond that was a distorted drawing that might have been the sign of projection, but the simple lines had been doubled and redoubled until the meaning was completely lost. The pilot frowned. None of the symbols was placed properly to call on any power. They were scattered at random, almost as though a child with a hieroglyphica had been allowed to scribble on the walls. If this was all the knowledge the gang possessed, she had already lost her gamble.

To her surprise, however, Efelay led them past the painted building, then through an increasingly complicated series of alleys, until at last they reached a narrow street almost blocked by fallen bricks and wood. Efelay turned into that maze, walking along the right-hand wall, and seemed to vanish as she ducked under a massive beam that slanted from the ruined upper story to the rubble below. Silence checked, startled, and Balthasar said, "Go on." The gang pressed close behind.

There was a note in his voice that allowed no argument. Silence did as she was told, running one hand lightly along the wall. As she reached the beam, the wall disappeared: there was an entrance hidden there, shadowed by the beam and the rubble, and further concealed by curtains hung to trap the light. She fought her way through the heavy fabric, swearing to herself, and emerged into a narrow corridor where the paint was peeling in great strips from the walls. Efelay was waiting at its end, at the top of a badly lit stairway. More curtains shrouded the landing, cutting off any light from below.

"Down here," she said, and beckoned.

Silence followed, glancing back only once to make sure the other star-travellers were at her back. The rest of Efelay's people trailed after, but she ignored them.

The gang's quarters were well below ground level, and cut off from the rest of the abandoned building by still more blind turns and elaborate light traps. The building had probably once been a factory, Silence thought, with these lower levels once used for transit access or for work that needed to be shielded from all outside influences, but the room in which they finally stopped had been changed beyond all recognition.

It was another long room, perhaps three times as long as it was wide, with poured-stone walls that seemed to exude a damp chill. Silence shivered once, and disciplined herself to be still. The first two-thirds of the room was almost empty, dismounted tables and folding chairs, all of brightly colored plastic, stacked against the walls. The walls at the far end of the room had been hung with thick curtains painted with some of the brightly colored symbols that she had seen on the building outside. Here, they seemed to have been arranged in a more considered order. She frowned, trying to trace the common theme, and then realized that the symbols had been ordered according to the ancient—and anciently discredited—zodiacal system. A low platform had been built up within the space enclosed by the curtains, its top painted black, and marked with more silver-grey symbols. From where she stood, it was hard to be sure, but the pilot thought she recognized a Ficinan-derived schema of the Earth system. She frowned, confused—a two-dimensional model was less than useless for operations of the Art, and not much use for star-travellers, either, even if the Earth natives knew anything about it—and Efelay cleared her throat.

"If you'll take your place, lady?"

Silence took a deep breath. This was the moment she had been dreading since she'd made the decision to go with the gang, the moment when she'd have to admit that she didn't have any idea what they wanted of her. Balthasar would bluff, she knew, and bluff magnificently, with no more information than she had. Or did she know more than she'd thought? she wondered abruptly. They'd spoken of the empress, as Quin Javerry said his father had done; predictors did tap into a common, if frequently silly and ultimately uncontrollable source, and she did know what the elder Javerry had seen. . . . She pitched her voice carefully, using the tones reserved for public—and therefore impressive—ritual, and said, "What is it you want of me?"

She heard an intake of breath behind her: neither Balthasar nor Chase Mago had heard her use that voice before. There was a murmur at once awed and unhappy from the gang members crowding the doorway. Efelay caught her breath, too, and answered, stammering a little, "To—to teach us, lady. That's why you've come?" Her voice trailed off at the end, and Silence lifted an eyebrow.

"Is it?"

Efelay hesitated, but rallied quickly. "So we were promised."

Silence smiled deliberately. "Are you certain of that?" Without waiting for Efelay's answer, she swept on, "Think: you saw that I—we—would come here, that I would be, as I am, a magus. You were promised nothing more." She held her breath again, hoping that she'd guessed right, that they hadn't seen anything more than the older Javerry. They couldn't've seen more, she told herself again, but her muscles tightened anyway, ready to fight or run.

Slowly, Efelay nodded, and Silence hid her own gasp of relief. From the crowd behind her came a second voice, a young man's this time. "I told you that was all, that this didn't have anything to do with the teacher."

In her state of heightened awareness, Silence could hear the first stirrings of skepticism in the young man's voice, and braced herself to meet it. Before she could speak, however, Efelay said, "She knew what was seen, didn't she?"

"Yeah, Fitch, you can't argue with that." The voice, too young to be surely either male or female, came from somewhere in the group on the stairs, and was echoed by a mutter of agreement.

"So?" The young man the others had called Fitch was quick to answer. Silence glanced sideways, and saw him shouldering his way out from among the others, a tall, skinny youth with the beginnings of a beard straggling across his jawline. In an attempt to make the fair hairs seem thicker, he had dyed them blue and orange; instead of making him look ridiculous, the patchy color somehow added to the menace.

"Fitch," Efelay said, with new formality, "is our anadvocate."

Silence nodded, wondering how that concept—the Contrary, the one required to speak for the unpopular side—had survived the centuries, when so much else had been lost.

"If she didn't come to teach us," Fitch said, "what's she here for?"

It was a pity, however, Silence thought remotely, that so many anadvocates seemed to enjoy the job. She could feel the other star-travellers' sudden tension at her side, and said, "I—we—are here for purposes of our own. That we encountered you I admit is a sort of good fortune. You have certain things that could help us, and we would be willing to trade knowledge, teaching, for them. But we were not—sent—to teach you, that I deny."

Fitch and Efelay exchanged glances, the woman expressionless, Fitch frowning, and then the anadvocate said, "I accept that."

Silence heard Chase Mago's soft sigh of relief, but there was something in Fitch's stance that stopped her from echoing it.

"But," Fitch said, "if this is just a matter of bargaining, what's the price for the three of us she killed, and the wounded?"

Silence raised an eyebrow, hiding the cold fear in her stomach. That they could escape, she had no doubt—she could still feel the harmonies, could still feel the powers waiting within her—but it could cost them dearly. She could not defend them all against the gang's mechanical weapons. "That was fair fight," she said, and smiled.

There was a long pause, and then, quite slowly, the anadvocate nodded. "Fair fight," he acknowledged, "but there should be a price." The crowd murmured in agreement.

Efelay clapped her hands, cutting off the noise. "Will you give rest?"

Silence hesitated, not knowing exactly what the other woman meant, and Fitch said, "The rite *thambhor*."

Silence bit off an instinctive refusal. At her back, Balthasar said, "Do it."

With an effort, Silence kept her face expressionless, forcing back her anger. *Thambhor* was another of the examples the magi on Solitudo used to point out the misuses of the Art, a simple, almost mechanical operation invested with a significance far greater than its real symbolic values. Still, she knew what the rite involved, if not the forms of the ritual; she could do what had to be done. And Balthasar was right; it was a small enough price to pay to win the gang's support. She took a deep breath, and said, as calmly as she could, "I'll do it, as you ask, as payment. But I'll tell you this, also as payment—as a first teaching. There's no virtue in this rite, except for the virtue—no, the necessity—of getting rid of the bodies."

There was a murmur at that, incredulous and tinged with anger, and Silence bit her lip, afraid she'd gone too far. Chase Mago stirred at her side. "Or such virtue as imparted to it by the good intentions of practitioner and witnesses," he said.

Silence gave him a startled glance—she hadn't expected that particular brand of metaphysics from the engineer—but nodded slowly.

"Let's go," Efelay said, and pointed toward the stairs.

The bodies had been left in yet another section of the warren, reached through another series of stairs and tunnels. Finally they had climbed the last stairway, and ducked through a carefully arranged light trap into a small, stone-paved courtyard. Half of its surface was covered with rubble, narrowing the space even further. In the center, piled awkwardly on a trestle table, lay the bodies of the gang members killed in the attack. No one had made any attempt to lay out the charred bodies properly; whoever had brought them had apparently decided he or she had done enough just by placing them on the table. Silence swallowed hard, sickened by what she'd done. She doubted she would have done any better, wasn't sure she would have done as much.

The gang had followed her up the stairs, had, without speaking, arranged themselves around the walls of the courtyard, with Efelay standing at the far side of the circle. Silence looked up sharply, and Efelay said, "Let's begin."

"Let's," Fitch echoed, and Silence was grateful for his acid voice. His anger steadied her; she put her own guilt and sorrow grimly aside, and concentrated on the work at hand. This was a work of simple dissolution—she would not think of it as *thambhor*—an operation controlled primarily by a world's lunar harmonies, and by the interaction of core notes and the distant, dissonant music of its moons. On a moonless world, one could use the music of the system's other planets, though that was a less effective expedient, and it was often better to use another operation altogether, but here. . . . Silence glanced up, and saw Earth's single moon, rising three-quarters full above the broken roofs of the surrounding factories. One moon—the first moon known to human beings, to the first magi—and one core harmony, a music that was becoming more familiar to her with every passing day. She murmured the First Cantation, letting herself slide into the familiar waiting state. It was becoming easier to block out the noise of the machines, though there seemed to be fewer of them in this part of the mainurb; she could feel the core notes almost at once, and let them rise around her. Then, very cautiously, she damped them down, as she would damp down the music of the harmonium, and reached instead for the music of the moon.

It was there, but very faint, despite the swollen shape in the sky. She listened for what seemed to be a very long time before she was sure she had it under control. Only then did she speak the Words that brought the two harmonies together. There was a sort of sigh in the courtyard's chill air, a buzzing that was almost like a human music. Faintly, Silence heard a murmur from the gang members lined up along the walls, and, as faintly, heard Balthasar telling them to be quiet.

The buzzing sigh swelled further, the sound taking form, a faint silver haze, just visible against the dark walls. Silence spoke again, shaping and directing the controlled dissonance. The haze moved, coalescing into a silver fog. She gestured, and it moved toward the table where the bodies lay. Slowly, moving under her direction, the fog formed itself into a ragged disk, and lowered itself toward the bodies. Tendrils formed, drooped, and touched the bodies, faint sparks showing here and there. Silence brought the disk closer, until it touched and enclosed the bodies, hiding them from sight. The sound shifted, darkened and deepened, and then returned to what it had been. Silence spoke a final Word, releasing the controlled harmonies. There was a sound almost like chimes, and the silvery light vanished. The bodies were gone as well.

Silence glanced around the circle, feeling the weariness that came from performing such an operation completely unsupported, but not daring to acknowledge it yet. "There," she said aloud, "what you asked is done."

"It's done," Efelay agreed, and, after a moment, Fitch nodded, too.

"It's done."

"And our bargain?" Silence asked. "My teaching in exchange for the use of your—what you call your forbidden tools?"

There was another, shorter pause, and then Efelay nodded. "It's a bargain, lady Silence."

"It's a bargain," the anadvocate echoed.

The gang provided them with a pair of rooms in one of the factory outbuildings, in a section set well apart from the gang's other holdings, and not too obtrusively guarded. The gang controlled the usable parts of at least four such structures, each one linked to the main building through a maze of tunnels. The tunnels had to antedate the abandoning of the factory, Silence thought—the gang didn't have the technical or mechanical skills to dig so deep in the Kills' unstable soil—but she could not figure out the tunnels' original purpose. They were convenient, though, allowing the gang to move from one part of the factory to another without being seen, and adding an additional layer of insulation against both mechanical sensors and the more sophisticated questers available to the Rose Worlders.

After the first few days, the gang was scrupulous in allowing them the appearance of privacy, though Balthasar swore they were still being watched. Silence did not doubt him: whatever else they might be, the gang, and Efelay in particular, was not noticeably naive. As an experiment, Silence enclosed their rooms in an aphonic ring; when none of the gang members mentioned the creation, she sealed off the space with a simonist lock, keyed only to the star-travellers. Its presence was unmistakable, unlike the ring's, and she waited nervously for Efelay or Fitch to comment on it. Neither mentioned it, however, and the pilot allowed herself to relax a little.

Efelay allowed the star-travellers access to the gang's collection of "forbidden tools" almost at once, and when Silence said she needed materials she had left at the hostel, sent a couple of gang members to fetch the carryalls. Looking at the materials the gang had collected, Silence was very glad she had a few things of her own. The gang's collection of tools was a very mixed bag, ranging from useful items such as the astrolabe to a child's toy, a Ficinan model of the Earth system enclosed in a sphere of crystal. The planets, surrounded by haloes of colored light representing the planetary harmonies, moved soundlessly along their orbits, the lights fuzzing and blending as the planets moved from opposition to conjunction. Silence appropriated that at once as a useful tool for her teaching, leaving the engineer to explore the rest of the cache.

She discovered almost at once that she had no talent for teaching, lacking the ability to restate a paradigm in order to make it comprehensible. To her surprise, however, both Balthasar and the anadvocate Fitch had that knack, and were able to translate for her. Her more complicated explanations tended to be filtered first through the Delian, and then through Fitch, who worked and reworked Balthasar's version until Efelay and a dark youth named T'la, who seemed to be the most naturally talented of the group, understood.

Taken as a group, the gang knew a surprising number of individual facts—among other things, they believed in what Fitch described, with a sardonic grin, as the "UFO heresy," that space travel is or was once possible, and that there were other intelligent beings on unnamed other planets, which made it easier for the star-travellers to explain the Rose Worlders' domination of Earth. They also had learned, from samizdat, the crude, hand-printed booklets that circulated at astronomical prices among the Kills' underworld, a surprising assortment of workable and unworkable operations. However, they lacked both an organizing principal and an awareness of the importance of such a principal. Silence, trying to take them through what she remembered of the Trivium as she had been taught it on Solitudo, was continually sidetracked by questions about the more sophisticated applications of the Three Arts, and frustrated by her own inability to explain why the basic structure was so important.

"Why don't we just write it all down, and then look it up when we need it?" a skinny boy—Larabee, his name was, Silence remembered, after a moment's thought—complained. It was a least the fourth time that day that someone had made the same objection. Silence took a deep breath, fighting back her anger.

"Because you may not have the books with you, or have time to look it up," she said, shortly, falling back on the one explanation that seemed to carry some weight with the Earth natives. There was more to it than that—a written chart was static, unable to express the multiple nexuses, the subtle and shifting connections between categories, all of which were governed by explicit symbolic rules. On Solitudo, she had learned those rules by rote, memorizing both those lists and the elaborate ordering methods, systems far more complicated than the comparatively simple rules for piloting, simply because she had been told to do it, because that was the way the Art was learned. She had been rewarded by the wonderful moment when everything suddenly became clear, the almost-epiphany when the systems began to function as they should, leading her mind automatically through the required conjunctions. She had tried explaining that, once, and Balthasar had done his best to translate, but even he hadn't fully understood. Silence had admitted defeat, and looked instead for the practical explanations that seemed to convince the students.

"But doesn't it take time to remember all that?" someone else, a girl this time, asked from the back of the group.

Sometimes, Silence thought, I'd almost believe the magi when they say women don't have the right sort of mind to appreciate the Art. She controlled her anger, and said, "No. The more you learn—the more you know, the faster it gets."

The girl scowled, and Fitch said, "Like a computer, sort of. The better you know the system, the faster you find things?" He looked at Silence with a sudden smile, pleased with the metaphor.

Nothing like a computer, Silence thought, with a shiver of distaste. A computer is non-thought, anti-thought; what it creates destroys the Art. . . . She put aside that knowledge with an effort, forced herself to contemplate the metaphor itself, as a metaphor, without the emotional resonances. After all, she herself had learned to use the information systems at the transport stations—which were computers—by making use of the techniques she had learned on Solitudo to analyze unfamiliar symbolic languages. Still, the equation of computer knowledge with the symbology that was the basis of the Art disturbed her on a very deep level. To make that association seemed somehow dangerous, inviting the computer's anti-thought to invade the Art at its most basic, and thus most vulnerable point. Fitch was waiting for his answer, the smile fading a little. Silence sighed. "Yes, that's true to a certain extent," she said. "But remember what I told you about computers before. They can't be used around the workings of the Art—they're like all mechanical creations, except worse. So it's a dangerous way to think of it, Fitch, even if it's true."

"But if it's just a metaphor," Larabee began, and Silence glared at him.

"Damn it, how many times do I have to tell you? Metaphors are *real*." She bit back the rest of her outburst, and went on, more calmly, "Metaphor is simply one class of symbol, do you see that? And symbols are the basis of the Art; symbols are the way we manipulate reality, and therefore symbols are—must be—real, too. Think about that for the rest of the day, understand it. We'll talk more about it tomorrow."

She pushed herself to her feet before anyone could protest at the abrupt ending, and stalked off toward the room where Chase Mago was working. She ignored Efelay's voice behind her, soothing and dismissing the others. After a moment, she became aware of Balthasar's presence at her elbow, and slowed apologetically. To her relief, however, the Delian didn't mention the day's lesson, saying instead, "How's Julie doing with the vox?"

Silence shrugged. "How would I know? I think he's still sorting out what works from the mess they've collected." She still sounded sour, and knew it. She glanced sideways with a half-smile of apology, and Balthasar nodded.

"Frustrating, I know. But it buys us time—and the use of their toys."

Silence smiled fully then in spite of herself. "Don't you feel old?"

Balthasar grinned back. "Not me."

Silence snorted, and then they had reached the painted curtain that covered the door of the gang's treasure room. The curtain was the result of the pilot's first attempt to teach the gang an elementary manipulation, before she'd realized how fragmentary their knowledge really was. She lifted her hand, feeling the warding music imprisoned in warp and weft, held by the painted pattern, and pushed it aside to step into the enclosed space. Chase Mago had set up a sort of workshop here, covering the walls and the floor and ceiling with crudely made baffles, but Silence could feel the leashed music trembling in the air around her. If the shielding ever failed, or if she and the engineer had been less skillful than they'd thought in preparing the baffles, the Rose Worlders could hardly miss the site. And the Rose Worlders did keep a watch for such things; she had learned that much in her time with the gang. Quin Javerry had been right; the Rose Worlders had attacked the farm because they'd discovered the senior Javerry's successful experiments. The farm, unshielded and set far away from the urban areas that might have provided some disguising dissonance, must have sung on their screens like a half-tuned keel. Silence winced, and put the thought aside.

Chase Mago had sorted the gang's collection of "forbidden tools" into several different categories, and objects were arranged along the walls and across the single work table in a complicated pattern. Most of the items had been set in a pile at the back of the room as useless. Silence recognized a ring from an orrery among the debris, and a couple of frayed strings that might once have belonged to a magus's monochord, but most of the things were no longer identifiable. What could the scraps of black cloth have been? she wondered. Durafelt, or some other material for baffles? She stooped to touch it, but felt only ordinary cloth.

The engineer grunted his agreement, and Silence looked up quickly.

"I'd like to know why they brought it, too," Chase Mago went on. "Hell, I'd like to know why they got most of this stuff, never mind where."

Balthasar laughed. "You can't expect them to tell you where they got it, Julie. They've got their trade secrets."

"I'd like to know—I need to know what some of this is." Chase Mago gestured to a handful of clear tubes spread out on the main table. They glittered and sparked in the glow from the fixed-fire lamp Silence had rigged for the work space. "Those, for instance. I could maybe use them for a tuner, but I haven't the faintest idea what the tolerances might be—from the look of them, they could be anything from ship's parts to something out of a homunculus, for God's sake. And I don't have enough of them to test them out—half of them are flawed anyway, and by the time I knew what I had, I'd've smashed them all."

He stopped, glaring at the other star-travellers, and Silence said quickly, "I think we might be able to talk Efelay into telling us what these things were being used for when they acquired them."

"If they know," Balthasar said. He leaned against the work-table, and picked up one of the thin tubes. He held it under the light, turning it so that reflected lights danced across the peeling walls. Chase Mago gave an exclamation of annoyance, and took it away from him.

"Do you want the counter-clash to shatter it? Leave my things alone."

The Delian shrugged, and looked at Silence. "I just wonder how much of this they're buying on the darkside, getting it third- or fourth-hand from people who don't know what it is, either."

Silence shook her head. "Not too much," she said, thoughtfully. "To make it worth buying, someone must know something. . . ." Her voice trailed off as she glanced at the objects littering the room. "No, that's not necessarily so, is it? There seems to be a market for anything the Rose Worlders use." She shook herself. "Still, why don't we try asking it that way, Denis? Put it as needing to know what things were being used for, not where they got it."

"We can try," Balthasar said, "but I'm not hopeful."

"It would be a help," Chase Mago said, with thinly disguised impatience.

"We'll try," Silence said, and touched his shoulder gently.

The engineer made a face, shrugging a little, but did not turn away. Before he could say anything, however, the bells sewn to the inside of the door curtain chimed, and one of the younger gang members stuck his head into the workshop.

"Sorry, guys—sieuri, I mean—but Efelay wants to see you right now, all of you. She says it's important."

Silence exchanged quick glances with the other star-travellers. It wasn't like Efelay to interrupt them—and it wasn't like her to overestimate a thing's importance, either. "We'll come. Where is she?"

"In the Out," the boy answered. "I'll take you."

The Out was the surviving half of a building set somewhat apart from the rest of the factory used by the gang. There was no tunnel leading from the last of the linked buildings to the Out; instead, the star-travellers followed their guide up a narrow stairway to a smelly, half-covered alley. It was the first time in several days that Silence had been outside, and she found herself glancing rather wistfully at the hazy sky.

The boy led them through a low arch half hidden by a carefully arranged pile of rubble, then through yet another series of light traps and into a narrow, badly lit hall. The walls were scribbled with more of the gang's orange and blue symbols, the symbols they used, Silence realized, to mark their "public" buildings, the ones from which they confronted strangers.

The hall ended abruptly in a curtained doorway. The boy paused there briefly, then swept the curtain up and back. Silence took a deep breath, suddenly aware of the theatricality of the gesture, and made her entrance.

The room was crowded, perhaps a third of the gang gathered in its center. Efelay turned as the star-travellers entered, and beckoned for them to join her, saying, "Lady Silence, I think this is a matter that concerns you."

"Oh?" The pilot came forward warily. The walls, painted with the overlapping orange and blue designs for perhaps three or four meters, only accentuated the height of the ceiling; it was like walking into the bottom of one of the crystal tubes that controlled Solitudo Hermae's atmosphere. The gang made way for her, and closed in again behind the star-travellers as they passed.

Efelay and Fitch were standing together at the center of the circle, staring thoughtfully at the man whose arms were pinioned by two more gang members. He stared back with a sort of frightened determination, licking at the blood that trickled from his split lip. He was young, Silence saw, not much older than most of the gang members, and handsome in a nervous, feral way. He wore a short, brocaded coat that glittered with multicolored metallic threads, and a brightly feathered mask lay crumpled at his feet. Rich boy, Silence thought, but then she saw the worn workcloth trousers, and the coat's carefully mended seams. Not rich, then, but fashionable beyond his means, and in a way she hadn't seen before.

"Lady Silence," Efelay said again. "This—person says he has business with you."

The prisoner took a half-step forward, and was hauled back by his guards. "You're the ones who bought my vox?" he said, and winced as the words jarred his cut mouth.

"Your vox?" Chase Mago said involuntarily.

Silence gestured for him to be quiet. "We bought a vox, from a man called Rafaiel."

"That was mine." There was a desperation in his voice that had nothing to do with the gang surrounding him, and Silence's attention sharpened further.

"I need—I want it back," the young man continued. "I'll pay you what you spent, and then some—or whatever you want. But I want my vox back."

"I say we put him down the shaft," Fitch said, and nodded toward a gaping doorway at the far end of the room. Silence saw the prisoner twitch, but he kept his eyes focussed on her face.

"That vox had to have come from off-world, Julie?" she asked, keeping her voice low.

The engineer nodded. "It isn't old enough to be pre-War," he answered, in the same soft tone, "and it couldn't've been made here. Not without magi's help, anyway."

Silence nodded, as much to herself as to Chase Mago, and the prisoner said, "Then you'll let me have it back?"

"Maybe." Silence paused deliberately, studying the young man. He was afraid of the gang, she knew, could read that in every movement of his body, but there was something else driving him—someone of whom he was more afraid, perhaps? It was impossible to be sure, and she put that question aside for the moment. "Where'd you get this vox?"

The young man jerked in his captors' hands, and Silence's eyes narrowed. That was not the question he had been expecting, of that she felt sure. "Answer me," she said, and put compulsion into her voice. It wasn't a technique that often worked, and she was not surprised when the young man shook his head convulsively.

"I can't," he said, and shook his head again. His voice wavered as he added, "Surely it's not important?"

That was the textbook counter to an attempt at compulsion,

Silence knew, the attempt to distract the questioner, to postpone the next question in order to allow one to rebuild one's defenses. An off-world vox, and knowledge of off-world techniques. . . .

"I still say we ought to drop him down the shaft," Fitch said again.

"Not yet," Silence said, with deliberate menace, and raised her left hand. Slowly, exaggerating each movement, she began to sketch the outline of a geas, the pentagram first, and then the warding crescents. She glanced at the prisoner—he had paled even further, and he was sweating—and started to close the geas. The young man threw himself violently backward, almost dragging the guards down with him. They hauled him upright again, swearing, and one of them punched him hard in the stomach, doubling him over in their arms. Silence murmured the Words that dismissed the geas half-formed, and waited until the prisoner had his breathing under control again.

"So," she said, and smiled thinly. "You recognized that, too. Where did you learn it—the same place you got your vox?"

The young man hesitated, trembling, and Silence lifted her hand again.

"Yes," the prisoner said quickly. "Yes, that's right."

"Where?" Silence asked.

"From—a friend," the young man answered, and flinched, anticipating a blow that did not come.

"He sleeps with the Unionists," Efelay observed.

"Does he, now?" Balthasar murmured, and Silence couldn't check her own satisfied smile. A connection with the Unionists—with the Rose Worlders—recognition of a geas in formation, and a real vox humana. . . .

"The vox came from off-world," she said aloud. "Who gave it to you?"

The prisoner flinched again. "He'll kill me."

"We'll kill you," Efelay said, dispassionately.

"Answer me," Silence said, and lifted her left hand again.

The prisoner pulled away, and the guards dragged him back. "Don't," he said, and took a quick breath. "He works on the Island, that's all, just a friend."

Silence shook her head. "I can read you," she said, and the young man made a face.

"He works on the Island," he said again, and added, sullenly, "His name's Radan."

"Kennet Radan?" Efelay said sharply, and Fitch whistled. "We've caught us an interesting fish this time."

Radan? Silence thought. She glanced at Efelay, not wanting to ask aloud, and the gang leader shrugged.

"Kennet Radan is a Unionist functionary, mid-rank or better—his title's havildar, I think."

The young man made a slight, involuntary movement, and Silence nodded to herself. "Havildar" was an old, old word, dropped from all but the most formal hierarchies within a century of the War's ending. Even the Hegemony no longer used it, except as an honorific. Once, however, it had signified the second most powerful post within a government department, a position that did not change with party or dynasty, but was held by a professional bureaucrat. All things considered, she thought, I doubt an Earth native could rise much higher—and I'm quite sure no Rose Worlder would give a native a vox humana. She glanced at Balthasar and saw him smiling, the calculation obvious in his face.

"All right," she said slowly. "What's your name, anyway?"

The prisoner did not answer, but Fitch said, "He calls himself Mikajaa. He's a musician, of sorts."

"Mikajaa, then." Silence nodded. "I'll name a price for returning your vox. I want to see Radan."

"Silence?" Chase Mago's voice was frankly appalled.

The pilot glanced at him, unsmiling. "Don't you see? He can get us a tuner—if he got this Mikajaa a vox humana, he can get us a tuner, and you won't have to fool around with these bits and pieces." She looked back at the prisoner. "Because if he doesn't get us a tuner, we can destroy him without ever harming ourselves."

"Wait a minute," Efelay said, her face hardening abruptly. "We had an agreement."

Silence turned to the other woman, cursing her own unguarded tongue. "I don't see that this affects it," she began.

Fitch cut in. "This wasn't part of the bargain, messing with the Unions directly."

Silence lifted an eyebrow in calculated disdain and said to Efelay, "This is our best chance to get the thing we need—the tuner—without having to take all of the tools you've collected. I'm offering exactly what I offered before; it's just your part that's changed—become easier, I'd say."

Fitch frowned at that, but Efelay gestured for him to be quiet. "What exactly do you want?"

"Your support—your backing—when we meet Radan."

Efelay nodded. "For your teaching," she said, "We'll do it."

Mikajaa took a deep breath, and capitulated. "All right. I can take you to him."

"Oh, no," Balthasar said. "Neutral ground."

"The Earth-born don't leave the island," Mikajaa answered. He licked nervously at his bloody lip, and jerked his head at Efelay and Fitch. "Ask them, if you don't know yourselves. If he—if I—betrayed you, you could still ruin him." He grimaced bitterly. "You'll get your chance to talk to him. He'll probably like it."

Silence nodded. It seemed logical enough—if I were the Rose Worlder in charge of the local help, she thought, I wouldn't let them out of my sight, either—and Mikajaa was being right about his chances of betraying them. The only way to stop them from telling any captors what Mikajaa's patron had done was to kill them, and it was highly unlikely that the musician would be able either to do it himself or to arrange their deaths before one of them could tell the Rose Worlders just what was going on. It was a risk worth taking, if it would get them a real tuner, and get them off Earth that much more quickly. . . . She nodded again, decisively. "We'll do it," she said aloud.

"Silence," Chase Mago said again. "I can retune with what we've got."

"And how long will it take you?" Balthasar retorted. "She's right, Julie."

"There's more involved here than just retuning," Silence said. She hesitated, then added, "Aili, remember?" She willed them to understand. Whatever happened with their contract or with Aili, once the Hegemon understood that Earth could be taken from the Rose Worlders' control, there would be an invasion, and the more information they could provide, the less chance there would be of being dragooned into the invasion fleet. All around her, the gang members did their best to look as though they'd heard nothing, but she was not deceived. She lifted an eyebrow at the anadvocate, who had the grace to blush and look away.

The engineer sighed. "All right."

"Some of us will go with you part of the way," Efelay said. "Just to keep him honest."

Silence considered that for a moment, then nodded. "Up to the bridges, then."

"It'll be a pleasure," Fitch said, and gestured to the youths holding Mikajaa's arms. They released him, and the musician stooped quickly to recover his broken half-mask.

"One thing, Mikajaa," Silence said, and the musician straightened warily. "Do the bridge Watchers scan for weapons—off-world weapons," she added, and saw Mikajaa wince at her casual mention of forbidden topics.

"Answer the Lady," Fitch growled.

Mikajaa nodded reluctantly. "They scan for everything," he said, after a moment.

Silence glanced at the other star-travellers. "Better leave the heylins, then." She held out her hand.

Chase Mago slipped his heylin out of the pocket of his coat without protest, but Balthasar hesitated. "Do you think that's wise?"

"Wiser than trying to sneak them in," Silence answered. The Delian made a face, but handed over the heylin. The pilot put her own heylin with the others, and frowned down at the piled weapons. She could sense the leashed fire in their chambers, and the distant harmonies of the planet: carefully but quickly, she wove the two together, sealing the heylins in a shell of frozen air. When she had finished, they seemed to float a few centimeters above her hands, the seal invisible but tangible. She offered the creation to Efelay, who took it warily, shivering as her hands touched the invisible solidity.

"I've sealed them because I don't want anyone trying to use them and getting hurt," Silence said. They all knew that was not the whole truth, but Efelay nodded anyway.

"We'll keep them safe," she said.

"Thank you," Silence said, and turned her attention to the musician. He was wiping the blood from his mouth with the sleeve of his undershirt, but stopped, feeling her eyes on him.

"A warning, Mikajaa," the pilot went on. "You know what I am—I'll know if you're trying to betray us, and I'll stop you." She sketched the opening gesture of a geas in the air between them, and saw the musician flinch away again.

"I understand," he whispered.

"Good," Silence said coldly, and suppressed the sudden feeling of guilt. She had been under geas herself; she should know better than to use those tactics. . . . I haven't put him under geas, she told herself firmly, and I won't, if I can frighten him without it. That's all that matters, getting him to cooperate. She looked at her husbands, reading her own determination in their faces. "Let's go."

It was a long walk to the bridge that linked the Kills to the Rose Worlders' main holding on Man's Island itself. One spur of the elevated train ran there, of course, but Balthasar vetoed that, for fear Mikajaa would find some way of alerting the Transit Authority. The musician looked sulky at the suggestion, but said nothing. Instead, Fitch led them through the uncrowded streets, occasionally pausing to point out some local landmark. Balthasar listened closely, obviously plotting escape routes, and Silence was just as glad to let him deal with it, and with the other gang members who were following a distance behind, ready to intervene if they were attacked. Instead, she watched Mikajaa, trying to read the thoughts behind the handsome face. The musician was more than he seemed, of that she felt certain—for one thing, she could not imagine taking the risk of revealing any part of the Rose Worlders' secrets to someone who was nothing more than a convenient bedmate—but she couldn't be sure what he was, or just how much he did know. He would have to be watched closely once they came into the Rose Worlders' domain, she decided, and marshalled all her powers. Once they were across the bridge, everything would depend on her.

"We're coming up on the Rosemont," Fitch said over his shoulder. He slowed down as they approached the next cross street, coming to a halt in front of a barred store window. "I don't think we should go any farther."

Balthasar nodded. "All right. What's beyond here?"

"More stores, houses, a couple of blocks of that," Fitch answered, "and then the Rosemont. You just follow this street and it'll bring you right up to the approach."

"Wonderful," Chase Mago muttered, and made a gesture of apology. "Sorry, Fitch, no insult intended."

The anadvocate shrugged.

"Thank you, Fitch," Silence said. "We'll go on alone from here."

"I'll have T'la wait for you, here by the fountains," Fitch answered, and turned away.

"Fountains?" Silence said, and then she saw, between two houses, the entrance to a sort of courtyard. A stone basin was just visible between the walls, though no water played over its dusty surface. "Oh, I see."

Fitch lifted his hand in farewell, and was gone.

Silence turned back to study the musician, who returned her stare with outward calm. "You understand what you have to do," she said.

Mikajaa nodded. "It's my own neck, and Radan's," he said. "I'll tell them you're part of a band; that'll be good enough."

"It had better be," Balthasar said, with silken menace.

The musician gave him a baleful glare. "Do you think I want to get killed?"

"We're trusting not," Silence said. "Come on."

The street curved gently as they approached the Rosemont, then widened into a sort of plaza. The open space was paved with square tiles of some dark-grey stone; beyond it was a low, white-painted fence, reaching only to the middle of her thigh. A grass-covered hill rose gently beyond that, sweeping up to support the massive pillar of the bridge. There were no pedestrians in sight: clearly this was an area that ordinary people avoided. Silence frowned thoughtfully, studying the arrangement. It was significant, of that she felt sure, each element a part of some hidden schema, but she was not certain of its purpose. Or rather, she corrected herself, she could guess it had protective intent, but she wasn't certain of its precise function. The stone looked familiar, though—like the treated chips of slate the magi used to animate their Watchers, she thought suddenly, and her attention sharpened. That slate was far from inexpensive, or easily made; no one would use it for paving without very good reason.

Frowning, she whispered the Words that allowed her to see the patterns imposed by the Art. For a moment, she saw nothing, but then a web of twisted lines became visible, floating just above the surface of the slates. She studied it dubiously, her steps slowing, but saw no traps concealed in its convoluted surface. It was a variation of the same schemae that created the Watchers, a warning device, and nothing more. Even so, she found she was holding her breath as she stepped onto the dark stones.

The moment that her foot touched the first slate, a door slammed open in the base of the bridge piling. Even though she'd been expecting something, Silence jumped, startled, and glanced quickly at her companions. Balthasar smiled back at her, one hand resting on Mikajaa's shoulder in a seemingly friendly gesture. The musician's face was impassive. After a moment, Balthasar released him, still smiling, but kept close to the younger man's side.

Two men were waiting in the doorway, rifles lowered at the ready. Seeing that, Silence frowned and said, "Are they always this suspicious?"

Mikajaa nodded. "Oh, yeah. They don't really like having the Earth-born on the Island—if they could put us anywhere else, they would. But don't worry, I can get us through."

"I see." Silence studied him warily. This was the first time Mikajaa had volunteered information, and also the first time he'd referred to himself as one of the "Earth-born." I wonder, the pilot thought, does that refer to any native, or just to the ones who serve the Rose Worlders? And if it's the latter, have we been—very neatly—manipulated?

There was no time to pursue the thought. They had reached the bottom of the little hill, and Mikajaa stopped at the opening in the fence, nodding to the man who came down the hill toward them. The guard nodded back politely enough, but his face was closed and wary.

"Papers?"

Silence pulled her own folder carefully from her pocket,

and the others did the same. The guard scanned them without haste, and then handed Mikajaa's folder back to him.

"I know you," he said. "What about the rest of you?"

"They're friends of mine," Mikajaa said. "Part of the band. Mir Radan wanted to meet them."

The guard lifted an eyebrow, and flipped through the papers again, scanning each set of ident stamps in turn. After what seemed like an interminable time, but was probably only a minute or so, he shrugged and handed them back to Mikajaa. The musician, face still carefully impassive, handed them to their owners. "Do we pass?" he asked.

The guard hesitated, and then sighed. "Yeah, go ahead. You'll be red-stamped at the other end of the bridge. Mikajaa can tell you what that means."

"Thanks," Silence murmured, and the others echoed her. The guard did something with the control box at his belt, and nodded. Mikajaa stepped carefully through the opening, and the guard beckoned to the star-travellers.

"One at a time, now," he said.

Silence stepped through the opening first, and felt the tingling of a leashed newtonian field. It came from the fencing to either side, she realized, and shivered. Anyone attempting to cross that ordinary-looking fence would be immobilized by the field—would be torn apart, if the power input were high enough. She glanced at the other star-travellers, wondering if they'd felt it, too. Chase Mago lifted an eyebrow as he stepped through the gate, but Balthasar, as always, was unreadable.

"This way," Mikajaa said, and pointed to the open door.

A spiral stairway led up through the center of the pillar. There were guards at the top and bottom, but they made no move to stop the newcomers. Silence could feel their eyes on her, curious and appraising, and wished suddenly for a veil. Lacking that, she met their stares as calmly as she could, and hoped they would attribute her nervousness to ordinary fear.

The bridge itself was surprisingly narrow, barely wide enough for two groundcars to pass abreast, and quite empty of traffic. There was no provision for vehicles, either; in fact, the paving was deliberately ridged in a pattern designed to disrupt a hoverfan. Silence stumbled on the first of the ridges, and swore irritably.

"Over here," Mikajaa said.

There was a smoothed path through the ridges, after all, small enough to force them to walk single file. Mikajaa took the lead, and Silence fell in behind him, wishing she had been able to bring her heylin. Still, she consoled herself, at this distance the Art would be able to control him.

The bridge seemed very long. To either side, support-steel cables dipped and rose between the twinned towers, smaller cables connecting that broad coil to the platform of the roadway. The water was very blue and choppy, the surface broken up by hundreds of little waves that appeared and vanished abruptly. There was no particular pattern to their movement, no current visible in the water. Silence studied it curiously. Some of the water would be coming downriver, mingling here with the tide from the great ocean that lay to the east. She thought she could pick out a brownish tinge to the water to her left, but it might have been only the reflection of the buildings lining the shore. She sighed and looked alway.

As they approached the bridge's central tower, Silence became aware of a faint sighing, like the noise of wind through narrow-leaf marryns. The sound grew stronger as she came closer to the tower, becoming more like running water, or the noise of a distant fire.

At her back, Chase Mago said, "Do you hear—?"

"I hear it," Silence said, and touched Mikajaa's shoulder. The musician did not turn.

"There's some kind of guard field coming up," he said. "It's normal."

"I don't like it," the engineer muttered, but said nothing more.

Silence shivered, and felt the hairs on her arms rise slowly. Whatever the field was—not another newtonian field, that much she knew, but she did not recognize the schema—it was very powerful. The dull, rushing noise seemed to come from the clear air to either side of the tower, not from the tower itself. It grew still louder as they came within a few meters of the structure, and Silence caught herself glancing back, looking for the approaching wind. She controlled herself angrily, forcing herself to consider it as an academic problem, even as Mikajaa said, "Relax."

"You'd better be right about this," Balthasar said again, and Silence could hear the fear beneath the threat.

"It feels like—" she began, and stopped abruptly, remembering that the Rose Worlders would have listeners set up along the span of the bridge.

"Oh, I know, it's all right," Balthasar said, but he did not sound appeased.

"Relax," Mikajaa said again.

Then they had reached the tower. Silence could feel the leashed power, far greater than anything she had handled. Even on the Earth-road, when she had manipulated those magnificent symbols, she had been assisting an existing process, channeling power into a path for which it already had an affinity. Whatever formed the basis of this field was unstable, barely controlled by the strict bonds laid upon it. The pilot could feel its restlessness, could almost hear, beneath the rushing noise, a voiceless moaning, something demanding to be free. She could almost smell sulphur, the most common by-product of working with the submaterial, and held her breath as she stepped under the tower's arch.

The noise eased slightly, and the feeling of tension faded. She glanced over her shoulder, and saw what seemed to be a wall of fog, filling the space between the towers and curving across the water to either side. That explained the instability, at least: the magus who had built the barrier had created it so that it was invisible from the outside, all the visual clues to its existence confined inside it. That sort of trick was inherently unbalanced, expensive and difficult to maintain—but, Silence thought, probably the only way the barrier could be created without betraying its origins.

Man's Island itself loomed ahead, very green after the poured-stone buildings of the rest of the mainurb. Silence smiled in spite of herself, but Balthasar said sourly, "Very pretty."

Chase Mago laughed, but Silence nodded, the smile fading from her face. The careful landscape was too pretty, too perfect to be trusted. She looked more closely, and began to see the pattern hidden in the apparently random arrangement of the long buildings, the overlapping fields of fire from the fantastically decorated towers to either side, and the hedges and trees placed to herd invaders into certain specific areas. She couldn't tell exactly what would be hidden there, but she was certain she didn't want to find out directly.

There was another guard post at the end of the bridge. This time, their papers were checked at the top of the spiral stairs, and again at the bottom, before the guard captain nodded reluctantly. At his gesture, a second guard came forward with an oddly shaped vial fitted with a wide nozzle. "Hold out your hands."

Mikajaa did as he was told, and the star-travellers copied him. The guard touched a button on the side of the vial, and Silence felt her hands bathed in a damp, invisible mist.

"That's the red stamp," the guard captain said. "If you enter any restricted areas—they're clearly marked as forbidden— the stain will show, and alarms will sound. The penalties for trespassing begin with death." He sighed. "I suppose Mir Radan knows what he's doing," he said, and handed the ID folders back to the musician, who distributed them without speaking. "But you're responsible for them, Mikajaa, remember that."

"I know," Mikajaa said, and made a face. "I'm not likely to forget, am I?"

Silence tensed at that, bracing herself for betrayal, but the guard captain laughed and motioned them through the gate. The star-travellers followed Mikajaa across an immaculately groomed lawn, and then through a series of interlocking gates, half living tree and half metal, until they finally reached a low-lying building. Mikajaa paused in the shadow of the overhanging doorway, fumbling in the pocket of his brocaded coat. Silence eyed him warily, and Balthasar said, "Lost your keys?"

The musician glanced angrily at him, but said nothing. Instead, he pulled out a paper-thin disk a little smaller than a woman's hand and slipped it into an almost invisible slot beside the door's lock mechanism. There was a distant chime, and a hatch slid back to reveal a small screen and keyboard. The screen was blank, but Mikajaa studied it for a moment anyway, his head tilted to one side, before typing in a quick series of commands. Silence, watching shamelessly over his shoulder, recognized the access and inquiry codes for the Hegemony's most common control system, and filed the information for later use. After a moment, the screen flashed a curt message, "entrance permitted", and the door unlocked itself noisily. Mikajaa pushed it open, motioning for the others to precede him into the building.

"After you," Silence said, firmly. The musician shrugged, and did as he was told. When nothing happened, the star-travellers followed.

The doorway opened onto a sort of low balcony that overlooked a sunken reception room. Silence caught her breath, recognizing goods from across human-settled space—handwoven rugs from Athlit laid over a much larger, darkly patterned carpet, a crystal carved in the shape of a Sareptan orchid, an immense platter that seemed to have been made from a single, meter-long piece of cloud-agate—and Mikajaa said, "This way."

"So you were right about this Radan importing things," Chase Mago murmured, and the pilot nodded.

"I hope I'm right about the rest." She followed the musician down the short ramp into the reception room, feeling her feet sink deep into the carpet's thick pile. A faint, cinnamony scent rose from it: chamaas, she realized, and whistled softly.

"Come now, sieura, I didn't think you'd be impressed."

The voice, with its perfectly accented coinë—the coinë of the star lanes, not of Earth—came from the left. Silence controlled her first reaction, made herself turn slowly to face the stranger. A man was standing in a door set just beyond the ramp, hidden from above by a carefully placed painted screen. He was not a particularly big man, a little above medium height, with greying hair and a strong, rather fleshy face. He was wearing a floor-length scarlet coat covered from hem to knee with gold embroidery: in the old days, Silence remembered, that had been the mark of a havildar.

"Sieur Radan," she said, and was pleased that her voice remained steady.

"Sieura—Silence? Surely that's not your only name." Radan stepped into the room, and Mikajaa came forward quickly, easing the coat from the havildar's shoulders. He slipped it onto the t-shaped stand that stood in one corner of the room, and returned with a crystal goblet, which he handed to Radan.

"It is my name," Silence said, and smiled.

"As you wish." The havildar gestured to the carved chairs that stood at studied intervals across the room. He had been wearing a plain tunic and workcloth trousers beneath the robe of office, Silence saw—an interesting affectation, she thought, as she seated herself in the chair closest to the door, but not necessarily significant.

"I'll stand," Balthasar said, with a grin, and leaned against the back of the pilot's chair. Chase Mago settled himself on the floor beside Silence without a word.

"Drinks?" Radan asked, and nodded to Mikajaa. The musician came forward with a tray on which stood four glasses. Silence took one, but did not drink. After a moment's hesitation, the other star-travellers copied her. Mikajaa retreated noiselessly to the table that held the liquor.

Radan sipped thoughtfully at his drink, watching the star-travellers over the rim of his glass. Silence met his stare with all the innocence she could muster, and after a moment, the havildar smiled. "I've been expecting you, sieura."

Silence smiled back. "I know," she lied. She heard Chase Mago stir slightly, and willed him not to give her away. "It seemed—useful to make your acquaintance."

Radan's smile widened. "Useful to me, certainly," he agreed.

"Possibly," Silence said.

Radan shrugged deliberately. "The crew of the foreign spaceship—forgive me, the *starship*—that broke through the barriers and then vanished could be extremely useful to me. You are that crew, are you not?"

His tone implied certainty, rather than any real doubt. Silence nodded slowly. "We are." This time it was Balthasar who shifted in protest; the pilot put out her hand, not looking at him, and gestured for him to be quiet.

Radan smiled again. "My—employers—are most anxious to 'contain the contagion', as they put it."

"It's a bit late for that," Balthasar muttered.

"Obviously they would be," Silence said. "After all, they've been controlling the Earth-road for—how many years? They

hardly want to lose their monopoly now." Radan started to
say something, but Silence continued, riding over the havildar's words, "I confess I'm surprised you haven't turned us
over to your masters—employers. I should think you'd be in
need of proofs of loyalty."

"How so?" Radan frowned. "Oh, the vox."

Silence gestured to the other off-world goods decorating
the room. "And all of this."

"Ah, well, that's permitted—an acceptable perquisite of
the position," Radan said.

When your position's weak, Silence thought, attack. She
nodded toward Mikajaa. "And him? I'm surprised he's been
allowed to see so much."

"Perhaps it is something of a gamble," Radan admitted,
"but he is a useful agent. As you've seen."

So it was all staged, the pawned vox and everything that
followed, Silence thought. Except the gang: I'm reasonably
sure Radan has no control there. She said, "Indeed. I
think we've made our points, Sieur Radan. We're mutually
vulnerable."

Radan nodded. "We are."

When he said nothing more, Silence sighed. "You brought
us here, havildar. What do you want of us?"

Radan set his goblet aside, and the pilot braced herself.
"Your starship," the havildar said. "All our reports indicate it
was rather badly damaged before we lost it, and I frankly
have to assume that your presence here confirms that—"

"We could be coming to overthrow the Rose Worlders,"
Balthasar said, and Radan shook his head.

"Three of you, alone? I hardly think so."

"Your estimate is a little low, havildar," Silence said, smiling to hide the cold knot of fear in her stomach. Radan was
guessing entirely too well for her comfort.

Radan smiled again. "If you say so, sieura. Nonetheless, I
do think the reports—visual as well as sensor scan—of exten-
sive damage to your ship are quite accurate." He leaned
forward slightly. "I would be willing to help you make your
repairs—for a price, of course."

"Oh, of course," Balthasar said.

"We might be willing to not tell the Rose Worlders

just what you've been doing," Silence said, deliberately misunderstanding.

Radan laughed. "That would hardly be to your advantage, sieura, really." He sobered quickly. "What I am offering is access to off-world equipment, things that will make your repairs much easier. In exchange, I'd ask your help, sieura, in one thing."

"And that is?" Silence asked.

"Help me to destroy the barrier enclosing Man's Island." Radan's lined face was completely serious now. "That's always been the crucial thing. I'm not a magus—none of the Earthborn are allowed to learn the Art—and it will take a magus's power to break through that field. You, sieura, are the first magus to reach Earth in hundreds of years who is not one of them. I want your help."

Silence blinked, startled by the sudden passion in the havildar's voice. "What good will it do to destroy the field?" she asked, buying time. "I understood the central control point was on another island, I forget the name."

"Ice Island," Mikajaa said, softly.

Radan made an impatient gesture. "Since the eruptions started again last year—it's a volcanic island, sieura—most of the operations have been transferred here. As to what good it will do. . . . We've been waiting for this chance for quite some time."

Silence nodded to herself. A number of things were being suddenly made clear. She said, slowly, "So you have something planned—" and Radan cut in quickly.

"Which, frankly, does not concern you."

"But it does," Balthasar said. "Very much so."

Radan frowned. "I can offer you the off-world—nonmechanical—tools you need to make repairs," he said again. "Whatever you need, I can get for you—if you'll do this one thing."

Chase Mago stirred for the first time since he'd entered the reception room. "But can you?" he asked softly. "Not that I doubt your word, of course, but if you rebel and lose—I assume that's what you're intending—I don't see how you can help us."

Radan murmured some answer, but Silence wasn't listen-

ing. A plan was forming in her mind, one that could—would—
solve all their difficulties; one that would get them safely back
out into human-settled space, and at the same time help Aili
and possibly even break the Rose Worlders' hold on Earth
itself, all with one simple move. Or relatively simple, she
amended, the elation fading a little. But if I can persuade
Radan, I think Aili and I between us can do the rest. She said
aloud, interrupting the havildar, "Sieur Radan, your plan
won't work, no matter how much support you have among
the other Earth-born."

"Why is that, sieura?" There was an edge to Radan's
invincible courtesy this time, and Silence chose her next
words carefully.

"Even if you succeed in taking over Man's Island, and I
admit you could probably do that, if I destroyed the barrier
for you, you won't beat the Rose Worlders." Radan started to
say something, and the pilot held up her hand. "Please, sieur
Radan, hear me out. I don't know how much you know about
star travel—"

"A little," Radan murmured, and gestured in apology. "I
beg your pardon, please continue."

Silence said, as if he hadn't spoken, "—or the precise
reasons that Earth hasn't been visited by people from outside
the Rose Worlds. In brief, the Rose Worlders have set up
siege engines that block the Earth-road, and we are the first
to figure out how to break through that interference. Now
that we know how to do it, of course, others will develop the
same techniques—especially since we're acting as agents for
his most serene majesty the Hegemon. His majesty has been
at odds with the Rose Worlds for some time." She took a
deep breath, measuring the dawning comprehension on Radan's
face. "If you were willing to cooperate with his majesty, to
coordinate your rebellion with an attack by his fleet. . . . It
would certainly increase the odds of your success."

Radan was watching her closely, and Silence made herself
meet his gaze without flinching. After a moment, the havildar
said, "And how will this fleet get past the—siege engines?"

Silence took another deep breath, steadying herself. When
she spoke, her voice was coldly calm. "I will destroy them."

She heard a soft gasp from Chase Mago, but did not glance

in his direction, fixing her eyes instead on the havildar. Very slowly, Radan nodded. "And can you promise me this alliance?"

Silence shook her head, and Radan's eyes narrowed. "I can't," the pilot said. "But there's someone on-planet who can."

"Aili—" Balthasar bit back the word almost before he'd finished speaking, and shook his head in apology.

"Forgive me, sieura," Radan said, "but how do I know this person has the authority to make this bargain?"

"Aili—the Princess Royal," Silence said coldly, "is the Hegemon's oldest—only legitimate—child."

Radan said nothing for a long moment, staring into space. "I'll want to speak with her myself," he said at last.

"That can be arranged." Silence met his searching look blandly, and after a moment, the havildar looked away.

"When?"

Silence shrugged.

"We'll contact you," Balthasar said.

Radan smiled thinly. "I'd prefer a little more in the way of guarantee."

"We are, as you pointed out, mutually vulnerable," Silence said. "Surely that's enough for you."

Radan sighed. "I gather it will have to be." He straightened abruptly. "I'm intrigued by your proposal, sieura— sieuri—but, as I said, I'll want to meet your princess before I commit myself to anything."

"How can we contact you?" Silence said.

"Through Mikajaa," Radan answered. The musician looked up sharply, his mouth opening as though he'd protest, but the havildar ignored him, and the younger man subsided. "He has a drop-box at a bar called the Elite, which he will check daily." He glanced at Mikajaa, who nodded unhappily. Radan turned his attention back to the star-travellers. "Will that suffice?"

"Yes," Silence answered, and pushed herself to her feet, setting aside her untouched drink. The other star-travellers copied her. Chase Mago drew himself up to his full height, and Silence was very grateful for his massive presence.

"Mikajaa will see you back to the Kills," Radan said.

Balthasar started to protest, but Silence shook her head at

him. "That will do," she said, and managed a chill smile. "Thank you for this meeting, sieur Radan."

The havildar bowed with almost courtly grace. "I'm delighted to have met you, sieura."

Outside the low building the air was sticky, but Silence found herself shivering despite the heat. She forced herself to relax, to think of nothing at all, and the shivering lessened. By the time they'd reached the bridge, she had herself under control; by the time they reached Rosemont on the far side, she was almost calm.

"So," Balthasar said, as they reached the edge of the slate plaza and stepped into the shadow of the street. "I think you've gone far enough." He was looking at Mikajaa, who stopped warily, just out of reach.

"You know where we're going," Silence said, almost gently, weaving a subtle thread of compulsion into her words. "You don't need to follow."

Mikajaa made a face—clearly, the pilot thought, my spells don't have much effect on him—but backed away from Balthasar's advance. "All right, I won't follow."

"Better get moving, then," the Delian said.

The musician hesitated a moment longer, then turned away, picking up speed as he moved down the street. Silence watched him out of sight, then glanced back at the others. "Thanks for backing me up."

"You're out of your mind, you know," Balthasar said, but he was grinning. "If this works. . . ."

"If," Silence said, grimly.

"Can you really destroy the siege engines?" Chase Mago asked.

The pilot hesitated. That had been the biggest uncertainty in her plan, but, in theory at least, there was no reason that the engines could not be shattered from Earth. "I think so," she said, and was not convinced. She made herself speak more firmly. "I think I can."

The engineer shook his head, but said, "If anyone can do it, Silence, you will." He glanced at Balthasar. "This still feels like one of your ideas, Denis."

The Delian laughed.

"Be grateful for it," Silence said, and glanced around again.

Mikajaa was long gone—she could not feel his presence anywhere nearby—and the shadowed street was empty. She
sighed, and nodded in the direction of the fountains where
T'la was waiting. "Let's go."

CHAPTER 9

T'la was sitting on the edge of the broken fountain, idly tossing chips of stone at a flowering weed. He looked up as the star-travellers appeared at the head of the alley, and smiled.

"I'm glad you made it."

So am I, Silence thought, but said only, "Sorry to have kept you waiting."

The boy shrugged. "No problem."

They returned to the gang's headquarters by a different, more direct route, and T'la, after a low-voiced conversation with the girls on guard duty at the main entrance, took them through the maze of tunnels to the painted basement room where they had first confronted Efelay. The gang leader was waiting there, sitting cross-legged on one of the dismounted tables, Fitch at her side. They looked up eagerly as the star-travellers appeared, and Efelay said, "Did you get what you wanted?"

Silence nodded, and seated herself on a table opposite the gang leader. "What can you tell me about Kennet Radan?"

Efelay shrugged, and glanced at Fitch. "You know more than I do," she said.

The anadvocate made a face. "What do you want to know? He's one of *them*—"

"Them?" Chase Mago asked. He leaned against the painted wall, apparently at ease, but Silence could see the tension in his movements, and was not deceived.

287

"The Unionists," Fitch said. "The ones who run things." He paused, looking back at Silence. "What do you want to know?" he said again.

"Who is he, where does he come from, what has he done?" Silence answered. "Anything you can tell me about him."

"All right." Fitch nodded. "It isn't much, though. He's a Unionist from way back. I don't know where he comes from, or anything like that, but he started out here as a recording sergeant, and gave everybody a whole lot of trouble."

"Recording sergeant?" Balthasar asked.

The anadvocate nodded again. "You know, the person in charge of keeping track of everybody in a district. He started out in the Kills, and did such a good job that he got promoted, taken into the hierarchy. He's been on the Island ever since—they say he's real important, but not the top man."

Silence nodded. That fitted in well with her own perception of the situation: Radan was intelligent, ambitious, extremely competent—and he could never rise beyond his present position, simply because he had had the misfortune to be born on Earth. "Is he—reliable?" she said aloud.

Fitch shrugged. "Define reliable."

"They say," Efelay began slowly, "they do say he had a deal with Rafaiel, back when they were starting out. And he hasn't done Rafaiel dirty yet, for all that everybody knows Rafaiel's a technologist, and that he runs their organization."

"What do you mean by a 'technologist'?" Silence asked.

Efelay grinned. "They don't believe in the Art," she said. "They think that their machines're going to save everybody."

"Well, of course Radan—or the Rose Worlders—wouldn't crack down on them," Chase Mago said. His voice held the startled note of sudden revelation. "The more machines there are, and the more complicated the individual machines are, the less chance there is of somebody stumbling onto any of the important discoveries."

That made a good deal of sense, Silence thought, was a very clever way to control Earth's natives, but it was hardly important at the moment. Before she could say anything, however, Fitch frowned.

"Rafaiel's not just a technologist," he said. "Or at least he's becoming something else. His people don't talk as much about it as they used to, anyway. I mean, it's almost like he's using that for cover." He looked up sharply, his face lighting with sudden knowledge. "*And* he's still in contact with Radan. I know that for a fact."

Is he, now? Silence thought. That cast a new and interesting light on both Radan and Rafaiel, and on the pawned vox. . . . "Can you find out any more about him—about Rafaiel's connections with the Island?" she said aloud.

"I can try," Fitch said, and Efelay corrected him.

"We can do it."

"Thanks," Silence said. She glanced at her husbands, and pushed herself to her feet. "The more we know about him, the more we can do."

"But what are you doing?" Efelay asked.

Silence smiled. "I intend to break the Rose Worlders' —your Unionists'—hold on Earth," she said. Without waiting for an answer, she turned and stalked toward the stairs that led to the tunnel that would take her back to her quarters. Balthasar and Chase Mago followed close at her heels.

Once they had reached the outbuilding, and the aphonic ring was safely sealed around them, Silence dropped into the most comfortable of the chairs the gang had provided, sighing to herself. Balthasar threw himself down on the wide bed, kicking off his shoes. Only the engineer remained standing, staring soberly at the others.

"Is it really fair," he said at last, "to tell these kids that?"

Silence looked away, ashamed, but Balthasar said, "Well, it's the truth, isn't it? If what I think she's planning works, we will break the Rose Worlders' hold."

"It's a pretty Delphic truth," Chase Mago said.

Silence sighed. The engineer was right: even if she were able to put everything together, persuade the Hegemon to send his fleet to secure Earth and persuade Radan to cooperate with him, it wouldn't free Earth. It would merely result in an exchange of masters, and that was wrong, too. Still, the more contact Earth had with the rest of human-settled space the better; the more chance there would be of the planet's obtaining real freedom. . . . The argument was not entirely convincing, even to herself, and she looked away again. On the other hand, she—they—didn't have a great deal of choice. No, she told herself firmly, that wasn't true at all. There would be no hiding behind that excuse. She could have avoided meeting with Radan, could have made Chase Mago build his tuner from the bits and pieces owned by the gang; it would not have been easy, but it certainly wouldn't've been impossible. She had chosen, deliberately and on her own, to play for higher stakes, to try to get the materials that would let them get off-world more quickly. She would have to take the consequences of her decision, and do whatever she could to see that things were at least no worse on Earth once the Hegemon's forces had arrived.

"I don't think it will be worse," she said, half to herself, and Balthasar frowned.

"Don't think what will be worse?" he asked.

Silence looked instead at Chase Mago. "I don't think I'm doing the wrong thing," she said. "Even if the Hegemon does take over here, he's still better than the Rose Worlders—and once the Earth-road is generally known, which it will be, very quickly, there'll be even more options available. I don't think I'm wrong."

The engineer sighed. "I hope you're right," he said. "I just hope you're right."

Balthasar gave the pilot a wary glance. "Just what is it you have in mind, Silence?"

"Exactly what I told Radan," the pilot answered. "I want to use Aili to contact her father—"

"How?" Chase Mago interrupted.

"Through the ship's systems, I suppose," Silence answered, "or even through the Rose Worlders' devices, if Radan has that kind of access. Once we've made contact, the Hegemon can bring his fleet in to support Radan's rebellion." She looked from one man to the other, from Balthasar's expression of thoughtful consideration to Chase Mago's frown of distaste, and burst out, "Good God, aren't you tired of being acted upon? I'm finally in a position to do something, and by God I'm going to arrange things my way for once."

Balthasar grinned. "All right, I'm with you," he said. "Hell, why not?"

"Julie?" Silence fixed her eyes on the big engineer.

Chase Mago said nothing for a long moment, then, slowly, shook his head. "I don't like the Hegemony," he said at last. Balthasar started to say something, and the engineer held up his hand. "I know, Denis, it's not the same people who destroyed Kesse, not precisely. I know it's irrational—but I don't particularly like handing Earth over to the government that did that."

"We never had much choice about that," Balthasar said, but gently. "The Hegemon was going to profit by it one way or another."

"I know." The engineer shook his head. "I said I was being irrational."

"I think," Silence said slowly, "I think it makes a difference that Radan will be involved, practically in charge of the rebellion here. He'll be able to treat with the Hegemon as something like an equal, which is something we can give him, and something he couldn't've done on his own."

"I know," Chase Mago said again. He sighed. "You're right, Silence. We'll do it your way."

"Thanks," Silence said.

There was a moment's pause, and then Balthasar pushed himself up off the bed. "Right," he said, a little too loudly. "Let's get communications set up."

The engineer nodded, and reached for the bag he'd left standing against the wall. Working quickly, he assembled the disguised bits and pieces into the communications unit, and, a little gingerly, keyed on the power. The tiny unit whined softly, but the crystal-lined dish remained clouded. The engineer made a face and adjusted the controls. Still nothing happened.

"Wait a minute," Silence said, and murmured the Word that dissolved the aphonic ring.

Chase Mago grunted. "That's better," he said, "but not wonderful."

Silence leaned over his shoulder. An image was beginning to take shape in the dish. Isambard's features, backed by the familiar shapes and colors of *Recusante*'s bulkheads, came clear, distorted only a little by the dish's curve. More annoying—more disturbing, Silence thought—was the haze, like a fog of tiny crystals, that washed back and forth across the image, threatening now and again to obscure it completely. "Can you do anything?" she asked aloud.

The engineer shook his head. "It's the machines."

Silence sighed, and leaned closer to the dish, staring into its foggy depths. She thought she could see Marcinik, standing behind the magus's shoulder, but Aili was nowhere to be seen. "Isambard."

"Silence." The magus bowed slowly in acknowledgement. "Everything's well here."

"And here," the pilot answered. "Something important's come up."

In the background, she could see Marcinik stiffen warily, but Isambard was less easily perturbed. "Indeed?"

"Is Aili there?" Silence asked, playing for time. "This concerns her, too."

"I'm here." The faint voice, heavily overlaid with the whispering of the fog, a noise softer and more distorting than true static, came from the corner behind Isambard.

Silence took a deep breath, bracing herself for the questions she knew would follow. "We've made contact with someone—an Earth native in the Rose Worlders' service, here on Man's Island. He already has some plan to overthrow the Rose Worlders, and wanted my help. I suggested that he ally with the Hegemon, through you, Aili, and that you—that we all work together to get rid of the Rose Worlders."

"Do you think that's wise?" Isambard asked.

Marcinik said, in almost the same instant, "But there's no way of knowing if his Majesty would agree. . . ."

"Of course he would," Balthasar muttered, and Silence waved for him to be quiet.

"I think it would be pretty foolish of him not to take advantage of the chance of creating a friendly local government," she said to the dish, and Marcinik nodded.

"Can we contact him?"

"I think so," Silence began, and Isambard cut her off.

"The ship's equipment is certainly capable of making such a transmission, and I believe it could be adjusted so that a brief message could even be sent without betraying the location of the sender."

"Or there's a chance we could even use the Rose Worlders'

own facilities," Silence said. "If Radan—that's the native; his name's Kennet Radan—has access to the communications facilities on the Island."

Marcinik nodded, accepting the technical decision, but said, "I wonder what this Radan wants from his Majesty?"

"I don't know," Silence said. "I thought it would be better if Aili dealt with that." She paused, and then said, "Are you willing to do this, your Serenity?"

There was a brief pause, the fog whispering across the face of the dish, and then Aili's voice said, "Oh, yes, I'm willing."

There was something in her tone that made Silence look up quickly, a note of calculation and of decision. Before she could say anything, however, Aili went on, "I think my father would accept it, too—as you said, Silence, he'd be a fool not to." She moved suddenly out of Marcinik's shadow, to lean over the dish, her veil held automatically in front of her face. "I'll talk to him, and to this Radan."

"It'll take time to get to the mainurb," Macinik said. "How do we find you once we're there?"

Isambard shook his head. "That will not be necessary," he said. "There is a quicker way."

Silence made a face. "The janus gate," she said, and the other magus nodded.

"It will be a strain on you, Silence, since you will have to hold it by yourself, at the end, but it is not impossible."

"We'll do it," Silence said, before she could change her mind. She glanced over her shoulder, but the other star-travellers were already moving away from the dish. "Be ready to help them through the gate," she said, and Chase Mago nodded. Satisfied, Silence looked back into the dish, and saw Isambard lift his hands, beginning the first part of the schema. She took a deep breath, and curled her own hands into the answering position, as though she cupped an invisible cylinder that rose from the edges of the dish itself.

"Are you ready?" Isambard asked.

Silence took a second deep breath, calming and controlling herself. She knew the schemae for the janus gate well—it was the first operation she had ever participated in, when they had been trapped on Mersaa Maia. There would be no difficulty in forming the gate, only in finding the sheer physical strength to hold it open alone while Isambard passed through it. But she would find it, somehow. She nodded. "I'm ready."

"Excellent." Isambard paused for a long moment, visibly calling on his own rituals to calm and center his power. "Then let us begin."

"Let's begin," Silence echoed.

Isambard spoke first, intoning a chain of sound that made the air thicken even at a distance. Silence spoke the confirming phrase, and felt the common air of the room thicken even further, the heat rising as new forces were set into motion. Isambard spoke again, Words of Earth and Air that framed a space above the dish, gave solidity and Form to the shape Silence had imagined. She answered with the Words that locked that Form to her own power, and thought she could see the shaped air like a ghostly shadow rising from her cupped hands. It was very hot in the room now, the power they had summoned hovering just outside the mundane world, held only by barriers that they themselves had weakened. The janus gate was a manipulation of purgatory, similar to but in the end very different from the act of piloting, capable of joining two places on the same landmass of the same planet. The power involved was tremendous, and the possible danger if they lost control of the confining Forms was very high. Silence was sweating heavily, but could not spare a hand to wipe her face. Isambard spoke again, and she answered; the skeleton of the gate was complete, waiting for the power to be channeled through it.

"Now," Isambard said, and gestured, reinforcing that movement with a Word like a crack of thunder.

Silence copied him, and felt the power blossom beneath her hands, scorching her palms. She blinked, but held steady, colors fountaining between her hands, to pour and reform into something resembling recognizable images. Slowly, the wavering shapes steadied, until she was looking directly into *Recusante*'s common room. She spoke the schema's final phrase, and felt the image lock firmly into place, the immense power of purgatory contained for now by the structure of the gate.

"It's done," she said, and Isambard nodded. The older magus looked almost as tired as she already felt, and the operation was not even half over yet. Silence shivered, and forced herself to concentrate.

"Now, your Serenity," Isambard said.

Aili moved warily toward the opening defined by the gate, still holding her veil across her face. Chase Mago stepped forward promptly, offering his hand in support. The Princess Royal reached through the gate and took it, and then, with no apparent hesitation, stepped over the gate's high threshold and into the little room. Marcinik followed, declining any help from Balthasar. The colonel's face was pale, the very lack of expression betraying his unease.

"Are you ready, Silence?" Isambard asked again.

The pilot nodded.

"Then I will transfer full control to you," Isambard answered. "We will do this in stages, as it was made."

Silence nodded again, soothed by the magus's steady voice, then braced herself.

"First, the threshold," Isambard said.

Silence closed her eyes. She controlled most of that already, its solidity a comfort against the shift and flux of purgatory contained within it. Slowly, as Isambard relinquished his hold, the shadowy threshold took on weight, became not a comfort but a burden, sliding away from her. Frightened, she reached out for it, caught and held it. When she was sure that she had stopped its fall, she eased it cautiously back into the structure they had so laboriously prepared. It clicked back into place, but the sense of weight remained, the feeling that she had to work to keep it there where it belonged.

"The sideposts," Isambard said. He released his hold very slowly, but even so, Silence had to struggle to keep them from tilting out of true. She could feel the heat rising again as she fought to control the unwieldy, invisible mass, heat that was another manifestation of the dissonance she could almost hear. At last, she had both columns under control, but she could feel her muscles trembling under the strain.

"The keystone," Isambard said, and Silence took a deep breath before she nodded. She could feel the keystone's heavy form already, a massive, triangular block poised, point downward, between the pillars above her head. As the older magus released his hold on it, Silence could feel the stone beginning to slip, grating against the pillars. The non-sound rasped at her nerves, flared like a sudden fire in the air above her. She fought it, sweating, and managed to stop the downward slide, but the stone was still out of true. The gate could not be used without danger until the Form was corrected. She ground her teeth together and, with her last gram of strength, pushed the invisible stone back into place.

"Now," she gasped, and Isambard nodded. He rose stiffly to his feet, and stepped ungracefully through the opening, almost stumbling over the high threshold. Chase Mago steadied him, but the magus waved him away.

"Dismiss it," he said, and his voice was almost gentle. "But slowly. Easily."

Silence released the breath she had been holding, and felt the entire structure tremble. Only a few more seconds, she promised herself, only a little longer. The janus gate had to be dismantled in much the same way that it had been constructed, or the pent-up energies would dissipate all at once, with an explosive force. She spoke the Words that damped down the conflicting harmonies, closing the opening into purgatory. *Recusante*'s familiar common room faded, became merely an image, and then vanished altogether. Then, cautiously, she called up Words of Unmaking, directed them at the keystone. Its weight faded, and then vanished. Unbalanced, the pillars wobbled; she controlled them, and, once they were steadied again, dismissed them as well. The threshold remained, a great weight in the air before her. She dismissed it, too, and sat staring at the unpainted floor. Exhaustion swept through her; she closed her eyes, and felt familiar arms around her, lifting her gently. She turned toward the embrace, and let herself fall into sleep.

She woke in her own improvised bed, her husbands to either side of her. The cool light of dawn was filtering in the room's single window, and she blinked up at it, momentarily disoriented. The janus gate had exhausted her more than she'd realized; she'd slept through the end of an afternoon and at least one night. Cautiously, not wanting to wake the others, she reached beneath the pillows for Chase Mago's chronograph, and touched the button that activated the date

display. By its reading, she'd slept through the next day as
well. Startled, she slid the chronograph back under the engineer's pillow, and wondered what to do next. She was fully
awake at last, though she thought she could remember waking briefly at some earlier time, and ravenously hungry.
Sighing, she eased herself free of the blankets. Balthasar
shifted, and opened his eyes. Silence made a face—the Delian
was never at his best on waking—but, to her surprise, Balthasar
managed a smile.

"Glad to see you awake again," he murmured. To his left
Chase Mago stirred, but did not wake.

"You're cheerful," Silence answered, reaching for her clothes.

Balthasar's smile widened. "There's a lot going on," he
said, and pushed himself out of bed.

Oh, wonderful, Silence thought, but said nothing. She
finished dressing, and went on into the outer room, where
the food was kept. Balthasar followed, shrugging on his heavy
jacket.

"I'll take care of coffee," he said, and stooped to adjust the
antique machine.

Silence let him fiddle with it, turning her attention to the
cold-storage chest that held the supplies. There was a woven-
paper bag full of the hard round rolls the gang favored, and a
tub of the soft cheese that went with it. The pilot busied
herself with those, and by the time she had finished, Balthasar
had poured two mugs of the steaming coffee. They ate without speaking, Silence concentrating on the sheer physical
pleasure of eating. She finished three of the chewy rolls before
finally leaning back, satisfied.

"So what is happening?" she asked.

Balthasar looked up with a quirky smile. "You know, Aili
really is something else," he said. "We told her what you had
in mind, and she really seemed to like the idea. She asked us
to set up a meeting with Radan as soon as possible—"

"And did you?" Silence asked.

The Delian nodded. "We—actually one of Efelay's kids—
left a note for Mikajaa like he said to, so we should be hearing
something soon."

"What does Isambard think of the idea?" Silence asked,

and was surprised at the sudden anxious fear in the pit of her stomach.

Balthasar sobered. "He agrees, the siege engines can be destroyed, but he's not so happy about trying to destroy that barrier. He wants to talk to you about it first, anyway, or maybe even see it for himself, before he says anything."

Silence frowned. "That doesn't make sense," she began— surely the barrier surrounding the island was a less massive creation than an engine capable of blocking a star road?—and Balthasar shrugged.

"It doesn't to me, but I'm not the magus."

"I'll talk to him," Silence said, and sighed. "When do you think we'll hear from Mikajaa?"

"Who knows?" Balthasar answered. "Fitch has been watching him, and he says Mikajaa checks his drop box regularly every evening. We should hear sometime today."

"Where are the others, anyway?" the pilot asked.

"Efelay put them in a couple of rooms next door," Balthasar began, but before he could finish, there was a tapping at the main door. Silence made the gesture that dissolved the lock, and the door swung open. Isambard, impeccable as always in his black robes, stood in the doorway.

"I'm glad to see that you're finally awake, Silence," he said.

The pilot made a face, but managed to answer politely enough, "I feel much recovered, thanks."

Isambard moved into the room and seated himself, stiffly, in the only chair. At Silence's frown Balthasar grimaced, and poured a third cup of coffee for the older magus, who accepted it with only a nod of thanks. "We need to discuss the details of this plan of yours," he said, and sipped at the scalding liquid.

Silence bit back an annoyed response. After all this—I brought him here, held open the gate for him, and what do I get out of it? she thought. Nothing, not even thanks—which is as usual, she added, so why am I surprised? She said only, "Denis tells me you're worried about the barrier around the island. I'd've thought the engines were more difficult."

"I expect they will be," Isambard answered, "at least in the sense that they require more strength—more power. But I do not know the schemae involved in creating this barrier of yours. Describe it for me."

It's not my barrier, Silence thought, and saw Balthasar scowling, ready to speak. That was enough to restore her sense of priorities. She shook her head at the Delian, and said, "I didn't recognize any particular schema. I'm certain a direct link to the submaterial was involved, probably as a power source, and the Art was employed to hide the visual spectrum of the field from an outside viewer. That's all I know." She was pleased at the professionalism of her voice, and realized suddenly that she shouldn't be angry at the magus's apparent unconcern. He was simply treating her as he would treat any other magus. It was not that he didn't care, but that he assumed he didn't need to care. It was a startling thought, pleasing and frightening at the same time.

"It sounds rather like one of the Alaruan branch schemae," Isambard said, and Silence dragged her attention back to the business at hand. "The Rose Worlders always favored his work."

"Can it be broken?" Silence asked.

"Oh, yes. 'Anything that can be created can be destroyed,'" Isambard quoted.

"Like the siege engines?" Balthasar asked.

Isambard gave him a rather annoyed glance. "Especially the siege engines, Captain Balthasar."

Before he could continue, there was another knock at the door, and it opened to admit Aili and Marcinik. The colonel in particular looked tired and ill-tempered—the result of dealing with Balthasar, Silence wondered, or just of having been cooped up aboard *Recusante* with Isambard for so long? To her surprise, however, Balthasar did not make any of his usual challenging remarks, mutely offering coffee and rolls instead. Isambard waited with ostentatious patience until the newcomers were settled, and then continued his lecture.

"The siege engines are an unnatural blockage, Captain. Metaphysically speaking, that road should be open—it *wants* to be open, one might even say. After all, it was the first star road to be discovered, and because of that it is still the Form on which all other roads are founded. All these other open roads create a tremendous and constant pressure on the engines, forcing them to expend a great deal of power to keep the Earth-road closed. We will be able to use that strain to shatter the engines."

"So if we can just repair the ship," Silence began, and Isambard shook his head.

"The engines can more easily be destroyed from here— from the surface of the planet, don't you see?"

"No, I don't," Silence snapped, and bit off the rest of her angry words. Nothing would be gained by losing her temper now, she told herself, and forced herself to remain calm.

Isambard sighed. "In a sense," he began, in the tones reserved for his more important lectures, "the ancients were right. Earth is the center of the universe, because it is the place where human beings first evolved. No matter how far into space the species has spread, it remains tied, physically and metaphysically, to the planet which gave it birth." He glanced expectantly at Silence, who nodded, curbing her annoyance at being lectured in front of the others.

"I see," she said, when it became clear that something more was expected of her, and dredged up a bastard-latin phrase she had stumbled across during her first weeks on Solitudo Hermae. "Not *umbilicus universi*, but *umbilicus universi nostri*— not the navel of the universe, but the navel of our universe."

Isambard was nodding eagerly. "Precisely. And the choice of the word 'navel' is equally significant, because it points up the nature of the metaphysical tie." He paused, as though he'd lost track of what he was saying, and resumed after a moment in a less elevated voice. "We are at the center of that metaphysical universe, and we are trying to restore things to their natural state: that will multiply the effects of our operation by—" He paused again, but shook his head. "I can't calculate the precise order of magnitude without more study, but certainly by a significant amount."

Silence took a swallow of her cooling coffee, trying to figure out exactly what this would mean for the workings of the Art. Certainly, being at the center of the human universe hadn't been much help in overcoming the effects of the machines that filled the planet—or had it? she wondered suddenly. She had been able to compensate for the interference rather better than she'd hoped. . . .

"Sieuri?" The voice came from outside the door. Silence thought she recognized it as belonging to one of Fitch's runners, and gestured. The door swung open, and Isambard frowned.

"That is a rather frivolous use of the Art, surely."

"It was necessary to maintain our privacy," Silence answered, rather sharply.

The girl in the doorway cleared her throat. "Excuse me, sieuri, but Fitch says he's got Mikajaa, if you want him."

"We do." Balthasar pulled himself to his feet. "Better wake Julie, Silence."

"I'm awake." The engineer appeared in the inside doorway, fastening the clasps of his coat. "Did you say Mikajaa was here?"

The runner nodded. "Yeah. He's in the Out."

"Sorry to interrupt breakfast," Balthasar began, and Marcinik nodded, setting aside his mug.

"We'd better go."

"Wait." That was Aili, and Silence gave her a rather startled glance. "The rest of you go ahead," the Princess Royal continued. "Arrange to meet with Radan today, if you can— I'll leave the details to you, you know the area best. But I have some things I need to discuss with Silence."

Marcinik started to protest, but seemed to think better of it as Aili shook her head slightly. Silence frowned. "Are you sure, your Serenity?"

"It's important," Aili said, firmly. "Please."

The pilot hesitated a moment longer, then shrugged. "All right, the rest of you go ahead. We'll join you when we can."

Balthasar raised an eyebrow, obviously ready to argue, but Chase Mago took him by the shoulder and turned him forcibly away. The others followed, leaving the two women alone together.

Aili waited until the door had closed firmly behind them before she spoke. "I want to be sure I understand the implications of this," she said, putting aside her veil in the gesture that indicated a desire to be completely clear, "and what you want from me."

Silence paused, still frowning. It seemed simple enough, she thought, and said, "To put it bluntly, this is my price for getting you declared his heir. I want you to call in the fleet—can you do it?"

Aili nodded. "I can. Yes, I can convince him to send a fleet, if Radan can convince me that he will support—that his people and his rebellion or whatever it is can support—our attack. I owe my father's people that much."

There was something in her voice that kept Silence from speaking. After a moment, the Princess Royal sighed and continued, more slowly, "It's—my question is, what will happen when Earth is freed?"

"Will it be freed?" Silence muttered.

Aili went on unheeding. "With the Earth-road open, and Earth restored to its proper place at the center of our universe, won't the person who controls Earth control that universe?" She fixed Silence with a sudden fierce stare. "I want to be that person."

The pilot froze. She had not thought of that possibility, had not considered anything beyond the metaphysical implications, the impact on her Art. Once stated, however, the political possibilities became frighteningly—possible. That might explain why the Rose Worlders had blocked the Earth-road, she thought, remotely. The Rose Worlds, the worlds of the ancient Ring, were even more closely bound to Earth than the rest of the planets in human-settled space—the fact that the Rose Worlds, and only the Rose Worlds, could be reached by means of the portolan was a clear demonstration of the metaphysical link. If Earth were free—if Earth's goods and knowledge could be traded freely, as they once had been, unmediated by the Rose Worlders—then the Rose Worlds themselves would become little more than a suburb of Earth itself. Who would go to the Rose Worlds, when he could come to Earth?

She shook herself away from that line of thought, forcing herself to look again at Aili's question. It was more than possible—it was even likely—that the person who controlled Earth would also come to control all of human-settled space. Which answered Chase Mago's fears of the Hegemony's taking over Earth, she thought, but doesn't make me any happier. I definitely don't like the idea of Radan running everything, and I'm not sure Aili could take and hold that kind of power. She looked again at the princess royal's face, and was no longer unsure. There was a strength behind the conventional beauty, a strength and a wisdom beyond Aili's years, an almost frightening awareness of self and of others. Silence shivered, and looked away.

"Whatever I do," she said, "you'll try it."

Aili nodded. "Yes."

Silence took a deep breath. "Better you than anyone else I've seen," she said, in an attempt at a lighter tone.

Aili nodded, quite seriously. "Yes," she said again. "I think so."

The confidence in her voice made Silence raise her eyebrows a little, but she nodded anyway. "Then you'll bargain with Radan?" she asked.

"You seem to think he's trustworthy enough," Aili answered. "But I'll want to see for myself."

"Then we'd better join the others," Silence said.

Aili nodded again, drawing the veil across her face. "Let's go."

The Out was less crowded than before, the extra gang members who had been hanging about to help intimidate the prisoner dismissed to other business. A wooden barrier had been pulled across the open elevator shaft, but Mikajaa, standing again in the middle of the room, had positioned himself so that he could keep an eye on it. Silence nodded a greeting to Efelay, who was sitting cross-legged on a table at the far side of the room, and wondered suddenly just how Balthasar had explained the others' arrival. Efelay smiled in response, and the pilot decided it didn't really matter. After all, she thought, they seem to be accepting it.

"So this is the woman?" Mikajaa's voice was a little shaky, despite the bravado of his words.

Fitch stared speculatively at him, flick-knife open in his hands. Balthasar said hastily, "Her Serenity the Princess Royal."

There were whispers from some of the gang members at that, their faces startled and impressed rather than disbelieving, and Efelay said, "Hush up."

Mikajaa eyed the princess royal warily, obviously taken aback by the veil. Silence didn't bother to hide her grin, and saw the musician flush. "They tell me you want to see Mir Radan," he said.

"Yes." Aili's voice was cool and pleasant, but her tone brooked no argument. "You're the one who arranges this?" She allowed a faint note of doubt to creep into her words, and Silence grinned again.

To his credit, however, Mikajaa did not rise to that bait. "That's right. When?"

"As soon as possible," Aili answered. Her voice sharpened on the next word. "Today."

Mikajaa made a hissing sound between his teeth. "I don't think I can manage that—"

"Radan said you could," Silence pointed out.

Mikajaa gave her an unfriendly glance. "If you wanted to go to him on the Island, sure. But they said you didn't want to." He nodded toward Balthasar and Marcinik.

"That's right," Silence said, and kept her face expressionless. She felt distinctly foolish, and knew that he had intended to make her feel so.

"How soon, then?" Aili asked, and the pilot dragged her attention back to the matter at hand.

Mikajaa shrugged. "Tonight, maybe, if he can get away."

"I think he'll want to," Silence murmured, and the musician made a face.

"We'll assume he can," Aili said. She looked at Efelay and then at Balthasar, including them in the question. "Where shall we meet with him?"

"There's a bar called the Elite," Mikajaa began, and Fitch cut in.

"Not on your life."

The musician shrugged again. "The fountains?"

Balthasar glanced at Fitch, who shrugged. "It's all right."

Aili said, "Are there other objections to it?" She looked to Efelay. "Sieura?"

The gang leader looked up quickly, startled and pleased by the coinë title. "The fountains is like a park, sort of. We can watch you there, no problem."

"Then that will do," Aili said, and looked back at Mikajaa. "When will your master be free?"

"He should be able to make it by ten," Mikajaa answered. "If it doesn't work out, I'll pass the word through Liu's."

"You'll come here and tell us," Balthasar corrected.

For a moment, Silence thought the musician would refuse, but then he nodded sullenly. "All right."

"If you don't come," Silence said, "and if no one's there, we'll assume Radan doesn't want to cooperate with us." She paused, watching Mikajaa's face, and saw that the musician understood.

"I'll let you know," he said again, and Efelay slid forward off the table.

"See him out, Fitch," she said. The anadvocate pushed himself to his feet, the flick-knife vanishing from his hand. Mikajaa followed him without a word, or a glance at the other gang members closing in behind him. Silence stared after him, wondering again if they should trust him, or Radan. This time, at least, they did have other options—but none as good, she reminded herself. Besides, it hardly seemed likely that the musician would be able to set up a meeting on such short notice, or that Radan would be willing to allow it. There would be time to think of alternate plans.

To the pilot's surprise, however, Mikajaa did not reappear to call off the meeting. She said as much to the others, sitting around the low table in the rooms that had been given to the new arrivals, and Marcinik grunted. "He wouldn't dare not come."

"We have something he wants," Aili amplified gently. "He'll be there."

Silence nodded, but privately she still had her doubts. Even so, she returned to the room she shared with Balthasar and Chase Mago and made herself lie down for most of the afternoon, just in case. She felt fully recovered from forming the janus gate, but there was no point in taking chances. The more rest she could get, the better. In the quiet of the closed room, she soon lost herself in waking dreams.

"Silence?" Balthasar was standing in the doorway.

The pilot shook herself fully awake, and sat up. "What is it?"

"Fitch says it's time to go." Balthasar held out a heavy dark-blue jacket trimmed with a single, palm-sized cluster of orange feathers. "You might want to wear this—it'll make you look like one of them."

Silence took it, belting it securely around her waist. Balthasar, too, was wearing the gang's colors pinned to the shoulder of his work-cloth jacket, and she wondered momentarily if the gang had managed to find something that would fit Chase Mago, or if the engineer had had to resort to the clip-on badges. She shook the thought away, and said, "I'm ready."

Balthasar nodded. "Isambard's staying here," he said. "But the rest of us are going. And Efelay's sending some people to escort us."

"Good," Silence said, and meant it. The more protection the better, in the Kills' unfamiliar streets.

As Fitch had promised, it wasn't very far to the fountains. Perhaps a dozen gang members walked with them for most of the way, moving surprisingly quietly through the dark streets. However, as they approached the entrance to the park, a filigreed metal arch spanning the width of the street, Fitch gave a low-voiced order, and the gang members melted away into the shadows, leaving the anadvocate alone with the star-travellers.

"They'll be keeping an eye on us," Fitch said. "No point in upsetting this Radan if we don't have to."

"Good enough," Balthasar said.

Silence said nothing, eyeing the empty gateway. Everything was in shadow beyond the metal arch, though she could just make out the outline of low trees. In the distance, she could hear the faint sound of running water. Nothing else seemed to be moving in the darkness.

Beside her, Marcinik stirred uneasily. "Lights?"

"I brought a hand torch," Fitch said, and reached into the pocket of his long coat. "Here." He held out the long cylinder, adjusting the screw so that the tube cast a soft wedge of light across the paving. The colonel took it thoughtfully, sweeping the beam across the entrance. For a long moment nothing happened, and then there was a movement to the left of the arch. Mikajaa stepped out of the shadows and beckoned without speaking.

"Here we go again," Balthasar murmured, and Chase Mago grunted his agreement. Silence said nothing, concentrating instead on the harmonies of the world around her. There were more machines here—she could feel their presence even though most of them were not in use, a sort of distracting tension in the air around her—but the park itself seemed clear of their influence. Overhead, the waning moon was just visible between the towers of two nearby buildings, its distant music offering neither help nor hindrance. The pilot shivered, then braced herself to follow the others.

Once past the gate and the encircling line of trees, the park was quite small. The noise of falling water was suddenly very loud. Silence looked toward it, and caught her breath in pleased surprise. The fountains from which the park had taken its name rose in the center of a paved circle, a three-tiered pyramid in the center, with smaller basins set at each of the compass points. A tiny stream wound between them, very dark in the moonlight; the same light glittered from the droplets falling from the central pyramid, turning them to strands of light.

Radan was sitting on the edge of the basin that surrounded the pyramid. At the star-travellers' approach, he rose easily to his feet, tilting his head to one side in thoughtful appraisal. He was wearing ordinary workman's clothes, a patched leather jacket over work-cloth trousers, and looked, Silence thought, like nothing so much as a common dock worker. It was a clever disguise, nothing like the magnificence they might have expected of one of the Rose Worlders' servants. She held her breath, hoping Aili would recognize the intelligence behind the craggy face and the rough clothes.

"So," Radan said. Mikajaa moved to join him, fading into the shadow of the central fountain. "You're the princess the sieura told me about."

"I am she." Aili stepped forward into the light from Fitch's torch. She had exchanged her veil for a feathered half-mask borrowed from Efelay, and the dark blue plumes nodded in the light. A triple strand of pearls fell from the mask, further hiding her face. Radan studied her curiously, and Silence thought she read a touch of uncertainty in his stance.

"She tells me you'd be willing to act as a go-between to the hegemon," the havildar said, after a moment's pause, and nodded toward Silence.

"Not precisely," Aili answered. Silence could almost see the thin smile on the other woman's face. "I'm willing to act as his representative."

"Can you?" Radan straightened slowly. "What precisely is your authority?"

"I am the princess royal," Aili said. "Until my father names another heir, I am the next in line for the throne."

Silence hid a smile. While what Aili said was quite true, it failed to mention that the hegemon wanted his son to inherit, not his daughter—but then, the pilot thought suddenly, neither the Rose Worlders nor Earth's natives seemed to restrict their women as much as the Hegemony did.

"But does that give you the right to act as his representative?" Radan continued, with a slight smile of his own.

"I'm here, am I not?" Aili countered. "And I can bring his fleet here, to support you—if you can convince me that I will not be bringing them into a hopeless fight."

Radan's smile widened reluctantly. "I have things in hand here," he admitted, "which I believe will succeed."

Aili started to answer, but her words were cut off by a sudden noise from the park wall, toward Silence's left. The pilot swung toward it instinctively, and saw Balthasar's heylin ready in his hand. Marcinik dropped into a fighting crouch, his heylin drawn as well.

"Silence!" It was Fitch's voice, coming from somewhere near the gate. "Get out, you're—"

He was cut off, but the pilot was already moving. She gestured, spoke a single Word, and felt hell open between her hands. She cupped that power, framing the phrases that would shape it to her needs, but left them unfinished, ready to be triggered by a single Word. Figures moved suddenly in the shadows, stepped out onto the pavement with lowered rifles, and a voice called, "Put down your weapons!"

The voice was vaguely familiar, Silence thought, and frowned at the irrelevant thought. The other star-travellers hesitated, and the voice called again, "Drop them, I said."

Reluctantly, Balthasar stooped and set his heylin on the stones at his feet. After a moment, both Chase Mago and

Marcinik copied him, the colonel taking a single quick step forward to place himself between Aili and the nearest gun. Silence stood quite still, her cupped hands, helped by the darkness, concealing the roiling patch of hell. Out of the corner of her eye, she saw Mikajaa draw back toward the fountain, into the deeper shadows, and held her breath, hoping he'd escape.

"Mikajaa," the voice said. "Don't try it."

The musician froze, and the voice added, "Put your gun down." Mikajaa hesitated, and then, very slowly, slid a gleaming gun—it looked like a heylin, but lacked the bulbous charging chamber near the butt—from his coat pocket and laid it on the edge of the fountain.

"Rafaiel!" That was Radan, his voice harsh with anger. "What the hell do you think you're doing?"

"What do I think I'm doing?" the voice mimicked. Rafaiel stepped out of the circle of the trees, rifle cradled loosely in his hands. "What are you doing, Kennet? We had an understanding, remember?" He raised the rifle until the barrel was centered on the havildar's chest.

Radan did not flinch. "We still do, as far as I'm concerned. What's your complaint?"

Rafaiel nodded toward the star-travellers. "Making a deal without me, that's what. I don't like it, Kennet, I don't like it at all."

"You'd've been informed when the time came," Radan said. "It was your safety I was thinking of."

"Bullshit," Rafaiel answered. "What are these, more of your foreign—excuse me, off-world—wizards?" His voice was thick with contempt.

"Don't start that technologists' crap again," Radan said, and Rafaiel cut him off.

"You've fooled me once too often, Kennet. Not again."

This has gone far enough, Silence thought. She opened her hands, and spoke aloud the Word that completed the schema. Rafaiel's people turned toward her, just as lightning exploded upward from between her hands. There had been time, this time, to control and modify her attack; the bolts were more light and sound than unbound elemental Fire. They curved down, dividing as they fell, to strike the lowered rifles, knocking most of them from their owners' hands. Thunder rolled through the park.

"If you're a technologist, Rafaiel, I suggest you reconsider your position," Silence said, into the sudden quiet. She lifted her hands, displaying the opening into the submaterial world, at the same time whispering a Word that set up a crackling dissonance along its outer edges. A few of Rafaiel's people stepped backward, in spite of themselves, and she thought she heard someone whisper, "The empress. . . ."

So that story's gained currency even with the technologists, she thought. She said, "We came here to reestablish contact with a lost world; we will do that, one way or another. This man—" She nodded toward Radan. "—says he wishes to be free of the Rose Worlders. Are you with us, or against us?"

There was a long pause, and through it the pilot could hear the noise of the fountains, and, beneath that, nervous mutterings from Rafaiel's people. She thought she heard, as well, faint scufflings from behind them, and hoped that, if it were Fitch and the rest of the gang, they would hold off just a little longer. Still Rafaiel said nothing, and, after a moment, Radan said, "I was counting on you, Rafaiel."

Rafaiel gave him a rather bitter glance. "You might have warned me."

Radan shrugged. "I admit my error." It was a formula, but Rafaiel nodded slowly.

"All right. What's in this for me and mine?"

"Is this your army?" Aili asked coolly, looking at Radan.

The havildar gave her a harassed look. "I was expecting their help, yes."

"And who are you?" Rafaiel demanded.

Aili turned her masked face toward him. "I am the princess royal."

Silence held her breath, but there was something in Aili's voice that cut off the technologists' comments.

"An off-worlder," Rafaiel said again. "And you'll break the Unionists?"

"*If* we come to some agreement," Aili answered.

Rafaiel hesitated, biting his lip, then nodded. "I want to sit in on the discussions," he said. "Will you come back to the BBC? We can talk there."

Silence started to refuse, but Radan spoke first. "What guarantee do you offer, after all this?" He gestured to Rafaiel's men.

"My word to you," Rafaiel answered, and, after a moment, Radan nodded.

"I'd accept it," he said.

"I'm not entirely sure we can," Marcinik said, and Balthasar nodded, a lop-sided grin on his face.

"We accept," Aili said firmly. Silence felt the Delian's eyes on her, and nodded. She was not completely happy with the idea, but she thought Aili knew what she was doing.

"Fitch!" she called, and heard a rustling in the underbrush. "Are you all right?"

There was more rustling, and the anadvocate appeared from behind the fountain, his own gun swung casually at his side. At his appearance, several of Rafaiel's men reached for their rifles, but Rafaiel gestured for them to stop.

"We're O.K.," Fitch said. There was a cut on his forearm and a bloody, scraped patch on the side of his face, but he moved easily enough.

"Come with us," Silence said, and the anadvocate nodded.

"We'll be with you," he said, with meaning, and the pilot smiled, knowing that her intent had been understood.

"Then we'll do as you say, Aili," she said aloud.

They made their way to Rafaiel's BBC through the back alleys, following the technologists' leader through the maze of streets. As they went, Silence glanced once at Fitch, and saw that the anadvocate seemed perfectly calm. The other gang members were following them, then, she thought, and in that moment Fitch saw her eyes on him, and nodded. She smiled back, grateful for the reassurance, and turned her attention to memorizing the route.

They entered the BBC through a side door, by a stairway that led down into a dimly lit basement. Silence caught a glimpse of the lights of the coffee shop, heard snatches of conversation and music, but then Rafaiel had said something to the burly man who seemed to be his lieutenant, and the lights and sounds vanished. The pilot stood very still, letting her eyes adjust to the new darkness, and felt something touch her arm. She started, and Balthasar said, very softly, "Julie and I are right beside you, with Marcinik and the princess."

Silence tensed—they were expecting trouble, but why? —and then the basement lights flashed on. She blinked, and felt Balthasar's hand relax. The room was almost square, the walls painted stark white, the floor just a naked slab of poured stone. The only touch of color was a fabric screen, patterned in abstract, multicolored stripes, that was folded back against the rear wall. It was intended to conceal a white-painted door. Even as Silence looked that way the door opened, and the dark-skinned woman who had been in charge of the coffee shop when the star-travellers had first come to the mainurb came into the room. She stared at the strangers, frankly curious, and Rafaiel beckoned to her, saying something in a voice too soft for the pilot to overhear. The dark woman nodded, and disappeared through the doorway again.

"Get the tables set up," Rafaiel went on, more loudly, "and then you can head upstairs, Jaan."

The burly man nodded, and moved toward the wall to the left of the screen. There was a compartment set into that space, Silence saw, cleverly camouflaged. Jaan set his hand in a slight depression at the center of the door, then yanked it open. Several of Rafaiel's men moved to help him set up the trestle table and the breakdown chairs.

Almost as soon as they'd finished, the dark woman returned, carrying a heavy tray; she was followed by a young man who held a shiny coffee service. At Rafaiel's nod, they set their burdens on the table, and vanished again. Jaan and his men followed more slowly, Jaan glancing unhappily over his shoulder. Rafaiel ignored him, and gestured toward the table.

"Please, people, have a seat. There's coffee, and food if you want it."

Silence chose a place toward the end of the table opposite Rafaiel, suddenly aware that she was very hungry. Aili took her place at the foot of the table as though by unquestioned right, Marcinik settling himself at her right hand. Rafaiel had already claimed the head of the table, and Radan grinned. He took the chair that stood in the center of the right-hand side, Mikajaa hovering at his shoulder, and glanced benevolently

from side to side. Balthasar and Chase Mago seated themselves beside Silence, and, after a moment, Fitch settled
reluctantly to Chase Mago's right, just below Aili.

"Coffee?" Rafaiel asked, and Radan nodded.

"Please."

Mikajaa moved to intercept the offered cup, and Silence
saw Marcinik give a wry smile. If the food or drink were
poisoned, there was nothing even Mikajaa's devoted service
could do to stop it. The coffee service and the tray of food—a
selection of the little sandwiches offered in the coffee shop—
made the rounds of the table. Silence took her share eagerly,
ignoring the other star-travellers' nervous looks, and ate without hesitation. There had been no time to poison the food; if
anything, they should be wary of the coffee—it was far easier
to poison a drink.

"Well, people," Rafaiel said. "I think we have some things
to discuss."

Radan nodded. "You and I had an agreement," he said.
"The lady—" He gestured to Aili. "—has an offer that may
improve our chances."

"Not precisely an offer," Aili said, as all eyes turned to her.
Silence saw the beads move as the princess royal drew a long
breath, and then the other woman had begun to speak, once
more outlining who she was and what she hoped to do. She
speaks well, Silence thought. Someone, somewhere, taught
her the basics of public speaking—but then, the pilot added
to herself, I saw myself that that kind of knowledge can come
in handy, in the Women's Palace. It wasn't all that surprising,
when you come to think of it.

"In brief," Aili finished, "I now need from you some
guarantee—no, better, some proof—that this plan of yours,
whatever it is, can work. As I've said before, I can't risk my
father's men without some chance of winning."

Rafaiel looked stubborn, but the havildar nodded again.
"That seems reasonable." Rafaiel started to protest, and
Radan gestured for him to be quiet. "As I said before, there've
been troubles with the Ice Island as a central depot, and most
control functions have been removed to Man's Island until
they—these Rose Worlders—can find some other remote
area on which to build their capital. Because the Earth-born

were never allowed on the Ice Island, there's been nothing we could do to break their hold, but now, with the facilities suddenly at hand—" He stopped abruptly, made himself continue in a less passionate voice, "This is our first, and possibly our last chance to seize control of the planet. There aren't many Rose Worlders in residence, perhaps a thousand or less, scattered across the world. There are more potential rebels in the Kills alone." He nodded to Rafaiel. "With his help, and with the help of some of the other gangs—yes, I was planning to contact your Efelay, boy—I could overrun Man's Island before anyone could move to stop me."

"Except for the barrier," Silence said.

"Except for the barrier," Radan agreed. "I had intended to gain access to its control point myself, and deactivate it—I believe I could have stretched my authority that far—but that was a risky activity. Better still to find a magus who could destroy it from the outside."

"So that's why you went through that whole charade," Rafaiel said, and made a gesture of apology. "Sorry, didn't mean to interrupt."

"Precisely," Radan said. He looked at Aili. "I think my plan would have succeeded anyway. With your magus's help, I can almost promise it."

The princess royal glanced at Marcinik, who nodded slowly. "They aren't a bad fighting force," he said. "If they cooperate."

Radan smiled. "They will."

After a moment, Rafaiel nodded. Fitch said, with a touch of belligerence, "If Silence says we should, all right."

"Then I think we have a bargain," Aili said.

"One thing disturbs me," Radan said. "How do you propose to contact your father?"

Aili smiled. "I rather thought you might be able to help us there, Sieur Radan, given your various contacts."

The havildar said nothing, clearly rather startled by the idea, and Silence saw suddenly that the princess royal was holding her breath. Then, slowly, Radan began to laugh. "Very well—your serenity? I think it can be managed."

"Excellent," Aili answered. Only the slight movement of her hand against the tabletop betrayed her relief.

"What do you intend?" Marcinik asked.

Radan gave him an appraising glance. "To be frank, I'm not entirely sure. It depends on what you need."

"What can you give us?" the colonel replied, grinning.

The havildar shrugged, his eyes flickering toward Rafaiel. "I have—contacts—outside the Rose Worlders' control," he said cautiously. "I also have access to the off-world transmitters."

Rafaiel looked up sharply, started to say something, and then closed his mouth again, scowling. There was something there, Silence thought—distrust of the off-worlders, or annoyance with Radan for not revealing that secret sooner—but she could not be sure just what.

"If you'll give me your message," the havildar went on, "I can see that it's passed along as intended."

Aili hesitated, and the pilot could read a sudden uncertainty in the other woman's face. She was being asked to commit herself completely, to trust someone whom she had no real reason to trust, and didn't like it. I don't blame you, Silence thought, but we haven't got much choice. If we use *Recusante* to try and reach one of the relays, we're almost certain to lose the ship—and there's no guarantee we'd get through.

"Your contact's reliable, I assume," Aili said, and waved aside Radan's answer. "No, of course he is, it was a foolish question." She sighed. "I'll give you the message."

"Then we're decided?" Radan asked, and the princess royal nodded.

"We are agreed."

CHAPTER 10

There wasn't much to be said after that, and the meeting broke up quickly. The star-travellers made their way back to the gang's quarters just ahead of the curfew, and paused just inside the main doorway while Fitch gave low-voiced orders to the group who'd accompanied him. The girl who was his apparent second-in-command nodded once, and vanished, drawing the others away with her. Fitch sighed, and looked at Silence.

"You'd better come with me," he said. "You'll want to tell Efelay what you've been planning."

There was a bitterness in his voice that made the pilot hesitate, suddenly aware of how much she'd counted on the gang's support, when she had no real right to speak for them. That kind of misjudgment might be enough to destroy her precarious hold over them, already undermined by her admission that she wasn't the empress, or, rather, that the empress was not quite what they had been expecting. . . . She shook the thought away, and said, "There wasn't time to consult with you. I'm sorry."

"You kind of took us for granted," Fitch said, and sighed. "But you're right, and I know it. Anything's worth it, if we can just drive them off."

To Silence's surprise, Efelay accepted the gang's place in the scheme without protest, and agreed to put her people under Radan's orders when the time came to attack the Island. Aili and Marcinik busied themselves with composing

317

the message to the hegemon, debating the effectiveness and importance of each phrase. Radan's access to the transmitters was limited, and there was less of a chance that a short message would be noticed and questioned; each word had to bear the maximum information possible. Most of the text, of necessity, was taken up with the description of the Earth-road: without that key, the hegemon's fleet could not hope to reach Earth in time, even if the magi had no difficulty in destroying the siege engines. Silence reluctantly recast the image from her *Gilded Stairs* into the symbolic language of the guilds, and gave the description to Aili. That was her own greatest gamble, the pilot knew, and her greatest fear was that the hegemon, having been given both the description of the voidmarks and the promise that rebels would move against the Rose Worlders, would simply ignore their appeal for support, and move in only after their attack had failed. But Adeben Kibbe was an honest man, she told herself grimly. He would not betray either his daughter or the people who had won him his throne.

She paused abruptly, staring into space. It had been she who'd beaten the old hegemon's fleet during Adeben's invasion of Asterion, and Adeben knew it. She had his formal admission of that debt, and his promise to pay it, signed and sealed before witnesses. The charter was sitting in *Recusante*'s strongbox even now, and there was another copy somewhere in the records house on Asterion itself. Maybe she could use that to secure the hegemon's cooperation. "Aili?"

The princess royal, bent over her books at the far end of the room, looked up sharply. "What's wrong?"

"Nothing's wrong," Silence said, and controlled her voice with an effort. "I've just thought of something, that's all. The charter his majesty signed, back on Asterion. Can you use that, make sure everyone knows he's bound to help us?"

Aili smiled rather shyly. "I'm afraid I already mentioned it," she said. "And I left instructions with my agents, too, as insurance. I hope you don't mind."

Silence shook her head, startled and a little annoyed by the other woman's action. But then, she told herself, Aili knows more about politics than I do; there's no shame in that. "It's just as well," she said aloud. "Good."

Aili gave her an appraising glance, but Marcinik called her name from the doorway, interrupting whatever she might have said. Silence gave a sigh of relief—she didn't really want to admit her momentary jealousies—and turned back to her work.

The magi faced two major projects, though Isambard hoped to develop some device, a variant of a siege engine, perhaps, which Radan could use to destroy the barrier. If not, he said, one of them would have to remain behind to manage the operation. Silence guessed which of them that would be, and, though she admitted the logic of Isambard's argument—she was, after all, the less experienced magus—she very much wanted to be a part of the greater operation.

Twice already in the five days since their meeting with Radan, Mikajaa had taken the magi to half-hidden lookouts, one on the cliffs behind the Kills, the other on a low bluff just south of the Rosemont, from which they could study the barrier. They could get closer, the musician had said sourly, but he did not recommend it. Isambard, apparently oblivious to the young man's dislike, had said he could make his observations well enough from a distance. He was back at the bluff right now, Silence knew, still studying the barrier, while she finished transcribing the voidmarks for the Earth-road.

She sighed, trying to concentrate on the work in front of her, but it was a merely mechanical task, and she found her thoughts wandering instead to the siege engines blocking the Earth-road. She wondered which of the schemae they could use—perhaps something based on the laws of sympathy would be best, would let them use the natural harmonies to greatest effect? She closed her eyes, a vague image taking shape in her mind. If it were a matter of sympathy, maybe the best model to use would be something based on an orrery. In modern terminology, of course, an orrery was merely a physcial model of a star system, articulated so that the planets and all the other subsolar bodies moved appropriately, but the original orreries had been models of Earth's system. They could use the orrery as a type—as a Form—to compel the larger system to return to its proper harmonies. . . .

"Silence." Isambard spoke from the doorway, interrupting her train of thought. "Have you finished the transcription?"

The pilot shook herself and nodded, putting aside the vague plans. "Here it is."

"Excellent. Her serenity is waiting for it."

Silence made a face, but collected her papers and rose stiffly to her feet. "I'll take it to her, then."

"Captain Balthasar can do that," Isambard answered. Silence saw the Delian, standing in the hallway behind the magus, roll his eyes in disgust, and did not hide her sympathetic grin.

"Thanks, Denis," she said.

Balthasar took the slip of paper with an unwilling smile. "I'll find you later," he said, and disappeared.

Silence stood looking after him, trying to suppress her feeling of disappointment. At the moment, she would far rather be with her husbands, not continuing the day's work. She glanced toward the single window, and saw that the sun had already set. "Do you need me, Isambard?"

"Yes." The older magus seated himself at the table, wincing as though he were suddenly very stiff. Silence frowned but said nothing, and, after a moment, Isambard went on, "I want to discuss with you the methods we shall use."

Silence sighed, but nodded and reseated herself. "All right."

"I have been studying the barrier," Isambard said, "and I believe I was correct in my first assessment. I am almost certain it is indeed based on one—the third, in fact—of the Alaurae branches, and therefore I am confident that I can destroy it. There is, however, a difficulty."

"I'm not surprised," Silence murmured, and added, more loudly, "What do you mean, difficulty?"

"The Alaurae branches are all based on a rather crude application of sheer power," Isambard answered. "When the Form of the barrier is altered, that power must be contained, and at once, or its release will devastate the surrounding areas. That is obviously undesirable."

"Obviously," Silence said. When the magus did not go on at once, she said, "Which means—?"

Isambard sighed. "I cannot build an engine to destroy it. I must do it myself."

"You?" Silence frowned, warily, looking for the hole in the argument. Was she going to get to take part in the destruction of the siege engines, after all? She put aside her excitement, and said, as calmly as she could, "That's going to create a problem with the timing, isn't it?"

"Perhaps not." Unaccountably, Isambard looked away, and Silence felt a sudden touch of fear. Something was wrong— she had never seen the other magus look so uncertain, or so old.

Isambard sighed again. "I must make a confession," he said at last, "one that is painful to me." He paused, bowing his head, and the pilot sat very still, not wanting to disturb him further. After a moment, Isambard lifted his head, and continued in a steady voice. "I do not know how to destroy the engines on the Earth-road; I have no vision or schema to guide me. And I do not know if I am capable of managing such a powerful operation anymore. If you have either the knowledge or the strength, I beg you to inform me."

Silence sat frozen, appalled by the old man's words. Not long ago, she had thought that she would give anything to become a greater magus than her teacher, and to force him to admit that fact. Now that it had happened, she wanted to run, to run away both from the terrifying responsibility and from the pain in the older magus's eyes. Why is it always me? she wondered again, and forced the thought away. It was on her shoulders now—this is why, she thought bitterly, this is why they tell you never to wish too much for anything. You may get it. She had wanted just to be a part of the destruction of the siege engines, not to have to do it all herself. Then she saw the matching bitterness in Isambard's face, and put those thoughts aside.

"I'd given the operation some thought," she said, choosing her words with almost painful care. "But I'd very much appreciate your advice." She waited until the older magus nodded before continuing. "I thought the laws of sympathy seemed to be what was needed, and that we might shape an orrery—a real orrery, a model of this system as it should be, and use that, somehow." She had been talking almost at random, trying to put words to the vague picture she'd developed earlier. Now she saw Isambard's expression sharpen, and braced herself for his response.

To her surprise, however, the older magus nodded, a smile spreading slowly across his face. "Yes, of course, I should have seen it. Oh, God, the advantages of a pilot's training!" He calmed himself with an effort, and went on. "But the orrery must not be tuned, Silence—or, rather, it must be deliberately mistuned to match the notes of the engines. And then, when the engine is brought into tune—"

Silence nodded, caught up in the same sudden excitement. "The siege engines, the ones blocking the road, will shatter. The whole system will be brought into its proper alignment."

"Yes!" Isambard's delight faded as quickly as it had appeared, to be replaced by a more sober assessment. "You are possibly the most talented student I have taught, Sieura Doctor. I congratulate you." The words were spoken with unconcealed bitterness.

As you said, Silence thought, I was trained as a pilot; it's easy for me to make those connections. She started to say as much, then stopped. It would sound too much like an apology, as though she did not properly value her own hard-won skills. She said, instead, "It can't be done inside the mainurb."

"No." Isambard's momentary jealousy vanished again, his mind already grappling with the practical aspects of the problem. "Perhaps this Radan knows of someplace suitable."

"Probably," Silence answered. "We can ask him when Marcinik delivers the message."

Once again, they met in the room beneath Rafaiel's BBC. This time, it was well after curfew—Radan had not been able to leave the island any earlier—and Silence could feel the tension in the escorting gang members as they made their way through the streets. Radan was there before them, as she'd half expected he would be, but the pilot was startled to see signs of strain in his face. He managed a smile as the star-travellers made their way down the narrow staircase, but it faded quickly.

"Is anything wrong?" Silence asked, tensing. Only she and Marcinik had come to the meeting this time, escorted again by Fitch, and she wondered for a brief moment if she'd made a bad mistake.

Radan shook his head. "No, sieura, nothing's wrong. We've just been rather busy, that's all."

Marcinik's eyes narrowed. "Why?"

Radan lifted an eyebrow, and Silence cursed the colonel's bluntness. After a moment, however, the havildar relaxed, and said, "Truthfully, I'm not sure. But it has nothing to do with us, in any case."

"I hope so," Marcinik said, and pulled the message disk from his pocket. "Here it is, as promised."

Radan took the transparent case, turning it thoughtfully in his hand before tucking it inside his battered jacket. "I'll see that it's transmitted," he said. "How long after it's received do you expect your fleet?"

"As we agreed," Marcinik said, "eight weeks, local."

The havildar nodded. "We'll be ready."

Silence stepped forward. "So should we be, but there are some things we need from you."

"Whatever I can offer," Radan answered, but his face was wary.

Silence hid a grin. "Doctor Isambard has decided to remain here in the mainurb to deal with the barrier for you. I'll be handling the siege engines." Marcinik gave her a quick, startled glance at that, but she ignored him. "To do it, though, I'll need someplace safe outside the mainurb—someplace away from mechanical influences. Can you do that?"

Radan paused, visibly considering the question. "You don't ask the easy things, do you, sieura doctor?" He sighed, chewing thoughtfully on his lower lip. "Possibly—yes, I think I can arrange it." He gave a fleeting smile. "One of the perqs of my position—I'm technically the owner of several tracts of farmland in the exurb; it's a way of calculating compensation for my services. It's crawling with machinery, of course, but all that could be deactivated—if that would be sufficient, sieura."

"Wouldn't that be noticed, if you turned all the farmers off?" Marcinik asked, before Silence could say anything.

"I can cover that," Radan said.

"How large an area are we talking about?" the pilot asked.

"Around five hundred hectares," Radan answered, indifferently.

Silence nodded, impressed in spite of herself. "That should be more than enough room," she said, "but how're we going to get there?"

The havildar smiled. "If either of your husbands can fly a mechanical flyer," he began, and Marcinik cut in.

"If they can't, I can."

"Then I'll get you one—we'll call it an inspection trip; we run them often enough, and that'll help cover any anomalous reports from that part of the exurb." Radan nodded, almost to himself. "Mikajaa can go with you, handle the communications."

The musician, waiting quietly in the corner until now, made a noise of protest, but the havildar ignored him. "Is that agreeable, sieura doctor?"

Silence paused, looking for any holes in the plan, but could find none. "That'll do."

Neither Balthasar nor Chase Mago offered any objections to the new plan, and even Isambard was dourly approving. As Silence had more than half expected, Balthasar admitted to knowing how to handle a mechanical flyer—they were in limited use on Delos, outside the port areas—and Mikajaa made arrangements to escort them to the landing field, on the western edge of the mainurb. Aili and Marcinik would remain in the Kills with Isambard, to coordinate the operation. Silence packed her belongings for what she hoped was the last time, and then turned her attention to helping Chase Mago tune the communications board he'd improvised from the gang's collection of miscellaneous material. At last they had it adjusted to the tuning of *Recusante*'s portable board, which they would leave with Isambard. The next day, as dawn was breaking, they made their way through the slowly brightening streets toward the tube-train station. The streets were more crowded than Silence had ever seen them. She said as much, yawning, and Balthasar shrugged.

"Day shift, on its way to work," Fitch said. He and T'la had insisted on accompanying the star-travellers to the field, to provide what protection they could. Silence was not entirely happy with the idea—two young men, one of them little more than a boy, were hardly much protection, and the bright gang livery drew more attention than it was worth—

but there had been no way to refuse, and she did her best to hide her unease.

"Factory workers?" Chase Mago asked. Of the five, he was easily the most alert, apparently unaffected by the early hour.

Fitch nodded. "Yeah. They make computers, things like that." He made a face. "Just what we need, more mechanics."

He sounds like one of us, Silence thought, and hid a smile.

They caught the tube-train from the Kills' only station. It was so crowded in the car that Silence found it difficult to breathe. She fixed her eyes on the monitor, trying to ignore the mob around her, and was very glad when the symbols for the terminus appeared in the screen. She shouldered her way out of the car after the others, and stood for a bewildered moment on the busy platform before Fitch caught her arm.

"This way." He pointed up the moving staircase, and Silence followed him obediently, clutching her bag close against her side. Balthasar and Chase Mago moved with them, efficiently shepherded by T'la. The anadvocate led them back to the plaza Silence remembered from their arrival in the mainurb, where he vanished briefly, to return a moment later with three booklets of tickets.

"Returns, too," he said, with a grin, and Balthasar nodded approvingly.

"Good thought."

Instead of taking them back to the circular northern platform by which they'd arrived, however, Fitch led them through a purple-bordered archway that bore the sign "Eastern Suburban Transit" and down a badly lit tunnel. The embarkation area at the end of the tunnel was smaller than the northern line, containing only five or six platforms. Strings of silver capsules were drawn up to each platform, and Fitch paused for a moment to consult the main notice board.

"The nonstop leaves from platform two," he said after a moment. "You're going to Nexa; it'll be the second stop."

Balthasar nodded, but Silence frowned. "I thought you said it was a nonstop?"

"Mostly." Fitch held out the ticket booklets. "It only stops at the big suburban stations. But the one you want is Nexa."

"All right," Silence said, and took the booklets from his hand. "Thanks, Fitch. This has been a help."

The anadvocate shrugged, and for a moment Silence thought she saw him blush. "Be careful, Lady—Sieura—all of you," he said, and T'la echoed, "Please."

"We will," Silence said, but they'd already turned away, and a moment later the crowd swallowed them. The pilot stood looking after them, feeling unaccountably lost, though she could not have said for certain why.

Chase Mago touched her shoulder. "Come on," he said gently. "Platform two?"

Silence nodded, and shook away the strange sense of loss. "Over there."

They found an empty car without too much trouble, and settled back on the padded benches to wait for the departure. Silence dozed, and was awakened by the sudden swaying as the trans jerked into motion. She glanced automatically at her husbands, and saw the same mix of emotions, fear and excitement and a certain amount of relief, in both their faces. She smiled, and, reluctantly, Bathasar smiled back.

"I guess it's almost over," he said, and Silence nodded. "I guess so."

It was not that long a ride to Nexa, but it seemed to take forever. The trans passed over kilometers of the heavily settled country that seemed to characterize the mainurb, and then, very slowly, the buildings began to thin out and patches of unused land began to appear. By the time the trans stopped at the first station, labelled Valon, the land was little different from the land around Diesmon. It was another half hour to Nexa, according to the announcer's rich voice, but even so Silence started to gather the bags together. She stopped, flushing, as Balthasar grinned. "Eager?"

The pilot glared at him, and Balthasar made a gesture of apology, the smile fading. "Sorry. So am I."

The Nexa station was very like the terminus at Diesmon, except that its single narrow platform was situated between two sets of tracks. Balthasar opened the capsule door, and they clambered out onto the metal flooring. Sunlight was pouring down the central stairway, and the star-travellers made for that, unspeaking. Silence could feel the tension settling in her shoulders, and tried to relax, but could not. If Mikajaa weren't waiting for them, if things had somehow gone wrong, and this were a trap—and even if it weren't, she thought, greyly, she still had the siege engines ahead of her. She shook herself, hard; the fear retreated, but it remained a cold presence at the back of her mind.

Mikajaa was waiting for them at the top of the stairs, lounging with apparent insouciance against one of the pillars that supported the station's roof. He nodded a greeting as they approached, but said nothing. Balthasar grinned and said, with silky menace, "Hello, Mikajaa."

"There's a car waiting," the musician said. "Over here."

"Stop it, Denis," Silence said. There was no point in antagonizing their only contact. Balthasar made a face, but nodded reluctant agreement.

Mikajaa led them down the long, open-sided station—there was a surprising amount of traffic, enough to make the star-travellers inconspicuous among the crowd—then out into the sunlight and across the hard-formed parking area to a battered four-wheeled runabout. Machines like it had been banished from most of the human-settled worlds for generations, but Mikajaa pointed to it with some pride.

"Here we are, people."

Silence struggled to hide a grin, and saw Chase Mago's eyebrows lift as he examined the dented frame. The engineer said nothing, however, and Silence breathed a sigh of relief.

Somewhat to her surprise, the runabout worked smoothly, the closed compartment comfortable despite the faintly unpleasant smell of the engine. Mikajaa handled it easily, swerving to avoid the patches of broken pavement. To either side of the road stood clusters of buildings, interrupted periodically by empty, neglected fields. One more sign of the Rose Worlders' insistence on Earth's natives staying in the urban areas, Silence realized. On any world in the Hegemony or in the Fringe, someone would have claimed those lots, used them either to supplement diet or their prestige.

As the runabout drew closer to the airfield, the clusters of buildings thinned out even further, until there were perhaps two or three buildings to every kilometer. Even out here, far from Unionist supervision, the buildings huddled together, with great stretches of open space in between: the prohibition had bitten deep.

The airfield itself wasn't much, just a paved runway and a single low hangar. The flyer had been wheeled out onto the pavement by the fueling stand, but there were no attendants in sight. No one appeared when Mikajaa pulled the runabout to a careful stop behind the hangar, and Silence frowned.

"Where is everybody?" Balthasar asked, before the pilot could say anything.

"Off duty, if they followed orders," Mikajaa answered. He shut off the runabout, and then tucked the control key carefully beneath the driver's seat. "Radan didn't want you to be seen, if we could help it."

"That makes sense," Chase Mago said, and pulled the star-travellers' bags from the runabout's luggage well.

The flyer was small, compared to the ones Silence was used to, and very noisy. It was not the ordinary, almost musical sound of a harmonium magnified through a sounding keel, either, but the coughing roar of a machine. The pilot winced, and pressed herself back against the padded seat as Balthasar ran the engine up to its full power, wishing there were some other way to reach the farmland.

The noise lessened once they were in the air, however, or at least, Silence thought, she became more used to it. She leaned forward, peering curiously out the little windows. They were flying below the thin cloud cover—below the Unionists' sensor net, Mikajaa had explained—and she could see the occasional opening in the forest that might have been a settlement like the Javerrys' but was more likely just a natural clearing. After perhaps an hour's flying, they crossed a low mountain range and turned fractionally south, heading out over empty country that became progressively flatter as they moved farther west. There were no settlements at all here, just acre upon acre of cropland, broken here and there by a flash of silver or the bone-white scar of a paved airstrip. Those were the repair stations for the AFMs, Mikajaa explained; the airfields were there so that flyers could land to collect the harvest. Once or twice, Silence thought she glimpsed the outline of ruined buildings, half hidden beneath the sea of grain, but the flyer passed over them before she could be sure. It wasn't impossible, she thought. Emma Javerry had said that all this land had once been heavily settled. She shivered at the thought of those massive relocations, and looked away.

They landed at Radan's holding a little after sunset, the flyer slanting down onto the paved strip that was the only sign of human activity for hundreds of kilometers in any direction. Silence climbed out into the purple twilight, stiff from the hours of travel, and stood staring at the sea of vegetation surrounding her. It was some sort of grass-like grain, growing almost as high as her waist, an oddly bright yellow in the fading light. Behind her, the flyer's engine coughed a final time and cut out, leaving an almost painful quiet.

"Over here," Mikajaa said, and Silence jumped. The musician was standing in the doorway of a metal-sided building, little more than a large shed. There was a second shed behind it, round-roofed—the machine-shed, Silence guessed, and shivered again. In their own way, she thought, the AFMs were worse than the homunculi. He beckoned again, impatiently, and Silence moved to join him, Chase Mago and Balthasar trailing behind her.

The interior of the shed was very dark. Mikajaa fumbled impatiently with the control box just inside the door, and the lights came on at last, throwing a cold glare across the single room. The place had never been intended for long-term visits, Silence saw at once, looking at the stacked cots and the crude mechanical kitchen. The only new-looking piece of equipment was the control console that filled one entire wall. She stared at the lights blinking on and off across the multiple boards, and Mikajaa crossed to stand in front of the least complicated of the control panels.

"I'm letting Radan know we've landed," he said, and touched a set of keys. After a moment, one set of lights turned green, and then a single light—the channel indicator, Silence guessed, though she could not be sure—turned from red to orange. Mikajaa nodded to himself, and lifted the headset that hung beneath the board. "Mir Radan," he said, and the orange light turned green. "Mir Radan, we're here."

"Acknowledged." Radan's voice was faint, choked by static. "Go ahead with the plan."

The light flickered out before Mikajaa could answer, and the musician nodded to himself.

"What now?" Chase Mago asked.

"You heard him," Mikajaa answered. "We shut down the machinery." Without waiting for a response, he moved to the main console, pulling a tattered notebook from the pocket of his coat. He flipped through its pages until he found the reference he wanted, then stood for a moment, studying the controls. Silence saw him take a deep breath, then reach for the first set of switches, flicking them off in a steady pattern. For a long time nothing happened, and then Balthasar whistled sharply.

The pilot turned. Balthasar was standing by the shed's rear window, staring out into the gloom. "Look at this," he said, and pointed. Silence moved to join him, and the engineer followed, warily.

Outside, in the almost-darkness, the AFMs were moving. The machine-shed door had opened, and the machines were rolling toward it, to vanish into its unlit depths. Some of them Silence recognized—tillers, another that was probably a harvester, its cutter bar cocked up behind it like a scorpion's sting, a little wheeled platform that carried the tank and bellows-pump of a duster—but most were alien, their functions unguessable. They moved almost noiselessly, the clank of their tracks and the rattle of the unsecured equipment almost inaudible through the walls of the shed.

"What the hell powers them?" Chase Mago murmured, almost to himself.

"Solar cells," Mikajaa said from behind them, and they all jumped. "Storage batteries at night."

The wave of machines was slowing already, Silence saw, and she frowned. "Surely that isn't all of them."

Mikajaa shook his head. "Not nearly. They'll be coming in all night, to here and to the other depots. By morning, though, they'll all be shut down."

And I can get to work, Silence thought. I just wish to hell I knew exactly what I was doing. She turned away, sighing, to look at the stacked cots and the crusted kitchen. "Let's get settled, then."

By morning, as Mikajaa had promised, all the AFMs had returned to their depots and the control console had gone dark. Silence stood for a long while, staring out into the brilliant sunlight, trying to decide what she should do next. She was vaguely aware of the others, watching her out of the corners of their eyes while they pretended to be busy with other things, but she put them out of her mind. Isambard had said that her idea would work—that she could use the Form of an orrery to destroy the siege engines—but she still was not fully certain how she should construct the schema. She closed her eyes, and whispered the first cantation, letting the local harmonies wash over her. For the first time since she'd come to Earth, there was no machine-made dissonance to interfere with the planetary music; the harmonies were at once unknown, and strangely familiar. It was like the Earth-road, she realized. There was a peculiar rightness to the music. And that, she told herself, would only work for her plan.

She turned away from the window, smiling distractedly at the others, still watching from beside the darkened console. "I'm going out, to get started," she said, and saw Balthasar take a deep breath.

"Is there anything we can do—?" he began, and Chase Mago laid a hand on his shoulder, cutting off the rest of the sentence.

"Good luck, Silence," he said.

The pilot nodded her thanks, and pushed through the shed door. Outside, the air was already very warm. She stood for a moment, squinting into the sunlight, then turned slowly, feeling for the harmonic lines. The two sheds, and the pavement of the airstrip itself were badly sited, lying at an angle to the music around them. She frowned, and started away from the airstrip, skirting the machine shed by a wide margin.

She walked west for perhaps two hundred meters, until she was free of the last traces of mechanical influence. She knelt in the center of the grain, the ground still damp with dew beneath her, and felt the stalks close in around her, hiding her completely. Julie will worry, she thought, and then shut the irrelevant thought away. She knelt there for a long time, listening to the faint, unfamiliar sounds of insects and birds, then slowly put those things aside, groping instead for the deeper music of the planet itself. Those harmonies swelled around her, enclosing her, until she felt that music deep within herself, stripping away the armor she had fashioned for herself against the dissonances of the mainurb, leaving her open to the music of the planet's core. Beneath that harmony, she could hear another, more distant dissonance— the natural dissonance caused by the clash of the other systemic harmonies, solar, lunar, planetary, against the dominant music of the world. She listened for a long time, until she was certain she understood it fully, and then, cautiously, reached beyond it to the supermaterial.

She chose the Form of the circle first, because it was the easiest, and brought it into existence, laying the harmonies against it and bending them to her will until at last she had a solid wall of sound, enclosing a space perhaps fifty meters in diameter. She spoke the Words that fixed that creation, and saw the grass within the circle shiver, bending toward her as though a wind were blowing from the invisible wall toward the center. She spoke again, and the grasses disappeared, leaving freshly plowed dirt beneath her feet. She touched it, feeling the rich loam crumble in her hands, and felt, too, the distant music of the planet. She could still smell the vanished grass, a strong, green scent, but even as she recognized it, the odor faded. She stood for a moment, surveying her handiwork, then spoke softly. The Words dismissed the created barrier but retained it in potential: she would need that wall again, when she began to create the orrery itself.

She sighed, studying both the land and its reflected harmonies. The proper material for an orrery was metal—metal considered as one Form of elemental Earth, the Form most responsive to harmony—but there was very little metal in the land beneath her. She could create it, of course, fuse some compound from the raw soil beneath her, but that would take time, and a great deal of power. She had neither to spare. She made a face, then, shaking her head at her own stupidity. There was metal and to spare back at the sheds, as long as the AFMs could be broken down into their component parts, and purged of the inescapably mechanical. If they could be purged, she added to herself, trying to control her rising excitement, but she could see no reason that they couldn't be. She looked up, trying to judge the time—to her surprise, the sun had slipped halfway down the western sky—then, sighing, started back toward the sheds.

The others were waiting by the machine sheds, idly examining one of the AFMs, but they looked up quickly at her approach. "How did it go?" Chase Mago asked, at last.

The pilot nodded. "Well enough," she said. "I still think it can be done."

"Well, that's a relief," Balthasar said, but he was smiling.

Silence smiled back at him. "I'll need your help—all of you," she began, and the engineer cut in quickly.

"Anything we can do, of course."

"The AFMs," Silence said. "I need the raw metal, to cast the orrery."

Mikajaa frowned. "Each one of them has a computer aboard," he began. "I don't see how—"

"I need the raw metal," Silence said again.

Chase Mago nodded. "I see. Yes, I think we can rip out all the computer components—will that be enough, or will the internal structure have been warped?"

"I don't think so," Silence answered. "Once the components have been removed, I should be able to reshape it all right." Mikajaaa still looked confused, and she elaborated, "The computers are antithetical to the Art. We have to take them out—and preferably get them away from here, though that's not absolutely vital—before I can get to work."

The musician nodded slowly. "I think I understand."

They spent the next four days disassembling a medium-sized tiller. Mikajaa proved invaluable at this, as he was able to point out minuscule components that the star-travellers might otherwise have missed, and the work progressed quickly. By mid-morning on the fifth day, all the irrevocably mechanical bits and pieces had been pulled out of the AFM, and the shell stood empty, waiting. Silence studied it, hands on hips, wondering if it wasn't too late to begin the work of transformation that day. She shook the thought away—if she allowed herself to delay now, for no better reason than fear, she would never finish—and said, "I think that does it."

Chase Mago nodded, wiping his arm across his sweating face. "I don't see anything else that has to come out."

Balthasar grimaced. "I suppose this means we have to move it out to that space you cleared," he said, and Silence nodded.

"That's right. And we'd better start now, before it gets any hotter."

The tiller was one of the smaller AFMs that ran on wheels rather than on tracks, which made it somewhat easier to move. Even so, and despite the fact that most of the heavy engine had been removed, it took all of their strength to push it into the circle Silence had cleared. The four sat on the ground for a long time after they'd gotten the AFM past the perimeter, panting, unable to say a word. Silence could feel her heart pounding, could feel the pain of a wrenched muscle in her shoulder.

"There's got to be a better way." That was Mikajaa, sprawled flat in the dirt just beyond the gutted machine. He sounded completely exhausted, and Silence felt a pang of guilt.

"I'll try to come up with something," she began, and Chase Mago shook his head.

"No," he said, "leave that to me. I've got a couple of ideas I can try."

"A little late with them, aren't you, Julie?" Balthasar grumbled, but he was the first to push himself to his feet. "We'll let you get on with it, Silence."

The engineer groaned as he stood up, then turned to pull Mikajaa to his feet. "Good luck," Chase Mago said, and, after a moment, the musician hesitantly echoed him.

Left to herself, Silence sat for a moment longer, gathering strength. When at last she felt fully recovered, she pushed herself to her feet, and turned to study the mass of metal. In its present state, it was useless to her; it would have to be transformed, and then reshaped into the various parts of the orrery. There was enough raw metal in this machine to form the centerpiece and the first ring. Well, then, she told herself, get on with it.

She took a deep breath, and spoke the Words that recalled

the barrier, sealing herself off from the fields around her. The harrmonies with which she would be working were dangerously powerful, could poison the land itself if she let her control slip. This way, at least, any errors would harm only herself. She felt the barrier close in around her, the air taking on the faintly lifeless quality that she associated with the isolation rings on Solitudo Hermae, where she had first learned the Art. Unpleasant though it was, the familiar feeling steadied her, and she regarded the stripped machine with more confidence. This would be a two-stage operation: first the metal would have to be transformed from its present, common state to a compound more receptive to the Art, and then that new metal would have to be forged into the orrery's centerpiece. The latter was easy; it was the transformation that worried her.

She took another deep breath, putting aside her doubts. Metals, compounded as they were of elemental Earth, the least volatile of the major elements, were notoriously difficult to work in the first stages of transformation, but once the original Form had been broken, were surprisingly easy to reshape. She fixed her eyes on the AFM, barely aware of the way the sun glinted off the unpainted surface, or of its heat against her back. She concentrated instead on the weight of the metal, on its solidity and its essential Form. When she was sure that the present Form was fixed in her mind, she spoke the Words of the first step of transformation. She felt heat flare in her mind, matching the sun's heat on her back; felt the same heat reflected from the AFM. This was calcination, the necessary death that bound the metal to its present state, and prepared it for the changes that were to come.

The heat rose, driving her back a step or two. She winced, but kept her eyes on the AFM. Outwardly, it was unchanged, but she could feel the heat rising within it, feel the first impure elements stir and shift, loosened from their place in the metal's structure. Then the AFM's outline seemed to waver, to loosen. Instantly, she spoke the next Words, banishing the heat, to leave the AFM shimmering in the sunlight, its outline as vaguely unstable as if she were viewing it through imperfect glass. She spoke again, and felt the metal solidify under the lash of the heavy syllables. Now, however, each lesser element was separate from the others, ready to be manipulated. She paused, gathering strength, watching the fixed metal for any signs of instability, then spoke the Words that opened a door into hell.

There was no true sound in answer, but she felt a kind of thunder shiver in the thick air. The patch of hell, roiling with the non-color that was all colors at once, grew between her hands. She whispered the phrases that controlled and shaped it, but did not stop its growth. The opening grew larger, shimmering like a silver platter; under her sure touch, it grew larger still, until it lay like a flat lake between her and the AFM, a shallow disk easily large enough to contain the entire machine. She spoke the Words that fixed it, then, and turned her attention to the AFM.

The machine seemed unchanged, the uncanny heat gone from its frame, but Silence could feel the difference in its response to her commands. She lifted her hands, balancing her awareness of the chaotic energies of hell against the arrested movement of the AFM's metal. With infinite care, she sent the disk of hell drifting away from her, until it hung suspended just above the AFM. Bracing herself, she lowered her hands, bringing the disk down over the machine.

Even though she had been expecting it, the explosion of released energy rocked her back on her heels. She swore, and swallowed the words unspoken, afraid of upsetting the delicate balance of forces around her. The disk sank lower, concealing and consuming the AFM. She fought to control the process, venting the unnatural energies back into the submaterial where they belonged. This was perhaps the most dangerous part of the transformation: the violent dissolution, followed by the digestion of the lesser elements into the chaotic state that was potentially any element, releasing its parts unevenly, throwing off dangerous bits and pieces of near-elemental matter. Those particles were inherently unstable, short-lived, but in their brief existence were capable of invading the more ordinary compounds, translating them into deadly poisons.

The disk sank lower still, until it had completely consumed the AFM, and its strange surface seemed to float only a few centimeters above the ground. There was a platform of stability here, and Silence seized it gratefully, wiping the sweat from her face. One more step, she told herself, one more step, and you're halfway there. She took a deep breath, and spoke the next Words.

There was another quivering in the air around her, a sense of shifting, but nothing else happened. She frowned, and spoke again, reinforcing her first command with a Word of even greater power. There was a groan, a sound deeper than the deepest notes of a ship's harmonium, and a noise like something tearing. Very slowly, a shape began to rise from the disk of hell. Silence spoke again, quickly, using Words that were the reflections of elemental Earth, and the shape stabilized into a dark, shimmering cube that hung just above the surface of the disk.

Silence sighed in relief—she was halfway finished now; she had broken the metal down to its elemental form, and now needed only to recast it into something more useful for her purposes—and dismissed the opening into hell. The cube remained in the air before her, a dark, oily-brown shape that sang with a power all its own. She tilted her head to one side, studying it a moment longer, then spoke the Words that began the next sequence. The surface of the cube shifted, darkened, then began to bubble gently. Wisps of matter rose from it like steam; she spoke again, softly now, and those wisps dissolved into the materials of common air, harmless and even beneficial. She spoke once again, drawing on the Form of the tetrahedron, dividing the interior volume from the planes of the surface. At another Word, those planes hardened, became a barrier between the near-elemental Earth within and the contaminating common air around it.

She paused again, breathing hard. The final three stages were the most difficult, primarily because the process proceeded so quickly once it had been initiated. She closed her eyes, visualizing first the completed orrery and then the specific pieces she would forge from this transformation, then spoke the Words that divided the substance within the cube from its Form. She could feel the surge of power, the rising music, not dissonant but not harmonious, either, and chanted the next phrase, the Words that were the schema, the definition, of the metallic compound illarion, the metal from which an orrery should be created. She could feel the substance shifting toward the metal, first a few tiny fragments bonding to form a lesser element, then another, and then those lesser elements shifting and reforming, joining one to another in an ever-increasing reaction that changed the Formless substance into a defined metal. She spoke again, phrases that shaped and defined the first parts of the orrery, tuning it to the true notes of the system around her, and felt the still-malleable metal changing state within the cube. She spoke a final Word, and the cube split open, to reveal the sun-sphere in its stand, and the ring-and-ball of the first planet. She gestured hurriedly, using the last of the rapidly dissipating energies to shift the newly made structure into the center of the ring, and then stood for a long moment, looking at it. I did it, she thought, and smiled. Around her, she could feel the last energies ebbing gently away. She waited for them to fade, listening to their soft reflection in the incomplete orrery. This part, at least, was properly in tune; the rest would be made deliberately out of tune, to allow her to break the engines, but this was perfect. She smiled again, savoring her success, then sighed, and turned to dismiss the barrier. She called up the last of her strength, and threw a shield of illusion around the circle, hiding it from any passing flyers, and then, fighting off the waves of exhaustion that suddenly threatened to overwhelm her, started back toward the sheds.

Over the next weeks, she performed that operation eight more times, casting each of the planetary rings. As the rings grew larger and more complex, it became harder to manipulate them; she had to struggle to force the unwieldy masses to take on the Forms she wanted. The deliberately dissonant tuning caused difficulties, too, and she had to cast a series of stasis fields to keep the disharmony from destroying the half-finished structure. At night, the buzzing of those fields haunted her dreams. Chase Mago and Balthasar, and even Mikajaa, did all they could to help, but there was little they could do, and Silence felt herself becoming remote from them, lost in a sort of waking dream. Things were progressing as planned in the mainurb, she gathered from the conversations she occasionally was aware of hearing, and Aili was making herself more than useful coordinating the various groups' activities, and mediating among their conflicting interests, but beyond that point she barely listened. She was too busy with the delicate process of creating the imperfect orrery to spare much thought for mere politics.

And then the last ring was in place. The dissonances were finally internally consistent, and she released the stasis fields with a sigh of relief. The tension, the nagging, sour sensation in the back of her mind, vanished, and she started back to the sheds feeling more alert than she had in days. Chase Mago greeted her with a smile and a nod, his eyes wary, but Balthasar grinned openly.

"It's finished, is it?" he asked. "Not before time, either."

Silence frowned, suddenly aware that she had lost all track of time. "When is it?"

Balthasar's grin widened. "If everything's gone according to plan—"

"There's no reason to think it hasn't," Chase Mago interjected.

"—the Hegemon's fleet will start the final leg tomorrow," the Delian finished.

"Oh, my God." Silence froze, putting a hand over her mouth. If it had taken another day—if she had waited any longer, or hesitated, or taken any steps over, the orrery would have been finished too late. She shook herself, pushing away the fear. She could not dwell on what might have happened; the orrery was finished, and she was ready to perform the final operation.

As if he'd read her doubts, Mikajaa said, "You are ready, aren't you?"

The pilot nodded, biting back a slightly hysterical laugh. "Oh, yes." She saw Balthasar's lifted eyebrow, and smiled. "Well, yes, Denis, I would've liked a day or two to rest, but it's no problem. Don't worry."

"But I do," the Delian said, surprisingly, then shrugged. "Like you say, there's no choice." He looked from Chase Mago to Mikajaa, who was waiting beside the communications console. "What now?"

It was the musician who answered first. "I'll tell Radan we're ready." Without waiting for an answer, he turned to the control board and began flipping switches.

Chase Mago said thoughtfully, "The plan so far has been

that we'll coordinate the destruction of the siege engines with Isambard's attack on the barrier. Is that still true, and, if so, how do we know?"

Mikajaa looked up from the flickering lights. "Radan will signal us when the barrier's down. Then I guess whoever's watching the console can signal Silence."

The pilot nodded. "That's simple enough," she said. Privately, she wished that the siege engines could be controlled from Man's Island—but it was a waste of time to wish that her enemies had been stupid, she told herself angrily. Of course they cast the engines to be independent, just in case there ever was a rebellion on Earth. Whatever else they might be, the Rose Worlders were not fools.

"Everything's set," Mikajaa reported, a few moments later. "They're planning on attacking just before dawn, just before the curfew lifts. Is that all right with you, Silence?"

"That's fine," the pilot said quickly, before she could change her mind. The actual time made very little difference to her. The orrery was already set to the approximate planetary positions relative to Earth; she could make whatever final adjustments were needed in the morning.

"You should get some rest," Chase Mago said gently, and Silence nodded again.

"I will," she said, without much hope.

Somewhat to her surprise, however, she slept heavily, and Balthasar had to shake her awake to give her her breakfast. Silence sipped cautiously at the dreadful coffee and stared at the wall in front of her, trying to clear her mind. In theory, at least, the operation was not that complex. As Isambard had repeated from the beginning, the siege engines imposed an unnatural dissonance on a system meant to be in harmony; the orrery was merely a tool to correct the situation. Still, the siege engines were very powerful—she could still remember the stresses that had destroyed the *Bruja*, and had almost destroyed *Recusante*; it would take a corresponding strength to overcome them.

"It's time," Chase Mago said, at her elbow.

Silence forced a smile, suddenly afraid. She was still relatively untried. . . . She pushed that thought away violently. She could not afford that kind of weakness, not today. She had thought of the operation; she would see it through. "I'm ready," she said aloud.

"Is there anything we can do?" the engineer went on.

Silence shook her head. "Once you've given the signal, stay inside, that's about it. I don't think there's any danger, but I'd rather not have to worry about you."

Chase Mago nodded, and the pilot reached for the magus's supplies Isambard had so carefully packed for her before she left *Recusante*. The only thing she needed from it today was the simple pitchfork, but she stopped abruptly. She only needed it to set the base notes, and there were better ways to do that. "Julie," she said aloud, "would you do me a favor? Let me borrow your pitch pipe."

The moment the words were out of her mouth, she cringed, expecting a refusal. An engineer's pitch pipe was the main tool of his trade, as personally valuable as a pilot's starbooks; Chase Mago wouldn't want to give it up, especially not for something as uncertain as this operation. To her surprise, however, the engineer reached into his shirt without a second's hesitation, and brought out the silvery egg. "Good luck," he said, and put the cord around Silence's neck.

The pilot touched it wonderingly, and managed a tremulous smile. "Thanks," she whispered, and impulsively threw her arms around him. "Thanks," she said again, and found herself close to tears.

"Hey," Balthasar said, and put his arms around them both. "It's time to go."

Silence nodded, fighting to get herself under control, and pushed herself away. "All right."

"Good luck," Balthasar said again, and gave his slow, lopsided smile. "So this is it."

"This is it," Silence said, and smiled back.

"We'll fire one of the flyer's flare-lights when the attack begins," Chase Mago said. "You can't miss that."

"I'll be watching for it," Silence said, and stepped out into the pre-dawn chill.

The light was still dim, but strangely clear, a few stars still showing on the western horizon. The dew was heavy in the thick grass, and Silence was soaked to the knees by the time she reached the clearing. She shivered, wishing she had thought to bring dry clothes, but then put that concern aside, and walked slowly around the orrery, checking one last time for defects. The dissonance was there, clearly audible in the way the concentric rings rang softly to her footsteps, but it was an intentional dissonance, not destructive. She stood for a moment longer, looking through the great silver rings, each one carrying a sphere that was a symbol of one of the first system's planets, to the larger central sphere that was the symbol of the sun. When the light hit it, she knew, it would gleam gold, the sun's metal, but for now it was just a slightly darker shape among the rings.

She looked toward the east then, past the dark shed, light glowing in its windows, toward the distant horizon. It was already growing lighter there, the sky fading toward sunrise. She shivered again, but knew this time it was tension, not the chill. Soon, now, she thought, very soon. . . .

Something moved by the sheds. She reached hastily for the pitch pipe dangling at her breast, but then curbed her impatience. She had to wait for the attack to begin on Man's Island, or she would almost certainly have to contend with extra interference, as the controllers there sought to drive her away from the siege engines. Even with the attack, she might have to face them, but, with any luck, Radan's agents would keep the Rose Worlders too busy for them to worry about anything but saving their own skins.

A light flared above the shed, rose and blossomed into a hundred stars. She stared for a moment, then realized abruptly what it was. The signal had been given; it was time to begin. She took a slow, deep breath, steadying her nerves, then lifted the pitch pipe to her lips. She sounded the first note, a low, dark note like the tolling of an immense bell, then spoke the Words that chained it to the outermost of the nine rings. She could feel the metal resisting, and spoke again, reinforcing those Words with other, more commanding sounds. With a strange, groaning noise the ring shifted, the metal realigning itself with the new, more perfect note she had sounded.

Silence stood for a moment, assessing the new internal harmonies she had created, and then sounded the second note. The first note still sounded, but more distantly; the second note cut through it as though it had not been there.

The next ring resisted, too, but then adjusted itself. The two correct notes blended into a sound that Silence recognized as the basis of the music she had heard when she finally travelled the Earth-road. The dissonance at the center of the orrery rose slightly, humming like a swarm of insects. Silence gave it a wary glance, ready to hold it static if she had to, but the humming stabilized at its new level. She waited a moment longer, and sounded the third note.

As she moved inward toward the sun-sphere, the rings' resistance increased. At the seventh ring, the Earth-ring, her note evoked a strange brassy cry, so weirdly tuned that she had to put both hands to her ears, the dissonance lashing at her. She shouted into it, binding it to her will, and, after a moment in which the entire universe seemed to hang suspended, the metal shifted, obeying her command. She stood for a moment, shaking, and felt the tension of the last two untuned rings, like a physical presence in the air around her. The combined music of the other rings surrounded her as well, a note almost too deep for human hearing, yet still somehow strangely muted. The dissonance of the remaining rings and spheres seemed to drown that perfection. She listened, wondering if the Rose Worlders were somehow affecting her operation, but could feel no signs of outside interference. She took a deep breath, and sounded the eighth note.

The sound seemed to hang in the air after she had lowered the pitch pipe, swelling toward some unimaginable climax. Hastily, she shouted the Words that turned it toward the proper ring, and felt that ominous pressure recede. No, not ominous, she corrected herself instantly, less threatening than unimaginably powerful. She sounded the next note, directing it to the last of the planetary rings, and felt the same power loom for a moment before her commands diverted it. That left only the sun-sphere, and the final operation itself.

The sun was rising now, its light glinting from the rings, which seemed to float along the central axis. It glowed from the sun-sphere as well, turning the metal to gold. All the conditions were right, Silence knew, and sounded the final note. It rose from the pipe, took on substance and weight, became visible as a spark of sun-colored light that soared through the orrery's rings to strike the central sphere. Silence braced herself, ready to speak the Words that would turn the orrery into a sympathetic model of the first system, and light exploded from the sun-sphere. It flashed outward, and with it came music. The sound was terrifyingly perfect, balanced between the notes of the sun and planets that blended into a systemic music that could never be forgotten, and the music of heaven itself, of the realm of Form beyond the material. The wave of sound struck Silence, knocking her backward onto the cleared ground. For a moment, she was aware only of pain, an agony like nothing she had ever imagined, and then the ground seemed to shift, or perhaps it was she who moved, and she hung gloriously suspended in the heart of the music.

She could feel it striking through her body, and through the core of Earth itself, waking the same glad echoes at its center; she felt the same notes reach up through the envelope of air and out into the vacuum of the first system, encompassing each planet in its course. Almost in passing, she felt the siege engines shriek and die, but it hardly seemed to matter, compared to the wonder of the music. The entire system sang with it, in perfect tune for the first time since the Millennial Wars, but the music reached still farther, resonating through purgatory until it seemed that all of human-settled space was encompassed in that song. And still the music continued, pulling away from her comprehension toward something that lay beyond the borders of the universe. She strained after it, fought to follow, but the music was failing now, or she was failing, the magnificent harmony slipping from her grasp. She thought she cried out, a wail of despair and loss, but the song had passed beyond her reach. She fell, and thought she wept.

And then she was lying in the shadow of the broken orrery, staring up into blazing sunlight. She moved her head cautiously, and winced at the pain in every limb.

"Silence?" That was Chase Mago's voice, thick with relief. The pilot turned her head, grimacing as the muscles of her neck protested the movement, and looked up into the engineer's familiar face. There were tears in his beard; she reached to touch them, frowning in concern.

"Are you all right?" the engineer continued. Behind his shoulder, Silence could see Balthasar. There were tears on the Delian's face as well, and her frown deepened.

"I'm fine," she said, and started to push herself up into a sitting position. The new pains in her arms and back made her swear, and she was grateful for the engineer's supporting arms. "At least, I think I am," she amended. "I feel as though I've wrenched every muscle in my body." The memory of the magnificent music was already fading to a bearable level; had she been able to remember it more clearly, she knew, she would not be able to bear its loss. She looked around deliberately, forcing herself to concentrate on mundane things. The sun was almost directly overhead, she realized, and the concerns of the morning came rushing back. "The engines were destroyed," she said slowly—somehow, she could not take credit for the effects of that glorious harmony—"but did the fleet get through? What happened?" She clutched the engineer's arm in sudden panic.

"It's all right," Balthasar said quickly. "Radan's people took the island, just the way he planned, and the fleet's through. It's moving in-system right now, and Aili's talking to it." He grinned suddenly. "The last Mikajaa heard, she was telling his most serene majesty where to get off." The smile faded a little. "Not that we were paying a whole lot of attention. We didn't dare move you, until we knew what had happened."

"Sieura!"

That was Mikajaa's voice, and Silence shifted in the engineer's embrace to stare blearily at the young musician.

"You're all right, I'm glad." Mikajaa seemed to see the other men's stares for the first time, and blushed faintly. "I thought you'd want to know," he went on after a moment, speaking now to all of them. "The hegemon's agreed, her serenity will have Earth—I don't know how she conned Radan into that—"

"Practice," Silence murmured, and saw Balthasar nod in wry agreement.

"Whatever," Mikajaa said. "And some prince—Azarian, or something like that—will inherit the Hegemony." His tone made it clear that he didn't understand how that was part of the issue.

Silence nodded. "So we've fulfilled our contract, too," she murmured.

"Were we mentioned at all?" Balthasar asked, and Chase Mago laughed.

"You're getting conceited, Denis."

Mikajaa grinned. "Not really, considering. Yes, you were. The hegemon wants you to enter his service, and so does her serenity. They're both offering you just about anything you could want."

Silence nodded again, smiling. "I don't know about you two," she said, "but my vote's for Aili."

"Let's see what she's offering," Balthasar demurred, and the engineer reached up to grab the slighter man's collar.

"It's two to one, Denis," he said firmly. "We'll stay." His determined expression softened slightly, and he released the Delian. "Think of it, man, we'll be based on Earth."

Balthasar smiled reluctantly. "All right," he said, "you win."

Silence relaxed slowly, leaning back into the engineer's arms. That was enough of a decision for now, she thought, smiling. There would be other decisions later, details to be settled—she still owed Efelay what knowledge she could share, and the Javerrys too deserved whatever help she could give—but for now, it was enough. She, and Balthasar, and Chase Mago, were free, truly free, for the first time since they had met—better than free, she thought suddenly, and better than just surviving. Whatever happens now, we're at the center, the center of human-settled space. We'll be a part of it, of this new time that's beginning. Her smile widened, as she stared into the blue of Earth's sky. That should be enough for anyone.

TRAVIS SHELTON LIKES BAEN BOOKS BECAUSE THEY TASTE GOOD

Recently we received this letter from Travis Shelton of Dayton, Texas:

> *I have come to associate Baen Books with Del Monte. Now what is that supposed to mean? Well, if you're in a strange store with a lot of different labels, you pick Del Monte because the product will be consistent and will not disappoint.*
>
> *Something I have noticed about Baen Books is that the stories are always fast-paced, exciting, action-filled and seem to be published because of content instead of who wrote the book. I now find myself glancing to see who published the book instead of reading the back or intro. If it's a Baen Book it's going to be good and exciting and will capture your spare reading moments.*
>
> *Another discovery I have recently made is that I don't have any Baen Books in my unread stacks—and I read four to seven books a week, so that in itself is a meaningful statistic.*